Seekers, Sinners & Simpletons

The Spirituality Players

Jim Lynch

ISBN: 0615758223
ISBN 13: 9780615758220

Dedication

To: Andrew, Lisa, Brendan, Holly, David, Christin, Kieran, Colin, JJ, Ryan, Courtney, Conor, Dylan, Liam, Declan, Bridget and the other family members yet to arrive, and most especially to my wife, Debbie, for making all of these wonderful relationships in my life possible.

I

The Spirituality Players

Patch Munson drove past the Christian Ascendancy Community Cemetery on the outskirts of Mobile, Alabama. Both of his parents were buried here during the past six months and the Munson family owned four additional plots nearby. Patch Munson was now the patriarch of the family. He had not yet reached his mid forties. His two older sisters, Marjorie and Gloria, were spinsters, with no prospects for marriage, today, tomorrow or yesterday. They were both heavy set, hardheaded and homely. Their one redeeming quality was that God had given heavenly voices to both the Munson girls. They sang at the Christian Ascendancy Community Church choir and they also volunteered one day a week to tidy up the rectory and church hall for Reverend Billy Brand.

Munson pulled his silver-ice colored Chevy Silverado over near the cemetery but didn't get out of the pickup truck. It was summertime in southern Alabama and it was sweltering hot. He decided he wouldn't walk to the gravesites. He was close enough. He would just say a few prayers from the roadside. His reverie was interrupted by the ringing of his cell phone.

"Patch, we need *sem thaangs* from Walmart, *whahle yer* out *an' 'bout*."

"*Lahke* what?"

"*Lahke* spray *t'* kill these ants in the kitchen. Seems *lahke they been multiplyin' o'er nahght*. We also need *sem flashlahght* batteries in case the *upcomin'* storm knocks out the *'lectricity* again.

"All right Maggie. *An'thaang* else?

"Not that *Ah cain thaank* of *rahght* now. *Yew* okay, Patch?"

"*Fahne*, Maggie. *Jes' fahne.*"

"*Yew* don't sound *fahne*. Where *'bouts* are *yew* now?"

"*Lahke yew* said; *'jes'* out *an' 'bout. Ah'll* be back soon. *Jes' doin' sem* stuff *wit' Harreh.*"

Harry or as Munson called him, *"Harreh,"* was his ever present tricolored mutt that was half Bassett Hound and half mixed breed hound. It was a bizarre turnaround of nomenclature, that some thought could only occur in Alabama. Harry Munson III, known as "Patch" since shortly after his fourteenth birthday, named his mutt "Harry" after himself – or at least after himself during his grammar school years. In some ways the dog served as more than just his companion. He was more like his alter ego. Some of Munson's friends believed that the dog was brighter than the master.

Maggie wanted to say more, but she felt that she had already asked her husband more questions than he was used to answering. She said goodbye and hoped that Munson would be true to his word and would return home soon. Over the last few months Patch Munson had not been the same man that she married. She worried about that.

Munson sat by the roadside for fifteen more minutes. He wondered about heaven and hell. He believed his parents had been rewarded for a hardworking, value based life; he just didn't know how to articulate that to himself, let alone others. He wanted his parents to look down from heaven favorably upon his own life. Patch Munson wasn't much of a talker, but he prayed a fair bit. Finally he pulled away from the graveyard and said, "Let's *git* home, *Harreh.*" He was talking to the dog.

Father Timothy Hanlon finished listening to the sinner's act of contrition while simultaneously saying the words of absolution and blessing his parishioner. He gave a penance of three rosaries even though the sins were not heinous or numerous. The Catholic Church in the 21st century had bigger problems than determining a suitable penance for particular violations of its canons, commandments and conventions.

As this parishioner finished his confession, got up from the kneeler and left the confessional, Father Hanlon waited to see if anyone else was in line. Soon he heard another person enter the confessional and kneel outside his chamber. The setup of the confessional at The Most Holy Tabernacle Church was similar to that of many Catholic churches worldwide. An element of privacy was accorded sinners as they confessed their offenses. They could kneel in the dark and speak through a small sliding doorway, while the priest would gaze steadfastly away from the sinner. However The Church also offered a face to face option for those who felt more comfortable sitting across from the priest and making human eye contact as sins were confessed to God, through his surrogate, the priest. This next sinner opted for the private sliding door.

"Bless me father for I have sinned. It has been two years since my last confession. These are my sins…" The sinner recited her preamble prayers. Father Hanlon immediately had the impression that this was not going to be a normal confession. It was not unusual to hear a sinner whisper her confession, but this sinner was trying to disguise her voice with her whisper. Also, when people came to confession during an ordinary week, not close to Christmas or Easter, and started by saying that it was their first confession in a long time, there generally was a salient reason for the confession. He also noticed that the woman might be having second thoughts or sudden anxiety concerning her confession because she suddenly stopped talking.

"You are God's daughter. He looks favorably upon your resolve. Please continue," he coaxed her.

"I'm not sure." The whisper was now barely audible, but the young priest would never ask her to speak up. God could hear every whisper.

"What is it you're unsure of, my sister? Surely you have no doubts about God's love for you and His willingness to forgive. Do you need help with your examination of conscience? Can I help you go through the commandments?

"No, Father, that's okay. I'm just nervous." Her voice had a familiar breathlessness to it, even as she whispered.

"All right, take your time. There doesn't seem to be many parishioners waiting for confession."

"These are my sins, Father …" She restarted but again the woman stopped in mid confession. She was having second thoughts.

"Sometimes we are embarrassed about our sins. That is only human. God already knows our sins. He doesn't …"

"Then why do I have to say them aloud to you?" It was an ironic whisper.

The confessional was not the place to conduct a class on Catholic doctrine. However he was listening to someone who might be returned to the state of grace. Therefore he had to do his job. He knew that it was peculiar to think of it that way – as a job.

"God will forgive your sins if you're truly contrite. I'm merely his minister. I'm here to listen to the recitation of your transgressions, and then to administer God's absolution of those sins. The Church asks that you articulate your most grievous sins. If you forget a sin or two, it doesn't matter, as long as you're contrite for *all* of your sins. When I administer absolution, I'm telling you that God absolves *all* of your sins, those spoken and those that are unspoken as well. My other role is to facilitate the recall of your transgressions against God and His Church. You have made a good start by acknowledging that you have been away from the sacrament of reconciliation for two years. Please continue." The priest knew that he had not directly answered her question.

"I have certain feelings for a man that I want to confess …" Her whisper tailed off and it was apparent that he might need to help her. She didn't need to be overly explicit. She only needed to recognize what was sinful and to express her contrition.

"We all have feelings. God created his children in his own image and likeness. We are emotional human beings. Did you take any action with respect to these feelings?"

Father Hanlon recognized that the most difficult sins to confess were sins of the flesh. For some reason people were more embarrassed to confess sexual misdeeds than they were to confess theft or assault or any other grievous sin. And most confessions easily incorporated issues such as anger, deceit, missing Mass, or spreading gossip, with a relatively more relaxed tone. It was the sins of the flesh that people struggled with, so he waited to hear what would be whispered next.

"Well … not exactly." It wasn't much of an answer. Father Hanlon strained to hear the whisper. He had an impression that the woman was young. He also knew from experience that a broad, almost technical definition of sins was helpful to the repentant sinner. If the priest used the words, the sinner could start by acknowledging the sins and quantifying the occurrences. She wouldn't have to say the words herself. Her answer of "not exactly" was an indication that she probably had not yet had physical intimacy with the unidentified man. He knew he should do what he could do dissuade the penitent sinner from moving forward with her desires. But his immediate responsibility was to help her to confess her sins.

"These inappropriate feelings, did they include self gratification?"

Father Hanlon knew that people had even more trouble confessing masturbation than they had in confessing illicit sexual behavior with others. For some reason, it was deemed demeaning and self degrading. He always felt that this was odd, because social scientists insisted that this sin was much more prevalent than what he heard in his confessional.

"In a way, yes." The whisper was an embarrassed one, so Father Hanlon pressed on without letting the awkwardness linger. However the young woman's interpretation of *self gratification* was somewhat different than Father Hanlon's perception.

"About how many times did you sin this way?"

"Constantly."

The one word murmur was enough. He needed to move on. He was concerned that there might be a looming marital problem that he could potentially derail.

"Is this man married?"

"No. No. Not at all." The woman was now quite embarrassed. She felt like she was playing a foolish game with hints and innuendoes.

This was not what she had intended. Her original intention was for a much more frank discussion. But she had lost her nerve and attempted to hide her identity. "I've said enough. I should leave now."

"You have to finish… I can only give you absolution if you…."

Carol Mays, the woman who was kneeling across from Father Hanlon stood up abruptly and exited the confessional. She didn't want him to stop her or – God forbid – come after her. She wondered if he recognized the voice she tried so hard to disguise. Mays felt like an absolute fool. *Why did I do that? Why did I approach the first man I ever loved … in a confessional of all places?* Her bronze face now reddened with self induced embarrassment.

Father Hanlon bent over at the stomach while still in his chair. He said a quick prayer for conditional absolution. He suddenly felt inadequate. In the past, he had felt a sense of spiritual elation when helping people through their confessions. Reconciliation was a terrific thing when it occurred between two people. It was even more uplifting when it occurred between God and a man or a woman. The failure of attempted reconciliation between two humans could be brutally disheartening. It was downright demoralizing when it involved the Deity.

Normally Father Hanlon would wait five or more minutes for additional penitents before he would get up to leave the confessional chamber. But he was mystified by the young woman who had just left. He stood up and walked around to the kneeler side of the confessional. There was something about her voice that was familiar. You can forget a face, he thought, but you never forget a voice. He felt that she sounded like Carol Mays. Then he thought his mind was simply playing tricks with him again. He knew that he thought about Carol much too often for his own good. As he went to leave the confessional his olfactory sense recognized a familiar scent. The nasal nostalgia tweaked the frontal cortex in his brain, but on a subconscious level he denied the recognition of the familiar perfume; or was it a familiar soap? Or was it just the recognizable scent of a familiar woman? As he slowly walked back to the rectory, he thought that the Sacrament of Reconciliation was the most emotional of all of the sacraments; more emotional than Baptism or Confirmation or Holy Communion. It was even more emotional than Matrimony. When Father Hanlon went to sleep that night he experienced a strange dream of reaching out with both arms and catching nothing.

Her job seemed so incongruous with her spiritual self. Julianne Carson was a thirty-one year old native Californian. She was a successful computer systems salesperson who logged more than 100,000 air miles each year traveling to various locations to consult with her clientele. Her company had twice offered her promotions to managerial positions within the firm and she had twice turned them down and kept her supercilious title of Executive Customer Advocate. On her income tax returns she listed her occupation as saleswoman.

Further examination of her tax returns told more of her story. Her personal donations exceeded twenty-five percent of her gross income. The fact that she claimed charitable deductions in excess of $50,000 a year had once caused her to have to produce documentation for all of her donations. The fastidious side of her brain was ready. She had kept every receipt and documented every donation. IRS never bothered her again.

The other side of her brain was less quantitative. Julianne was a spiritual woman. She read three or four books on spirituality each and every month. She was a seeker. She attended yoga classes regularly and even took vacation time to attend Caribbean yoga retreats in Turks & Caicos and near the coral reef off the coast of Belize. Julianne aspired toward true self actualization. She simply wanted to call it something else. She wasn't a big Maslow fan. Recently she was making an effort at a more simple approach. She wanted to be more spontaneous in her activities even while she remained more contemplative in her morning meditation. She resolved not to second guess first impressions as she had done in the past.

Julianne rehashed the evening's events in her mind. She had done something that she hadn't done in several years. She had asked a man out on a dinner date. And odder still, it was someone she had met only hours earlier. Bertrand "Hawk" Richter was a guest speaker at one of her company's customer appreciation events. Richter was a controversial 39 year old blind German scientist and orator who was an avowed atheist. He was also a captivating after dinner speaker who was both witty and engaging. Richter was a well known university educator, who had attempted to make quantum physics digestible for the common man. Julianne was instantly fascinated by Richter and went up to talk to him after he spoke. She challenged his stance that science and theology were mutually exclusive, citing some of her reading of the works of the Dalai Lama. She challenged the speaker to continue the debate with her over dinner when she would be visiting his home town of Tampa, Florida in a few weeks. To her surprise and delight he accepted her invitation, and they exchanged contact information.

Professor Melech Katz had just left the Tampa office of his psychotherapist, Abe Elowitz. He liked Elowitz and felt that he was making some progress in his private sessions with the analyst. However Katz still couldn't talk about the war or about Palestine and Israel, at least not in any detail. All he could deal with at this point was the outlook he had now, seven years after leaving the Israeli Defense Forces. His feelings about his tour of duty in the IDF were cold, dispassionate and occasionally mind numbing. Elowitz had been specific in his diagnosis of Katz. He was suffering from PTSD, posttraumatic stress disorder. However Abe Elowitz had not yet prescribed a specific regimen of treatment that might bring Melech Katz back to the life he knew before joining the hostilities between Palestinians and Israelis after getting his BS and MBA degrees in the United States.

One thing that Elowitz had done for Katz was to tell him stories about the concentration camp that Elowitz' own father had escaped from during World War II. Elowitz had also given Katz a copy of Victor Frankel's book, <u>Man's Search for Meaning</u>. The book was short and Katz read it three times. Katz was also searching for meaning but his search was proving to be elusive.

Elowitz' most recent suggestion, however, didn't sit well with Katz. Elowitz invited Katz to join his group therapy session that met every other Saturday afternoon. Katz didn't say yes and he didn't say no. Katz told Elowitz that he would think about it.

Reverend Billy Brand climbed to the pulpit of the Christian Ascendancy Community Church and smiled out at his congregation. His telltale kinesics displayed a controlled energy that would gradually progress to a fully animated hard charging delivery of his sermon. The demonstrative cleric's persona came right out of central casting for a fire and brimstone preacher. This morning the congregation was suspicious of the smile.

"Good *mornin' mah* fellow Christian *worshipehs*. Let us thank the Lord *fur grantin'* us all *anotheh* week on His green earth *t'* fulfill His *divahne* will." As he spoke the 42 year old minister waved his right arm from his far left to his far right over the entirety of his congregation. He did this with his palm facing upwards, open to heavenly grace. He began to elevate his arm slightly as he slowly finished his broad sweeping gesture. By the time his arm reached its elevated destination his hand was above his shoulder and he began to clench his open hand into a fist. He held the fist out from his body about head high, while his left arm remained at his side. He then paused to capture the attention of all those in the church, and he gradually let the smile fade from his visage.

"*Y'all* know that from one week *t' 'notheh* the Lord will *d'sahde* which *o* us *t'* call home to His *heavenleh* kingdom, *an'* which among us will be left *behahnd t'continya* our work in His *holeh* name. This decision is the Lord's *an'* the Lord's alone." Reverend Brand was no longer smiling. "*Quahte unfortunateleh* … *Ah* mean *t'* say … *quahte sinfulleh* … there are those who believe that they *cain* usurp this *divahne rahght* from our *heavenleh* father. There are men in our midst who believe that they *cain* take a *lahfe* at its *vereh* inception *an' murderousleh* interrupt that *lahfe* from its mission."

The congregation settled back and listened as Billy Brand lambasted the people and organizations that were responsible for more than a million abortions that were performed in the United States each year, including as many as 14,000 in the State of Alabama, alone. They listened as Billy told them that their neighboring state of Florida was among the most sinful of states with more than 81,000 abortions including 2700 that were performed at the Fein Center for Women, in nearby Tampa. Billy reminded his congregation that Dr. Aaron Fein, a transplanted New Yorker, also planned to open a clinic nearby in Mobile and that this fact made Billy "*maddeh* than a wet hen."

Brand pronounced Fein's name with a heavy Alabama accent, which treated all "long I's" as though they sounded like "*ah*." This caused the word "I" to be pronounced as "*Ah*," the word "right" to be spoken as "*rahght*," and Aaron Fein's name to sound like "*Fahne*" rather than the Yankee pronunciation as "*Fine*." The southern Alabama dialect also reconstructed the sounds at the ends of words by occasionally dropping "g" sounds and lifting words that ended in an "r" or in a "y" to sound as though they ended with an "h" so that "brother" became *brotheh* and "only" became *onleh*. Finally the southern Alabama accent caused the "short I's" to be dragged out as though they were elongated "short A's" thereby creating the word "*thaank*" to mean "think" as in "*Ah thaank yer rahght*."

Billy Brand's non-denominational Christian congregation was unusual in that it was comprised of both whites and blacks in significant numbers. More than 25 per cent of his congregation was black. There was a small group of Latino parishioners and the remaining were working class white Americans, most with deep roots in the Deep South. There was some effort at fellowship between the different ethnic groups after Sunday services but it didn't transition to interracial social interaction beyond the parish property. However at a bare minimum, parishioners recognized one another around town and were generally civil and respectful of one another when their paths crossed.

Billy Brand was continuing the work of his father, The Reverend Will Brand, in trying to get his congregation ever more solidly integrated on a social basis. Together they had already created a great deal of moral harmony over the years that they had shepherded the Christian Ascendancy Community Church of Jesus Christ. They had also built the Brand brand into a recognizable trademark for their books, beads and even a Billy Brand Bobblehead. They marketed their ministry across the southern United States and their weekly services were televised across a thirteen state area. But the Brands practiced what they preached. Their ministry took in more than twenty-eight million dollars annually and they redistributed these funds to a wide group of charities that were associated with churches, synagogues, mosques and other houses of worship across the South. Their well audited largesse gave them credibility with their congregation and for that matter with other Southern congregations also. And although his sermons were often filled with fire and brimstone, Billy Brand was quite affable and approachable beyond the pulpit. He was full of southern charm and used southern idioms and witticisms in his every day dialogue as well as in his sermons. He and his wife, Sarah Anne, were generally loved and respected by all members of his congregation. Will Brand now operated in the shadow of his son and had done so for several years following the death of Ellen Brand, Will's wife and Billy's mother. Recently Will Brand had been diagnosed with Alzheimer's Disease and even though he was only seventy-four, the disease appeared to be advancing rapidly. Meanwhile, Billy and his wife had not yet been blessed with any children although thirty-nine year old Sarah Anne had suffered through three miscarriages.

Among the members of the congregation who were listening to Reverend Brand were Patch and Maggie Munson. They shared some of the pain that Brand and his wife felt because they too were childless, and Maggie had also suffered through a miscarriage. However the Munsons were different from the Brands in that they thought of themselves as being several years beyond the child rearing years of their lives, and there was no prospect of a change in that status. For that matter they had only had sexual intercourse a few times in the past two years.

As Patch Munson listened to Billy Brand continuing to disparage the likes of Aaron Fein and other abortionists, he began to feel sorry for himself. Munson had never had the son he wanted, the boy who would go hunting and fishing with him, the boy who would have children of his own to carry on the Munson name. He was sad that there would be no Harry Munson IV or for that matter there would not be another Munson at all in his family tree. (Of course, Harry the hound didn't register at all in this equation.) Munson had never considered adoption. Maggie had brought up the topic once or twice and when Munson rejected her entreaty the topic was never broached again.

"*Onleh* God *almahghteh* knows what causes men *lahke* Aaron *Fahne t' continya t'* prosper in the sinful pursuit of profits, *whahle ignorin'* the innocent infants whose *incubatin'* existence *continyas t'* enlarge, expand and develop in the wombs of their *mothehs*."

Billy Brand had now been preaching about the dignity of life and the sanctity of the unborn soul for half an hour. He had started by harshly criticizing a specific abortion clinic in Florida and now was concluding by returning to the same villainous venue. His voice was loud and powerful. "But, *Ah'll* tell *yew* this, *mah brothehs* in Christ. God waits *'til* the end of life *t'* pass judgment on those who eschew his message of *merceh t'* all. But God does not tell us the *tahme* frame for that end of *lahfe* judgment. It could come *fur aneh* one *o* us in *thirteh* years, or in *thirteh* days or in *thirteh* minutes. But Judgment Day will *arrahve fur* each *an' evereh* one *o* us ... of that *y'all cain* be certain."

As Brand wound down his sermon, Patch Munson sat soberly in his pew. He marveled that Brand was able to put into words, some of the very thoughts that Munson himself held dear. Brand preached on a wide variety of topics and Munson wasn't enamored with all of them. He was sensitive about Brand's frequent critical remarks about people's attachment to physical assets, like land and money. But for the most part Munson was in sync with Brand's teachings. Billy Brand had also been solicitous of the spiritual well being of Munson and his sisters after the recent passing of both of their parents. On the topic of abortion, Patch Munson was 100 percent aligned with Billy Brand.

Aaron Fein opened the door to his office and admitted the reporter. Fein believed that Priscilla Stengel was on his side. He thought that Stengel would write an article that was favorable to the FCW, the Fein Center for Women. He had met Priscilla before, but he didn't know her well. She had already written a pro-choice article for her paper several years earlier after the initial demonstrations by pro-life groups against the expansion of the Fein Center.

"Come in and have a seat, Priscilla. Can we get you some coffee or a soft drink?"

"No, to the coffee, but I will take some water if you don't mind."

Stengel situated herself on a couch in Fein's office and immediately noticed that there was a general plush feeling to Fein's office that was incongruous with the more austere offices that she had visited in other parts of the Fein Center. Fein's professional looking secretary brought in a glass with ice and a bottle of water and handed them to Stengel before leaving the room and shutting the door behind her.

"Well, I must say that it's awfully nice of you and your editor to want to do an article on the FCW. How can I help?"

"Actually, as I indicated on the phone, we wanted to focus more on you, Dr. Fein. We are doing a series on businessmen and businesswomen in the Greater Tampa area, who have created job opportunities during the last five years. The series takes a human interest approach to discussing the people behind the businesses rather than the actual businesses themselves."

"I see. That could be tricky. Will I be able to review the article before it goes to print?"

"I will send you a courtesy copy the night before publication, if you would like."

Fein was really asking whether or not he could have advance editorial control before the article was published. They both knew that the answer to that unasked question was "no." However, Fein figured that there was no harm in asking.

"I'm not a publicity hound, although I don't mind discussing my work. I just don't like to get too personal."

"Why don't we just try a few questions and see where it takes us. Naturally you can answer whatever you'd like to answer, and refrain from answering anything you might find too delicate."

"Fair enough. What would you like to know?"

As a reporter Priscilla Stengel knew to ask open-ended soft background questions at first. These were a prelude to more probing personal questions that might give more insight into Fein's personality and feelings about the issues surrounding his business. "Could you tell me about your childhood and when you decided that you wanted to be a physician?"

"I grew up in Cedarhurst, New York, which is on the South Shore of Long Island. I was an only child. If you know anything about growing up Jewish on Long Island, you will know that a medical profession was chosen for you by your mother even before your Bar Mitzvah. Every Jewish mother has to have a doctor in the family and I was her only option." Fein tried to be humorous, but Stengel just stared and waited for the delivery of more details.

"Let's see. What else can I tell you? I went to NYU for my undergraduate degree, and then to Vanderbilt School of Medicine in Tennessee. After doing my gynecology residency back up in New York, I opened my first private practice in Queens, New York. That was twenty-six years ago." He paused and then asked, "Is this the kind of thing you're looking for?" He noticed that she was taking out a small recorder.

"That's fine for starters." She tittered self-consciously as she realized that she had unwittingly punned. Her hand went briefly toward her mouth.

"Yes, you might well say that's *Fein* for starters. What else would you like to know?"

Stengel quickly recovered her balance by temporarily suspending eye contact and then asking her next question. "Why did you choose an obstetrics and gynecology specialty? Why not cardiology or radiology or neurology?"

"I'd like to tell you that I had a calling for women's health right from the beginning, but that would be less than truthful. Somewhere along the line I realized that there was a significant demand for women's health services and I believed that it was a good business to be in. In all candor, I liked the idea of dealing with young women of a child bearing age."

Priscilla Stengel paused to consider Dr. Fein's answer. On the surface it sounded blasé enough. However she had always believed that Fein had a sleazy side to him that was hard for many people to detect. She had no proof or evidence of untoward behavior. She just had this feeling. She always trusted her feelings, even when they had betrayed her in the past. She decided to move further along on her unveiling of the Fein resume.

"So as I understand it, your facility in Queens, New York, dealt exclusively with women's issues surrounding conception."

"No. That wouldn't be accurate. We dealt with the whole realm of women's health issues. However if you wanted to surmise that the majority of these issues dealt with pregnancies I would acknowledge that as an accurate assessment."

"Would you also say that the majority of your revenue came from performing abortions?"

"We didn't start that way. But yes, over time terminations for unwanted pregnancies became a large part of our practice. Women would be referred to our center because we came to be known and acknowledged as understanding and empathetic practitioners. We treated our clientele with dignity and privacy, just as we do now in the Fein Center for Women here in Tampa."

"Okay Dr. Fein. And as I understand it, your first partner up in New York, was Dr. Leslie Wolf, who was also your first wife. Do I have my facts straight?"

"Why is this important? I thought you wanted to do an article about Tampa based businesses. We're talking here about a part of my career that was more than 20 years ago."

"This is simply background. Remember this article will be about you and your career and how you came to be a large employer in Tampa."

"Yes. But I told you before that I'm not all that comfortable dealing with personal items. I'd prefer to leave my personal relationships out of it entirely."

"But Dr. Wolf was more than your first wife; she was also your first business partner. Don't you think that she had some bearing on your career?"

Aaron Fein did not like the way this interview was heading. He had expected something entirely different. Maybe a puff piece about how much good the FCW was doing for the community was too much to hope for. However the reason he agreed to do the interview in the first place was because Stengel had been even-handed in her reporting in the past. He didn't want to see his personal life exposed, even if it could, in some convoluted way, prove to be positive for his business.

"Both of my ex-wives were involved in my business in the past. But I have not seen either of them in more than a dozen years. I'd strongly like to avoid any reference to these women in any article that you might write. Can you promise me that much?"

"This won't be an article about your ex-wives. Nor will it be about your current wife, Amanda. Although I believe Amanda is a nurse and administrator here at the clinic. Is that right?"

Fein gave a nod of affirmation without answering her question aloud. Stengel didn't wait for a comment. She just continued because she didn't want to promise anything to Fein.

"This will be an article about Aaron Fein, the man who owns the Fein Center for Women. However as a human interest article, our readers will be captivated by some simple facts, like whether you are married and whether you have children. We want to portray the human side to the businessman as well as the business side of the employer."

"And that last part is what is truly important. Is it not? The fact that we employ almost 400 people from the greater Tampa area should be what interests most people."

"That is the baseline for our series. Entrepreneurial employers are important to the community. We are simply trying to shed some light on what these people are all about."

"Well the fact that I've been married three times and have no children has nothing whatsoever to do with my ability to run a successful woman's health facility."

"Maybe the readers should make that decision for themselves. You've been married three times and divorced twice. Many people have been through turbulent marriages and they have a perspective about those who have had a similar failure. I'm a single parent and that gives me a perspective on those who are parents and those who are not. Your business often deals with a decision about whether or not to become a parent. This makes your personal experience a matter of interest to those who might be your clientele."

Priscilla vaguely referenced her own experience simply to lend credibility to her line of inquiry. She was glad that the self-absorbed person she was interviewing would never ask her for any more personal revelation.

"I think you're stretching there, Priscilla. Why don't we stick to my business credentials and the success of the Fein Center? And leave my ex-wives and Amanda out of it."

Stengel realized that she would need to get to the Fein Center sooner than she might have liked, but she was prepared to ask difficult questions here as well.

"Estimates have been made that the Fein Center performed as many as 3000 abortions a year during the last three years. Would you say that this is about right?"

"No. The number is a vast overestimate. And as you know the term abortion has a negative connotation. We have had more than 5000 women utilize the services of our women's center each year for the past few years. There is a wide variety of services that we provide. Among the procedures that are offered at the center are methods for preventing and limiting unwanted pregnancies. Within this group we have some patients who elect to terminate a pregnancy. The vast majority of this group realizes that these terminations differ significantly depending upon the trimester as well as time within a trimester."

"That still doesn't answer the question of how many abortions you and your colleagues perform at the Fein Center every year. If the number 3000 is too many, what is the real number?"

"Very few women come here and have a late term pregnancy abortion."

"However you and your colleagues will perform an abortion at any time during a pregnancy. Am I right about that?"

"Our center protects the rights as well as the privacy of young women. Unfortunately some young women go through a protracted period of indecision prior to making their decision to terminate their pregnancies. Naturally this makes the procedure more complicated. But once again we put the rights and privacy of our clientele ahead of any dissemination of information to the general public."

"I'm certainly not looking to abrogate or abridge the rights of any of your patients. As a reporter I would like to enhance those rights by providing access to more information about your clinic and the services you provide. However I'm also looking to put these services in a proper perspective."

"Can't we do that without reigniting a referendum on the topic of women's healthcare rights?"

"I recognize that abortion is an emotionally charged topic and my role is not to reinvigorate the debate. However I would like to write a fact based article about the Fein Center for Women as one of Tampa's growing employers. And I will discuss the different services that you provide. However I also want to provide this information in an appropriate context and perspective. That's why I'm talking to you and not just to your publicist. The building has your name on the door. Who is better to characterize what you do here than Aaron Fein?"

The interview lasted another twenty minutes and Aaron Fein managed to move the focus away from the topic of pregnancy terminations and onto some of the ancillary services that the Center provided. Priscilla Stengel was satisfied that she had fulfilled her reporter's obligation to give her interviewee an opportunity to provide context for the subject matter of the article that she was about to write. And although she wasn't able to pin him down on exact numbers for any of the procedures that they performed, he didn't deny the volume figures that she suggested either.

During the interview there was one impression that came across to Stengel in an overwhelming way. There was a stark depersonalization to almost every remark that Fein made. It was almost as though he went out of his way to separate himself from his clientele. He never once cited any customer satisfaction surveys or follow-up care programs that were unique or distinctive. For that matter he seemed oblivious to the fact that one of his clients had been interviewing him right there in his office.

After Sunday services at the Christian Ascendancy Community Church, Patch and Maggie spent a few minutes at the fellowship reception under the backyard tent on the church property. The parishioners brought homemade biscuits, coffee cakes, fruit bars and other treats, while the church provided coffee, tea and soft drinks. Fellowship generally lasted about forty-five minutes, but the Munsons rarely stayed longer than fifteen minutes before Patch Munson walked over and started the engine to his pickup. Invariably Harry would be faithfully waiting leashed onto the rear platform of the Silverado. This routine had played out in a similar fashion for quite some time.

On this particular Sunday, Munson was standing by himself with a mug of coffee while Maggie conversed with a few of her lady friends. He looked up and saw his two large sisters, Gloria and Marjorie standing near the courtyard gate after singing in the choir during the service. They both were wearing large loose black dresses and Munson couldn't help thinking they looked like two Hefty Bags ready to be stuffed with the leftover garbage from the fellowship. But then again the equally rotund Patch Munson was not exactly an example of sartorial splendor. Munson walked over to where they were standing. He listened as Gloria complained about the one flaw in Reverend Brand's weekly services, the fact that he was inept at leading his congregation in song.

"*Billeh Bran' cudden carreh* a tune *iffin* he had a bucket *wit'* a lid on it." The ladies all put their fingers in front of their mouths to hide their giggles as Patch Munson approached. He ignored the other women but greeted his sisters perfunctorily. The giggling stopped and the women's demeanor grew more somber.

"Marge; Gloria." Patch Munson offered a two word greeting but it was enough to engage them.

"So *wuddid y'all thaank 'bout* Reverend *Billeh's* message *'bout dat A-bortion* guy?" Gloria was by far the most vocal of the Munson siblings. However it seemed absurd to hear such a melodious voice coming from such a sad sack of a body. Her voice may have been easy on the ear, but her figure was not easy on the eye.

"*Billeh's gat* his way." Munson answered Gloria's question while looking back and forth at the two Hefty Bags. One was now animated. The other didn't move.

"That *Fahne* fellow *betteh* keep *hisse'f* in *Floor'da, an' furget 'bout comin'* up our way. Tell *yew dat.*"

"*Ah* agree. We don't need his *kahnd 'round* here."

"*Yew thaank Billeh's gunna* organize *sem kahnd o* protest at City Hall like he *dun* when they had that atheist *professeh speakin'* at the college graduation?"

"*Wudden'* be *surprahsed,*" Patch answered his rotund sister. "*Billeh dudden' cotton* much *t'* outsiders *comin'* into our neck *o* the woods *an' tellin'* us how *thaangs* should be. And he's *fahred* up *'bout* this Jew *wantin' t'* come here *an'* kill babies. *Ah* am too. *Billeh jes'* says it better *'an* me."

"*Ah wudden worreh* too much *'bout* it." Gloria said with an air of finality. "The Lord has a way of *lettin'* us know what *t'* do, when, where *an' whah.*" She then waddled over next to her sister Hefty Bag with her nose in the air in an attempt to distance herself from discussion about someone she considered to be white trash.

II

Terrifying Thursday

Hawk Richter was looking forward to his dinner with Julianne Carson. He wondered about her motives. Behavior was always driven by motives, he thought. His driver was winding his way through the early evening traffic near the west end of Interstate Rte 4 where it spills into Rte 275 heading southwest toward Tampa Airport.

"Why is the traffic so heavy tonight, Paul?"

"Not sure, Professor Richter."

"It's always slow around here though isn't it?"

"Yeah, I guess you're right." The driver hoped that Richter was merely making small talk, and he tried to be agreeable with the physicist-professor. He knew that Richter had a habit of turning the most mundane topic such as automobile traffic into a scientific dissertation without much provocation whatsoever.

Bertrand "Hawk" Richter didn't believe in God. He was a physicist by training, a university professor and public orator by occupation and he was sometimes characterized as an ethicist through his writings. He adhered to no unsubstantiated beliefs. He lived in a world of empirical fact. Beliefs were simply unproven theories. He had contempt for organized religion which he disrespected as a salve for the intellectually challenged or tortured. But holding no "unsubstantiated beliefs" did not mean that Hawk Richter didn't have any values. And it didn't mean he had no opinions.

"We're all such creatures of habit. Aren't we, Paul? Traffic is a classic example … people all leaving somewhere around the same time, heading in the same direction."

"That's not such a bad thing, is it?" As soon as he took the bait he wanted to spit the hook. Richter had caught him again. The lecture was about to ensue.

"That depends on what arguments you want to make about the superiority of the human race. What's so different about humans? Aren't we essentially like lemmings or like the swallows who return to Capistrano every year on St Joseph's Day? Are we any better off than the migrating animals around us?"

"No. We migrate twice a day and call it commuting." Paul gave a snippy answer to Richter's rhetorical questions. He did his best to avoid being challenging even though he knew that Richter would like that more than the simple resignation of agreement, which Paul was offering.

"So you don't want to debate, I see. You should argue more, Paul. It's good stimulation for your brain."

"If you say so, Boss." Paul attempted to head off the rest of the lecture while still remaining civil. But for his own satisfaction, he raised his right hand and extended his middle finger to punctuate his annoyance. He knew that the blind man wouldn't be able to see his gesture.

In the back seat Hawk Richter thought that, *Paul is probably giving me the finger again.* The blind lecturer had an uncanny ability to sense such things and that was what made him such a complex person. On the one hand he professed to be an empiricist. On the other hand because of his physical blindness he was often forced to make assumptions about things that were not visible to him. The irony of this dichotomy amused him more than it befuddled him.

The traffic picked up a bit as they started down Rte 275. Paul put both hands back on the wheel and changed the subject, before Richter went back to lecture mode.

"So what time do you want me to pick you up, after your dinner?"

"I've only met this woman once, so I'm not sure what to expect. Just be ready around 9 PM and we can take it from there. If I need you sooner, I'll call. Even if this woman is a total bore, Armani's is a great restaurant with a wonderful atmosphere. I can't see finishing dinner in less than two hours. Nevertheless, if I'm not down by 9:30 then come up to the restaurant and get me. We are such slaves to time and schedules though. Aren't we?" Paul was flabbergasted that he still couldn't shake Richter's philosophical approach to anything and everything.

"You once said that every minute of every hour is important and that every hour of every day is precious."

"That I did dear Paul, but I have probably been less than an effective teacher for you in this regard. The minutes, hours and days are indeed all precious. That's why we shouldn't waste time counting them or relentlessly ordering them. A bit of disarray is a good thing."

"If you say so, Boss." It was Paul's favorite rejoinder although it never stopped Richter from lecturing.

"Did you know that there wasn't always twenty-four hours in the day or seven days in a week? In the seventeenth century we had ten hour days."

"That's not possible. Isn't time controlled by the earth's relationship with the sun and the moon?" Paul was hopelessly ensnared. "Each day lasts twenty-four hours because that's how long it takes for the earth to spin on its axis. Each year is 365 days because that's how long it takes for the earth to revolve around the sun."

"Beware of conventional thinking about the demarcation of time dear Paul."

"What do you mean?"

"Who decides that there are twenty-four hours in a day and sixty minutes in an hour? Time, like many other facets of life is a relative convention. Yes there's a span of time that it takes for the earth to turn on its axis and for the earth to travel around the sun, but within these cycles of life the demarcations of minutes, hours, weeks and months are due to mortal beings configuring allotments of time."

"I see." Richter and his driver both knew that Paul's two word response wouldn't stop the lecture. But the truth of the matter was that occasionally Paul was enthralled by Hawk Richter.

"After the French Revolution in the eighteenth century there was more change afoot than a simple political transition. There was a movement towards a pervasive cultural revolution as well. France had traditionally been a Roman Catholic country. The French had conventionally utilized the same Gregorian calendar that is the international standard today. The Gregorian Calendar was named after Pope Gregory XIII, who ran the political entity known as the Roman Catholic Church in the latter part of the sixteenth century. Among many changes the French wanted to make, they attempted to bring the metric system of measurements to all facets of everyday life. This included decimal measures of time. They introduced the French Republican Calendar and decreed that there would be ten hours each day."

"So they had shorter days?"

"No. They had 100 minutes in each hour and 100 seconds within each minute. Therefore they had hours that contained a time span that was more than twice the elapsed time that we currently call an hour."

"And the math works out that simply? They just rounded off each day by making longer minutes and hours? I can't believe that it would work out that flawlessly. Did God create a perfect day that fit perfectly into the metric system?" Paul thought that this was the ideal rejoinder to Richter's lecture and his poorly-veiled criticism of Catholicism. He also thought it was a good rebuttal to Richter's atheistic convictions. However Paul was in over his head when it came to having an intellectual debate with Richter. The professor laughed and made an honest but futile effort not to be condescending in the process.

"You theists need to work harder for explanations. You can't simply chalk things up to 'the will of god.' There's a scientific basis for everything. As for the French Republican Calendar, the secret to making the math work was in the smallest measure of time. Each second of the metric minute was slightly shorter than what we know as a second today." The blind man paused for a conventional second or two to ensure that Paul was still following his dissertation. "Each second was the equivalent of 0.864 Gregorian seconds. You see, the answers are almost always found in the most diminutive details. This is why I'm so fond of quantum physics. But that's a whole other story."

A quantum physics harangue was not high on Paul's list of lectures to endure. Besides he still didn't quite understand all of the implications of the French Republican Calendar, so he went back to the topic. "What about the other measures of time, like the weeks, and months? How did the Frogs squeeze these together to fit into a year? I'm assuming that the years were the same length."

"Yes, years were approximately the same length, with the actual time span being determined by the day of the occurrence of the autumnal equinox each year. Subtending the designation of the time span of each year was the determination that each month would have three weeks … the French called them, décades … and each week, or décade, would have ten days. Each month therefore would have exactly thirty days rather than the varied lengths of the Gregorian months."

"That doesn't seem precise and scientific, Hawk. Even with twelve months like we have today it would create a short year of 360 days. We now have 365 and a quarter days. Right?" Paul was unwittingly caught up in the debate that he didn't want to enter. Richter, the scientist/professor was thrilled that he had ensnared his driver/student.

"This is true. However just like we do in our awkward Gregorian calendar, the Frogs found methods to account for the extra days to round out a year. The French, by the way, did have 12 months in their year. These calculations were meant to approximate the phases of the moon. However their calculations were every bit as imprecise as those of the Gregorian calendar. We get a full moon every twenty-seven and a third days, and we get 13.3 full moons each time the earth makes its annual orbit of the sun."

Paul was now totally bewildered. He inadvertently made a reverberating noise with his lips and felt like the frustrated AFLAC duck. Fortunately traffic was now moving at a normal pace and he decided not to reengage in the conversation. He hoped that he would be able to ride out the last three miles to the hotel without enduring more philosophical or historical instruction from his employer. So he changed the topic.

"We'll be coming up on the Hyatt in about five minutes, Hawk."

The blind man took that as his cue to finish up his lecture.

"Just a couple more quick points I wanted to make about time and calendars. First let me say something about moons and months. Because there are approximately 13 moons in the year, it is rare to have two full moons in the same month. Over time the second full moon within a month became known as a "blue moon." That's how the expression 'once in a blue moon' came to depict a very rare event."

Paul was now pulling into the long driveway of the Hyatt, and Richter could sense from the turns that they were fast approaching the main doorway of the hotel. So he hurriedly imparted one last pearl of wisdom.

"You know Paul; the French Republican Calendar was only in use for about a dozen years. Napoleon finally gave in to the Catholic Church and reestablished the Gregorian Calendar in 1806. So for all practical purposes it was merely a short episode in the way people measure time. If you want to dig deeper on how people have historically measured time, you might investigate one of the many other calendars that have been in use over more extended periods. The Chinese Calendar, the Jewish Calendar and the Islamic Calendar are all in use to some degree today."

Paul got out of the car, quickly circled around the back and opened the rear passenger side door to allow Richter to exit with his cane, as a doorman approached to assist him. Once standing outside the car, Richter concluded his lecture on calendars and time keeping by saying, "Forget about these other modern calendars. If you want to find some interesting thinking about time, check out the ancient calendars, particularly the Mayan Calendar. It'll be right up your alley. It's very spiritual."

The driver was finally able to terminate his lesson by passing Richter off to the doorman. He then wondered if Richter's dinner date knew what she would have to suffer through. *Poor woman*, he thought. Paul then drove under a light in the parking lot and picked up the book he intended to begin reading while he waited for Richter. He opened The Rhapsody Players and turned the first few pages and came to the Foreword. It contained an interesting quote from an unknown philosopher:

"Time is an illusion. There is no beginning. There is no end. Life is simply a series of snapshots without a plot. If you flip them together quickly the mind creates the mirage of motion and motion creates the illusion of time."

The drive from Mobile, Alabama to Tampa, Florida was an opportunity for Patch Munson to think about many things over an eight hour stretch. Some of his thinking was unrelated to his self-appointed mission. And then some thoughts were specifically related to the tactical execution of his duty. His mission was for the betterment of society, but it was an undertaking that he needed to execute furtively. He kept counsel to himself alone. Sure he had heard his friend Bubba Looney declare that Yankees like Aaron Fein deserved to be 'hung by *der* balls *'til* they *dah*.' But for all his bravado *big ole* Officer Bubba Looney was a finger pointer more than a fist pounder. Bubba had been Munson's friend since childhood, but now that Bubba was a police detective he was getting pretty damn uppity. No, this was definitely a mission he would carry out alone ... except naturally Harry the hound would be riding shotgun.

Munson left Mobile with $350 in cash. This would enable him to avoid using any credit cards that could help trace his path, if it ever came to that. Even the cash was not an obvious recent withdrawal. It was part of his fishing trip money that he kept hidden in a metal box in the bomb shelter.

Munson figured that he would be gone for three days. It would take him one day to get to Tampa, one day to carry out his mission and one day to drive back to Alabama. He would be staying over two nights near Tampa if all went according to plan. He didn't want to be on the road when the police department would be on high alert for anything suspicious. He also didn't want to register at any hotel. He knew that campsites were less particular about taking identification and license plate numbers and generally just accepted whatever was filled out on the registration form. He had targeted a campsite a half hour north of The Fein Center. Munson had two hunting rifles in the back of his Silverado that were legitimately registered in Alabama. He had no intention of using either one of them on this trip. He was also carrying one unregistered and untraceable handgun. This weapon could be jettisoned immediately after the mission had been completed.

Munson had told Maggie that he was "*goin' fishin'*" for a couple of days" and as was typical of his wife, she posed no questions. However Maggie did wonder why her husband enjoyed his fishing trips so much when he didn't even know how to swim. She guessed that he never worried about falling overboard.

After driving past Pensacola and Tallahassee, Patch then preceded south along I 75 towards Gainesville, Ocala and ultimately towards Tampa. He arrived at the campsite in New Port Richey, Florida at 2:00 PM and paid the proprietor in cash. He scribbled his name and license plate in an illegible manner on the registration form and then drove back to his allotted spot near the rear of the campsite. He was 35 miles north of downtown Tampa and 24 miles northwest of The Fein Center for Women. He set up his tent quickly and prepared himself for the task ahead. Then he went back to his Silverado and retrieved two Budweisers to calm his nerves.

Carol Mays was back in New York City. She had just left the midtown studio after the cover shoot for *New York Nights* magazine. She hated the term *supermodel* that was often affixed to the elite of her profession, not because her own credentials fell slightly short of that designation, but because she found the term itself to be pretentious. Modeling was hard work and most careers were relatively short. One day there is an attentive media and an adoring public, limousine rides and red carpets. The next day there is an occasional gossip column reference, an isolated autograph request, taxi cabs and hard wood floors. From there the downward trajectory often became a rapid slide into oblivion. An intelligent professional would have saved enough money from her halcyon days to avoid the troubled lives of many of those who clung to their glory days. Mays had a keen awareness of these facts and also knew that as an African American model the opportunities were fewer and the decline could be more rapid, unless she handled herself and her career with an ardent appreciation of the opportunity she had.

"Hey baby. How was your trip back home?" Jude Royale, a prototypical New York fashion aficionado, was also Carol Mays trusted friend. She loved his sense of humor even more than his flair for fashion. Jude was also at the forefront of the party scene in New York for the artsy folks who knew no difference between a weekday night and a weekend night in the summer. However this was a sultry summer afternoon and the two friends were enjoying lunch together at "Pera" an interesting Mediterranean eatery on Madison Avenue.

"It was all right … a week out of the craziness of Manhattan is good for the soul." Mays knew that she had to be upbeat and carefree around Jude. He would be able to detect the slightest hint of sadness and would be probing for responses to questions that Mays didn't want to answer.

"So did you spend some quality time with Mom and Dad? Aren't they so proud of their rich, sophisticated daughter who undoubtedly is the talk of the town back in Birmingham?" Mays didn't want to lie to Jude about her trip down south, but she didn't want to get into details either. She chose to ignore his first question and give lip service to the second inquiry.

"My parents don't understand what I do. They have no idea how much money I make, and they don't care. They love me for who I am and that's that."

"I'll bet they loved seeing their grandson."

Mays didn't bother telling Jude that her trip to Alabama didn't include an extended visit with Russell's grandparents. After a short stopover in Birmingham, she had driven down to Mobile with the crazy idea of introducing Russell to his father. But she lost her nerve in the confessional, while she left her seven year old son at the hotel day care facility. After her faux-confession, she returned to get her son and Russell had no real concern because she hadn't confided in him beforehand.

"Mom and Dad love Russell to death. They always look forward to seeing him." Mays quickly changed the subject and had no intention of returning to it. "What are you going to have for lunch?"

"What's not to like about Russ? He's seven years old and already gorgeous, like his Mom. He's polite and he's smart as a whip. He's going to make somebody very happy some day." Royale wouldn't be moved off the topic.

"He already makes *me* happy. And he also loves his Uncle Jude."

"Sometimes I wish I was his real uncle."

"What's that supposed to mean? Being an uncle is more about being there for someone than it is about biology."

"In that case, why shouldn't I just be his father? I'm sure I spend more time with him than his father does." Jude couldn't help himself. He was always hoping that sooner or later Carol would confide in him regarding the identity of Russell's biological father. Carol still wanted to change the subject.

"Russell's father is a good man. He just isn't in a position to spend time with Russell. Can we change the subject?"

"Certainly, dearest. Which museum did we decide on for our date with Russ next week?"

"You love MOMA, Jude, and I love The Met, but I think that Russell will enjoy the Museum of Natural History the most, with all of the dinosaurs and whatnot. If you have some time this afternoon we could preview it together. I hear they've got a great exhibit on the human brain. Are you up for it?"

"That would be wonderful …a nice compromise." Royale finally focused on the menus that they had in front of them. "So what will you have for lunch? There are so many good things on the carte du jour."

"All of the small plates and mezes look great. But I think I'm just going to have the watermelon and feta salad. What are you going to have?"

"The Turkish smoked lamb tacos and some grape leaves are wonderful. This place has the most interesting lunch menu. I always have something different." Royale then smiled at his dear friend. "Isn't this the greatest city in the world? You can get different food every day of the year if you like."

"At least it's nice to look at the different menu items. But some of us have to watch what we eat. You know?"

"We all choose our own professions."

"And exactly what is it that you do again, Jude?" Mays chided her friend only because she knew that he wouldn't take her criticism personally. They both knew that Jude Royale made his income simply by being Jude Royale. He had been left a small fortune as an inheritance from his parents who were in the Asian textile industry and died several years earlier. Royale loved the fashion industry, the shows, the models, the glamour, each and every facet of it. He also enjoyed appearing on several television shows as a fashion expert, who was always ready with a quick quip or criticism.

"Lest you forget, Darling, I make my living by commenting on the apparel which you wear when you strut up and down the runway at the behest of those who write your paycheck. But that's OK. If you want to be snippy, I'll just let you pick up the check for lunch."

The banter went back and forth between the two friends and although most of the conversation was superficial in nature, Mays realized what a good friend she had in Jude Royale. She even contemplated whether she should reconsider telling him about Russell's father. She needed to give it a more thought.

Father Timothy Hanlon was reading the Liturgy of the Hours from his breviary in the den of the rectory. The daily ritual was part of being a Catholic priest. On some days Hanlon found it to be a tedious and monotonous task. He tried hard to derive significant understanding from the translated verbiage and it was difficult work. On other days he read the breviary in a more relaxed and intellectually unencumbered manner. On those days his mind and spirit wandered as his eyes floated lightly across each sentence of the text. He thought about his parishioners, especially those who were down on their luck; those who were sick and those who were lonely; those who were poor and those who were too proud to reach out for help. They were all his charges. On his good days Hanlon knew that he made a difference in their lives. On more difficult days he prayed for the strength to keep doing what he was doing. In order to conquer those more difficult days, he had to overcome his own doubts and uncertainties. Lately the doubts and uncertainties were winning.

The housekeeper, Bernadette, stopped by the study and tried to gauge Father Hanlon's mood. She would not interrupt him in his prayerful meditation. But she knew that he would sometimes pause of his own volition and speak to her if it met his fancy. He could simply sense her presence.

"Good morning Bernadette."

"Good morning, Father Hanlon."

Hanlon had been daydreaming while he read his breviary, so he pulled the ribbon bookmark into place and looked up at Bernadette. She had been the rectory housekeeper for more than 35 years, and she had not been given a salary increase since Hanlon had arrived in the parish. However she never breathed a word of this to Hanlon.

There were two priests in the rectory. The pastor, Father George Goethe, was a rather officious sixty year old man, who only seemed interested in Bernadette as the cook/housekeeper. But Father Hanlon was a tall handsome young priest, who was more in touch with the parishioners. Bernadette had a feeling about everything that went on in the rectory. Without being told she knew when a new priest was about to arrive or when an existing cleric was about to complete his service to the parish. She knew when the relationship between Father Goethe and any of the young assistant priests was not going according to plan. Bernadette also knew how Father Goethe perceived each of his assistants. She realized that Father Goethe respected Father Hanlon more than the last two or three assistant pastors. She respected Hanlon as well. He was different from most of the other priests that had been assigned to the parish during her tenure as the housekeeper. For one thing Hanlon was straight and tall. Nearly all of the other priests that had been assigned to the parish were short. And she worried that the few tall priests were not straight.

"Father Goethe went into town to make his deposits at the bank. He said to tell you that he'd be back in twenty minutes. Can I get you something to eat for breakfast, Father Hanlon?"

"No, thank you. But a cup of coffee would be great, however." Hanlon put down his breviary and decided that he would return to reading it after his conversation with Father Goethe. He had to think things through before that conversation took place. Bernadette returned with the coffee at about the same time as the front door to the rectory opened and the pastor came in.

Goethe appeared slightly haggard and worn out, which was unusual. Normally he held his head high and made a valiant effort at conveying confident dignity. On this morning, however he appeared tired and resigned. It was as though he already knew why Hanlon wanted to talk with him. He didn't waste any time after his entry. He walked towards Hanlon sitting in the den. He noted the breviary in Hanlon's lap and thought that it was a hopeful sign.

"Are you ready to talk now?"

"Yes. I think now is good." The younger priest answered in a non-confrontational tone.

The den in the rectory was a warm room, wood paneled and thickly carpeted. There was a leather couch lining one wall. A rectangular wooden coffee table separated the couch from two plush brown leather armchairs. Further back in the room there was a desk that was used by both priests. Facing the desk in a catty-cornered fashion were two smaller and lighter leather chairs. Behind the desk was a swivel leather chair which was the largest of all the chairs in the room. Neither priest approached the desk. Hanlon had been seated in one of the leather chairs across from the couch. Goethe walked over and turned the matching chair so that he could face Hanlon with both men being on the interior side of the room.

"I sense that the topic of our discussion may be troubling to us both." Goethe didn't procrastinate. "Should I get my stole?" Goethe referred to the purple silk, scarf-like vestment that priests wore to hear confessions, including those of other priests.

"Not now. I think we should have a *business* discussion before I try to deal with my *business* in an appropriate spiritual manner. Reconciliation on a secular level may need to take place before I will be able to seek reconciliation on a sacramental basis."

"It's never too soon to seek forgiveness from God."

"At this point, I'm seeking understanding, rather than forgiveness."

"There are some things that we will never understand, Father Hanlon." Goethe addressed his colleague formally rather than calling him by his given name, Tim, as he more frequently did around the rectory. He was thereby subconsciously setting the parameters of the discourse to follow. "God knows everything, and while we can appeal to him for knowledge and understanding, He will only reveal to us that which he chooses to reveal."

"I agree. Of course," he hesitated, "that doesn't mean I understand." He paused again reflectively. "Maybe this lack of understanding is what we need to talk about. I'm not certain that my vocation was God's choice. Maybe I have made a mistake. Maybe I should not have become a priest. And maybe it's time for me to leave the priesthood."

"That's a lot of 'maybes,' Father Hanlon. You don't seem certain about any of this. What is it that is causing your doubt? Is it a secular matter or a spiritual concern?"

"It's a bit of both."

"Explain that to me."

"My faith is weaker than I'd like to believe. And my fortitude is also not what it needs to be. Every day I have questions and concerns about my vows. Most particularly I'm concerned about my vow of abstinence."

"If there is a transgression that concerns you, we could handle it within the context of the sacrament of reconciliation and there would be no need for me to discuss it with the bishop or any of the other members of the liturgical hierarchy." It was apparent to Hanlon what Goethe wanted to hear. He knew that Goethe was hoping to hear about a transgression that could be forgiven rather than something more profound and enduring.

"It's not something that I've done that I want to discuss. It's more about how I feel about my vows of abstinence in general."

"We are all human, Father Hanlon. It is natural for us to desire sexual congregation with women. It is a beautiful part of the human existence. That's why The Church recognizes marriage as a most blessed sacrament. The Church also says that sexual relationships outside of the sacrament of matrimony are sinful. The Church does not permit its priests to marry and therefore it requires a vow of abstinence. But again, we are human. We are fallible. If we repent for our failures, God will forgive us."

Hanlon felt his Adam's apple bob in his throat. Then he swallowed hard and cut to the chase. "Excuse me, George, for being so direct. However, speaking as one human being to another, I find it hard to believe that a loving God would ask us to take a vow of celibacy. Although I have kept my vow since entering the priesthood, I have strong misgivings about this. I don't believe it is natural. I have had many thoughts about what I have done. After some of thought and prayer, I have come to the conclusion that I want to leave the priesthood."

Joseph Clinton was every bit as deranged as his predecessors, Charles Joseph Whitman and Seung Hui Cho. Like Whitman, at the University of Texas at Austin in August of 1966, and Cho at Virginia Tech in April of 2007, Clinton was bent on mass murder. His venue was the campus of Baker-Browning Institute of Technology, Science and Yon, also known as BITSY.

Clinton began the morning by writing one last chapter in his "Manifesto for the New Recognition of Individualism," a rambling and disjointed dissertation on Clinton's views of the world that was unfathomable to anyone other than Clinton. In his writings Joseph Clinton referred to himself as JC and at various points in his 1000 page treatise likened himself to Jesus Christ. In other parts of his manifesto he likened himself to Buddha and Mohammed. In some sections of the manifesto he equally defamed many of the great religions of the world while cursing himself in the process. Elsewhere in his manifesto he slammed organized religion entirely. At the beginning of his Manifesto he was in favor of women's rights, toward the middle he cursed the practice of abortion, and then toward the end he had a whole mishmash of opinions on the topic. He was also against big business, big government and major philanthropic organizations. The emotional swing of his writings was as far flung as his contradictory viewpoints. He was a madman.

The early evening hours on this Thursday in July found Clinton in his off campus apartment loading his various weapons into a stolen golf bag that had a weather protecting cover for the club heads. But now the bag and cover simply served as a concealing encasement for his assault rifle, a Barrett REC7, which was a 2007 vintage "reliability-enhanced" carbine. He placed three loaded handguns and additional magazines for the REC7 in the side pockets of the golf bag. Clinton had never played golf in his life, but he had recently studied the mannerisms and habits of those who did.

The campus golf course was just north of the BITSY campus. The six story science building, the tallest building on campus was immediately south of the thirteenth green and the fourteenth tee box on the BITSY links. There had been many late night amorous interludes on these holes by college students that were driven more by testosterone and estrogen than by a long two-iron. But on this occasion amore was not in play. Joseph Clinton was about to unleash all of the anger, animosity, rage and resentment that had been building inside him for years.

Clinton took a taxi with his golf bag to the golf course clubhouse. Then he flashed his student ID at the starter and said he was going to hit some balls from the driving range. He put his bag on the back of a golf cart and headed in the direction of the driving range. When he got near the range there were a handful of golfers smacking practices shots into what remained of the setting sun. The sky was rapidly darkening in front of an impending storm. Clinton didn't stop but simply made a left turn and kept following the cart path toward the 10th hole. There were no golfers on the hole, nor were there any on eleven. He could hear voices ahead of him but he still hadn't seen anyone, nor had anyone had seen him. He drove off the cart path and saw a foursome holing out on the thirteenth green and getting ready to move on to fourteen. They were the last foursome of the day. His timing was good.

Behind the tree lined south end of the golf course there was a gate that led to the service road to the campus buildings. The newest buildings, including the science building were able to receive supplies through a tunnel under the buildings that ran along the service road. Clinton stopped on the golf course side of the gate and took one of the handguns from the side pocket of his golf bag. When he noticed that the gate was unlocked and was simply held together by a slip bar, he left the gun on the seat of the cart, got out and removed the slip bar. He opened the gate, got back in the cart and drove onto the campus service road.

Campus security guard George Lafler was reading a book as he sat in the guard booth outside the underground tunnel. He looked up as he saw the approaching golf cart. It was unusual but not entirely unprecedented to get a delivery via a golf cart. He was curious but not worried. When he saw Joseph Clinton brandishing a hand gun, fear began to overcome him.

"Open the door." Clinton nodded toward the garage type double door that permitted access to the underground roadway.

"Yes, sure, okay. Just be careful where you point that thing." Lafler didn't hesitate for even a second in pushing the automatic garage door opener. As the door slowly rose, he simply waited to see what Clinton wanted next. He kept his hands in front of him as though he might try to block a bullet. Clinton stared at him while the door cranked open. Then Clinton fired two loud shots into the head of George Lafler and drove down under the science building.

Clinton drove straight to the service elevator in the basement of the science building. He waited patiently for the elevator to reach the basement floor. He drove the golf cart onto the steel floor of the service elevator and pushed the button for the sixth floor. The door shut just as Clinton began to hear shouting near the garage door area. The elevator moved past the first three floors and slowed down near the fourth floor. Meanwhile Clinton sat calmly in the golf cart holding his hand gun facing the door. The passenger elevators were near the front of the building. However, occasionally students and faculty members took the freight elevator for convenience sake when they were at the rear of the building. As the doorway opened on the fourth floor two young female students and one male professor attempted to gain access. They were quite surprised to see a golf cart blocking their way and even more surprised when Clinton used his last four bullets to shoot all three of them at point blank range. The professor was down but still moving so Clinton threw his empty gun at him.

The rapid loud echo of the shots was in deafening contrast to the deliberate grinding noise of the elevator as the doors slowly closed and the lift continued its upward journey. Meanwhile Clinton remained somewhat dispassionate as he simply removed another handgun from his golf bag. When the elevator reached the sixth floor, the doors opened and Clinton pulled the golf cart into the hallway, just outside of the physics lab. There was no one in sight at first, but he could hear voices saying something about "awfully loud to be fireworks; sounded more like gunshots."

Clinton drove his golf cart down the hallway and made a left turn. He then came upon two male students wearing baseball caps backwards.

"What the fuck....?" One of the students began to laugh at the appearance of the cart, and temporarily forgot about the gunshots. His humor was ephemeral. Clinton fired off three more shots and felled both students. He then threw this still loaded handgun at his victims just as he had done two floors below. He would only need his rifles now. He continued down the hallway to a sign marked "rooftop exit." Clinton got out of the cart and dragged his golf bag up the stairway to the roof. He pushed open the emergency exit door and went out into the cloud-shrouded setting sun.

Back on the sixth floor Professor Melech Katz raced around the corner after he heard the shots and the subsequent moans from one of his students. The ex-IDF professor saw a scene unlike anything he had seen since his days in the Palestine-Israeli conflict. He saw the door leading to the roof close across from the golf cart in the middle of the floor. He also saw the two bodies laying on the floor further down the hallway. One was entirely motionless and one was moaning. He grabbed his cell phone from his pocket as he carefully passed by the golf cart and exit door and went down the hallway towards the bodies. He dialed 911 as he was moving down the hall.

"This is Mel Katz, over at BITSY on the 6th floor of the science building. Two students have been shot and I heard several other gunshots that sounded like they came from elsewhere in the building. Send help fast, please, please. Please send help as fast as you can." There was blood everywhere and Katz had a flashback to the Gaza Strip. Time stood still. It was a bad dream. It wasn't like a movie. It was more like a series of still shots being flipped quickly. Each separate photo was more horrid than the one before it.

Katz felt like he was moving in slow motion. His feet felt like they were carting 50 pound ankle weights. He fell to his knees and he watched as life expired from the second of the two students who were shot. Then he was filled with rage that he hadn't felt in more than eight years. It was a rage that he had been trained to control and channel while he was training at Mitzpe Ramon and while he was on the battlefields in Gaza. Katz picked up the handgun that had been discarded by Clinton and started toward the stairway to the roof.

Clinton moved across the roof of the science building and removed the cap from his golf bag. He pulled out the piston-operated Barrett REC7. It had a 30 round magazine and a 600 meter effective range. He quickly readied his weapon and pointed it down into the courtyard in front of the science building. The building had a modified U-shape as it lay out on the campus. All six floors shared this layout. The front door of the building was at the bottom or center of the U which stretched more than 150 feet wide. The small, or modified, arms of the U-structure were a shorter 75 feet each. When Clinton set up on the roof he moved from the bottom of the U to the top of the right arm of the U. He had a clear vision of the entire courtyard as well as the front door to the building. He began firing randomly at students standing and seated around the fountain in the center of the courtyard. Almost simultaneously sirens and the university alarm horn began sounding all around. Although the alarm horn was meant to warn people to stay indoors, several students were shot as they rushed from the front door of the science building. Within two minutes fourteen additional casualties had been claimed by rifle shots.

Katz hustled up the stairway and as he reached the doorway leading out on the rooftop, he stopped and took a deep breath. He had checked the chamber of the handgun and realized that he had only 3 bullets left in the gun. Meanwhile he heard the rapid retort of Clinton's assault rifle as he began firing down on the courtyard. Katz took a deep breath and opened the door. He saw that there was a large cubic air conditioning unit twenty feet in front of him and he could also visually see Clinton ahead of him looking down into the courtyard as he aimed his weapon at the innocent students down below. The noise of the gunfire and the sirens and the alarm horn allowed Katz to get to the 7 foot cubic AC unit without being heard. He paused behind the cube with his heart pounding in his chest. It began to rain lightly.

There were two other similar cubes to his right and two to his left. He needed to go right to get to Clinton, but he was scared beyond belief to pit his unknown handgun and three bullets against the automatic weapon that Clinton was now reloading with a new magazine. Clinton began firing once again and his full attention was down below him. His firing was now sporadic as people had taken cover and there was a general awareness of the location of the shooter. Katz made it over to the second cube just as Clinton stopped firing for several seconds. Katz had no way of knowing whether or not he had been detected by the deranged gunman. The sirens were louder and more numerous than before. When Katz heard Clinton begin firing again he ran over to the last cube, twenty feet from Clinton, who had his back to him. The rain intensified.

Katz made it behind the last cube. Now he heard return fire from the ground up towards the gunman. He also heard the motor of a helicopter in the air nearby. He waited about fifteen seconds and then peered around the edge of the cube. Clinton was moving away from the edge and it appeared that he might pass near the other side of the cube. Katz sucked in his breath and continued hiding behind the cube. Another fifteen seconds passed and then Katz saw Clinton with his back toward him, moving toward the center of the roof. He was no more than ten feet away, and then he began turning with his rifle toward the ex-Israeli Defense Forces professor. Katz braced with both hands on the handgun and fired the last three rounds into Clinton's forehead killing him instantly. He then walked over to the body to make certain that it was lifeless. He picked up the rifle and began to move it away from the body when the stairway door opened and two Florida State Policemen barged through the door, with their guns pointed directly at Katz.

"Drop your weapon," the lead officer commanded as he cocked his own gun ready to fire it at a moment's notice. Katz put his gun down immediately as a Florida State policemen ran over and quickly handcuffed him before he could explain who he was and what had occurred. One police officer could be heard speaking into his radio: "Two shooters on the roof … one has apparently been hit by return fire. The other shooter has been apprehended. Situation is secured." The rains then poured down heavily.

"This is not what I expected when you told me that you would be writing about our Center." Aaron Fein narrowed his eyes in disbelief and disgust as he stared across his long desk at Priscilla Stengel. This is certainly a less than complimentary article." His understated assessment of the negative nature of the article did nothing to hide his distain.

"Everything I have written is true. The growth in jobs at The Fein Center for Women is directly correlated to the growth in the number of abortions performed in the center."

"You say almost nothing about the other services that we perform for women at FCW. You have turned the article on job growth into a referendum on pregnancy terminations."

"The matter is simple enough. Job growth at your center has nothing at all to do with other services. It is purely a matter of the increased demand for abortions at the Fein Center at a time when abortions are decreasing in number on a national level. The truth of the matter is that the Fein Center does little of a positive nature to help the economy of greater Tampa and it brings a certain notoriety along with it, especially among the pro-life groups of the state."

"And from the tone of your article, you obviously now count yourself in that group?" Fein stated his inquiry rather than asking it.

"I didn't say that."

"You didn't have to."

For the next twenty minutes Fein and Stengel argued about her article. The piece also indicated that much of the job growth went to people who were recruited from outside the Tampa area and the fact that Fein himself was a carpetbagger from New York. As their conversation went longer Fein grew angrier. He couldn't fathom why Stengel had turned on him, after previously being supportive. Finally he ended their conversation because he had agreed to pick up his wife out at the airport. Amanda Fein was flying in from a short vacation in Brazil that included the recruitment of physicians to work at the Fein Center.

☙❦❧

Tampa, Florida was a big city as far as Patch Munson was concerned. He had been there a few times in the past. He thought that the city life of Tampa was too fast paced for his liking. In his mind it was a sinful city, but at least he understood that sentiment. Five years earlier, he had spent a weekend in Tampa with his pal Bubba Looney and a few of their fishing buddies and they proceeded to get drunk both Friday and Saturday nights. On the second night they went to one of the strip clubs on Dale Mabry Highway. His memory of that evening included visions of young women who were the most beautiful he had ever seen, almost angels. One of these almost angels had given him his first ever lap-dance and he had foolishly spent over $150 in the process of achieving ecstasy in his own underwear. He never thought of the transaction as abusive of women. He simply thought the prices were abusive of men. He also never attempted to reconcile these activities with the sermons and teachings of Reverend Billy Brand that he listened to each Sunday. But his last trip to Tampa was then and this was now.

This trip to Tampa was for a different reason. Patch Munson had a specific goal in mind and he didn't think of it as sinful. He was now just north of the city in a parking lot of a strip mall across from the Fein Center for Women. He could clearly see the executive parking lot behind the FCW. The strip mall faced west with its parking lot behind it to the east. There was a narrow wooded area and a six foot wide stream separating the small parking lot from the executive parking lot at the FCW. The larger general parking lot was on the other side of the Fein Center completely out of sight. It was early evening but Munson still had an excellent view of the FCW through his binoculars. Only a few cars remained in the lot. There was no mistaking which vehicle belonged to Aaron Fein. The black Mercedes Benz had a license plate that was as obnoxious as any vanity plate he had ever seen: 1 FEIN MAN. Ironically Fein's car was parked near a spray painting on the side of the building that said: "Murder, Inc." Protesters had snuck into the lot three nights earlier. They had annotated the western wall of the FCW with their views of what went on inside. The maintenance crew had already started removing the graffiti but the outline shadow of the words was still legible.

After an hour or so of waiting patiently while quietly talking to Harry, Patch Munson finally saw his mark. Aaron Fein left the building accompanied by a frumpy looking woman with short dark hair and an oversized butt. Her shoulders were narrower than her hips, and her overall physique reminded Munson of a weeble. They were talking in a manner that appeared to be argumentative. They stopped near Fein's Mercedes and exchanged a final few words. Neither of them seemed happy. They didn't shake hands. There was no kiss on the cheek to say goodbye. There wasn't even a slight hand wave. They stood almost five feet apart as they talked. Their body language suggested acrimony. Finally Aaron Fein got into his car and the frumpy woman walked across the lot and got into a rusted five year old red Chevrolet Camaro. In sharp contrast to the sight of the company executive easing into his luxury automobile, the frumpy weeble-woman looked like she was getting into one of those tiny open-windowed weeble-mobiles. Fein pulled out of the lot first and frumpy weeble-woman was right behind him in her red Camaro. Patch Munson saw his opportunity.

Munson started the engine to his pickup and pulled out of the mall and headed toward the FCW. He let Fein's Mercedes pass in front of him and then turned right and began to follow him, cutting off the Camaro in the process. When he looked in the mirror he saw frumpy weeble-woman giving him the finger. Munson kept his Silverado close behind the Mercedes – almost too close – and the little weeble-mobile was practically tailgating his pickup, as they all headed toward Interstate 4. Harry was now sitting on his haunches in the passenger seat and began to growl excitedly as he sensed something exhilarating occurring. Fein headed west while Munson followed. The Camaro finally turned off in the opposite direction when they got to Interstate 4 but not before the weeble-woman gave Munson the finger one last time. The commercial jingle began running through Munson's head in a mindless repetitive manner: *Weebles wobble but they don't fall down;* He was glad when she turned off. Harry also seemed glad and stopped growling.

When Fein began heading southwest on the Interstate, Munson was concerned that they were headed towards Tampa Airport. Munson worried that he wouldn't be able to accomplish his mission at such a crowded venue.

Fein's iPhone lit up with a message from the airline. Amanda's flight was delayed an hour and forty-five minutes because of weather in Rio de Janeiro. "Damn," he said aloud to no one but himself. He wished he had checked on her flight before he left the office. His first reaction was to continue down to the airport and to wait there, but then thought better of it. He couldn't be certain that there wouldn't be an even longer delay, because the weather wasn't so great in Tampa either. It had begun to rain and he could hear the low rumble of thunder. Fein made the fatal mistake of turning around and heading back to the office. He was oblivious to anyone else on the road, completely consumed with his own thoughts.

Munson followed as Aaron Fein's Mercedes turned off the Interstate and circled around heading back in the direction from which he had come from the office. *Oh no*, Munson thought. *He knows Ah'm followin' 'im.* Munson allowed two cars to come between the Mercedes and his Silverado. When Fein's Mercedes got off at the exit and headed north it was nearly 7:45. Munson had become less paranoid about being noticed. Fein didn't appear to be in a hurry, and Munson assumed that Fein must have forgotten something at the office, as he continued in that direction. The rain intensified and the thunder grew louder as frequent flashes of lightning illuminated the sky. Harry sat next to Munson with his tongue hanging out, growling at Mother Nature.

When Fein arrived at the FCW he used his pass card at the simple unattended electronic gate and pulled back into the executive parking area. There were no other cars in the lot. Once the boss had departed for the evening the remaining executives had followed suit.

Patch Munson saw that Aaron Fein parked close to the rear door of the building. He was sitting in his car waiting for the rain to subside. Munson realized that the building was probably surrounded by security cameras so once again he was watching Fein from the strip mall parking lot about 140 feet away. There was a black slatted wrought iron fence on the other side of the small stream between the two parking lots. The fence surrounded the executive parking lot which only had twenty five parking spots, including six visitor's spots for VIP visitors, like Priscilla Stengel, who had to be cleared by Fein personally. Munson was not aware of any of these particulars. He was only interested in being able to get close enough to Fein to accomplish his mission without being detected by perimeter security cameras. He wanted to use his handgun and not one of his hunting rifles, because he knew no one would be able to trace the handgun, a twenty year old Colt .38 Super, that he had purchased for cash in the parking lot of a gun show without giving any identification.

As the Floridian storm continued to pelt the parking lots, Munson's visibility into the other parking lot was being hampered. Meanwhile Harry began growling again at the lightning and thunder. But Munson had this surreal feeling that this was now the time to complete his mission. He grabbed his Colt, got out of the Silverado and walked down the slightly declining bank to the shallow stream that separated the two parking lots. His camouflage hunting jacket helped him blend into the otherwise sparse foliage between the two parking areas. Fortunately the stream was not deep and Munson was able to quickly splash through it in two long steps without getting soaked in the process, and without attracting attention. Fein's car was directly in front of him through the fence, facing in the other direction. He could now clearly see Fein still seated in the car. However as Munson approached the fence on the opposite side of the stream, he crouched low so that he would be below the sight line of Fein's rear view mirror. He was now a mere 25 feet from the back of Fein's Mercedes. There was some additional seclusion provided by two large trash dumpsters at the perimeter of the strip mall lot behind him, and by some short foliage on the Fein Center side of the stream just outside of the fence. Nonetheless Munson was worried when the lightning continued to periodically illuminate the landscape.

The rain didn't abate much but at the first sign of a slackening, Aaron Fein's car door opened and he emerged moving quickly around his car in the direction of the rear door to the building. Patch Munson didn't waste any time thinking about what he was doing. All of the conjecture and contemplation was a thing of the past. He simply aimed his Colt .38 Super at the gynecologist/businessman and began firing. He fired a total of five bullets and hit Fein with all five shots. Fein was killed instantly by the second bullet that went directly through his brain. The gunshot sounds were different from the rolling thunder that accompanied them, but no one came around and discovered Fein's body during the next forty five minutes. By that time, Munson had re-crossed the stream; returned to his Silverado; driven back to his campsite; and crawled into his tent with Harry.

Julianne Carson arrived at the Grand Hyatt Hotel at 3 PM, after flying in from San Francisco. She checked into her room and clicked through her emails on her iPad. She had thirty two messages, mostly from business colleagues. There was one message from Hawk Richter confirming their 7 PM dinner at Armani's Restaurant on the top floor of the hotel. She reflected once again on how different this evening might be from many other "dates" she had navigated her way through during the past several months. This was a date that she had requested and that she wanted to have. This was unlike the many times that she had acquiesced to the requests of men that she found to be less than scintillating dates. She wasn't sure what it was that had attracted her to Bertrand Richter but he certainly fit the bill as being different. He was eight years older than she was. She knew from his well publicized biography that he had been married once before and that he was a widower. However Julianne was more interested in differences beyond variances of the circumstantial kind. She was intrigued by the way that Richter viewed life in general. It was extremely different from her own viewpoints. Therefore she was going into this date fully realizing that it could possibly be unpleasant. But that was what was exciting about this opportunity for Julianne. She was clearly going out of her comfort zone to learn new and different things about herself. And she was being spontaneous, living in the here and now, just as she had promised herself she would.

After an invigorating shower, followed by a power nap, Julianne got ready for dinner. She put on a simple black dress and very little makeup. She realized that Bertrand Richter was blind but she still wanted to look good when she looked in the mirror. Julianne had her own pride to deal with, and she had learned long ago that you never knew who you might run into from time to time.

"Good evening. I'm Julianne Carson and I have a reservation for two people at 7:00 PM." Julianne had walked off the elevator 5 minutes before the reservation time and was standing in the front foyer of the restaurant. The maître d' stood behind a narrow podium checking the list of dinner guests expected for the evening.

"Good evening to you as well Ms. Carson. Has the other party arrived yet?"

"Not that I'm aware of. I was about to ask you the same thing."

"No. I believe that you're the first to arrive. Would you like to be seated in our anteroom?" He gestured towards some comfortable couches near several low tables in the waiting area. Julianne nodded her assent and the maître d' walked her to a small table near a window overlooking the water. Before he could even ask her if she wanted a drink, Julianne spotted Bertrand Richter navigating his way from the elevator to the maître d's podium.

"I see my dinner guest has arrived," Julianne said and stood right back up after being seated for less than 10 seconds.

"You didn't tell me that your guest was Hawk Richter. He dines with us frequently and we are honored to have you both with us as patrons this evening, Ms. Carson."

Julianne paid little heed to the maître d' and walked past him to greet her guest.

"Hello Professor Richter. I'm glad to see that you made it here without difficulty."

"Yes I usually manage to find my way." Julianne reddened as she realized that her comment could possibly be misconstrued as a statement about Richter's handicap. Richter's smiling mouth and lower face alleviated that concern. However his sightless eyes remained expressionless behind a pair of wraparound sunglasses. They stood facing one another for an uncomfortable moment until Richter added, "You can dispense with the Professor Richter stuff. Please call me Bertrand ...or if you prefer ... Hawk. Most people call me, Hawk."

That was the last awkward moment of the evening. The thirty-nine year old professor looked older than his age. The thirty-one year old saleswoman appeared younger than her age. They proceeded to enjoy the evening as though they had been longtime friends. After they were quietly seated in a rear corner of the restaurant the discourse began to flow fluidly. Julianne made a few initial comments about her interest in Richter's theories, postulates and writings. Richter made a halfhearted attempt at humility by saying that he was "always learning something new, from someone new, every new day of the year." Neither of them allowed the conversation to get too philosophically arduous before they could learn a little more about one another. Richter was at a distinct disadvantage in this exchange because he was a well known lecturer and his tablemate was an unknown acolyte of spiritual exploration.

"So you've told me what you know about me. I'd like to know more about you. Besides being a sales rep for a computer company, what do you do with your time?"

"Well, I travel quite a bit with my job, but mostly within the United States. When I get vacation time I like to travel abroad. I've been to Europe twice and then last summer I spent three straight weeks traveling throughout China, Japan, Singapore and India. But when I only have a short amount of time to travel I usually go to one of the Caribbean Islands."

"So you've told me *where* you spend your time, but you haven't told me *how* you spend your time."

"Well, no matter where I go I try to spend some time working on keeping my body in shape and some time in meditation to keep my mind crisp and alert."

"How interesting ... and do you do this as a matter of a regimen of some kind?"

"I try to vary my approach so that it doesn't become a regimen or routine, especially the meditation part. I want to have a certain amount of command over my time and yet I want a freedom of association in order to maximize my exposure to new ideas."

"And how do you go about doing that?"

"I just try to stay away from any one particular, religion, philosophy or spiritual approach, to the exclusion of other lines of inquiry."

"How interesting ... don't you find it frustrating to have no specific belief system?"

"That itself is an interesting question coming from a self-proclaimed atheist."

"Being an atheist doesn't mean I don't have any beliefs. There are many things that I believe to be true, for which I have no empirical proof."

"But you don't believe in God ... a supreme being ... if you will. I'm not talking about the God of any specific religion ... not Yahweh, or Allah or Jesus Christ. I'm just asking if you believe in some form of higher power than the human species."

"Well that last part is somewhat of a different spin than believing in a specific God."

"Then tell me what the concept of God means to you?"

"Those of you ...you meaning all theists ... who gravitate toward the concept of God, generally construe that to mean some all-powerful, all-knowing essence. This belief is usually correlated with the concept of some type of heaven or nirvana and a reciprocal punitive concept of hell or some other version of eternal damnation. All of these generic notions are hopelessly encompassed in some perception of an afterlife. Obviously there are hundreds of permeations of theistic notions. Frankly I find them all to be nonsensical."

"But you said you do have beliefs. Right?"

"The beliefs I hold are not what you characterize as religious or even spiritual beliefs. They are simply unproven hypotheses that over time will be proven or disproven through concerted scientific thought, detection and discovery. Look how long it took Christians to accept Darwin's theories of evolution. Some churches still don't accept some of these scientific facts." The blind man spoke with a strong passion in his voice. However what Julianne heard was a man trying too hard to be convincing. *Was his zeal really covering a lack of true conviction?* She thought not. But Julianne was not a wall flower that was easily cowed. She found Richter fascinating even though she found his atheism to be flawed.

"So then it sounds like the roots of your atheism are grounded in what you call scientific facts. But some of these so called facts have been disproven over time and then they were relegated to the realm of myths. What seems to be a fact one day is a mistake the next day. Am I right?"

"It's true that in the broad realm of scientific discovery, errors are often committed. However, over time corrections are made, errors are eliminated and a broader body of knowledge takes root. That's what mankind's progress has been about for thousands of years."

As they spoke to one another in the corner of the restaurant, a raging lightning and thunder storm lit up the summer sky over southern Tampa. Richter could barely hear the thunder through the thick large glass windows, but he was oblivious to the exhilarating light show that flared from the heavens outside and danced across the rooftop restaurant. Meanwhile they both were unaware of the carnage that had just taken place slightly north of the city.

Julianne stopped watching the lightning and looked hard at Richter. She still had this overwhelming sense that the scientist/ professor was trying hard to convert her to his secular line of thinking. Nonetheless she enjoyed his company. There was something about the man that she found enthralling. Maybe it was the idea that Richter was a seeker, just as Julianne, herself was a seeker. They both seemed to be looking for something profound and neither of them had found it yet. Richter asked Julianne about her work and appeared genuinely interested in her answers. As the multi-course dinner was served the conversation grew lighter. Gentle probes about one another's background were interspersed with commentary about the delicious food as well as some light chatter about life in the greater Tampa area. When the main course was completed Hawk Richter had an idea about what he wanted to do next.

"Let's go out on the back veranda. We can have a cognac in the night breeze."

"I don't know. Half an hour ago there was more going on than just 'the night breeze.' But it looks like the storm has faded away. So let's try your idea of a cognac on the veranda. But I'll let you have the cognac. I'll just finish my glass of wine."

There was a small glass-paned door in the center of the back wall that led to the back veranda. As soon as they stepped out they could feel the breeze. The cement deck was wet with wind-blown rain, and they were the only two people on the terrace.

The veranda behind Armani's Restaurant on the top floor of the Grand Hyatt Hotel was one of Hawk Richter's favorite spots to smoke a cigar. It was almost always windswept, and it was a significant contrast to climate controlled atmosphere of the restaurant itself. Small portions of the veranda were canopy-covered but open on the sides. The remainder of the space was entirely open to the elements. It was usually quite breezy and this night was no exception. There was still a lightning flash in the distance but the rain had stopped. Richter held onto Julianne's arm as they entered the dimly lit terrace.

"Doesn't that breeze feel nice? You can also smell the salt water from the bay."

"Yes it's nice out here. Do you always come out here when you dine at Armani's?"

"Yes, usually … Armani's doesn't promote the idea of coming out here, but you can't smoke a cigar inside so people do come out here occasionally."

The door to the veranda opened once again and the waiter came out with a small tray holding Julianne's refilled glass of wine and a cognac in a snifter for the physicist. The waiter handed them their drinks and returned into the restaurant leaving them alone. There was a small cement half wall that served as a high table to rest their drinks and both Julianne and Richter immediately put their drinks down. The young saleswoman found the atmosphere to be oddly alluring and exotically different from the rigors of her business day.

"Are you going to smoke a cigar, now?"

Richter paused and then responded, "No. I'm just going to enjoy the salt water in the air and pretend I'm smoking this." He unraveled an Alec Bradley Nicaraguan cigar and held it in his teeth. "I'll smoke it later." It was an unspecified timeframe.

"You can smoke it now, if you'd like. I don't mind."

"Certainly you mind. People who don't smoke, don't enjoy being around cigar smokers, when we are puffing away. Of course, I'm assuming you don't smoke."

"No, I don't smoke." Julianne said this rather sheepishly because she was more interested in the way that Richter assumed things rather than what he actually said. The man exuded a virile self confidence. She moved closer to him on the terrace so that they could speak in lighter tones and not have to speak over the slight whistling of the wind.

"You've come closer. I like that." Richter took the cigar out of his mouth and for the moment tucked it into the breast pocket of his sport jacket. But it was Julianne who touched Richter first as she lightly grasped the hand that was now free from the cigar.

A silent moment, that was more affectionate than awkward, was broken when Richter said, "Can I *feel* what you look like?"

Julianne was not sure what Richter was implying by the word "feel," so she wasn't quite certain how to answer. She also wasn't sure whether or not the question was simply a rhetorical inquiry. However she felt the conviviality of the evening pushing her to say "yes," regardless. She didn't answer verbally, but she also didn't retreat from her new friend as he raised his right hand to touch her face, while Julianne still held his other hand. As he did so the conviviality morphed into a tenderness that surprised Julianne. She let go of his other hand and brought both of her own hands up and covered the back of Richter's fingers. She immediately noticed his warm fingers grow rigid. She sensed that Richter was perceiving rejection in her movement. She finally spoke ...softly, "It's okay. Please, go ahead. Feel whatever you want to feel."

Julianne was instantly self-flummoxed. She turned scarlet red as she listened to the self-conscious words of permission stumble from her own lips. She was glad that Richter couldn't see her embarrassment and was not yet aware that Richter could *feel* her reddening visage. He said nothing. However he quickly brought his other hand to Julianne's face as well. He allowed Julianne to adjust her palms to cover the backs of both of his hands.

He waited about five seconds and then began to move his hands. First she felt his thumbs move softly in opposite directions away from her nose. Then she felt the soft pleasant touch of his other fingers along her cheekbones just beneath her ears. He shifted his hands slightly and ran his thumbs to her chin while his other fingers probed her slanting jaw line and cheekbones. His touch was paradoxically both soft and firm. His fingers were steady in their movement as the tactile receptors traced both the shape and the texture of her face. She knew that he could sense exactly where her makeup had been applied.

Richter removed his hands to a position about an inch away from her face and whispered, "Don't move." His words were both soft and firm like his touch had been. His momentary tactile hesitation was simply a transitory one as he repositioned his fingers to her temples and his thumbs to her forehead. As he did so Julianne stared into his face. She could see some sense of satisfaction in his mouth and lips that were slightly ajar, but she was unable to discern much more because his eyes were still shaded behind his glasses.

It was Julianne's turn to be more direct in her approach. "Take off your glasses." She imitated his soft but firm approach and he was momentarily startled. She could feel his puzzlement in his fingertips. This surprised her. Maybe he wasn't so cocksure of himself after all. It was almost as though she had said, "Take off your pants."

Richter was getting all types of vibes about his new friend. He could *feel* that she was pretty and young, younger than he had thought.

One of the problems with being deprived of his sight was that his perception about personal characteristics, such as age, was occasionally askew. He removed his glasses and exposed his sightless eyes. Julianne immediately saw that the scientist's eyes were vacuous vessels and feeble feelers. She now understood why he wore his glasses.

Before they could say another word to one another, the back door to the restaurant opened and the waiter returned. Richter hesitantly put his glasses back in place just as the waiter addressed him.

"I'm sorry to interrupt you Professor Richter, but your driver, Paul, is here, and he said that he has some sad news that he needs to discuss with you."

"Well, tell him to come out here and join us."

As the waiter retreated to the restaurant area, Richter turned to Julianne and said, "I'm sorry about the disruption but Paul doesn't usually trouble me unless it's something important." Hawk Richter was not being entirely truthful in one respect. He often asked Paul to pick him up at a location where his driver might be able to observe the person or persons with whom he was meeting. In a sense this allowed Richter to query Paul later about the stature and appearance of the people he met. Nevertheless he was surprised by Paul's pushiness on this occasion. When Paul opened the door to the veranda Richter was no longer surprised by his pushiness.

"I guess you haven't heard the news reports, Professor Richter. It's been an awful night. There has been a mass murder back on the BITSY campus, and in a completely different event Aaron Fein has been shot dead at the Fein Center for Women."

"Oh my God …" Julianne reacted first. Meanwhile Hawk Richter's jaw dropped open and he was uncharacteristically speechless. Besides he couldn't utter the deity's name in vain, because he didn't believe in a deity.

Billy Brand enjoyed his work. But then again he didn't consider it work. He considered it his calling. He had felt that way since he was a young boy. It had seemed inevitable that he would take over his father's ministry. When Billy prayed he felt as though he were talking directly to God. His supplications to the Lord were direct and he heard the Lord's answers ring out in his own mind. Sometimes however the Lord would answer him in different ways. In his mind he would simply hear the voice of God say, *"Look for the sign."* Alternatively the voice might say, *"I have sent you the sign."* On these occasions Billy would search his world with all five of his senses to find the Lord's Sign. Invariably it was there, and when Billy returned to prayer he thanked the Lord for sending him the answer.

The first sign that Billy remembered vividly embracing was when he was seventeen years old. That was when he first received God's calling to his ministry. Billy's father was well known through southern Alabama, and eastern Mississippi, and throughout the Florida panhandle. Billy was shunned by some young men in his age bracket, not so much because of his father's profession, but because Billy mingled with Black youth as easily as he interacted with white teenagers. Some of the non-church-going youth even intimated that Billy must have some black blood in him somewhere along the line, because he was the fastest white man they ever knew, breaking local county records for the 50 yard dash, the 100 yard dash and even the quarter mile. After his junior year in high school, scholarship offers to major colleges began to line up. Billy was confused by all of the sudden attention that had shifted from his father to him. He had been dating Sarah Anne Cooley – a young parishioner at the Ascendancy Church – since his freshman year in high school. Brand's life was replete with yet to be fulfilled promises.

Then came the accident. Billy was walking Sarah Anne home from school when a pickup truck came barreling up along the state highway. Three young people were squeezed in the front seat. The windows were down and the radio was blaring loudly. Despite the fact that it was the middle of the afternoon, the three youngsters were obviously drunk. Billy and Sarah heard the truck coming when it was still a good two hundred feet away. They saw a beer can go whistling out of the passenger side window and back into the low brush along the roadside, joining fifty or more similarly situated empty containers.

The truck was swerving as the two young men were paying more attention to grabbing at the girl who sat between them, than they were to the road in front of them.

Billy reacted quickly but not quite quickly enough. When he spotted the truck bearing down on them, he grabbed Sarah Anne and pulled her with him up on the grass by the roadside, well off the shoulder. When the driver in the pickup saw the fear in Billy's eyes he decided to scare him further by swerving onto the shoulder. When Sarah Anne saw the truck bearing down on them she panicked thinking it would hit them head on. She started toward the road. The driver though turned the truck back off the shoulder, even as his pal in the passenger seat hung out the side window. Billy again grabbed Sarah Anne and tried to pull her further away from the roadside. As he did so, he inadvertently spun around and got side swiped by the truck's passenger side mirror. Although it was a glancing blow to his shoulder, the speed of the truck caused the impact on his neck and shoulder to be so significant that he also twisted his knee as he fell trying to keep the truck from hitting Sarah Anne. In the process Billy tore the ACL, the meniscus and the knee cap of his left knee. The aspirations for a track career dissipated quickly as Billy suffered through a longer than normal rehab of both his knee and shoulder.

Billy became convinced that the accident was a sign from God to follow in his father's ministry. They never did find the drunk drivers who ran them down but Billy forgave them anyway. He and Sarah Anne got married when they were both nineteen. The Brands all felt that it was the preordained wishes of God. The Christian Doctrine Divinity School offered a track scholarship that Ole Miss and Alabama couldn't offer. The track at CDDS led to a heavenly reward while scholarship offers from Ole Miss and the Crimson Tide at Alabama would have simply had Billy Brand running in circles.

III

The Queasies

Patch Munson was troubled. He didn't expect to feel so queasy about everything. Yes, he thought, that was the word for it, "queasy." He didn't feel sorry. He didn't feel glad. He didn't feel frightened and he didn't feel fulfilled. He simply felt queasy. Or maybe the word for his feelings was unbalanced. *Yes, that's it*, he thought. *Ah feel unbalanced, or maybeh jes' uncomfortable. It's a physical thaang. Ah cain feel it in my gut.* No matter what word he used to explain or rationalize his feelings, Patch Munson knew that he was queasy. And what exactly was this "queasy" thing? It was a nauseous and unsettled feeling that was vaguely reminiscent of sea sickness.

The return trip from Tampa to Mobile had been somewhat surreal. After killing Aaron Fein, Munson had simply returned to his campsite north of Tampa and crawled into his sleeping bag inside his tent. Harry had nestled in next to him, and remained docile throughout the night. Meanwhile Munson slept in a silent cocoon of deepest REM sleep. Upon awakening he recalled none of his dreams. He did, however, recall each and every detail of his activities the night before. That was when the queasiness began. Although Munson was a quiet man who normally kept his own counsel, he suddenly wanted someone to confide in, someone besides Harry. It was an unusual and uncomfortable reaction for Munson. His thinking process normally was swaddled in a quiet self assurance, even righteousness. It was weird to be overcome suddenly and succinctly by a morose self-doubt. Where did this feeling emanate from? Munson wasn't sure.

After leaving the campsite, Munson took his time returning to Mobile. He drove along the back roads of Florida for several hundred miles, avoiding toll roads and bridges and all other possible points of electronic surveillance. He had filled up his gas tank the previous afternoon and only stopped once more in the town of Perry, Florida to refuel. On both occasions he paid cash. He also paid cash when he stopped for a greasy hamburger at a fast food drive-through along the way. The burger only made the queasiness more acute. By the time he reached the Alabama border, he was ready to refuel again and he was also ready to vomit. He knew he would be able to purge the greasy burger, but he was still unsure how to disgorge the queasy sinfulness of the murder he had committed and that he now accepted as reality. He tried to convince himself that he'd done the right thing but his mental fortitude was still weakened by uncertainty. His self doubt didn't abate at all until he summoned all of his courage as he passed into the city of Mobile just after 5 PM on Friday. Fatigue was not a factor as he drove up outside his father's gravesite and said a prayer before returning to his house.

Munson didn't answer Maggie when she asked him; "How's the *fishin'* Patch?" And she was unconcerned about his simple answer: "So, so." But she persisted in her questioning regardless.

Munson knew he wouldn't confide in Maggie. He then had a thought about sharing his secret with Bubba Looney. After all he had been keeping Bubba's secret for a long time. Good-ole-boys didn't squeal on one another. But Munson thought that confiding in Looney was much too risky. Looney was always shit-faced and sometimes got loose lipped. No he would have to find some other way. Then he suddenly had an idea about how he might rid himself of the *queasies*. He would talk to Billy Brand. Meanwhile Munson could hear his wife babbling on.

"*Yew gunna* tell *meh 'bout* the *fishin'* or not?"

"*Nuthin' t'* tell, Maggie. *Nuthin' t'* tell." He walked through the back door and out on the lawn leading toward the family farm. He knew the topic wouldn't resurface.

By Friday morning the Florida State Police were now dealing with two widely reported murderous proceedings: the mass murders that had occurred at BITSY and the execution style homicide of Aaron Fein. The events appeared to be entirely unrelated but had taken place within five miles of one another. Both events had also occurred within twenty minutes of one another. Both stories were sensationalized nationally. The lead detective assigned to the Fein investigation was twenty-two year veteran of the Florida state police, Ismail Kanasani, a quietly efficient Muslim investigator, who was respected within the ranks of the state police, not only for his investigative talents, but also for his tenacity. Whenever Kanasani was the lead on an investigation, it was a dead-on certainty that no stone would be left unturned in the search for the perpetrator.

While the Fein murder was a wide open case, the mass murders committed by Joseph Clinton received even more national media attention. The mix-up arrest of Professor Melech Katz had been quickly straightened out back at the police station, but not before the media reported his arrest. The ensuing embarrassment for the Florida State Police was putting more heat on the organization to solve the Fein case to help restore its reputation. Meanwhile Katz was being lionized as a superhero and a Rambo-esque Israeli freedom fighter who single-handedly took down the mass-murdering madman, Joseph Clinton. The preliminary perusal of Clinton's manifesto indicated that he was originally intent on blowing up several buildings before he went on his shooting rampage. But like many other convoluted ideas in the writings, his scheme got altered along the way. So while media outlets were tripping over one another in an attempt to interview Katz, they were also pressing the police to release more information from Clinton's manifesto.

All of the attention that was given to the Clinton murders by the overnight media was okay by Detective Kanasani. It allowed him to conduct his investigation of the Fein murder with a little less scrutiny. There already was enough internal pressure to resolve this case as quickly as possible. He thought they had developed a few quick leads that he would follow up on immediately. There was the *Murder, Inc* graffiti and there was the Stengel woman, the female reporter who had been Fein's last appointment on Thursday evening. Kanasani intended to run these leads down immediately.

⚜

It was an unusual place for a rendezvous after a hiatus of almost eight years. But the circumstances in both of their lives called for a low key location where they could just talk to each other with no strings attached. They drove to the diner in separate cars.

"Hello Tim. It's been a long time."

"In some ways it seems like a long time, Carol. In other ways it doesn't."

"I know."

"I always think about you."

"Even after you became a priest?"

"Especially after I entered the priesthood …"

"I always think about you also."

Carol Mays looked down at the table between them in the diner. She was speaking softly. She chose her words selectively and she wasn't sure exactly what she wanted to accomplish in meeting her former lover. She wasn't even sure she would tell him about Russell … at least not right away. For the moment she was content simply to be with Tim. She couldn't think of him as Father Tim. Regardless of what ensued, she knew she would never think of him as Father Tim. However there was a part of her that felt sinister about their meeting. It was not her purpose to erase Tim Hanlon's vocation. But there were certain things that she believed Tim had a right to know and there were certain things she would like to know herself. She looked back up at Tim just as the waitress came over for the third time and asked if they were ready to order yet.

"Scrambled eggs, bacon and grits," Hanlon said. Then he added, "But we're not in a hurry." There weren't many patrons in the diner anyway.

"Oatmeal and fruit," Mays said. It was a big breakfast for her.

The middle aged waitress momentarily stared at young couple. It was no longer unusual to see a mixed racial couple in the South, but it didn't mean that they had earned any special treatment either. She also noticed that neither of them had an Alabama accent. The waitress had no way of knowing how many classes Carol Mays had taken in New York to try to neutralize her accent, even though her agent had told her that her accent could be an asset. The waitress did notice begrudgingly that both the tall dark haired man and the thin black woman were very good-looking. She wondered briefly why they couldn't find attractive mates of their own respective races. She didn't let the thought linger, but simply flipped her pad back to the top page and went about her business of placing the order, while the young couple continued to look goo-goo-eyed at one another.

"So tell me Carol. Why did you call after all of these years?"

"I simply wanted to see you. I wanted to see how life was treating you. I don't know. There may have been another reason, also. But first I wanted to see you, to see how you were doing with God's work." She knew she was being disingenuous at the outset, but she didn't want to rush into things. "What about you? Why did you agree to meet me for breakfast?"

"Well, to be perfectly truthful, I know that you came to speak to me in the confessional a few weeks back. I didn't realize it was you until after you left. I didn't see you, and I didn't think it was appropriate to seek you out. But as I said, I never stopped thinking about you. When you called you didn't mention the confessional, so I assumed that you were simply calling me as a friend and not as a priest. It was an offer that was hard to pass up. Obviously I picked a location on the outskirts of town and I didn't wear my collar or even dress in black. But a parish priest is often visible to people he doesn't recognize.

That's why I refrained from even a friendly kiss hello when I came over to your table."

Mays blushed at his mention of the confessional, but she also recognized that little by little the intimacy of their relationship was returning, even if the physical intimacy was now verboten. They each had their own secret to share but neither Carol nor Tim was ready to make their respective disclosure immediately. "I know that your vocation makes our past relationship somewhat awkward, but it doesn't preclude us from renewing our friendship. Does it?"

"I don't know and to some extent I don't care. I have always tried to do the right thing, but I don't always know what the right thing is. For now, let's just say that I'm glad that you called and I'm happy to be having breakfast with you." Even as he said this he reflected back on the text of the conversation in the confessional and felt bizarre about the line of questioning he had pursued at that time.

They sat silently for a few seconds, but anyone who observed the way they looked into each other's eyes would quickly realize that this was more there than a simple friendship. Hanlon finally broke the silence. "Do you go back to Birmingham often?"

"Actually I was just there a few weeks ago to see my parents." Mays was still blushing slightly as she added, "It was right before I tried to see you in the confessional."

Hanlon felt like he should ask her, "*Were you there to see me or were you there to seek forgiveness from God?*" But he thought that he already knew the answer to the question and so he didn't ask it. Instead he explored a simpler line of questioning. "How are your parents doing?"

"They are doing well. They want to see me more often and they want to see Russell more often as well."

"Russell?"

"Yes, I have a son named Russell."

"Oh." Hanlon didn't know why he felt disappointed to hear this. He added, "You didn't mention that you were married."

"I'm not married."

"Oh." This time he added nothing.

"I try to maintain a private personal life. That doesn't help my career much. It helps me keep my sanity, but it drives my publicist crazy. Also, I don't use the social media to contact my friends. I pick up the phone and call them."

"Or just show up in their confessionals." Hanlon laughed quickly to let Mays know that he was only teasing her.

"Okay, let's clear that up first. I am still a Catholic and I do go to church on Sundays. And yes I did have a baby out of wedlock, but no one is condemning me for that. And Russell is the biggest joy of my life. Like many people who say they are Catholics, I don't go to confession often. I had the stupid idea that if I confessed my feelings anonymously to you in confession I might be able to rationalize why I still feel the way I do about you. I know. It was a bad idea. Can you forgive me … er …personally, I mean?"

Hanlon took a deep breath. He was tempted to make a light-hearted remark, because he often found that humor was an easy way to handle discomfort. But he knew that it was a serious moment. Before he could make a statement of any kind, their conversation was interrupted by the waitress coming over and pouring more coffee. The respite gave Hanlon an opportunity to survey the face of his former lover. She appeared to be more beautiful than ever. In addition there was a mysterious aspect to her countenance that he hadn't known in the past. And even in her casual apparel she exuded a raw sexuality that was impossible for her to hide. She was tall and slender but in a healthy way, not like some of the NYC Fashion Avenue models whose appearance always seemed to border on anorexia. Hanlon remembered every curve of her body well.

The waitress moved on to the next table and the priest finally answered the model's request for exculpation. "Naturally I forgive you. Otherwise why would we be sitting here?"

Carol Mays knew that she had another transgression to confess and one that might not be as easily pardoned. It was a sin of omission rather than a sin of commission. She didn't know quite how to say what was on her mind, but Hanlon led her right down the path with a few simple probes.

"Tell me more about your son, Russell. How old is he?"

This is it. It is all going to come to light in the next few seconds, Mays thought. *I hope he'll forgive me for not telling him earlier.*

"He is seven."

"Seven?"

"Yes, seven … he'll be eight at the end of July."

"At the end of July? Hmm … ahh …"

"You're doing memory math? I'll save you the trouble. Russell is your son. There, I've said it." Mays locked her eyes on the priest's eyeballs and attempted to see his soul.

"Wow." It was all he could say. Mays strained her ear to catch an inflection that just wasn't there at first.

"Was that a good 'wow' or bad 'wow'?"

Priscilla Stengel was stunned by the news of Aaron Fein's murder. Apparently it took place less than a half an hour after she had left his office. She saw the details on the news right after she got in bed and couldn't sleep most of the night. At 9 AM the following morning, she was ready to call the police to tell them that she had seen Fein shortly before he was murdered. But first they arrived at her front door to ask questions.

"Priscilla Stengel?"

"Yes"

"Hello. I'm Detective Ismail Kanasani, and this is Detective Loretta Chambers. We are investigating the shooting at the Fein Center last night. We'd like to ask you a few questions if that would be alright. Can we come in?" The detectives both showed their identification in the doorway, close enough to Stengel that she would be hard pressed not to allow them entry into her home.

Stengel was not surprised by the appearance of the detectives on her doorstep. She was merely surprised by how fast they had gotten there.

"Do I need a lawyer?"

"Not if you haven't done anything wrong. You do not have to talk with us if you don't want to. But we are trying to solve a crime and we believe you can help."

"All right, come in. But I don't have all day. My son is at his friend's house for a sleep over. But if he returns early, the interview is over. We can talk at another time. I just don't want Michael to be upset."

"That sounds fair enough."

Both of the detectives entered Priscilla Stengel's house in the city of Winston, Florida, about 20 miles inland from Tampa. Ismail Kanasani glanced all around the living room as soon as they entered the small house. His instincts told him that this Stengel woman was not the murderer. Although she seemed nervous, her anxiety level was nowhere near that of a murderer who was about to be questioned. Still Kanasani was careful because he knew that whoever the murderer was, he or she was armed and dangerous. Kanasani and his partner, Loretta Chambers, sat next to one another on the worn out living room couch, while Stengel occupied a beaten-up rocking chair across from the couch.

"Now, how can I help you? I saw the news about Aaron Fein last night and I was shocked. I'm sure you know that I knew him and that's what you're here to talk about."

"I read the newspaper article several days ago, so I have an idea about how you felt about the man and his business."

"Well you probably already know that I was at the FCW speaking with Dr. Fein shortly before he was shot."

Kanasani was satisfied that Stengel wanted to be cooperative. He led with the idea about the newspaper article and not the detail that she had been at the center the prior evening. The fact that she immediately disclosed this information relieved the detective.

"Yes we are aware of your meeting with the deceased last night. But we don't have any of the details of that meeting and we'd like you to fill us in with as much as you care to tell us."

"Do you mind if I record our conversation? It's just one of those reporters' things. I try to record as much as I can of my conversations so that they don't get misconstrued at a later date." As she said this she got up out of the rocking chair, walked into the kitchen and returned shortly thereafter with a small handheld Sony recorder.

"No. We don't mind at all," was Kanasani's delayed response. "I think that's good practice." Actually Kanasani didn't care much for the idea of having their conversation recorded by a reporter. However it did offer him the opportunity to place his own recorder between them without asking for permission.

"So when did you last see Aaron Fein?"

"He wasn't overly happy with the article that I wrote for the paper last week. I think he was expecting much more of a puff piece about the FCW. He asked me to come see him once again. And I'm not sure exactly why. It's not like we were going to print a retraction. And truthfully I think the article was balanced. You said you read it. What's your opinion? "

"I'd rather just go back to the facts of the meeting. When your meeting ended was anybody waiting to see him?"

"Actually we walked out of the building together. He got in his car and I got in mine. I will tell you this much though. Fein was not a happy camper. He tried to make me feel like a little girl who had gone to the principal's office. After he was through criticizing my article, I believe he was finished with his work for the day. He said something about having to go to the airport to pick up his wife. I saw him getting in his car and leaving. But from what I heard on the news he must have come back."

"Are you absolutely sure it was Aaron Fein who left in the car? Could it have been someone else?"

"No. I'm sure it was Fein. He was parked in the VIP parking lot. When he called and asked me to come in for our talk he also gave me permission to park there. I think that there were fewer than a half dozen cars in the lot, but I can't be absolutely sure of that. We walked past his car first and I saw him get into the driver's seat."

"Do you remember what type car he was driving?"

"It was a Benz. No mistaking the car. I even remember the plate: '1 FEIN MAN.' Fein had some ego!"

"Is it possible that there was someone else in the car waiting for him?"

"Well it was getting dark and it looked like it would begin raining any minute and as I recall the windows to his car were lightly tinted. But I'm almost positive that no one else was in the car. As I think back on it, I remember him pulling out of the parking lot in front of me and heading in the direction of the airport. That's why I was so surprised to hear that he was shot back in the FCW parking lot."

"And did you come right home after leaving the Fein Center?"

"Yes. The only stop I made was right here in Winston to get gas. I was running low and just stopped for a routine fill up. Then I came right home."

"So then if you came directly here into town from the FCW, you would also have taken Interstate Route 4. And of course, Fein would have taken Interstate Route 4 to the Airport. Correct?"

"Yes, I guess that's accurate. Except for the fact that when we got to Interstate Route 4 we would've headed in opposite directions."

"Naturally."

"I'm not sure why but I don't remember seeing which way his car went shortly after we left the center."

Priscilla Stengel stopped abruptly and tried to visualize the events from the previous evening. Kanasani and Chambers studied her closely. Stengel was generally a nondescript individual, the kind of person who can get lost in a crowd of two. She was overweight and misshapen but not terribly obese. Her face was oval shaped in a more narrow fashion than the rest of her body. It gave her the appearance of someone who was continuously trying to lose weight and for some unfathomable reason was only able to accomplish this feat from the shoulders up. Still she seemed to be an intelligent woman and the two detectives were willing to give her the time to recall whatever she could from the previous evening. While they were waiting for her to say more she began to shake her head in some type of imperceptible annoyance.

"What is it, Priscilla? You never know. Sometimes the smallest details can make a difference." It was Chambers who spoke and tried to make a connection.

"No, it's nothing important. I just remembered why I didn't see which way Fein went after he left the center. I got cut off by some asshole in a pickup truck. And I ended up following this asshole all the way to Interstate 4."

"So this guy in the pickup was between you and Fein all way to Route 4?"

"That's the thing. I'm not sure that Fein was still in front of me. I guess I was fixated on the asshole in the pick up."

"What we know is that Fein eventually returned to the FCW. So it's difficult for us to say what's important and what isn't. Maybe this guy in the pickup had something to do with Fein."

"I doubt it. He was just some jerk who cut me off. I gave him the finger a couple of times and he eventually went in the opposite direction."

"You mean that he went southwest on Interstate 4? And if Fein was still in front of him that could mean that your asshole friend was following Fein. Am I right?"

"I guess anything is possible. But to tell you the truth I have no reason to believe that the asshole in the pickup had anything to do with Aaron Fein.

"Why don't you leave that determination up to us? We can run it down without a problem. Do you remember what kind of a pickup the *asshole* was driving? And do you remember what the *asshole* looked like?"

"I don't know. I can't be sure. It was a good sized pickup. It could have been a Chevy Silverado or maybe a Dodge Ram. I'm just not sure. I got a quick look at the driver, but not enough to identify him. But he wasn't a kid. He was probably in his forties … maybe his fifties or even older. I just can't say. I remember that he had a very big head, and that there might have been a dog of some kind on the seat next to him. If we weren't here talking about this right now, in the context of Aaron Fein's murder, I'm sure I would have forgotten about it in no time flat. You know what I mean. There are assholes everywhere."

"I'll ask the obvious question, knowing the answer. But I have to ask. Did you happen to get his license plate number?"

"No I didn't. But come to think of it, I seem to recall that he had an out of state plate. It might have been Georgia or Alabama, or some-place else for that matter. I can't say for sure. I just seem to remember that he wasn't from Florida."

Even though they were recording the conversation Detective Chambers continued habitually, to take handwritten notes. As she noted the last comment or two, Detective Kanasani picked up the line of questioning.

"Ms. Stengel, you mentioned that you stopped here in town to get gas. You don't happen to have a receipt from the gas station?"

"No, I never keep those things. Besides what does that have to do with the Fein murder? If you believe that I'm a suspect in this murder, then maybe I should get a lawyer."

"You can always get a lawyer if you'd like. We're not saying that you're a suspect in this case. I guess the way we view you at this point is that you're 'a person of interest.' How would we look at it any other way? After all you're one of the last people to have seen Aaron Fein alive. So anyway, if you don't have the receipt from the gas station, can you at least tell us whether you put it on a credit card? It might help us establish the overall timeframe for the events of last evening."

"Yes I put it on my American Express card."

The two detectives continued to ask Priscilla Stengel numerous questions regarding the previous evening. Then after about 20 minutes are so, they turned the questioning to a more detailed review of her overall relationship with Aaron Fein. They also picked up the fact that the recent article which Stengel had written was not the first article that she had written about the Fein Center for Women. They made a note of this fact so they could review all of the articles later in the day.

After they left the Stengel home Chambers turned to Kanasani and asked, "So what did you think?"

"For the most part she's telling us the truth. She didn't shoot Fein. But that doesn't mean she didn't have somebody do it for her. Frankly, I don't believe that's the case either. Even though she mentioned a lawyer a few times she never seriously considered calling one. That would have been an expensive proposition for an innocent woman. If she had nothing to do with the murder, then why go to the expense of hiring an attorney? Still I get the sense that she was hiding something that I couldn't quite put my finger on."

Shortly after the two detectives had left her house, Priscilla Stengel's son returned home. Michael Stengel was now nine years old. He was autistic. Priscilla loved him more than a rooster loved the sunrise. Two years before Michael was born, Priscilla had made a mistake. She had never been quite able to forgive herself for her first visit to the Fein Center for Women. But it was only recently that she had come to realize this fact. She was ecstatic to have Michael in her life, but recently she had begun to whimsically wonder what life might have been like had Michael had an older brother or sister.

Billy Brand was standing before his congregation, while television cameras recorded his sermon for distribution throughout the South. His jet black hair was neatly combed back off his forehead and his large round eyes shown out across his church like two beacons searching the sea for floundering ships. He knew what he wanted to say and he needed little preparation to say it. As much as he found the work of Aaron Fein to be despicable, he also knew that there was no way to condone the senseless shooting of the abortionist. He knew that members of his congregation could be conflicted about the message that he had been preaching. Pure and simply abortion was murder. His message was clear. But two wrongs did not make a right. He wanted to get this message across to his congregation, not just those seated in front of him, but to his whole television congregation throughout the south. He couldn't be sure that it wasn't a member of this extended congregation who murdered Aaron Fein in Tampa. Brand's Sunday sermons were carried on cable TV throughout Florida, and an electronic disciple could possibly have been the person who executed Fein. The preacher made a few opening remarks welcoming his congregation before launching into his message.

"This past *Thursdeh nahght* a gunman took the *lahfe o* Aaron *Fahne*, a man who has taken the *lahves o* so *maneh* humans, that the exact total is unknown. Now it's possible that *y'all mahght* view this as vindication, a just end to the *horrifyin'* slaughter *o* God's most innocent children; unborn babies, who were *bein'* nurtured in their mommas' wombs. *Yew* have heard *meh* call *fur* the end *t'* this slaughter on *maneh, maneh* occasions, *an' yew* will *continya t'* hear *meh* say *exactleh* the same *thaang* as long as *Ah cain* preach. *Y'all cain cut off my legs an' call me Shorty b'faw Ah'll* budge an inch on this topic. *A-bortion* is *murdeh ... unequivocalleh, murdeh.*"

The preacher paused and moved his eyes from one section to another around the faces in the congregation. He saw heads bobbing in agreement, chins steeling in support, and ears perking for the next sound bite.

"Now *Ah* know that *Ah cain sem'tahmes* get wound up *tighteh* than an eight day clock, when *Ah* speak *'bout* these villainous acts. *Howeveh*, on the same *Terrifahin' Thursdeh* that Aaron *Fahne* was gunned down in the *parkin'* lot of his *A-bortion* clinic, seven innocent babies were *A-borted* on the *otheh sahde o* that *buildin's* walls. These seven innocent children were *deprahved o* their God given *rahght t'* walk on His earth. Now Aaron *Fahne* may not have performed these *A-bortions hisse'f ...* although he has *fessed-up t' personalleh performin' maneh* such executions in the past ... but Aaron *Fahne* facilitated these *killin's jes'* as he has facilitated thousands upon thousands of *killin's* in the past. Of course the *A-bortionists* don't refer to these hideous offenses as 'executions' or '*killin's.* They don't even tolerate the term *A-bortion.* They prefer *t'* call these horrible sins '*terminations.*' So sad ... so *vereh vereh* sad."

The preacher punctuated his remarks by several different hand gestures. He raised two fingers on either hand in symbolic quotation marks as he uttered the word "terminations." And he shook his head from side to side to emphasize the word "sad." Some in the congregation had unwittingly taken to shaking their own heads along with the

Reverend Brand. One of those in the pews shaking his head was Patch Munson, attending services three days after he had taken his Thursday night excursion to Tampa.

"Now as sinful and atrocious as all of these *A-bortions* have been, the Lord has granted each of us the free will *t'* determine *fur ourse'ves* the passageway *t'* heaven or a *slippereh* slope *t'* hell. We know that those who profiteer from the slaughter of unborn children have chosen the *slippereh* slope. They have taken a route that will lead straight *t'e-ternal* damnation. But it is *not* the job *o aneh* one *o* us *t'* send *'em* on their way ahead *o* the Lord's schedule. In Romans 12:19 it is written:

> *'Dearly beloved, avenge not yerse'ves, but rather give place unto wrath: fur it is written, Vengeance is mahne; Ah will repay, saith the Lord.'*

"We must let the Lord work in His *all-knowin' tahmeframe*. There are *maneh* who have repented *durin'* their *lahfetimes an'* embraced the Lord. We need *t'* give these *sinnehs* a chance *t'* do that. Yes, we should protest the evil *doehs an'* the carnage they wreak. We should demonstrate against the *spahneless* political officeholders who are too weak *t'* stand up against the terrorism *an' tyranneh* of *A-bortion*. We should make our voices heard in *evereh* social *venyew*, in *evereh* business office, in *evereh* municipal building, in *evereh* sports arena, in *evereh* printed paper, in *evereh* internet blog, *an' anehwhere* else where we *mahght* be heard. But we must not turn *t' vah'lence ourse'ves*. We must not join the Godless *murderehs* on their own *playin'* field. We *should* not; we *cain* not; and we *may* not, *murdeh t'* prevent *murdeh*. In Matthew 26:52 it is written:

> *'Put yer sword back in its place,' Jesus said t' him, 'fur all who draw the sword will dah bah the sword.'*

"One of the greatest ministers of our *tahme*, the Reverend Martin Luther King said it in a simple way:

'Hate begets hate; vah'lence begets vah'lence;
toughness begets a greater toughness. We must
meet the forces o hate wit' the poweh o love...'
So Ah too say t' each of y'all, yew should hate
the sin but love the sinneh, b'cause even the
sinneh is a chahld of God.'

"Now we all know that on this past *Thursdeh evenin'*, *sum'un decahded* that Aaron *Fahne* would breathe his last breath in the *parkin'* lot of the *vereh buildin'* where he has taken the *lahves* of thousands of children of God. *Y'all* have heard me condemn the actions of Aaron *Fahne* from this pulpit on *maneh* occasions. *Fahne* was akin to Adolf Hitler in his *wahd'spread slaughteh* of human *lahfe*. *Fahne* would tell tales of how he was *helpin'* damsels in distress. His *litaneh* of *lahs an'* deceptions has been well chronicled from this pulpit. And *Ah* have also spoken out against *Fahne's play'un t'* expand the *companeh* that *Ah* have often referred *t'* as '*Murdeh*, Inc,' into the great State of *Al'bama*.

"*Howeveh y'all* have also heard me preach against the evil of *cap'tal* punishment. It is never proper *fur* the state *t'* take a man's life, no matter how heinous his *crahmes* may have been. Now *Ah* know *maneh o yew* have expressed concern *'bout mah* strong opposition *t' cap'tal* punishment. *An' Ah'm vereh* troubled *bah yer* concerns. But *Ah* stand *bah mah* convictions. *Ah* stand *bah mah* faith. And *Ah* stand *bah mah* Lord and Savior, Jesus Christ, who was *hisse'f* a victim *o cap'tal* punishment *fur* perceived *crahmes* against the state."

Billy's voice was a tower of strength. He was reinforcing all of his points with strong body language and facial expressions. He seemed to be much larger in stature than his 5'11", 165 pound frame. His audience in the pews of the Christian Ascendancy Community Church, along with his regional television audience, was riveted to every word Billy said. Billy was conscious of his impact but he was also aware that his sermon was now drifting. He didn't usually like to rail against abortion and capital punishment in the same sermon. But he believed he had a point which needed to be emphasized. So he moved quickly to connect the dots.

"So then as much as *Ah despahse* the works *o* the now deceased Aaron *Fahne an'* as much as *Ah* will *continya t' fahght* against the *possibiliteh* of his awful legacy *reachin'* the outskirts of Mobile *Al'bama, Ah cainnot* condone the cold blooded *murdeh o* the cold blooded *murdeh-eh.*

"Even as we reach outside the parameters of our Christian faith, we *cain fahnd* the *teachin's* of *othehs* who are *lahke mahnded* in spirit. It was Gandhi who said; '*Victoreh* attained *bah vah'lence* is tantamount *t'* a defeat, *fur* it is *momentareh.*' Therefore we must *realahze* that even though Aaron *Fahne* is no *longeh* the main face of *A-bortion,* here in the south, there are others who are *waitin' t'* take his place. Aaron *Fahne* may be dead but *unfortunateleh* the *Fahne Cenneh fur* Women lives on. *An'* nowhere in our Christian faith or in our Christian scriptures do we *fahnd readin's* that disallow the destruction *an' killin'* of heinous institutions such as the FCW in *Tamper.* But we need to bring down these evil institutions *wit'out stoopin' t' vah'lence.*

By the time Billy Brand had left his pulpit many members of his congregation had repositioned their venom towards the institution and away from its deceased leader. Patch Munson may not have been the only member of the congregation who believed that there was more work to be done down in Tampa but he was troubled and conflicted by the words of the Reverend Billy Brand.

Aaron Fein's death had been disturbing to Hawk Richter. Richter didn't know Fein all that well but he considered him to be a brazen sort of soul. Fein had been fearless in defending his position against all of the Right-to-Life critics that he had encountered. The problem was that it was highly likely that Fein had been murdered by one of those critics, someone who had taken the criticism to the extreme and had decided to end the life of Aaron Fein.

What troubled Richter even more was that the crazy person who killed Aaron Fein might not stop killing. Ideologues were known to risk a great deal in order to get their way. In view of the fact that

Richter was one of a small group of limited partners in the Fein Center for Women, he had to consider the fact that he too might become a target of the deranged gunman. Richter was not a stranger to protest or controversy. He had endured his share of criticism because of his pronounced atheistic views. However he had never before been embroiled in the abortion hubbub. He had his opinions but they generally weren't part of his repertoire of activist causes. His involvement with the FCW was simply a financial investment.

Richter was even more stunned by the mass murders that took place on the same night at BITSY. Apparently the authorities had that situation under control, even though the tragedy had claimed the lives of thirteen people and injured another fourteen innocent people. The BITSY murders took place in a building where Richter lectured in the only class that he was teaching that semester. Although he didn't personally know any of the students who were killed, he was casually acquainted with Melech Katz, who was in his first year teaching at the university.

The whole Tampa community was in shock over these two nearly simultaneous acts of deranged terrorism. There was absolutely no evidence that connected the two events and in some way that made these events even more horrific. *Was random violence getting completely out of control?* Hawk Richter didn't know the answer, and nothing was more unsettling to the scientist than not knowing answers.

It was Sunday morning and Richter sat in front of his television set listening to the political talk show *Face the Nation*. The Tampa murders were mentioned as breaking news but they were not treated as the main subject area of the talk show. Richter simply stared sightlessly at his TV, but paid little attention to the content. His mind was in another place. He was roused from his reverie by a ringing telephone.

"Hello?"

"Hello Hawk … It's me, Julianne. I just wanted to see how you doing today." Julianne had spoken on the phone to Richter on Friday morning before her flight back home to San Francisco, but the discussion was brief. On Saturday she had called again, but only got his answering machine. He hadn't yet returned the call.

"Hi Julianne … Thanks for calling. I'm doing OK I guess. How are you?"

"I had nice evening on Thursday. I'm sorry it ended in such a sad way."

"Yes. I was enjoying myself as well. It certainly is a strange world we live in. Isn't it? I was not super close to Aaron Fein. But I did like the guy. He might have been obsessed with the success of his business but that didn't make him a bad person."

"People are saying that he was killed *because* of his business. Do you think that was the case?

"That's probably an accurate hypothesis. But I'd rather just let the police worry about that. I'm sure they'll find the guy quickly, prosecute him and then incarcerate him." After a moment he continued, "I don't think Aaron left much family behind. He has a young wife, Amanda, whom I met once at a board meeting. I heard that she is a stunningly beautiful woman."

For a second or two, Julianne wondered what beautiful meant to Richter. Was it a physical thing? Once again she recalled the moment out on the veranda when Richter was softly fondling her facial features. Julianne remembered the fleeting titillation of those few awkward moments. It could not have felt more intimate if he had been caressing her breasts instead of her face. She felt warm all over once again. Julianne thought about Amanda Fein, and the fact that Hawk had *heard* that she was *stunningly beautiful*. How did Hawk form these perceptions, she wondered. He didn't seem to be the type to simply take someone else's word as gospel. She already knew what Richter thought about so called gospel.

"Did you go to services for your friend?"

"No I didn't think that would have been appropriate. Obviously it would be rather hypocritical for me to go to see Amanda and try to comfort her by telling her that Aaron will be okay and that he's in 'a better place.' That's lot of nonsense. He's dead. He's gone. End of story."

"Well couldn't you just stop by to see Amanda, you know, sit Shiva and all that. Pay your condolences? I don't know … talk about the future or something comforting … in some way?" It was more of an inquiry than a suggestion.

"As I said, I'm not good at that kind of thing. Think about it. Would you like someone to come into your home and tell you what you already intuitively know … that your loved one is gone forever? Right, wrong or indifferently, our society still likes to be supported by myths. Believe me. My ego is not that big that I feel a compulsion to go into people's homes and make sure that they realize that there is no God. Sometimes it's best to just let things be."

"Has anybody contacted you with respect to your investment in the Fein Center? Are you at all worried that the loon who killed Aaron Fein might want to continue the bloodshed?"

"No. There are a dozen different investors in the Fein Center. But the only name that's out in the public domain is that of Aaron Fein."

"What about the other murders? They're all over the news here in California. It must be crazy back in Tampa."

"Yes. It's all very sad. The whole campus is in mourning. Many students have left to go home. It was better that this happened during the summer. There were fewer students on campus."

There was an awkward silence on the phone as both parties began to ponder others topics. Neither person cared to continue the conversation in the direction it was going. Their friendship was too nascent to handle such tragedy in a simple phone conversation. And then unexpectedly an idea occurred to Hawk Richter.

"Let me change gears for a second, Julianne. Do you have any vacation time that you can take from your job?"

"Sure. My company is liberal with its vacation policies for its better performers. I enjoy my vacation time so I make sure to take all of it that I can. Why do you ask?"

"In two weeks I'll be going to Barbados for a convention. I was thinking about extending my stay for three days and I would love to have some company. Can I interest you in joining me?"

Julianne was surprised by this request. She was still trying to fathom what she thought about their dinner date the past Thursday evening. But she knew how she felt about it. She felt mystified. For the past couple of years she had learned to trust her feelings.

"That sounds delightful."

Melech Katz was sitting at the large bar of Charley's Steak House on West Cypress Street. In two hours he was scheduled to take a flight to New York City. He was beginning to wish that he hadn't agreed to do the shows. He had already done more than a dozen short news interviews, all via communications connections from his home on the outskirts of Tampa. Now he was being asked to make two live appearances on morning news shows in New York City for more extensive interviews. He was also going to do a segment on Kenneth Brady's cable TV show, *The Brady Focus*. Katz didn't want this to be his fifteen minutes of fame. But his thinking process had been somewhat paralyzed over the past three days. In fact, he was barely thinking at all. He had been simply reacting, ever since he reacted to the Clinton madness on Thursday night. It was similar to the firefight in Gaza Strip, when he merely reacted for fourteen hours straight. But now he didn't want to think about that either. He ordered another shot of bourbon and a beer chaser.

The bar area of the upscale restaurant was spacious but it was crowded with young men and women in their twenties and thirties. A svelte young single lady sidled up next to Katz.

"Aren't you that hero professor that's been on TV?" The sylphlike blonde haired young woman smiled beautifully as she spoke. Normally, Katz would have sensed opportunity knocking in a heartbeat, but his heart just wasn't beating that way at this time.

"No, just a look alike." He didn't smile or offer any encouragement to the willowy blonde. He just kept his eyes on his beer and tried to focus. He was trying to recover his brain, before he got onto his flight. He was also reconsidering Dr Abe Elowitz offer for group psychotherapy. Maybe that would help. Elowitz had told him it was a small group of eight people and at least one other person suffered with PTSD. It might be worth a try he thought.

Patch Munson had some strange ideas over the years, but this one was crazier than most. He wanted to talk to someone about the fact that he had taken the life of Aaron Fein. He had no second thoughts about it being the right thing to do. Fein was a murderer and the Bible stipulated that an "eye for an eye" was a just punishment. For a while he had entertained the idea of going to see his minister, Billy Brand. Brand had long railed against the horrors of abortion and had even mentioned Aaron Fein by name as being one of the country's most prolific baby murderers. However after listening to Brand's most recent Sunday sermon Munson was disinclined to speak with the minister. The problem with that decision was that once he decided not to talk to Billy Brand, the *queasies* returned. That's what caused his newest crazy idea.

Father Tim Hanlon was still a Catholic cleric. After his discussion with Father Goethe, the pastor had persuaded Hanlon to pray about his decision and to continue to say Mass and administer the sacraments. Goethe promised that he would speak to the bishop immediately and together they would pray about the decision for the best course of action. Ten days had gone by. Hanlon had not heard back from Goethe other than Goethe's pressure to continue in his ministry during the waiting period. Hanlon had done just that. He had prayed every morning as he said Mass. And he had much to pray about. He believed that God might be sending him answers and he needed to pay attention. Three days after his discussion with Goethe he had received a call from Carol Mays. Two days later he'd met Mays in the diner and learned that he was a *father* in more ways than one. Life was coming at him quickly. And that was not about to change.

Hanlon had been sitting in his confessional listening as his parishioners filed in to tell God about their transgressions. This experience had changed for Hanlon since Carol Mays visited his confessional. He was about to have an even more transformative experience in the confessional. And he would wonder why God continued to test him.

The sliding door between the kneeling penitent and the seated priest slid open with a wooden sound. The voice that Hanlon heard was one he had never heard before.

"*Fatheh, Ah wanna* make a confession." Hanlon recognized that this was going to be another one of those unusual confessions. It didn't start with the normal formality of a designation of the time frame since the penitent's last confession. What he was about to hear would confirm his assumption.

"Yes, my son. God will rejoice in heaven if you are truly sorry for your sins. How long has it been since your last confession?"

"*Ah* don't *wanna* beat *'round* the bush *'bout* this, *Fatheh*. Last week *Ah* killed *sum'un* in *Tamper. Ah* don't know *iffin* it makes a *diff'ence 'bout* how long it's *'bin* since *Ah 'bin* to confession, 'cause *Ah ain't neveh bin* here *b'faw.*" Patch Munson was obviously anxious to just blurt out what had been troubling him. He was willing to do almost anything to get rid of the *queasies*.

Father Tim Hanlon was nearly speechless. This was a rare occurrence for him in the confessional because he had a duty to be responsive. He didn't want to delay replying for an inordinate amount of time, but he was truly speechless.

On the kneeler side of the sliding wooden window, Patch Munson didn't know what to say next either, even though the *queasies* had begun to subside somewhat. *What was takin' this priest so long t' talk? He must hear thaangs lahke this from tahme t' tahme. Sureleh, Ah'm not the first person t' eveh confess killin' sum'un.*

"You say that you've never been to confession before. Are you Catholic?"

Many things raced through Munson's mind. *Did priests' vow of silence apply only to confessions from Cat'licks? Maybeh Ah should tell him Ah'm Cat'lick.*

"*Ah'm Cat'lick*, all right. *Ah* just *ain't 'bin t'* church in a long time, *an' Ah* don't remember *doin'* much *confessin'* when *Ah* was a kid. It's still all right *t'* confess stuff now. *Ain't* it?"

Again there was a delay before the priest spoke. Munson was worried. He was about to get up and run out of the confessional when Father Hanlon finally responded.

Meanwhile Father Tim Hanlon was trying to gain his composure. There was something odd about the man on the other side of the wall. What concerned the priest most was the fact that the man in the confessional didn't sound contrite. He sounded more like a defendant pleading his case to a judge or jury. Still Hanlon wanted to help. He decided to accept the man's declaration of his Catholicism and move on. He also wanted to put the man at ease to confess all his sins and to ask for God's forgiveness.

"God is always open to your confession. There is no timetable associated with his forgiveness. So please go on. Tell me how you killed this man in Tampa. Was it an accident? Was it an emotional response? Was it vengeance?"

"He was an evil man. He was a baby *killeh*. He deserved *t' dah*. *Ah* shot him and killed him and now he won't be *murderin' no* more babies."

Father Hanlon's ears were ringing with this confession. This man kneeling across from him had apparently murdered Aaron Fein. Hanlon noticed that he himself was now shaking. This shocking disclosure was unlike anything that he had ever heard before in the confessional. Everyone had heard about this murder. It was a far reaching national story. The news media continued to cover developments in the story several times daily. And now there was someone two feet away from him who was claiming to be the gunman. But Hanlon had a job to do.

"Regardless of the evil that this man has caused, we're not at liberty to avenge his violence, with violent acts of our own. I assume that you realize this and that's why you have come to confession. Am I right? Are you sorry that you took the life of another man?"

"Aaron *Fahne* was a *terr'ble* person. He was far worse *'an* Hitler *'cause* he killed *maneh o* these babies *wit'* his own hands. Thousands of babies were *bein' murdehed ever'* year *bah* this animal."

"I understand the emotion behind your actions. But are you sorry for taking another man's life?" The priest was whispering in his well-practiced confessional tone.

"*Ah* don't *un'erstand* the question. *Yer sayin'* the same *thaang* as Reverend *Billeh.*"

"And what would that be?"

"Reverend Brand is *lahke* all *yew Cat'lick* preachers. He goes on *an'* on *'bout* how horrible *A-bortion* is … even called *Fahne*, a *murdereh.* Then when *sum'un* takes *Fahne* out, he starts *preachin' 'bout* how we *shudden* be *eliminatin'* this beast."

"Taking the life of another human being is never the right thing to do. It is always sinful. But we are all human beings. We sometimes sin out of anger or frustration. We do bad things, sometimes grievously bad things, or terribly immoral things. But if we are truly sorry for our sins, God will forgive us no matter what we have done."

Hearing these words, Munson was now somewhat conflicted. He certainly wanted to be forgiven. He believed that forgiveness would help with the *queasies*. However there was a big part of him that could not be dissuaded from the self-righteous opinion that he had done the proper thing. He hadn't acted immorally, maybe illegally, but not immorally. He wondered; *What comes next in this confessin' process?* He wasn't sure. Father Hanlon prodded him along.

"Are you sorry for killing this man?" The tone of the priest's voice was kind enough. His manner was somewhat soothing.

"*Ah* am *sorreh.*" Patch said it, but he didn't mean it. He thought for a second and then backed off his statement of contrition.

"*Yew* know what *Ah jes'* don't *git*. There were two mass *murdehs* in *Tamper* last *Thursdeh*. They're *sayin'* that the *Fahne Cenneh* performed multiple *A-bortions* on the same day that *Fahne* was killed. That was mass *murdeh* number one. Then that lunatic Clinton shoots all *them* people at the university. That was mass *murdeh* number two. *Rahght*? So this ex-Jew freedom-*faghter*/professor takes out Clinton and he's considered a hero all *oveh* the country … as he should be. No more Clinton. No more dead students. *Rahght*?"

Munson didn't wait for an answer he simply continued; *"Meanwhahle Ah* take out Aaron *Fahne.* No more *Fahne.* No more dead babies. *Rahght?* Yet there's a manhunt out *t' git meh. S'plain t' meh* what's the *diff'ence."*

"The confessional is not the right place to have a political discussion on the appropriateness of abortion. Besides, we both view abortion as a hideous sin. I'd be happy to discuss the matter with you at length in the rectory, or even here in an extended private confession, that we could schedule. But for now, the key issue is whether or not you feel sorry for killing one of God's children."

"Ah alreadeh said *Ah'm sorreh."*

Now it was Father Hanlon's turn to make a choice. He had never made a determination that someone wasn't penitent when they verbally expressed sorrow and regret for the commission of a sin. Then again, no one ever came into his confessional and confessed a murder before. He deferred his decision a little longer.

"We have spent a lot of time on one sin, for which you have said you are sorry. Are there other sins that you would like to confess?"

"Nope. That's *'bout* it."

"I'll remind you that in order to make a true confession and to receive absolution, you need to be truly sorry for *all* of your sins. And although it is not necessary to confess each and every sin, you need to make an honest effort to recall your most grievous sins, your mortal sins, and confess those transgressions. Do you need help in recalling these sins? Should we quickly run through the commandments?"

"Tell *meh* this Father. *Iffin Ah* tell *yew* that *Ah'm sorreh fur* all of *mah* sins do *yew furgive 'em? An'* also … *yew ain't* allowed *t'* tell *nobody 'bout* what *Ah* tell *yew.* That *rahght?"*

"Your confession is between you and God. God forgives your sins. I am simply His emissary, administering absolution on God's behalf. And yes, as his minister, I've taken a vow not to disclose anything that I hear in the confessional."

The young priest was still struggling with his decision. He now began to think once again that the man in his confessional may not be a Catholic. And for that matter he may not even be truly sorry for murdering Aaron Fein. On one hand this man seemed to be simple minded, or at least single-minded. But he wasn't a simpleton. He had certainly thought through the comparison between his own actions and those of Melech Katz. *Then again*, thought Hanlon, *maybe we're all simpletons.*

Father Hanlon decided to take the man at his word. Over the next three minutes or so Patch Munson clumsily confessed several other minor transgressions. They finally began winding down and Hanlon told him that for his penance he should say the Lord's Prayer twenty-five times and write it out on a piece of paper five times. He asked him to pay particular attention to the words: *Forgive us our sins, as we forgive those who sin against us. And lead us not into temptation, but deliver us from evil.*

When it came time to say his act of contrition, Munson had no clue about how to proceed, but Father Hanlon walked him through it phrase by phrase. The entire confession took about twenty-five minutes.

As he stepped out of the confessional Munson looked around and saw that there was only one other person in the church, a thin young black woman, who was sitting too close to the confessional for Munson's liking. This young lady looked up at him briefly and then simply gazed out towards the altar. No one else was waiting to go to confession. Munson didn't waste any time saying prayers inside of the church. He figured that he could handle that at home, privately. When it was over and he stepped out of the church, Munson felt much lighter. The *queasies* were gone, at least for the moment. Back inside of the confessional Father Hanlon now had the *queasies*.

The Munson family farm was originally more than 3500 acres in size and had been in the family since the post Civil War period. Sharecropping in the latter part of the nineteenth century had reduced the Munson family farm to 1750 acres. At the time Alabama was known as the "Cotton State," and the Munson family farm produced more than its fair share of cotton. In the early twentieth century however the Munsons' cotton farm was nearly destroyed by the arrival of the Mexican boll weevil. They survived this blight. However more of the farm area was sold off and many family members retreated from the farming industry to work in the shipping industry in the port of Mobile. By 1925 the family farm was the sole property of Harry Munson Sr. It had dwindled to less than 1500 acres, and the family had diversified its efforts away from cotton farming. They started growing corn, peaches and pecans as well as cotton.

Harry Munson Sr. had one son and one daughter. His daughter died from consumption at the age of eight, and Harry Sr. and his wife also both died relatively early in life, neither reaching the age of fifty. The Munson farm was then in the hands of Harry Munson Jr, who was always known simply as "Junior." Right after World War II and over the ensuing twenty years, Junior sold off more of the property. With the remaining farmland Junior began to convert to citrus fruit farming. With the help of his wife and their son, Harry III, and their two daughters, Gloria and Marjorie, Junior made a respectable living.

But Junior also had other interests. He dabbled in local county politics and he also had an interest in what went on in the world outside of Mobile. During the early part of the Cold War years, he was frequently the purveyor of fright to others in the community with his concerns about the possibility of a nuclear attack by the Soviet Union. He went so far as to build two concrete bomb shelters in different sections of his property. With the help of Harry III (*who at the time was called "Lit'le Harreh" but would later be given the moniker of "Patch,"*) Junior would periodically stock and restock these shelters with food and munitions. Junior's wife and his two daughters thought he was paranoid, so they never participated in his survivalist mania. Over time Junior and young Harry III, or Patch as he was now called, also became less concerned about fallout from nuclear attacks by the Russians. Then after the demise of the Soviet Union in December of 1991, they stopped the mindless restocking of their fallout shelters.

Meanwhile the family farming business continued to evolve. The main residence on the farm had been expanded several times. For a while Junior and his wife lived in this house with their three children.

After Patch Munson married Maggie in 1997, the family made a decision. The farm was now still over 900 acres, and in recent years its most profitable crop had been soybeans, but Junior was beginning to show signs of deteriorating health. After much discussion among the family members it was decided that they would sell 450 acres, essentially half of the farm, to a development company that wanted to put up single family homes in the neighborhood.

The real estate market was not yet in full bloom but it was quite healthy nonetheless. The Munsons were offered $1.1 million for the 450 acres. Junior negotiated with the developers and settled for a one million dollar cash payment plus ownership of the largest new house in the new development.

The family's agreement provided that Junior and his wife and two daughters would move into the new home in the new development. Patch Munson and his wife, Maggie, would remain in the big farmhouse and continue to work the farm.

The deal that Junior made with the developers came at just the right time. A couple years later there was a drastic decline in soybean prices and almost overnight there were many farms on the market and prices were significantly depressed.

Once again the family farming business evolved and the Munson farm was now the habitat for six broiler-chicken houses. These chicken houses produced meat chicken under a contract with a large regional chicken production company. Collectively these broiler-chicken houses were able to produce as many as 120,000 chickens every six weeks. The minimal amount of labor that was required was also contracted directly from the regional company. It was almost as though the family was renting the farm to the chicken company. There was not a lot of work required of the Munsons but the income was not exorbitant either. There was still a little extra income that accrued from a few acres that were devoted to citrus farming, but it was more of a hobby than a profession for Patch Munson.

All of this simply meant that unlike Bubba Looney and some of Munson's other fishing buddies, the chicken farmer had a good bit of spare time on his hands. So when his parents recently died within weeks of one another, Munson began to see the world in a different light.

Patch Munson had always been close to his father, Junior Munson. All of the Munsons had long been churchgoing Christians. They believed that a harmonious eternal afterlife would be their recompense for living a virtuous and moral lifestyle and they were highly suspicious of others who were less inclined to heed the teachings of The Church. At least that was the way things appeared at first glance. However like many of their supposedly abstemious neighbors, they would hide the alcohol under the fruit and vegetables at the market, and tell the checkout clerks that they were buying it to keep the farm workers happy. Although the Munsons made a working class living off their farm income, they were also frugal people. They rarely travelled and seldom ate out at restaurants. But they were not unhappy people. They simply lived in expectation of their eventual heavenly reward.

After Junior Munson passed away, Patch Munson began thinking about his life in a more holistic way. He began to become concerned with what his life was all about. He started taking the sermons that he heard in church quite seriously. However he was somewhat selective in which sermons he listened to and heeded. His disillusionment with Billy Brand's most recent sermon was the deciding factor that led him to seek absolution from a Catholic priest. And as he left church after his confession he began to become equally skeptical of Father Hanlon. He decided to watch him to see what he could learn about the priest's comings and goings. He simply didn't know what else to do and he had some time on his hands. He needed additional information and he didn't want to *queasies* to return.

Patch Munson watched and waited for Father Tim Hanlon to come out of the church. After about 10 minutes, the thin young black woman whom Munson had observed sitting outside of the confessional, came through the church doorway and meandered slowly down the four church steps. She was not in any hurry and when she got to the bottom of the steps, she stopped and appeared to be waiting for someone. Munson was parked in his Silverado about 80 feet down the road on the opposite side of the street. His vehicle was facing toward the church. The woman didn't look around much and didn't appear to be looking down the street for a car to pick her up. But she was definitely waiting for someone.

Five minutes later Father Hanlon came out the front door and stopped at the top of the steps. He looked somewhat surprised to see the black lady but regardless he met her at the bottom of the 4 foot stairway in short order. Their conversation appeared to be animated but amicable. Munson couldn't tell much more about the conversation from where he was watching, but he sensed a friendly rapport. Still he was extremely intrigued by what they might have been talking about. He was reasonably certain that it wasn't about his confession, because the woman didn't seem at all astonished by anything that the priest said. Whatever the conversation was about, however, the priest appeared to be very interested. The woman was doing most of the talking and the priest was leaning in, as though he didn't want to miss a word of what she said. They talked for more than ten minutes before they headed in opposite directions. Hanlon walked back towards the rectory while the thin black woman walked down the street toward the spot where Munson was still parked in clandestine observation. He watched as the young lady walked right past his truck and he got a better look at her. She was tall and attractive and she flashed a broad toothy smile as she turned after talking with Father Hanlon. The smile had not faded entirely by the time she walked past Munson. In fact the farmer thought that she was the most attractive black woman he had ever seen. He had no idea why she interested him so much, and he knew that his concerns should have been more about Father Hanlon. He resolved that the situation just needed more observation.

Carol Mays was happy, walking away from the church. Tim Hanlon had agreed to meet his son, even though he was troubled by something she couldn't quite put her finger on. Maybe it was a bad idea to meet him after confession. However she didn't want to call him. She wanted to see him in person. But she didn't want to be scheduled at the rectory for an official visit. She realized that the potential for problems for Tim was lessened if others didn't know she was talking to him. Regardless, during their brief conversation at the bottom of the church steps Tim Hanlon had satisfied Carol that he wanted to meet Russell. When she had asked him what was bothering him, he quickly smiled, albeit a sad smile, and said he simply had a lot on his mind. But then he said that *"his heart and soul had been delighted by the knowledge that they had had a child together."* The way he said it, and the words he chose, sent a thrill through her whole being that she hadn't felt in several years. That was all she wanted to hear. She assumed that his consternation was related to other matters.

There was one thing that bothered her however. As she walked down the street towards her car, she noticed a seedy-looking man staring at her. As a professional model, with a certain modicum of success, Carol Mays was used to having people leer at her. However this was somehow different. The thick-bodied, unkempt, stubble-bearded man had an extra large head. He was sitting in a truck trying to hide the fact that he was looking at her. Then she realized that he was the same heavily perspiring man who had come out of the confessional after an extended period of time, while she was waiting for confessions to end. The man gave her the creeps.

When he returned to the rectory, Father Tim Hanlon took off his collar and his black shirt and walked into the bathroom. He stared at his face in the mirror over the sink. He wondered whether or not his son Russell would bear any facial resemblance to him. He was about to find out very soon.

IV

The State Park and the Island Paradise

alk show host Kenneth Brady was used to people whose moment in the sunshine was fleeting. His cable news show had garnered excellent ratings for several years running. *The Brady Focus* was now a staple of primetime TV in many households throughout the nation. The young talk show host had a controversial personal background in that he was bisexual and made no pretense at being a conventional newsperson. He was brash and opinionated and his show, *The Brady Focus*, was often the program that people watched to get a different spin on emerging news developments. You could expect the unexpected when you watched *The Brady Focus.*

Brady's guest for a ten minute segment of his show this evening was Professor Melech Katz, the hero professor from Tampa, who had shot and killed Joseph Clinton on the BITSY science building rooftop.

"Thanks for coming on our show this evening Professor Katz, and a special thanks for coming into the studio to do our interview live."

"It's not a problem. This is the third program I've done today, here in New York."

Brady wasn't thrilled to hear Katz speak about the other shows. He wasn't even sure if he liked Katz. As a slapdash young egocentric commentator, Brady generally wanted the show to be more about him than about his guests. Because of this Brady frequently looked upon as guests in an adversarial manner.

"It's been four days now since you shot Joseph Clinton in Tampa and ended his rampage through the BITSY campus. What have the last four days been like for you?"

"Strange … very strange … I don't think I can begin to tell you how weird it's been. I feel so terrible about the students and professors who were shot at BITSY. Along with many other people I'm grieving for their families." Katz stated his grief and anguish but he knew truthfully that he had a hard time feeling it. He simply felt numbness.

"But for you personally, how has this all played out? The media has branded you as a hero amidst the heartbreak of an agonizing tragedy. How do you feel about that?"

"Frankly, I'm not sure how I feel about it. At this point I'm just trying to do whatever I can to bring some solace to the affected families. I don't know if talking about what happened is helpful to them. But that's what I'd sincerely like to achieve. This whole business about being a hero doesn't make much sense to me. Frankly I was scared to death when all of this went down."

"So let's talk about that for a minute … if it's not too painful. The way that the story has emerged is that you were on the sixth floor of the science building when you heard shots ring out and then you found two dead bodies on the floor. You saw that Clinton had somehow driven his cart to the rooftop stairway. Do I have that correct so far?'

"Well not exactly. There were two students that were shot, but one was still moving. The other was motionless, and I presumed he was dead."

"That's interesting I didn't know that. One of the students was still alive."

"Yes, but unfortunately he was bleeding profusely, and he later died also."

"Did you try to help him?"

"I called 911 and asked them to send help ASAP. I'm not a doctor, but I knew that it was likely that the second student would also die. As I said he was bleeding profusely."

"All right let's leave that for a moment. As I understand it, you then picked up a hand gun that was discarded by Clinton and went up after him on the rooftop of the building. Is that right?"

"Yes."

"What were you planning on doing?"

Katz stopped and took a deep breath. It was almost as though he were reliving these events for the hundredth time. However other than the original police interrogation, he hadn't gone into the gruesome detail in the way that Brady was leading him. Most of the other media coverage dealt with the fact that he had risked his life to save the lives of others. They had been effusive in their praise for his bravery. But Brady was different. He wasn't assuming anything. He was looking for details as well as nuance and rationale. Katz wasn't quite sure how to answer without re-reflecting on what was going through his mind last Thursday night.

"I guess I was planning on shooting this crazy guy Clinton, before he killed anyone else. So yes I took the gun and went upstairs after him."

"Didn't you think that this was an enormously dangerous course of action?"

"The situation was already extremely dangerous. I believed that if I could get to the gunman, I could make the situation much less dangerous for everyone. The thing that I didn't know, at the time, was how many people were involved in the shooting."

"You mean that you didn't know whether or not there was more than one shooter?"

"Yes, precisely."

"So when you finally made it up to the rooftop what did you see?"

"I saw this guy, who was later identified as Joseph Clinton, firing an assault rifle down into the courtyard in front of the building."

"So then when you saw Clinton you just began firing at him and managed to kill him, thereby stopping further bloodshed. Is that the way it was?"

"It didn't happen exactly that fast. When I first saw him on the rooftop he was a good distance away. So I had to sneak up on him.

There was a lot of noise at the time. Besides the noise of the gunfire there were sirens going off everywhere. So I managed to get up closer to him before I shot him."

"Did you call out to him at all? Did you ask him to put down his rifle?"

"No I didn't. He had an automatic rifle; I had an unknown handgun. Frankly I just wanted to stop him anyway that I could. And I didn't want to call any attention to myself before I stopped him."

"It is interesting to note, Professor Katz, that right after you shot Joseph Clinton, the Florida State police mistook you for the gunman. Am I right about that?"

"Yes, that's right."

"I guess you could say that it's a good thing that they called out to you before they began shooting."

Katz was unsettled with the direction of Kenneth Brady's questioning. He knew he had to answer these questions from the police when they investigated the shootings, but he never expected this type of grilling from a news commentator.

"I don't know if you've ever been in combat, Mr. Brady. What happens is that you are forced to make instantaneous life and death decisions. Those of us who have been trained in combat situations understand these risks and the decisions that come along with them."

"No. I was not in the military. But in the course of my career as a newsman, I have been up close and personal in several combat situations. And sometimes I have witnessed remarkable restraint on the part of the American military men and women."

The interview was now obviously quite tense. And the time allotted by *The Brady Focus* for this segment was running out. Kenneth Brady had successfully irritated his guest to the point where Melech Katz was growing red with rage. But before Katz could respond again to the commentator, Brady simply wrapped up the segment with a comment of his own.

"So there you have it, before we go to break, the thought processes of the vigilante professor, who says that he saved the lives of many additional people by taking the life of a deranged unstable gunman."

Tim Hanlon was very excited, but also very worried. It had been five days since he first learned about the existence of his son, Russell. And it had only been one day since he had heard back from Father Goethe that the bishop was considering his request to be laicized. In addition to these major life altering events, he had recently heard the confession of a man who had claimed to have murdered Aaron Fein. The tumult in his life had never been so pervasive. He thought that this must be the Hand of God working in his life. He was anxious to do the right thing in each of these episodes of his life's journey. He just didn't have a clear understanding of what the right thing was. And so he prayed for guidance.

Through prayerful meditation, Tim Hanlon had come to believe that it was time to leave the clerical priesthood, and he believed that God was re-sending Carol Mays to him as a sign of His divine will. Hanlon's mind played tricks with him as he considered whether his interpretation of this sign was simply a rationale for his own desires. And if this paradox wasn't enough to keep him on edge, he had the added complexity of the murder confession. What was he supposed to do about that? In the past he rarely transported the failings of others from the confessional to the outside world. His job was to hear the recitation of transgressions and to administer absolution. But now, for some odd reason, he felt the need to evaluate as well. He never saw the man who killed Aaron Fein, but he remembered the troubled voice quite vividly. He sounded like a man who needed help desperately. Father Hanlon considered the fact that someone could actually confess his sins, make peace with God and still be very needy in a secular way. What if this man decided to kill again? Hanlon realized that he had done nothing to intercept that possibility. If the troubled man decided that there was another abortionist who needed to be eliminated, what would he do? Maybe it wasn't just abortion that he was looking to remedy. Were there other transgressions that this man might attempt to rectify? Maybe this man needed significant psychological counseling as well as religious reconciliation. Hanlon felt that he had failed. He hadn't made a substantial effort to get the man to see him outside of the confessional. In a different venue he might have been able to persuade the sinner to get secular help, in addition to spiritual help.

These were some of the many thoughts that went through Tim Hanlon's mind as he drove north from Mobile to meet Carol Mays in Montgomery. He flipped them over in his mind one way and then another, without any clear resolution.

But then he thought about Russell. Having a son brought a very new joy to his life, but Hanlon knew that Russell was going to cause more than a little consternation on the part of the church hierarchy. Then again there were plenty of other things for the church hierarchy not to like. This started with the fact that parish priest Tim Hanlon was still in love with the mother of his child. The fact that she was African American added to the intrigue but would be less concerning to the powers that be within the church. But all of these things were issues that Hanlon felt he could deal with over time. Right now, what interested him the most was the fact that he was about to meet his son. There was no question in his mind that he also wanted to renew his intimate relationship with Carol Mays. However he wasn't sure how Mays might feel about that idea. He pulled up outside of the Marriott Courtyard and took a deep breath. He was about to find out. With all of these things on his mind he was oblivious to the fact that a silver-ice colored Chevy Silverado followed him into the lot.

Carol Mays and her son, Russell, were staying at a Marriott Courtyard about halfway between Mobile and Birmingham Alabama, in the city of Montgomery. She could afford to stay in a fancier place, but she liked the quiet comfort of the Courtyard. The motel style lay-out allowed her to drive up to the hotel and park right near her room. The hotel also held some history for her, as she had been there several times in the past. There was a time nearly nine years earlier when she and Tim Hanlon had shared a very intimate affair. He was in his early twenties, classically tall, dark and handsome, although admittedly not as dark as Carol herself. He also had an engaging sense of humor and a far stretching desire to do good things for the world. He often talked about the need for unanimity amongst individuals with different economic backgrounds, different religions, and different races. They met by chance when he was a junior at Spring Hill College in Mobile and she was still 19 year old freshman at Auburn University. The venue for that chance meeting was at a symposium at Rosa Parks Museum and Civil Rights Memorial, right there in Montgomery Alabama. Montgomery was roughly 50 miles closer to Mobile than was Auburn, so they met at that same Marriott Courtyard multiple times over the twenty-five months of their relationship.

Although Mays was thrilled with the thought that her little boy was about to meet his father, she was anxious that the experience might somehow not turn out as she hoped. Mays was at an all time emotional high. She had taken so many risks during the last week that she was reeling from the excitement.

Before going to Mobile she went to Birmingham to see her parents, Lawson and Ella Mays, and told them that she was bringing Russell to meet his father. That had been very troubling to her parents. They were the only people besides Carol who knew that Russell's father was Tim Hanlon. And they didn't care much for the Catholic priest, who had impregnated their daughter and then ran off to hide behind a Roman collar. Of course that was their version of what happened. Deep down they knew that Hanlon was unaware of their daughter's child, and they wanted to keep it that way. Nevertheless they had given in to the repeated entreaties on Carol's part to accept her wish to seek out Hanlon and disclose her secret. A few weeks earlier when she returned to Birmingham after misconnecting with Hanlon, Mays' parents presumed that her misguided ardor for introducing Hanlon to his son had run its course. Privately they had hoped that he would never find out.

Now as Mays went down to Montgomery, she was excited about the way things were working out. She was very anxious for the long-awaited meeting that was about to ensue. She felt confident that things would go well, but she was nervous nonetheless.

"Hi Carol. Hello Russell. Do you know who I am?" Hanlon looked right past Mays and into the eyes of a seven year old boy. He could instantly sense that his son was smart, self confident and charming. The eyes said it all. However Hanlon was surprised at the size of the seven year old. He was just a few inches under five feet tall, a long and lean seven year old. He had his mother's soft dark complexion and smallish ears. But he had his father's eyes, nose mouth and chin. He had been blessed with the best features of each of his parents.

"Yes. I think so. Mom told me that I was going to meet my father. Are you my father?

"Yes, I am."

"Well then hello, Father."

Hanlon had previously considered the potential awkwardness of this moment. He knew that a potential inelegance might display itself in many different ways. He hadn't spent much time conjecturing about what he wanted his son to call him, but he knew that the answer definitely wasn't "Father."

"Maybe you should just call me …."

"Russell? You should call your father, *Dad*." Mays quickly interrupted Hanlon before he offered to let their son refer to him as Tim, or Uncle Tim, or any other such innocuous name. She tensed for a moment as she gave her son this instruction. However the young boy answered quickly putting both adults at ease. This self confidence that Hanlon had noticed in the boy shone through immediately.

"All right … Hello Dad, nice to meet you."

"Well it certainly is wonderful to finally meet you Russell."

"You can call me Russ. Only Mom and my teachers call me Russell." Russ had a very appealing smile. He was engaging and precocious well beyond his almost eight years of age.

The party of three was seated in the small dining area of the hotel. There was a self-serve buffet breakfast arrayed on nearby counter tops and there were several hotel guests busily availing themselves of the morning cuisine. It wasn't the ideal place for a conversation of any length or depth. But Hanlon and Mays had agreed to make a cursory introduction over breakfast and then leave quickly for a picnic where everyone could get to know each other better. Still even these few words of greeting raised the interest of the other guests who couldn't help but be intrigued by a white father meeting his dark-skinned son for the first time. The fact that the young parents were attractive people made the whole scenario even more fascinating to the others, who remained impassively stone-faced as they filled their plates and sat at other tables.

Mays realized that she probably should have chosen a different venue for the initial introductions, because one of the hotel guests appeared to recognize her, but what was done was done. The one thing that she knew about her son, Russell, was that he was always hungry. So she wanted to make sure he had something to eat before they left for the day. She occasionally worried about his voracious appetite. If she tried to eat a fraction of what her seven year old son consumed, she would undoubtedly lose her job.

"Is it okay if I get something to eat?" The focus of the boy's attention changed rapidly as he saw an attendant refill the pancake chafing dish. "I'm starving!"

"Yes, all right. But don't overdo it Russell. We'll have plenty to eat at the picnic."

Tim Hanlon was now growing more aware of the surroundings and he suddenly turned quiet. He simply looked at Mays and smiled. Then in a soft voice he said, "He's a beautiful boy if boys can be beautiful."

"I would say thank you for the compliment, but you have to realize that you're complimenting yourself as well."

"I hope he's a fast eater. I'd like to get going so that we can have more time together, just the three of us." He said this nodding towards the false insouciance of the other hotel guests.

Russell came back to the table and wolfed down his breakfast without much conversation, other than a debate about how much syrup he was allowed to bathe onto his pancakes. Shortly thereafter they left via the front door of the hotel.

❦

Patch Munson was very surprised by what he saw.

"Now, *lookit* this *Harreh*," he said to his hound. "Looks *t' meh lahke* this priest's *gat sem confessin' o* his own to do."

Father Tim Hanlon was leaving the hotel where he had picked up the same black woman that Munson had seen at the church. As a precaution Munson had been following Father Hanlon off and on for the last several days. He wanted to make sure that Hanlon didn't go to the police or to some church authority to report what he had heard in the confessional. Munson had been kicking himself ever since he executed his scatter-brained idea of going to a Catholic confession. How could he have been so stupid as to trust his secret to a Catholic priest? There's a reason people have grown wary of priests, he thought. He shook his head with a private shudder for about the tenth time since his confession. *"What was Ah thaankin'?"* was the question he couldn't get out of his mind. But to his dog he simply said, "Well *Harreh, maybeh* we *gat ourse'ves sem in*-surance or *maybeh* we *gat* a problem." He couldn't decide which it was and Harry just looked at him sadly.

Munson noted that Hanlon looked nothing at all like a priest. He was dressed in Khaki shorts and a short sleeved white polo shirt that had a red trim on the sleeves and the bottom of the collar. What was surprising to Munson was that the black woman with Hanlon had a young boy accompanying her. *Her son*, he thought. Hanlon had been in the hotel for more than 45 minutes. If it were not for the young boy, Munson might have thought that the priest was in a hotel room playing slide-the-salami with his dark-skinned lover or whatever she was. Munson couldn't quite figure it all out.

But Patch Munson also noted the apparel of the black lady. She too was very casually dressed in shorts and a modified halter top. She was even more attractive than he remembered when he saw her a few days earlier. She was very tall but still more than 5 inches shorter than the 6 foot 3 inch priest. He saw that the woman was carrying a picnic basket, and toting an oversized handbag. From the way she dressed and the way she carried herself, Munson believed that she was not a local black woman. He also noticed that she was quite slender, although still somewhat shapely. He observed the way the priest walked close by her. It suggested a degree of intimacy. He waited to see if the priest would take her by the hand. That didn't happen. However he did treat her in a gentlemanly way, by opening the passenger side door and ushering her into her seat before closing the door behind her. He also opened the back seat for the young boy and closed the door after he had buckled the seat belt. There was something about their general demeanor that made Munson think of them as a family, but he didn't believe that could possibly be true. When the priest pulled out of the hotel lot, Patch Munson followed in his Silverado. And that was another thing that made Munson think. What was a priest doing driving an $85,000 black Range Rover? He continued to follow them as they drove north along Interstate 65 in the direction of Birmingham. He was intrigued and he had little else to do.

The hour ride north from Montgomery to Oak Mountain State Park seemed shorter to Tim Hanlon. He felt like he was floating up along the interstate on a cloud. It was an odd feeling of euphoria however. He knew that he was blocking out the more ominous aspects of his decision to simply enjoy the pleasure of spending time with his lover and his son. He was assuming a lot. He had spoken on the phone to Carol every day for the last five days. And he had found it difficult waiting to see her again and having this opportunity to meet his son. But he hadn't yet told her of his plan to leave the clerical priesthood. There were many reasons for that decision and he didn't want Carol to assume that she and Russell were the only reason he had asked to be laicized. He implicitly knew that this was a discussion he was about to have today. But things were happening so fast that he could hardly keep his emotions in check.

They turned off Interstate 65 at exit 246 and drove down along Alabama route 119 for a short distance and then on into the park.

Patch Munson was beginning to think that this was just another of his bad ideas. He had been following Hanlon all morning long. He had no hint where they might be headed now and he had no idea who the woman and child were. They were heading north along the Interstate and Munson was running low on gas. With less than an eighth of a tank left, he was probably going to stop following them within the next exit or two. So he thought he had been running a fool's errand all morning long. What was he trying to learn? What did he want to accomplish? Munson didn't know the precise answers to these questions. He also wondered why he had brought his guns with him. He had no intention of using them. They were simply his security blanket. He had permits for *most* of his guns ... so why shouldn't he carry them? He still hadn't disposed of the handgun he had used on Aaron Fein, although he had designs on throwing it in some lake or river. This was a recurring urge since last Thursday night, but he had yet to take action on this inclination.

Finally he saw Hanlon's Range Rover turn off the interstate. Maybe he needs gas also, Munson thought. There were a couple of cars in front of him but they kept going straight, so that when Munson turned onto the exit ramp he was directly behind the priest. He tried to slow down to allow room between the vehicles and was satisfied when he saw the priest turn onto route 119. But he was nearly out of gas at this point and didn't know how much further he could go. He watched Hanlon make the turn into Oak Mountain State Park, and thought that this was his opportunity to fill up his tank. *How big could the park be? How hard would it be to find the preacher's black Range Rover?*

If you can't beat them, join them. Priscilla Stengel was now investigating the murder of Aaron Fein, from a reporter's perspective. As a freelance journalist Priscilla covered a variety of different news topics on her own terms and in her own timeframe. Sure she had to adhere to deadlines when she contracted out a story in advance. But if she was working on a story for future sale she danced with her own footwork. With respect to the Fein murder, she had more than a passing interest. She felt that she was actually a suspect. How tragically ironic it all seemed.

Life had not always been so easy for Priscilla Stengel. Her first pregnancy occurred when she was 19 years old. She and her boyfriend, Kevin Stengel, weren't ready to have a child. They loved one another but they were very scared. Neither Priscilla's parents nor Kevin's parents knew about the pregnancy. Other than the young couple no one else knew about the pregnancy. They had heard about the new women's center that had just opened up outside of Tampa and a very frightened young woman went there in the fourth month of her pregnancy and had an abortion. Both Kevin and Priscilla had agreed upon the procedure and both felt relief after the procedure had been performed. Over the next several months however they both began to feel grief. They were able to deal with heartache in some respects through sheer denial. But neither of them could obscure the fact that their denial did little to remove the guilt and grief. The odd comfort of sharing a secret trapped the couple in one respect. They were helplessly bound to one another.

Kevin Stengel continued his courtship of his girlfriend Priscilla, but the physicality of their lovemaking was lackluster. They tumbled toward marriage without knowing why they wanted to tie the knot. Maybe it had just seemed like the right thing to do. Even on their wedding day their shared secret put a very perceptible damper on the proceedings. Soon after they became husband and wife, Kevin and Priscilla Stengel began to drink heavily. Kevin worked construction and got into a few scrapes on the job. Priscilla was equally dissatisfied at her job. But at least they had each other. They never discussed the abortion with anyone else, and for that matter they rarely spoke about it with each other. But independently they both thought about it constantly.

Kevin and Priscilla worked at their marriage for the next 15 months. Regardless of their less than passionate lovemaking, Priscilla managed to get pregnant once again. Kevin was slightly surprised by this turn of events but made a good show of being happy with the expectation of their second child. Priscilla stopped drinking, but Kevin took his drinking to a whole new level. Almost on a daily basis Kevin would leave work and head directly to Holden's Bar and Grill, his favorite watering hole. One afternoon he arrived at Holden's at 3:30 PM and left for home around 7:00 PM. He never made it home. Kevin Stengel crashed his car into a telephone pole at 55 miles an hour, in a single vehicle accident. His blood alcohol level was more than twice the legal limit. His pregnant wife Priscilla was now a widow.

Priscilla's memories of her husband Kevin were mostly good ones. However she was worried that Kevin had never had a chance to come to grips with the biggest mistake of his life. For several years this realization had haunted Priscilla, because now not only could she not have her first child back, but she couldn't have her husband back either. By the time she was 25 Priscilla Stengel had had a lot of life that she wanted to put behind her. She wanted to get beyond the hurt and pain.

When she reflected on it Stengel realized that the main reason she had an abortion was because of some false sense of stigma attached to having a child out of wedlock. Her parents, as well as Kevin's parents, were Catholics. Her mother had frequently lectured her about the evils and perils of premarital sex. Both her parents believed that conjugal relationships belonged in the marriage bedroom and nowhere else. Kevin's parents might have been more open minded but Priscilla and Kevin never took the opportunity to find out. They had simply followed the primrose path that led to the Fein Center for Women. To further complicate her life, Priscilla's mother died shortly after Kevin's accident, and Priscilla's father began to drown his sorrow in alcohol. A lifelong smoker and drinker, his health began to deteriorate rapidly. Priscilla often wondered why God had dealt her such an unfair hand. She hoped that her natural investigative instincts would help her find answers to these questions.

Priscilla had always liked to write. She dreamed that one day she would be a famous suspense novelist. But she had to make a living and so she wrote articles for her local paper. Her wages were barely at the subsistence level but she wasn't living a life of luxury anyway. Priscilla was making her daily visit to her father's house which was less than a mile from her own home. When she opened his front door she could immediately smell the stale tobacco smoke and feel the sticky humidity of the living room area where her father spent at least eight hours a day watching television. He was slowly dying from cancer and cirrhosis of the liver. He was now down to less than 120 pounds, and had trouble standing by himself. But he was mentally alert and sharp enough to know that his days were numbered and the number was not in the triple digits.

"Good morning Priscilla. Aren't you too busy to be stopping by here every day? Michael needs you at home." Frank Malone, Priscilla's father was a very gifted man. However he never pushed himself and was contented to see his daughter do well in the world. He had operated a small accounting business in the area, assisting some local attorneys in estate planning and tax filings. He considered himself to be semi-retired for the last ten years. For the last ten months he was fully retired and dying.

"I'm never too busy to see you Dad, and I never will be."

"So when you were here on Monday you said that you're investigating that murder that took place over in Tampa. How's that going?"

"I have a few ideas. But I've got a good bit of digging to do. I was already starting down this path with my most recent article about the Fein Center."

"Yes. I think you did a much better job this time than in the last article that you wrote about that place. I don't like to say this about anyone. However I will make an exception in Fein's case. The man was a scum of the earth. I'm sure there are plenty of people who were glad to see him die and very few people who miss him."

"Well he has two ex-wives and a widow that he left behind. He never had any children."

"Thank God for that. I believe that some people were meant to be parents and some people are not. That bastard Fein certainly fits into the latter category." Frank Malone coughed out these words and it took maximum effort to do so.

"I have a source that works at the Center and she is helping me get some information about the employees, owners and suppliers for the center. Apparently there is no shortage of people who worked with Aaron Fein who hated his guts."

"So you think it's an inside job, then? You should remember that people in the community hated him also. And you've also got that 'Murder Inc' lead to work on."

"Don't worry Dad. I'll cover all of the bases. Remember this is what I do for a living and I happen to think I'm good at it. Let's change the topic. What have you eaten today?"

"The lady from hospice was here this morning. She brought me some soup and a turkey sandwich?"

"Did you eat it?" Her father didn't answer. Priscilla ambled around the living room and on into the kitchen. She made some noise getting herself a glass of water and at the same time surreptitiously glanced into the garbage where she spotted three quarters of the turkey sandwich. Maybe he at least had the soup, she hoped. She returned to the living room with two glasses of water and gave one to her father.

"Have you taken your pills?"

"Yes, definitely, the hospice lady stood right next to me while I took all eleven of them. You can call her and ask her if you'd like." Priscilla knew from her father's tone that verification was not needed. Nonetheless she was saddened that her relationship with her father had become so mundane. She preferred to remember him as a passionate human being with a terrific sense of humor. But ever since his wife died of breast cancer several years earlier, Frank Malone had seen his own health stifle his interactions with his family and friends as he slowly approached his own demise. He rarely ventured outside of his home and even stopped going to Sunday Mass. Priscilla wondered if he even thought about God. Her own thoughts on the subject were mixed. She questioned how a kind and loving God could allow her father to suffer in such misery.

It was a beautiful mid-summer afternoon in Oak Mountain State Park, Alabama. Carol Mays, Tim Hanlon and their son Russell were walking leisurely through the Double Oak Lake section of the nearly 10,000 acre park. They had been strolling casually for about 25 minutes with no particular direction in mind.

"There's an open table. We can eat there. I'm getting hungry again."

"You certainly can work up an appetite very quickly Russ."

"Why don't you go swimming before you eat your lunch? You just finished your breakfast less than 2 hours ago." Carol Mays looked lovingly at her son. She was so proud of him. He was a gorgeous boy inside and out. Because he was tall and relatively mature for his age, many people mistook him for being older than seven. However to Carol, Russell was still her baby. Until she recently decided that she wanted to see Tim Hanlon again, Mays' whole life revolved around her son.

Russell ran off to the edge of the lake and splashed in the shallow water as his parents watched from a short distance away. Mays and Hanlon moved from the picnic table to a blanket closer to the beachfront and called out to Russell to make certain that he saw them move.

"There was a time when I envisioned a similar scenario … you and I and our son out at a picnic, by the lake. Although I must admit my day dreaming included a daughter as well."

"And you probably envisioned a different occupation for his father."

Carol didn't answer. She simply sighed somewhat satisfactorily, resigning herself to enjoying what was real, rather than what might have been.

Patch Munson hadn't realized the size of Oak Mountain State Park. He'd been driving around now for nearly forty-five minutes. There were countless parking areas throughout the park and numerous vehicles were parked in each lot. But then he got lucky. He saw Hanlon's Range Rover, parked in the Double Oak Lake section. He pulled his Silverado into the lakeside lot and suddenly realized that his bladder needed relief. He was careful not to park too close to the Range Rover, but he was still less than 150 feet away. Munson figured that Hanlon and the black woman were probably nearby, but he still had no idea why that mattered. *What am Ah goin' t' do 'bout it?* He had no answer as he made his way past several sheltered wooden picnic tables and over to the shed-like building that housed the toilet facilities. For no apparent reason he took his unregistered handgun along with him.

The undercurrent of anxiety that Tim Hanlon had felt for most of the day had started to dissipate. He was growing more comfortable with his son, Russ, as well as with his lover, Carol. He still felt a slight nervousness but it was a pleasant nervousness. He intended to tell Carol about his big decision and he was just about to get to it. He was glad that it was a conversation that he could have outside of Russ's earshot. He thought that Carol would be supportive but he knew that the issue deserved discussion and not just disclosure. Russ continued to splash in the shallow water as his parents gazed affectionately towards him.

"He's a very happy young boy. It's hard for me to believe that I've missed so much of his life already."

"But you didn't know, Tim. You couldn't be expected to help out in a situation that you didn't know about."

They both stayed quiet for a few seconds before Tim responded. "There's something I want to talk to you about. But before I get into it, I want you to know that my decision predated our reconnecting."

Intuitively Mays knew where the discussion was headed. She didn't say a word but made sure that she made warm eye contact. She wanted him to know that whatever he wanted to say, she wouldn't be judgmental.

"I'm planning on leaving my ministry. I have already applied to the bishop for release from my vows. I'm having difficulty rationalizing many of the positions that The Church takes on several different social issues."

"Like celibacy?"

"Yes celibacy is certainly an issue. This was not a prerequisite for the priesthood that was established by Christ."

"Christ never married."

"That may be true but he didn't make that a requirement of priest-hood. He appointed Peter as the first pope and Peter was a married man. Of the 266 popes that have led The Church there is evidence that as many as thirty-nine of them were married. This whole idea of celibacy was something that church leaders made mandatory in the eleventh century. There may have been celibate priests before that but there were many married priests also. Anyway, celibacy is not the only issue. The trouble is that The Church is very prescriptive in how it wants us to think."

"Isn't that what they mean by having faith? Isn't that what faith is all about? And isn't that what led you to the priesthood in the first place?"

"All of these are very good questions. I do have faith. I believe in God. And I believe that Jesus Christ is the son of God who came down to earth as our savior. I can't prove these things but I believe them. I have studied the Bible thoroughly especially the New Testament. And I have read multiple other accounts of the life of Jesus, besides those written by Matthew, Mark, Luke and John. All of these accounts of the life of Jesus indicate that he was much more than just a man. But still he was a man … and to most people … Christians and non-Christians alike, he was the most fascinating man ever to walk the face of the earth. But I also believe that God gave us free will. And I have come to believe that the hierarchy of the Roman Catholic Church has impinged upon this free will, in a manner that Jesus hadn't intended."

"So beside celibacy what are some of the other issues that concern you so much that you want to leave the priesthood?"

"Well, there's more to the idea of celibacy than simply refraining from sexual relationships. It goes to the very core of the human rela-tionship between a man and woman. I believe that the genders are dif-ferent but equal. I think that it hurts The Church that they don't allow priests to marry. In many ways The Church is quite sexist. Women cannot become priests nor can they have a sexually intimate relation-ship with a priest. The Church has essentially shut them out."

"But you knew all of these things when you took your vows several years ago. What has made you change your mind?"

"Before I answer that question, I should tell you that the vow that troubles me most is the vow of obedience to the bishop. This is where we priests surrender our free will. If we think differently on a topic, we are required to stay silent about our opinions and to put forth the positions of the Catholic Church as they are distilled through the bishop."

"Can you give me an example of what you're talking about?"

"Contraception …I don't agree with The Church's position on contraception. I believe that abortion is a terrible crime against God and man, and some forms of contraception, like the morning-after pill, embody abortion techniques. These are obviously terribly wrong. However I believe many forms of contraception and family planning make more sense than The Church will allow us to believe."

"Can't you work within The Church for reform of this kind of thinking?

"Frankly, no." Hanlon's frustration was evident and Mays simply let him vent. "The whole contraception issue is precisely why The Church loses its credibility on abortion. The Church is slow to examine and embrace scientific breakthroughs to the point where it risks becoming irrelevant. For example The Church should be making a stand on selective abortions that take place during the in vitro fertilization process, rather than admonishing Catholics that rhythm is the only acceptable method of contraception. Pregnancy prevention is much different from the slaughter of embryos."

Mays and Hanlon continued their discussion, going back and forth on several different topics, while they watched their son splash in the shallow water at the edge of the lake. Before too long Mays excused herself and started walking in the direction of the restroom facilities.

A few years earlier Julianne Carson might have felt that she was moving too fast with her latest relationship. She would have examined and re-examined; evaluated and re-evaluated every step along the way. She would have given in to her misgivings and canceled her trip to Barbados with Hawk Richter. After all she knew him less than a month.

There was an emotional intimacy associated with their fledgling relationship. However that intimacy had not been reaffirmed in any physical manner, or at least not in a sexually physical manner. Did that matter? Sure it matters, Julianne thought. Her sexuality was extremely important to her and at times her sexual exploration had been as diverse as her spiritual exploration.

However this was a different Julianne Carson than the young lady of a few years back. Julianne looked at many things in a different light these days. Each and every day, Julianne spent at least an hour in private meditation. Her level of introspection had progressed to the point where she felt that true happiness was merely a half step away. But she wasn't sure how to take that last half step forward. Julianne knew now that she was a seeker. As a seeker she viewed every day as an adventure. And as a seeker there was meaning to every nuance of life, to every morsel she tasted, to every song that she heard, to every flower she smelled, to every prayer that she prayed, and to every person that she met.

Also as a seeker Julianne felt things. She felt the wind even on a still day. She could feel moisture in the sunshine and dry heat in the rain. She felt goose bumps when she read ghost stories and sorrow when she read sad stories, but she could also find happiness in sorrowful situations and meaning in seemingly meaningless events. She felt other things too. She felt grief for the forlorn when she met them. She felt hunger for those who didn't know how to seek. And Julianne felt bliss whenever she met a fellow seeker who was traveling down the same wavelength in the same timeframe. And in the last few years she had also found and felt an explosive awareness in her own sexuality.

For Julianne every synapse in her being was now geared toward her search for her soul. She felt that it was a meaningful and happy search.

But Julianne had not always been a seeker. There was a time in her life when rain was simply wet, the sun was simply hot, night was simply dark, grey didn't come in shades thereof and prayers were only said in church. It was a far less nuanced time of her life. More recently she was a much more perspicacious person. But still she was a seeker.

And now here she was waiting for her new found friend, Bertrand "Hawk" Richter, to meet her at their hotel room. This was the last day of his conference and the first day of their mini-vacation in Barbados. Julianne flew in directly from a client meeting in Miami that she had deliberately scheduled for its convenient proximity to the Caribbean. After entering their room she checked out the arrangements immediately. There were two queen sized beds, although one was part of a fold-up couch in the living room of the small suite. There was only one formal bedroom. There was one full sized bathroom and a half-kitchen facility. The deck outside of their second story room was angled toward the ocean which was a mere 50 feet away. Julianne walked out onto the deck and stared at the ocean. What, if anything, did these accommodations say about Richter's plans for this weekend? All of his clothing was in the bedroom. The maid had just finished servicing the room. Richter was due back within an hour. Julianne decided that she would shower and clean up. It was still only 2 PM, and they would have plenty of time to enjoy the rest of the day as soon as Richter returned.

When Carol Mays neared the small wooden building that housed the rest room facilities, she noticed a thickset slightly disheveled looking man coming out of the men's room. At first she paid no attention whatsoever. But when the bulky man saw her, he appeared to be temporarily startled. His eyes locked on her momentarily. Then he turned away and began walking at a faster pace towards the parking lot. Mays stared after him for a second. He looked familiar. *Do I know him? Haven't I seen him some place before?* At first she wasn't sure. Then cognition came to her. He was the man that she saw in The Most Holy Tabernacle Catholic Church in Mobile. He was also waiting outside the church in his truck and staring at her when she finished her conversation with Tim. She suddenly felt quite uneasy. *Is that the same man? Or is my mind playing tricks on me?* She walked to the other side of the restroom area and watched the man as he hurried through the parking lot. Then her suspicions were confirmed. He was heading toward a truck that looked exactly like the one he had been seated in outside of the church. She shivered. *Why is he watching me? Or is it Tim that he is following?* She saw a hound dog jump up to greet him as he opened the car door. The dog jarred something loose around the man's waistband. She trembled as she saw him take a handgun out from his belt area and put it under his seat before he got into the truck.

Bertrand "Hawk" Richter was exhausted. But he was looking forward to spending the next few days relaxing with his new friend, Julianne Carson, on the beaches of Barbados. The first three days of his trip were spent in a small conference room with the other physicists who were planning the agenda for the following year's Solvay Conference. The Solvay Conferences had been held at three year intervals since the first conference in Brussels in 1911. Occasionally the meetings leading up to the conferences were as intriguing as the conferences themselves. At these pre-conference meetings the physicists could spend personal time with one another, exploring each other's theories in a semi social atmosphere. And although Richter felt exhausted, he also felt exhilarated. These conferences and planning sessions were the only times that Richter ever felt intellectually challenged. These fellow physicists were his peers; his comrades in thought; his best source of intellectual stimulation.

This gathering was different from some of the more recent meetings. The seven physicists chose to explore the social implications of their scientific postulates rather than arguing proof of the hypotheses themselves. Now that the conference had concluded, Richter was looking for a different kind of stimulation. In the past he had found that if he let his mind rest after these meetings, his subconscious would often surface a different way of looking at life in general. This was not to say that Richter would engage in inane banter with significantly inferior minds. He was still quite selective in how he spent his time and with whom he spent it. Richter said his goodbyes to the other scientists, grabbed his cane and made his way back in the direction of his hotel room. Based on past experience and knowing that Richter relished a strong sense of independence, none of the other conferees offered to assist him back to his room.

Richter waved his cane back and forth and made a mental note of the distance that he travelled down the second floor corridor without needing to count his steps exactly. He had been blind for seventeen years and the dimensions of distance had become part of his intuitive memory once he had travelled these lengths a time or two. He waved his cane merely to detect variable obstructions, such as the maid's cleaning carts, discarded room service trays or other capricious impediments. Once he had covered the distance to his room, he felt for the door handle. Then he quickly located the slot for the plastic keycard. He inserted his card and opened the door to the faint elusive scent of a woman.

"Julianne?" Instead of a verbal response, he heard the sound of the running shower in the bathroom. He entered the suite and let the door close behind him as he nestled his body onto a sofa. As he heard the shower water continue, he called out once again, "Julianne, I'm back." When he didn't get a response right away he began fumbling for the remote to the TV/entertainment system hoping to find some music to his liking. When he found it he inadvertently moved the volume up very high before turning the stereo on. The resulting blast startled Julianne in the shower and she quickly turned the faucet off. At first she was shocked but then logically presumed that Richter had returned to the suite. For confirmation she called out to him, as she heard the musical commotion subside.

"Hawk? Is that you?" Simultaneously she reached for a towel to wrap around her.

"Yes, I'm back."

"Are you alone?" Given her current state of dishabille she felt that it was a logical question to ask.

"No, my dear, I'm no longer alone. I'm now here with you."

Julianne perceived a slight hint of sarcasm in Richter's answer. However after quickly wrapping one towel around her body and twisting a second towel around her hair, she opened the door to the bathroom and walked over towards Richter. The physicist could sense her still moist body as she approached. His heightened tactile acuity could discern a denser dampness to the air as she drew near. It was different from the clammy humidity that was carried by the island breeze. Julianne had left the sliding glass door to the smallish deck ajar. Still wrapped in her towels, Julianne sauntered past Richter and shut the sliding door. The air conditioning automatically restarted.

"You startled me. I didn't think you'd be back so soon."

"You might say that I was in a hurry to *see* you. And of course that wouldn't be accurate." Once again Julianne perceived the hint of playful sarcasm. She realized that he was simultaneously mocking his own disability while deriding her feeble anxiety.

Julianne decided not to verbally spar with Richter. Instead she moved over and sat in a chair across from him. "I'll disregard any cynical connotation to your greeting and simply tell you that I'm glad to be here and I'm glad to *see* you. And I'm looking forward to the next three days." She flashed a broad invisible smile.

"I can hear the smile in your voice. And kidding aside I'm also happy that you're here with me. Can I get a kiss, hello?"

Julianne thought for a second, then got up and sat next to Richter on the couch. She leaned her mouth over and kissed him quickly on the lips. It was a kiss of greeting not a kiss of passion. However in their now mutually heightened corporeal attentiveness, they were both aware that lips were still lips. It felt good. Julianne's lips lingered only a second or two, and then she stood up quickly.

"I'm going to finish getting ready to go out for a walk around the property. Then you can get ready to come with me. Okay?" She appreciated the reality that they both wanted more than a passing greeting, but she just wasn't ready to go that fast. She wanted to savor the moment when it came to pass. Nevertheless Julianne had her own sense of playfulness. As she got up from the couch, she stripped the damp towel off her body, and threw it gently into Richter's lap. "Here, catch."

Carol Mays didn't want to upset her son and she didn't want to break the mood of the picnic, but she knew she had to tell Tim about the man at the rest room. She was grateful that Russell went down to the waterside once again so that she could speak freely. She didn't have to initiate the conversation.

"What is it Carol? You look like you've just seen a ghost."

"I… I…I… I don't know what to tell you."

"Please Carol, what is it?" Tim Hanlon's alarm needle now registered full alert. "What happened at the ladies room?"

"Somebody has been watching us, Tim. I saw him before at the church. He is a horrid evil looking man … and he has a gun."

"Whoa, whoa … slow down Carol. Just tell me what's going on."

Although the closest blanket to where they were seated was more than 30 feet away, Carol labored to keep her voice from getting too loud. She stared directly at Hanlon and swallowed her anxiety to best of her ability. Then she blurted out her thoughts.

"When I went up to the bathroom, I saw this man staring at me. It's not like I haven't been stared at before. But this was different. As I kept walking I knew I'd seen this man before. The other day when I met you outside the church after confessions, this man was watching us from his car. I don't know what it is about him, but he gives me the creeps."

"Are you sure it's the same man? And what's the issue with a gun? How do you know that he has a gun?"

"I saw it, Tim. I saw him put the gun back under the seat of his truck. This is not some type of hallucination on my part. I know what I'm talking about." She took a deep breath and tried to slow down. "The other day when I went to a meet you at the church, I went inside first. I wanted to see how long the line was for confession and how long it would be before you would be coming out. I saw this man leaving the confessional and then leaving the church. At first I thought nothing of it. But later when we were talking at the bottom of the church steps, he was watching us. When we finished our conversation I walked back toward my car and I saw him sitting in his truck. I walked right past him. I knew that he was staring at me at first, but as I passed his truck, he turned his eyes up the street and it looked like he was watching *you*. I immediately realized that he was the guy who had come out of the confessional. Normally this wouldn't have stuck with me, but the guy had a certain creepy look about him. For one thing, he didn't have that unburdened glow that people seem to have when they leave the confessional."

"And you're sure that this was the same man that you just saw near the restrooms."

"Absolutely sure. And I think he was worried that I knew who he was."

"Why would he worry about that?"

"Tim, damn it … don't you get it? He had a gun." Mays was once again getting ahead of her story. "He's worried because he was probably going to do something wrong, and he didn't want me to be able to identify him." Mays listened to her own words and suddenly questioned her own intuition. "Am I just being paranoid or what?"

"Carol, maybe you have just spent too much time up in the northeast. You grew up here in the South. Remember? Lots of people own and carry their own guns down here." Hanlon had effectuated the calming tone that was reflective of his work as a clergyman. He was trying to appear composed, but in reality he was anxious. There was only one person that Carol Mays could be talking about and that person was the confessed killer of Aaron Fein. He thought before he asked the next question because he knew he was beginning to tread on the edge of his priestly vows. He couldn't talk about confession, or those who sought absolution for their sins.

"What did this man look like? Is it possible that he just looked something like the man you saw at church?"

"No Tim. That's not possible. It was the same man. He's dumpy looking. He has a huge head, a big gut and big heavy looking legs. He is either my height or maybe an inch taller or shorter. I don't know. And remember we're more than three hours away from Mobile. So either it was an amazing coincidence that our paths crossed once again or he followed you from Mobile to Montgomery, and then followed us up here from Montgomery. Why would he do that Tim?"

Billy Brand was a strong young man. He didn't change his opinions or alter his sermons because of any social pressure that that might be brought to bear. He was more than a little bit annoyed however, when the Muslim detective from Tampa suggested that his sermons may somehow have contributed to the murder of Aaron Fein. Nevertheless he had taken the phone call from Detective Kanasani and had even gone so far as to invite the detective up to Mobile to visit with him at the Christian Ascendancy Community Church.

Meanwhile Detective Kanasani was not very pleased with the Reverend Brand's dismissive attitude when it came to accepting responsibility for inflaming the abortion debate. After reviewing numerous tapes of the televised sermons which Brand had given over the last few years, Kanasani had counted at least twenty-three different times when Brand took on the abortion issue. He also mentioned Aaron Fein by name on nineteen of these twenty-three occasions. More importantly Brand had coined the phrase "Murder Incorporated," to describe Fein's business at his FCW. This of course was the exact phrase which was spray painted on the side wall to the center only days before Aaron Fein was shot. Reverend Brand had used this moniker in every sermon that he mentioned Fein. Every one of those sermons was broadcast on a Tampa Christian cable network each Sunday morning. In Detective Kanasani's mind, Brand had not only inflamed the people of Alabama, he had created equal unrest among the citizens of Tampa. He believed that Reverend Billy Brand had contributed to the murder of Aaron Fine.

Over the phone Reverend Brand indicated that it was his *"responsibiliteh t' agitate against A-bortion"* and that he had no intention of turning down his rhetoric on this topic. It would be fair to say that the first conversation between these two strong willed men was not very conciliatory on the part of either of them. However Kanasani decided to take Brand up on his offer to visit the Christian Ascendancy Community Church, and he flew up to Mobile to question the preacher.

When he arrived at the church, Kanasani was greeted by the stiff-haired but gentle speaking Sarah Anne Brand. Mrs. Brand was sugary cordial as she explained that Billy was going to be "just a tad late" to their scheduled 10:30 AM meeting. Apparently he was visiting a sick member of the congregation, whose family was experiencing some financial hardship. Kanasani instantly wished that he had brought Detective Chambers along with him for the meeting. He viewed Sarah Anne as a typical southern "steel magnolia," sweet and delicate as can be on the outside and steel willed on the inside. He believed that Chambers might have done a better job neutralizing Sarah Anne's saccharine surface. Nevertheless he walked along with Sarah Anne as she gave him a tour of the church property. He noticed that the campus was impeccably well kept and the church itself was immaculately clean. There was a flat one story office building at the rear of the property and a shipping platform at the back of the office building. Behind the platform there was a storage facility for the various products that the church shipped to its constituency in return for the donations that they offered to the church. The business building was by far the busiest place on the church campus. Numerous shipments of books, tapes and trinkets that were dispatched each day to various locations across the south. Billy Brand's personal workplace was not in the office building. His office was in the 7000 square foot rectory.

After the 20 minute tour was completed, Sarah Anne led Detective Kanasani back to her husband's office in the church rectory. Billy Brand had made it back from his visit with his parishioner. He stood up as his wife and Kanasani came into his office.

"Good *mornin'* Detective Kanasani. *Ah'm sorreh* that *Ah gat* delayed. But a *membeh* of our congregation needed *sem he'p wit'* respect *t'* her *dahin'* wishes."

Kanasani couldn't help but wonder if these dying wishes had anything to do with a bequest to the Christian Ascendancy Community Church. He couldn't help but feel that the Brands were living at a much different level of affluence than their constituents in the church. But he wanted to get off on the right footing with Brand so he greeted him amiably.

"Good morning, Reverend Brand. How are you today?

"*Ah'm jes' fahne … fahneh* than a frog's hair, *Ah'd* say."

Before he could respond to the preacher, Sarah Anne took her leave. "*Ah* guess *Ah'll* leave *y'all t'yer* business. *Ah* have *sem* errands *t'* run." Kanasani then sat down in rectory office wistfully wondering what *errands* Sarah Anne Brand would be running. Somehow he believed that those errands meant an appointment at the local beauty parlor where the preacher's wife could get her golden locks re-stiffened.

"Thank you for inviting me up to Mobile, Reverend Brand. It's my very first time in your fine town." Kanasani was trying to start out their conversation in a non-confrontational manner.

"*Ah'm* glad *yew* could come up here *t'git* a feel *fur* what we do. *Yew* would *git* a much better *ahdea* of our *blessin's* if *yew* would stay *fur* the weekend services."

"I know that you're busy on weekends and I just wanted to be able to talk face-to-face about the Fein matter." Kanasani didn't want to be distracted by his surroundings and yet he wanted to absorb the ambience of the church environment so that he would have a context for evaluating whatever it was that Reverend Brand might tell him. Nonetheless he wanted to get the Fein matter on the table at the earliest possibility.

"Oh, yes. Aaron *Fahne*. In *maneh* ways it's a shame that he's still *causin'* trouble, even *afteh* his death."

"Could you explain what you mean by that?"

"When *Fahne* was still *livin'* he was one *o* the most prolific *A-bortionists* in the *countreh*. *An' yew* know he was *play'unin'* to expand his operations into *Southern Al'bama*. Lord knows *whah* he chose this area of the *countreh fur* his projected expansion … made no sense *whatsoeveh*. He knew he would *git signif'cant* resistance from Christian ministers *an'* priests throughout *Al'bama*. *Mah* belief is that he *purposeleh* sought out this confrontation as a *weh* of *promotin'* his business on a national basis. But that's *simpleh mah* belief. *Ah didden'* know the man. *Ah neveh* met *'im*. And *fur* that *matteh Ah neveh* even spoke *t' 'im* on the phone. He *certainleh didden* seek out *mah* counsel."

"Did you ever feel that it was your responsibility to reach out to him? Sometimes in the police work that I do I'm astounded by what might have been avoided if people were just able to talk to one another before a situation turned violent."

"Yes. As a matter of fact Detective Kanasani, *Ah've agonahzed oveh jes'* that question *eveh* since *Fahne* was killed. *Ah didden'* do *'nough t' he'p 'im b'faw* he *dahed*. *Ah neveh* did reach out *t' 'im personalleh t' trah t'* convince *'im o* the error in his ways. *An' Ah'm sorreh 'bout* that."

Detective Kanasani was surprised by the answer that he got from the Billy Brand. The answer seemed both sincere and spontaneous. Just the way he spoke gave Kanasani a very different feeling about Brand. He had expected someone who was pompous and self-righteous. Brand was neither. He was simply a man of strong convictions, who was secure enough to reflect upon his own shortcomings.

"I've listened to numerous tapes of your sermons where you mention Aaron Fein. You don't cut him any slack in any of those sermons. You go right after him as though he were the devil incarnate. Don't you worry that this type of inflammatory rhetoric could cause some poor deranged soul to go off the deep end and kill Fein?"

"*Yew* need *t'* listen *t' all* of *mah* sermons in order *t'* put the *Fahne* references in perspective. While *Ah* have railed against *A-bortion Ah* have also spoken out against *vah'lence* of *aneh* sort. One of man's most monstrous *failin's* has been his perpetual penchant towards *vah'lence*."

Detective Kanasani thought about Brand's response. It was true that he hadn't listened to the tapes of the preacher's other sermons. The staff back at police headquarters had only provided him with the tapes of the sermons that mentioned Aaron Fein. It certainly was possible that Brand espoused a nonviolent approach. However his rhetoric was still extremely inflammatory. Comparing Aaron Fein to Adolf Hitler was far from a gentle touch. The same could be said about the "Murder Inc" references.

"Let me ask you a different question. You must get feedback from your constituents about your sermons. Is there any particular piece of feedback that caught your attention as showing a potential for violence against Aaron Fein?"

Brand was now sitting upright in his swivel chair. His lean physique was angled forward towards Kanasani, who was seated across the desk from the preacher. Both men found the other man to be forthright in their discussion. Neither of them had anticipated liking the other person. But the conversation progressed in a straightforward fashion as each of the men was conciliatory toward the other person's perceived sincerity. In that spirit, Brand replied to Kanasani's question.

"We *git 'bout fifteh t' hun'red* pieces *o* correspondence *evereh* week. This *dudden* count the *maneh* donations that are accompanied *bah* a sentence or two of *grat'tude*. This correspondence includes emails, letters and an occasional phone call. Most of this … *Ah wudden* say *hun'red* percent, but most of it … is logged in *bah* our business staff. *Ah* don't see *evereh* piece of correspondence. *Sem* of it is vetted *bah* the staff. But *Ah* would venture a guess that *Ah* see *'bout* half the correspondence. *Sem 'tahmes Ah* dictate individual responses, but more often *Ah* allow the staff *t'* respond *fur* me. Our process calls *fur* these responses *t'* be approved *bah* one of three people; *meh, mah wahfe* or *mah fatheh*. This *ain't* a perfect system, but it works *fur* us. And *t' git t' yer* specific concern, *Ah've neveh* seen *aneh* indication of a threat against Aaron *Fahne. Converseleh, oveh* the *yeahs*, we've received *maneh* threats *t' membehs* of our family."

"Yet you have often called for the destruction of the organization which you refer to as Murder Incorporated. I think that I'm quoting your words nearly verbatim. And if so, that is violent language. Isn't it?"

"*Possibleh ... howeveh* it *certainleh idden espousin' vah'lence* against people, *mereleh* against evil institutions. *An'* the destruction of a malevolent institution is a virtuous accomplishment."

"Do you think that the death of Aaron Fein will destroy the FCW in Tampa?"

"No *unfortunateleh Ah* do not believe that'll be the case at all. In fact, *Ah* believe that *jes'* the opposite could be true. The *killin'* of Aaron *Fahne* may embolden the opposition. *Sem* may feel the urge to paint the whole *Rahght - t'- Lahfe* movement *wit'* a broad brush, *an'* refer to all of us as deranged *ahdeologues.*"

"In order to avoid such a possibility, would you consider toning down your anti-abortion rhetoric?"

"*Absoluteleh* not ... *Ah thaank yer missin'* the point, Detective Kanasani. The person who killed Aaron *Fahne* was wrong *t'* do so. *Howeveh* that *dudden'* change the fact that *Fahne hisse'f* was an affluent murderous miscreant who *prospehed* off the *suffurin' o othehs.*"

"Well that certainly answers my question emphatically enough. But let me get back to the question about the correspondence. You said that you keep a record of most of this stuff. I imagine that some of these messages come from outside Alabama. Maybe even some of it comes from the Tampa area where your services are shown on cable TV every Sunday morning. Would that be accurate?"

"It's fair *t'* say that *sem o* our correspondence comes from *outsahde* the Mobile area. *Ah'm* sure we do *git sem* correspondence from *Floor'da an' probableh* from the *Tamper* area. However *yew* must *remembeh* that this correspondence is privileged. So if *yer fixin' t'* secure *aneh copehs*, transcripts etc, please expect a *vig'rous* court battle. *Ah'm* not *lookin'* to be uncooperative. *Ah actualleh* hope *yew* capture *Fahne's* assailant. *An' Ah* hope our court system affords that *misguahded* soul more compassion than *Fahne eveh offehed* to the unborn babies that he *slaughtehed. Ah* don't believe in *cap'tal* punishment *an'more 'an Ah* believe in *A-bortion.*"

"I'm aware of that Reverend Brand. As I said before, I have listened to a number of your sermons." Kanasani had pretty much accomplished what he wanted to accomplish, and he thought that he had at least opened up a dialogue with the preacher so that he could ask more questions at a later date if he needed to. "Thank you for your time and hospitality. Maybe our paths will cross again down the line."

"*Ah'll* see *yew* then, Good Lord *willin' an'* the creek *don't rahse.*"

Julianne looked past Hawk Richter toward the setting sun on the ocean horizon behind them. It was a beautiful evening and they were enjoying finger food at Tapas Restaurant, along the south shore boardwalk of the island. The sun was brilliant so Julianne wore her sunglasses as they sat in the open air bar area on the bottom floor of the restaurant. Richter's shades were more or less an ongoing accessory to his wardrobe. Julianne felt pretty as she sat at their beach side corner table wearing a red flowered sundress. Richter was more simply attired in tan shorts and a collared navy blue polo shirt. They munched on tuna carpaccio and vegetable spring rolls and were delighted not to be surrounded by a throng of people. It was all very serene.

"I'm very glad that you asked me to spend some time with you. This is a very lovely island and I've never been here before. Is it your first time as well?"

"Yes. And I agree it's a great place. The restaurants are good. The people are very friendly. And the island even has some interesting history."

By now Julianne was attuned to Richter's "perceptions" of things. As a result she was even more aware of her own way of perceiving things. She knew that when she said Barbados was a lovely island, her first perceptions were visual ones. She had never before given much thought to the priority of her sensual perceptions.

"I just got here. So why don't you tell me what you've learned about Barbados history. I didn't have much time to research it on my way here."

"Odd … that you would use the word 'research.' However I'll let that go for now. I think of you more as an intuitive type person, not someone who's necessarily given to research. Of course that makes you different from me. I research everything to death."

"That approach goes along with your profession. Doesn't it? Anyway, tell me what you learned about Barbados' history."

"Well for starters, it has an interesting intersection with American history. Apparently a 19 year old George Washington spent about six months here trying to get healthcare for his older brother, Lawrence, who was suffering from tuberculosis. George Washington remained in Barbados for more than four months before returning to Virginia and later becoming the first President of United States."

"You seem to have a thirst for this kind of trivia."

"Yes it's true. I admit it. But I find all of this stuff very fascinating. So, for example, this fellow, Lawrence Washington, was not only George Washington's half brother but also his surrogate father after George Washington's father had passed away. Through various land grants from the British government and rapid fire land auction deals and other such shenanigans Laurence Washington came into ownership of a vast amount of real estate that today comprises Mount Vernon and Alexandria, as well as thousands of Virginian acres between Alexandria and modern day Fredericksburg, Virginia. After leaving Barbados and returning to the US, Laurence Washington died at the ripe old age of 32 and when Laurence's wife passed on shortly thereafter, through inheritance and marriage, George Washington became an enormously wealthy land owner. As American presidents go, Washington was by far the wealthiest of all. His material assets would dwarf the wealth of JFK, both of the Roosevelts, and Thomas Jefferson combined. In relative terms he may have been one of the hundred wealthiest people in history of the world. And yet throughout his whole life, the only time he ever left the United States was to travel to Barbados."

"Sounds like brother Laurence did all of the hard work, died at an early age, left his fortune and potential fame to be inherited by his half brother, George. Makes you wonder what Laurence Washington might have accomplished himself had he lived longer."

"Yes it does. But throughout history there are plenty of examples of people who left their mark on the world even though they died young. Alexander the Great comes to mind pretty quickly. He conquered a good part of the world before dying at age 32. Vincent Willem van Gogh was 37. In spite of his everlasting search for the fountain of youth, Juan Ponce de León died at the relatively young age of 46. Attila the Hun also died at 46. The great English poet, John Keats, died from tuberculosis at age 25 and Elvis Presley was 42. Some women also made historical contributions before dying early. Marie Antoinette was Queen of France at 19 but died at the age of 38. Cleopatra, Queen of the Nile died at 39. Joan of Arc was a mere 19 when she was executed. Marilyn Monroe died at age 36. Janis Joplin was gone at 27. And, besides these men and women, of course, we can't forget Jesus Christ who died at age 33." Richter rattled off this litany of names as though he were reading it from a pre-written script, but he also gave the impression that he could go on for another dozen or two names if he were so inclined.

"You are one strange man Hawk Richter. Why on earth do you keep track of such minutiae?"

"My dear Julianne … this is not minutiae. These people are cultural markers along the course of modern history. Why do you dismiss their relevance as minutiae or worse yet as trivia?"

Julianne was beginning to see a repetitive challenge in her ongoing discourse with Richter. He simply loved the debating process. It was a game to him. She could also see that Richter liked to play the game with a full arsenal of facts and factoids and he didn't care that other players didn't possess a similar cache of intellectual tidbit weaponry. He always wanted to win. She assumed that her best strategy was surrender.

"Alright Bertrand, you win. I simply asked you what you learned about Barbados history and you gave me an onslaught of information about the short longevity of famous people." She hoped that calling him by his given name might put him off.

"*Short longevity* is an oxymoron, my dear, Julianne." He still wanted to grapple intellects, but Julianne would have none of it. He thought for a second about telling Julianne that he himself had lived a lot of life at an early age. He was married at the age of 19 and widowed at the age of 22, but he didn't want to get into personal matters just yet and he simply let Julianne respond to his comment.

"I want to change the subject."

"Hmm … I guess I can *see* that."

Julianne suppressed a giggle as Richter once again punned about his disability, but the professor could sense his victory nonetheless.

"Gotcha …didn't I?" Now it was Richter who offered to alter the discussion. He realized that he was no longer debating with his fellow scientists, as he had been the last few days. But he still controlled the direction of their conversation. "Thanks for coming down to be with me. I'm still wound up from the conference over the last few days, but even more so about the murders in Tampa. I can't seem to get those out of my mind."

"I hope that your negative thoughts don't translate to me because that night in Tampa was the first time we spent any time together."

"No, that's not a problem. You must know that. My mind simply registers cause and effect. Coincidence can easily flourish outside the realm of causality. Our having dinner together that night was mere coincidence and as a standalone event it was magnificent."

"What about the murders, themselves? Do you also believe that these were simply coincidental as well?"

"All manner of inquiry seems to point in that direction. These murders were very close to one another in time and space. However the similarities end there. Still there is something about these events that troubles me still, even two weeks after they happened."

"Maybe that's because as a scientist, you don't truly believe that things just 'happen.' Go back to what you just told me about cause and effect. Your curious mind is looking beyond the realm of coincidence. And maybe what bothers you is that in an odd way, you, Hawk Richter, are one of the connecting threads in the murders. You teach at BITSY and you're a part owner of the Fein Center. Maybe that's what has you rankled."

"I'm not sure I want to talk about this anymore. It's a depressing topic at best. Let's just enjoy the beautiful evening and each other's company. Tell me some things about yourself. Why did you agree to meet me down here? You're young and bright and beautiful. You could do whatever you want with your time. Tell me why you chose to spend it with me."

"Does your ego really need that much stroking?" Julianne answered him in the teasing tone but she wasn't teasing.

"Fair question. The answer is no. I don't need to hear things that are complementary to me. At the same time I'm looking to find out what makes you tick. At this point I still find you to be a fascinating person."

"I guess I should assume that that's a good thing. But are you saying that if you find out what makes me tick, then I will be less fascinating to you? In that case I'd rather remain a mystery for a while longer. But I don't like playing games for a long time. So tell me more about Bertrand Richter, first?"

"For starters, no one calls me Bertrand anymore. But I don't mind it if you do. It reminds me of Part 1 of my life."

"Part 1?"

"I think of Part 1 as when I could see."

"Do you want to talk about that?"

Richter relented and decided that it would be alright to have this conversation after all. "I don't mind. I graduated from college when I was 17 and started going blind right before I got married and was fully blind after an unsuccessful eye operation when I had just turned 22. I was married at the age of 19 and my wife died when I was 22. There was a lot happening in my life all at the same time."

"What caused you to go blind?"

"I can tell you that it wasn't excessive masturbation."

Julianne appreciated Richter's sense of humor, but she was still looking for an honest answer. Regardless she decided to play along with Richter's little game. "How do you know that?"

"Because I would have been blind by the age of 13, if that was the issue." He laughed at the fact that Julianne was willing to play straight man for his juvenile humor and then he delivered a more serious answer to her inquiry.

"I have a condition that is known as acute papillitis. It is an infection of the optic nerve. I didn't know that I had this condition until after I had graduated from college and obtained my master's degree. When I first experienced a slight vision loss I thought it might be from simple eye fatigue from excessive reading. I had no idea how bad things might get at the time and I was getting ready to get married. At the same time I was working on a doctoral thesis. Life was stressful and I refused to admit that I had a significant vision problem. Things got much worse when I suffered a retinal detachment and several other complications after a car accident following my 22nd birthday. That's when I had the disastrous operation. That botched operation left me totally blind. So now I have been blind for the last seventeen years."

"Is there any possibility for a recovery of your sight? Numerous medical breakthroughs have taken place over the last quarter century."

"I have several layers of problems with my vision. Remember I was suffering from acute papillitis with poor visual prospects at the time of the car accident. After suffering the traumatic retinal detachment, that became the *focus* … no pun intended … of the treatment … make that mistreatment … that I received. There were other physical issues as well. But I'd rather not get into all of these details right now."

"Did your vision impairment contribute to the car accident?" Julianne allowed her primal curiosity to take the conversation one step further.

"I wasn't driving. My wife was driving. She died in the accident. We were living in Germany and I was the youngest member of the faculty at University of Hamburg at the time. Life was quite good there for a while."

"Oh …" Julianne was speechless. She recognized that she might have finally pushed this discussion too far.

"None of this matters that much anymore. I have accepted the fact that I will never see again. But I don't consider this a disability." He seemed to have much more to say on the topic but for the moment he refrained from delineating his thoughts on the matter in more detail.

"That's so tragic about your wife. I'm sure you miss her dearly."

"She's gone. It's a shame, but she's gone."

After he dropped Carol and Russ back in Montgomery, Tim Hanlon began the last leg of his trip back to Mobile. It had been a very long day. He had been up at 5 AM and left after the 6:30 AM Mass for the ride up to Montgomery. And after a late breakfast and another hour ride north to Oak Mountain State Park, he had driven 250 miles. The trip north seemed to fly by with the exhilaration of expectation. The trip back to Mobile took forever. In total he had driven nearly 500 miles, in one bewildering day. But life was becoming more bizarre by the moment. He had tried to convince Carol that her imagination was playing games with her and that he had no idea who would want to follow them. However he was troubled by the realization that it might have been Aaron Fein's murderer, the mystery man who had recently entered his confessional. Paradoxically, Hanlon prayed to God to lead him in the right direction.

At least Hanlon had a partial plan in place. Carol was going to return to New York for about a week and then she was going to return to Alabama and go with him to talk to the bishop. They hoped that this would help expedite the process of laitization. One way or another it was going to happen. Hanlon simply wanted the process to allow him to remain in the Catholic Church and to receive the sacraments. However he had to wonder how much this really meant if he was willing to flat out leave The Church if he had no alternative. And if that was the way things unfolded, would he still honor the privacy of the confessional, especially if someone else's life was in danger. This thought process became even more troubling as he recognized the fact that those in danger included himself, his son and his lover. What were his responsibilities to his faith and to God if he no longer was a part of The Church? Father Tim Hanlon was now down to the basics. He was asking himself; *Who is Tim Hanlon?* His curiosity alone kept him awake at the wheel until he arrived at the rectory in Mobile.

Back at their hotel suite after dinner, Julianne was beginning to feel the effects of the three glasses of wine that she had with dinner. A pleasant glow radiated from her body and Richter couldn't see it but he could feel it.

Over dinner they had both learned things about each other. As the evening unfolded they each felt primordial premonitions about the sexual exploits they knew would eventually ensue. And each looked forward to that experience. They had talked a lot at dinner, but said little on the cab ride back to the hotel and on the walk up to their room.

Inside the room Julianne grabbed Richter's cane and threw it on the couch. She then took him by the hand and led him into the bedroom. While standing near the bed, Richter reached both of his arms around Julianne and hugged her to his body.

"You're taller than I realized." Julianne spoke these innocuous words into Richter's chest as he held her.

"And you are exactly the shape I knew you would be." As he said these words Richter moved his hands from behind Julianne and down to her waist, nestling his hands at the narrowest part of her body. Julianne sensed that Richter was tactilely tracing a mental image of her body and she was glad that his tentacles explored her finest physical asset first. His touch was deliberate but soft and sensuous. Simultaneously Julianne allowed her arms to wrap around Richter's back. She arched her head and kissed him softly on the lips, lingering long enough to allow the next move to be in Richter's hands.

"What color is your sundress?" He spoke softly as he reached his hands to the back of her neckline in search of a fastener. He found two ends of the halter that were tied behind her neck. He untied the two ends and Julianne stepped back and allowed the dress to fall away from her bare breasts.

"Red."

"What's that?"

"Red. The color of my dress is red."

That was a beginning. Julianne stepped out of her dress and kicked it to the side. She kicked her shoes in the same direction for good measure and then stepped back into her embrace with Hawk Richter. He continued to explore her body softly, as they tumbled into the nearby bed. She knew that he was registering all the information positively.

She removed his glasses but his eyes were closed. His chin had settled lower toward his chest, with his mouth slightly ajar. Julianne was amazed at the way Richter communicated with his hands and his mouth. In the past she had been hit upon by loquacious men who wagged their tongues to deliver garrulous gibberish that inevitably was relegated to the scrap heap of jejune come-ons. Over the next several hours Julianne was fascinated to find out at least one man knew how to use his tongue in much more imaginative ways.

V

Righteousness

"So tell me, dearest, what did this fellow, Tim Hanlon, have to say when you told him that you had borne him a son?"

"He's not just a *fellow*, Jude, he's Russell's father and he's also a Catholic priest."

"But from what you've told me, it doesn't appear like he'll be a priest for long."

"That's probably true, but things are more complicated than that."

"Speaking of complications, dearest, all of a sudden you've gotten your life to be more than just a little bit convoluted. You have two important cover shoots in the next three weeks and yet you're ready to run right back down to Alabama to help your man renege on his vows."

"I'm not asking you to understand this situation. I'm merely asking you to watch Russell for a few days. I'll be back Monday night. It's just that things are happening faster between Tim and me than I originally thought. We just need a weekend alone without the company of a seven year old. I'll be back at work Tuesday morning. Tim's planning to come up to New York as soon as he can get away. I think that will be soon but I don't want Tim to do anything until he's ready to do it."

"You know I love Russ. So of course I'll watch over him. I've enjoyed all of the weekends that we've have spent together in the past.

I just want to make sure that Russ's mom has her head on straight. That's all."

"Don't worry about that. And thank you for being such a friend and caring so much about my well being. I know that you're surprised by all of this. But things happen for a reason."

"People use that foolish phrase all the time. It's just an excuse for not telling me what's up, or why you are doing what you're doing. Whatever you do, don't fool yourself, Dearest. The highway to hell is littered with fools, fabricators and their friends. You should have a damn good reason before you going running back to this mystic."

"He's not a mystic, Jude. I told you. He's a priest and he's Russell's father."

"Priest, Rabbi, Minister, Brahmin, Imam, Magician, Mystic. They're all the same to me."

Mays suppressed a laugh. She knew that Jude had a spiritual side to his life. But he didn't discuss it much and preferred to create an imaginary moat around his psychic castle.

"You're so irreverent, Jude. But I adore you anyway.

"Whatever you say, dearest … whatever you say."

Professor Melech Katz wasn't sure he wanted to continue teaching at the university. He wasn't sure he wanted to live in Tampa. In fact he wasn't sure of anything lately. He also was extremely tired, and yet he couldn't sleep more than a few hours at a time. He felt jittery, irritated and anxious most of the time and he frequently had a feeling that something horrible was right around the corner. His one outlet for all of these feelings was his workouts at the gym. For the past two weeks, he was spending as much as three hours a day in the gym, lifting weights, doing cardio exercises to the point of exhaustion and attempting to get his body in perfect shape, because he felt like his mind was deteriorating rapidly. He just couldn't concentrate on anything.

The last interview that Katz did with respect to the BITSY shootings was on *The Brady Focus*, but that interview had created a landslide of requests for additional media appearances. His cell phone jammed with voice mail messages to the point that no one could leave a message. He had so many text messages that he had grown tired of emptying them out without responding. He had a difficult time finding personal email messages amongst the litter of messages from the media. He vaguely understood that he was undergoing a relapse of the posttraumatic stress disorder that had haunted him intermittently since leaving the war zone in Israel. He was so fearful that this might happen after the BITSY shootings that he went out of his way to continue to talk to people as a way of avoiding the re-onset of the condition. He talked to the police and school authorities. He talked to local reporters and did a few radio interviews. Then he even flew up to New York to do three television interviews. But after the Brady interview he just couldn't do it anymore.

Intriguingly Brady had started a media debate among talk show hosts. The majority of them attacked Brady for attacking Katz. But a few of them opened up the discussion about whether or not Katz had acted legally, morally or prudently. Katz was incapable of watching or listening to any of this. He had simply returned to his apartment near the BITSY campus just outside of Tampa. He talked to almost no one.

One person that he had agreed to talk with was his analyst, Abe Elowitz. Elowitz had been a rock of support throughout the recent madness, and had encouraged Katz to attend the group session, even if he just listened at first. Katz was still considering it.

Ismail Kanasani was getting tired of dead end leads. Although he was the head investigator on the Fein murder, he also had more than a passing interest in the Clinton slaughter that took place on the BITSY campus the same evening. One of the tasks he undertook was to try to read through the rambling 1172 page Clinton Manifesto. This was no easy task to perform. The manifesto seemed to start in the middle of nowhere; bypass the edge of somewhere; and land back in the middle of nowhere again. There was no real pathway through the document. It was a lengthy jumble of unrelated feelings, political sympathies, sophomoric ideologies and disjointed calls for revolution. The author frequently changed course in the middle of his manifesto. Detective Kanasani noted for example that Joseph Clinton professed to be pro life with respect to the abortion debate and then 75 pages later he indicated that the United States should adopt the Chinese abortion procedure for limiting family size to one child.

As he perused Joseph Clinton's manifesto, Kanasani utilized some computerized tools to reconfigure the manifesto and align portions of the document along topical lines. He was interested in any cross over into his investigation of the Fein murder, so Kanasani was particularly careful to find all of the references to abortion and women's rights that appeared in a document. He was surprised to find that there were fifty-one such references, including one reference to "Murder Inc." In order to see how this stacked up against other topics he searched for references to China and the Chinese, as well as to Muslims, Arabs, and the Russians. Remarkably there was approximately the same number of references for each of these topics, when he cross counted the references with each data sort. This fact undercut the remote possibility that there was a connection between the BITSY murders and the murder of Aaron Fein. The only outlier among the various topics that pervaded the manifesto was capitalism, which had 582 references. The document was also spiced up with expletives and obscenities and Kanasani's search engine collected 7328 utilizations of the word "fuck" and derivative versions of the word. This amounted to nearly seven such usages per page for this one obscenity alone.

Regardless of the fact that the manifesto disparaged many different races, religions, ethnic groups, institutions and ideologies, Kanasani focused in on the fifty one references to abortion and women's rights. There was one passing reference to the Fein Center for Women in the document although it used the acronym version, FCW, to refer to the institution. Kanasani reread that short disjointed passage:

*"Women should beware that the fucking capi-
talistic clowns who operate institutions like
Planned Parenthood; Tampa's own Murder
Incorporated, the FCW; Orlando's EPOC
Clinic; and ACOL. These shitheads are responsible for 30 million fucking abortions since
1973."*

Expletives aside, this statement itself was quite clear. However four paragraphs later Clinton seemingly contradicted himself by stating:

*"Government has no right telling women what
to do with their vaginas. They can fuck whoever they want to fuck, even themselves. If they
want to murder their unborn kids, they have the
fucking right to do so."*

Then about 40 pages later Clinton in a calmer tone suggests that:

*"It's about time that our government acts
responsibly and repeals Roe v Wade."*

Kanasani shook his head at the incongruity of the Clinton Manifesto. But he figured he would run down the references anyway. He knew what Planned Parenthood was and what it did. He was also aware of the activities and services of the Orlando EPOC Clinic, because it had been under close surveillance ever since Aaron Fein had been shot. He was not aware of what ACOL was at first. However he learned that this was a reference to Abortion Clinics Online, a state by state abortion referral service that facilitated the location of practitioners in every state who would perform abortions.

Kanasani realized that he may be grasping at straws to try to find some connection between the BITSY murders and the Fein execution. To begin with he knew that it was a different person who performed each crime because they happened concurrently. And in spite of the many references to abortion in the Clinton Manifesto, it was certainly not Clinton's only peeve. He railed against capitalism far more than he obsessed against abortion.

When Kanasani grew weary of cross referencing the work of a mad man, he went back to his other notes on the Fein investigation. However Clinton's obsession with anti-capitalism and alternating views on abortion gave him another thought. Fein's killer may think the same way as Clinton. Maybe he would want to kill other capitalists who sponsored abortion. It might have been Aaron Fein's name that was on the doors to the FCW but there were other investors as well. He pulled up the names of those investors from his computerized notes and found one interesting piece of information. One of the minority investors in the FCW, Bertrand "Hawk" Richter, was also a member of the faculty at BITSY. He allowed his search tools to go back over the manifesto and search for mentions of Hawk Richter by name. He found two such conflicting references. However both references were with respect to Richter's atheism and not to his investment in the FCW. It wasn't much of a lead, he thought, but Kanasani figured that he would run it to ground anyway.

Patch Munson was growing more and more dissatisfied with his life. After his parents passed away Munson became the family patriarch. This meant little beyond being the only surviving male in the family. His sisters, Gloria and Marjorie, never ventured far from Mobile and his wife, Maggie's idea of a big vacation was a few days "down the 'Bama shore." There was no next generation of Munsons on the horizon. The Munson farm, which had evolved faster than the Munson family itself, would likely prosper in some form or fashion long after the current crop of Munsons moved on to the heavenly harvest.

Until recently Patch Munson had led a remarkably mundane life. It was getting increasingly hard for him to understand the unforeseen feelings that he had about himself after he shot Aaron Fein. It wasn't remorse that he felt. It was more of a simple upturn in aggressive attitude that had him perplexed. He was annoyed with himself for trusting the priest with his secret. He was now determined not to trust anyone else, not his sisters and not his wife. He was also beginning to feel an overwhelming compulsion to ensure that the priest would never tell anyone. He didn't want to harm the priest because so far the priest had apparently kept his secret. But he couldn't be sure. He temporarily put these thoughts aside and decided to take his weekly walk over to back end of the farm to talk to the foreman of the chicken houses. Harry waddled along slowly behind him, sniffing the ground along the way.

"*Mornin'* Patch. *Yew an' Harreh* out *fur* a walk?"

"*Mornin'* Bobby Joe. Looks *lahke* it's *gunna* be *'nother fahne summeh* day. How're the chickens *doin'*?"

"We're *rahght* on schedule. We're *truckin'* the birds from the grow-out houses *t'* the *processin'* center on *Mundeh nahght*. We *gat* all the contract *he'p readeh t'* go. We're *havin'* a *li'l* trouble *wit'* the plow pushers, so the *boys'll* be *stuffin'* a lot *o* the chicken boxes *bah* hand. *Goin' t'* be noisy around here *tomorrah evenin'*. *Yew* best be *havin'* a few brewskis back in the big house *wit'* Mrs. Munson."

"She's *headin'* down the *'Bama* shore, *wit' mah* sisters *fur* a week. She'll be *leavin' tomorrah afteh* services at the church. So *Ah mahght jes* come *bah t'* watch *thaangs* on *Mundeh nahght*."

"Suit *yerse'f. Ain't* much *t'* watch. We're *sendin'* out *'bout* 100,000 birds. We had *sem* trouble *wit'* the temperature in House #6. We isolated those chicks *fur* local slaughter. *Ain't* worth *nuthin' an'way*." We *gat* 120,000 newly hatched chicks *comin' oveh* from incubation on *Tuesdeh*. We should have the temperature straightened out in House #6 *bah* then."

Munson was chewing on a piece of straw as he listened to his foreman. He never interfered with his work. The few times that he chose to watch anything was simply when he was bored.

There were only three men who worked full time at the grow-out houses at the back end of the Munson farm. But once every six weeks they would hire five or six additional men to help with the restocking process. This included the movement of the 3 week old newborn chicks onto the farm from the regional chicken company's hatchery and incubation facilities. These chicks replaced the outgoing birds right after the farm hands gathered up the "grown-out" nine week old, four pound chickens that would be trucked back to the regional company for de-feathering, processing and slaughter.

Bobby Joe was the foreman of the Munson chicken farm. He and the other two full time workers entered the rear entrance to the Munson farm on a daily basis and always stayed on the rear or northern end of the farm which was now a total of 450 acres. All six of the 400 x 50 ft chicken grow-out houses were located on this back 120 acres, which was quartered off by a narrow private road and a broken-down post and rail fence. On the south side of the fence there were nearly seven hundred citrus trees all in a single grove area situated between the chicken houses and the Munson residential lawn area. The citrus grove was also separated from the residential lawn area by another post and rail fence. This second fence was better kept and it encircled the residential lawn area out to the main road. It was in the rear of this residential area that Patch Munson's father, Junior Munson, had built the two bomb shelters in the 1970's.

"How'd the temperature get so *out o whack* in House 6?" Munson didn't really care because he had a contract with the regional company for the maintenance of the houses. He would get paid for the full complement of chickens regardless of the yield.

"Ventilator motors broke down. We're *s'posed t'* keep the temperature at 85° F, but it *gat* up *oveh* 110° *fur* more than two days last week. *Wuddah* moved the chicks but we're *full-up* in the *otheh* houses and that *wuddah* added heat *iffin* we crowded *'em*. In the middle of the mess the company *vet'narian* shows up and says *t'* keep Building 6 quarantined. He *didden'* want *t'* mess *wit'* the *otheh* houses. *Them* birds have an average of less than one square foot each as it is. That's the second *tahme* we had this problem this year. The vet says that the company may want *t'* talk *t' y'all 'bout buildin'* a spare house. He says it would be cheaper than the cost *o losin'* so *maneh* birds several *tahmes* a year."

Harry began sniffing up Bobby Joe's pants leg and the foreman bent down and cuffed the dog gently around its large floppy ears, until Harry pulled away from the playful torment. Patch Munson just watched in a bemused manner, because Bobby Joe was the only other person alive who could play with Harry's ears and not get snapped at. Harry chose his human friends selectively.

"Guess we *kinda* cooked *them* broilers *b'faw* their time." Munson made a haphazard attempt at being amusing. Generally he had no sense of humor.

"*Them* birds *ain't* worth *nuthin'*. They may be cooked, but they smell *gawd-awful*. We couldn't even hack *'em* up and feed *'em* to the *niggeh*s on the *otheh sahde* of town. *Sem* of *'em* are *alreadeh* dead. They're covered *wit'* all *kinda* maggots *an'* shit. We're *jes' gunna* burn *'em* up and plow *'em* under once we clean the place up and spray it all down."

"All right. Good *t'* see *y'all gat ever'thaan' undeh* control. *Ah'll* be *headin'* out. *Gid* day." Munson liked Bobby Joe but he didn't care much for his racist attitude or the fact that Bobby Joe assumed that Munson shared Bobby Joe's biases. Munson knew that he was not exactly an ambassador of good will, but he didn't consider himself a racist. He even managed to indulge in a thought or two about the priest's black girl friend. He considered her a fine enough looking woman for a roll in the hay. The problem was that Munson hadn't had a roll in the hay with anyone including Maggie for quite some time.

Munson made the slow walk back across his property, past the barrier fence to the chicken farm, past the private dirt road, through the citrus grove, through the gate to the residential lawn and on across the low brush that covered about twenty acres and obscured the two fallout shelters which were about a quarter mile apart and about 400 yards from the farm house. As he approached the rear door to his house there were four large 100 year old magnolia trees, with a family of song birds chirping away near the top of the southernmost tree. Some parts of Alabama would live forever he thought as he walked into the back door of his home. His next thought was more tactical: *Now what should Ah do 'bout that priest and his girlfriend?*

"Good morning Julianne. It's been a *vhile* since *vee* have seen you." Yogi Dawa Trashi smiled in greeting.

"I've been spending a lot of time on the East Coast."

"The job has had you running around. I take it."

"You might say that."

"*Vell velcome* back to The Rhapsody Lifestyle Center and our Shambhala meditation hub. I'm sure that you *vill* readjust rapidly." Dawa Trashi was a yoga/meditation instructor at the center. He and Boddhidharma, another spiritual guide had worked extensively with Julianne over several years with her Shambhala training, during multiple weekend meditation retreats. It was there that she learned the basics of meditation and acquired the ability to meditate when sitting or standing in a group setting, while still remaining centered on her own self-awareness. On this occasion however she was anxious to separate herself from others and renew her quest for enlightenment. She carried her zabuton tucked up under her arm.

It was early in the morning in California, but the east coast had been awake for a while. Julianne had resisted the temptation to call Hawk Richter when she awoke in her home just south of San Francisco. She needed some time to think about what she was doing with Richter. Her relationship with him was incomplete. He was significantly different from most men she knew. He was much more intellectual but much less spiritual. His intelligence intrigued her. But his spiritual shortcomings shrouded his intellect. For the time being, his physicality was the tie-breaker. Despite his blindness he was very sensory and that made him very sensual as well. All together that gave him a quite captivating aura, which was ironic because Richter derided that very word as being "too mystical to be meaningful."

But for the next 90 minutes Julianne was going to spend time exclusively with Julianne. She needed to relax as much as she needed to make decisions, maybe even more so. She was wearing tan full length yoga pants and a matching belted wrap-around top that she wore over a loose t shirt. She also enjoyed the comfort of bralessness. She took off the wrap-around top that she brought with her to wear following her meditation when her body temperature cooled down. She sat on the edge of her zabuton and assumed the lotus position. She could feel her mind and body reflexively entering their meditation mode. Earlier these had been two separate transitions, but through iteration this had been narrowed to a single personal transformation. The mind and body grew comfortable together and time stopped ticking.

Julianne felt the wonderful drift of her psyche in the general direction of Shambhala, the mythical hidden kingdom, and the focal point of her meditative endeavors. Her seeking of Shambhala was personal and unreflective of the others near and around her at that moment and hour or in the surrounding days and weeks. She also was aware of her strengths and weaknesses in this spiritual quest. She was an accomplished seeker on a personal level, but she knew that she did not possess the requisite spiritual skillfulness and intellectual dexterity to share her expertise as a seeker with others. That was the work of the Dawa Trashi's and Boddhidharma's of the world. She respected their skills as instructors, but knew that her search for Shambhala was her own and it needed to come from within her.

At its best Julianne's reflective meditation evolved in a different dimension than time itself. Before long her physical body seemed to float effortlessly next to her spirit. Intuitively she knew that even the concept of "floating" was a mere metaphor for her awareness. The wondrous experience was unique and yet in some way repeatable. She was able to return to this marvelous place in sequential meditative sessions, and yet every time she returned the feeling had a uniqueness to it that was indescribably enchanting.

Her body was a featherweight. And her intellect was not an impediment either. The pleasure was simply otherworldly. The intrusion came on mildly with the first chimes from her enzo clock. The awareness gradually brought Julianne back from the edges of her search for Shambhala. Regrettably, in the "real world" seeking had a place and meditation had a finite duration. When her 90 minutes of meditation came to an end, Julianne felt a slight chill. She also felt the other familiar physical changes. Her whole nervous system was relaxed yet refreshed. Her body felt the dichotomy of softness and hardness. The nipples on her breasts were erect and her skeletal structure returned to its more rigid formality. However her slight body perspiration was now a chilled dampness and her skin felt soft to the touch. Her musculature felt sinewy and although she still felt an overall sensation of relaxation, she felt very little fatigue, and enough exhilaration to start her west coast work day.

Julianne showered and got redressed in the locker room at the Rhapsody Lifestyle Center. As she was leaving Julianne felt renewed and refreshed … a new woman. She had even put on her makeup and a new frame of mind. She passed Dawa Trashi once again on her way out.

"Good day. *Vill ve* be seeing you again soon?" Her instructor intoned.

"I'll be back next week. I'm heading to Tampa tomorrow night." Julianne was now moving quickly and spoke over her shoulder as she hurried by. She noticed that Trashi was staring longingly at her butt, as she moved by. How ironic, she thought. She knew that the literal translation of Dawa Trashi, her instructor's name was *auspicious moon.* Boys will forever be boys, she concluded.

As she drove away from the Rhapsody Lifestyle Center, thoughts of Hawk Richter came back to mind. She wasn't ready to go there right away, so she flipped on the radio. Ironically the first song she heard was Three Dog Night crooning their old song, "On the Road to Shambala." She hated the song. She didn't like the pop culture invasion of the spiritual search. She knew that the recording artists even opted for the westernized spelling of Shambhala. Normally she would have simply flipped the station and been done with it. But this time she decided to listen.

"Wash away my troubles, wash away my pain
With the rain in Shambala.
Wash away my sorrow, wash away my shame
With the rain in Shambala.

Ah, ooh, yeah, yeah, yeah, yeah, yeah, yeah
Ah, ooh, yeah, yeah, yeah, yeah, yeah, yeah

Everyone is helpful, everyone is kind
On the road to Shambala.
Everyone is lucky; everyone is so kind
On the road to Shambala.

Ah, ooh, yeah, yeah, yeah, yeah, yeah, yeah
Ah, ooh, yeah, yeah, yeah, yeah, yeah, yeah

How does your light shine, in the halls of
Shambala?
How does your light shine, in the halls of
Shambala?

I can tell my sister by the flowers in her eyes
On the road to Shambala.
I can tell my brother by the flowers in his eyes
On the road to Shambala.

How does your light shine, in the halls of
Shambala?
How does your light shine, in the halls of
Shambala?

Julianne wondered why she found the song distasteful. The song, the lyrics and the artists' rendition of their music all predated her introduction to Buddhist spirituality. *Was it a personal flaw? Could she not accept the happiness of other seekers? Could she not accept the commercialization of the search? Yes, maybe that was it.* She resolved to think about this more at a later time. She needed to get her mind ready for work. But as she drove to the office she didn't think about work. Her thoughts simply returned to Hawk Richter. She wondered why her mind kept going back in that direction and causing her to feel a semi-sexual experience of arousal. She repressed the feelings as best she could, but she knew that she would visit with Richter once again in two days. She didn't expect that it would be "the lights shining in the halls of Shambhala." It was more likely to be lights out for simply scintillating sex.

"*T'day* we'll talk *'bout rahghteousness*. *Ah* call *yer* attention to the dilemma posed in Psalm 11:3 where we're asked:

'If the foundations are destroyed, what cain the rahghteous do?'

"Well *Ah* will tell *yew* that the Lord has called us all to *un'erstand an' t'* do the *rahght thaang* in *all* our *earthleh* interactions. *An'* we should all be worried *'bout* our foundations" Billy Brand thundered as he said the word "*rahghteousness*" simultaneously utilizing a sweeping motion of his right hand to symbolize the vast dominion encompassed by the term "*all* our *earthleh* interactions."

Those seated in the Christian Ascendancy Community Church were immediately drawn in and focused on how Reverend Brand would proceed to define "righteousness." The television audience throughout the South was also affixing its attention to the young minister. Viewing from their respective homes in the greater Tampa area were Detective Ismail Kanasani and Priscilla Stengel. Kanasani's interest was professional. Stengel's interest was of a more personal nature.

"It's not *'nough* to be *rahghteous* in our own actions *an'* in our own thoughts. We need *t'* be *discahples* of *rahghteousness*. We *cain't* be true Christians if we have molasses in our britches. We need to affirm the Lord's way. When we see an injustice we need *t' crah* out in indignation. When we see an immoral *activiteh bein'* tolerated, or worse yet *bein'* sponsored, we should raise our voices in repudiation.

"Allow *meh t'* focus on the abhorrent practice in *sem o* the northern states of *permittin'* same sex marriage. This is *absoluteleh* repugnant to the Lord. From the *beginnin'* of *tahme* the Lord has stipulated that a marriage was between a man *an'* a woman. *An'* although the great state *o Al'bama* has a constitutional ban on gay marriage, there are *otheh* states in our union that have blasphemed the Lord. They have endorsed the illicit union *b'tween* two men or *b'tween* two women.

This is a hideous abomination. Vermont, *Mass'chusetts*, New York, New *Hampsheh*, Connecticut and *Ahowa*, *y'all* should be *'shamed o yehse'ves*. New Jersey, Maryland *an'* Washington DC, *yer alreadeh slahdin'* on the *slippereh* slope. *Fortunateleh* we are solid in the South. Not only here in *Al'bama*, but also in Arkansas, *Floor'da*, *Jaw'gia*, *Mississippeh*, *Lews'yanah*, North *Car'lina*, South *Car'lina*, *Tenn'see*, Texas *an' Virginyer*, we have constitutionally *defahned* marriage as a union *b'tween* a man and a woman and we have *collectiveleh* banned same sex marriage. Still there are those who agitate against our common sense *an' digniteh*. We *cainnot* allow their perverse *ahdeas t'* permeate our subconscious. So even *whahle* we have *solidleh furbidden* this perversion in the South, there are *oh-pinion* polls *bein'* conducted that indicate a small but *growin'* number of citizens in each of our states are *becomin'* more tolerant of this depraved *an'* immoral practice.

"The *bahble*, at its very *beginnin'* teaches us *'bout* marriage. Allow *meh* to quote Genesis 2: 18-24:

> *The LORD God said, 'It is not good fur the man t' be alone. Ah will make a helpeh suitable fur him.'*
>
> *Now the LORD God had formed out of the ground all the wahld animals and all the birds in the skah. He brought them to the man t' see what he would name 'em; an' whatever the man called each livin' creature, that was its name. So the man gave names t' all the lahvestock, the birds in the skah an' all the wahld animals.*
>
> *But fur Adam no suitable helpeh was found. So the LORD God caused the man t' fall into a deep sleep; an' whahle he was sleepin', he took one o the man's ribs an' then closed up the place wit' flesh. Then the LORD God made a woman from the rib he had taken out o the man, an' he brought her to the man.*

The man said: 'This is now bone of mah bones and flesh of my flesh; she shall be called 'woman,' fur she was taken out o man.'

That is whah a man leaves his father an' mother an' is unahted to his wahfe, an' they become one flesh.

"The *bahble* tells us more *wit'* even *greateh clariteh* in Leviticus 18:22:

Thou shalt not lah with mankahnd, as wit' womankahnd: it is an abomination."

Billy Brand rambled on for the next twenty minutes about righteousness and virtue and the need for rectitude in fending off the man made evils of the world. In addition to same sex marriage he took umbrage against atheism, religious intolerance, prostitution and the erosion of family values. Under the broad-rimmed umbrella of righteousness, he also attacked one of his favorite offenses, abortion.

"In *closin'* our thoughts *fur t'day*, let me point out that there are those in our midst who offend us on more than one of these *mattehs*. Take *fur* example the so-called *educateh* from *Floor'da*, Bertrand *Richteh*. *Y'all* remember when he had the *audaciteh t'* promote his blasphemous atheistic *ahdeology* on the campus of the University *o* South *Al'bama*. The *rahghteous* amongst us protested in large numbers *t'* shout down his damnable dogma. Did *y'all* know that this man is also one of the principle investors in the *Fahne Cenneh fur* Women? Yes it's sad but true. This man has been *busieh* than a one-legged man in a butt *kickin'* contest. But he has been *doin'* the work of Satan. Even though Aaron *Fahne* was sent to his grave in an attempt *t'* stop his murderous bloodshed of babies in *Floor'da*, his illicit legacy lives on in the work of other evil doers like Hawk *Richteh*, Amanda *Fahne an'* the other corrupt capitalists who use *theiah fahnancial* resources *t'* slay unborn *chil'ren*. Now *Ah* have said *b'faw* that we need *t'* stop the *promotehs an'* kill the program, not the *otheh weh 'round*. As *yew cain plainleh* see *despahte* the *killin' o* Aaron *Fahne*, this atrocious program lives on. The *rahgh-teous* among us need *t'* kill the program."

In Tampa, Detective Kanasani was riveted to his TV. After meeting Billy Brand, he now had a better understanding of his charisma. This sermon confirmed Kanasani's intention to meet with Hawk Richter, if for no other reason than to warn him. He was fascinated by this turn of events. First he discovered a weak connection between the two atrocities committed on what was now nationally known as "Terrifying Thursday." And almost immediately thereafter Billy Brand was preaching about the same connection in his Sunday sermon. As a Muslim, Kanasani also regarded abortion as *haram* or forbidden. He was beginning to wonder whether he was being sent a sign of some sort. Generally Kanasani followed his Muslim faith, but he didn't proselytize or attempt to impose his views on others. He quietly prayed 5 times a day in accordance with his faith. He also fasted during Ramadan, but he had yet to make a pilgrimage or demonstrate any public passion and zeal for his faith. His wife was also a Muslim, but she was even less ardent in her faith than her husband. Still whenever Kanasani came across odd occurrences in his investigative pursuits, he often wondered if he was receiving a message from Allah.

About twenty miles outside of Tampa, Priscilla Stengel was also listening intently to Billy Brand. She had become a devotee of his weekly program during the last several years and often found comfort in his convictions, when they were similar to her own. His preaching had been an impetus for her 180° turnaround in her position on abortion. However she worried that he may also unwittingly have been an impetus behind the murder of Aaron Fein. She wasn't sure how she felt about all of that. She thought she might take up the issue with her psychotherapy group. At the very least she simply needed to think more about it, maybe even pray about it.

Rumors move quickly in Mobile Alabama and the scuttlebutt at the fellowship hour after services at the Christian Ascendancy Community Church was that across town, one of the Catholic priests was leaving his ministry to get married. No one would attest to the veracity of the rumor and no one seemed to know the name of the parishioner who was responsible for the defection of the young priest. But everybody seemed to know that the priest was Father Tim Hanlon. At least one member of the Christian Ascendancy Community Church congregation hinted that she had an impeccable source and other rumors led folks to believe that the source was Bernadette, the housekeeper at the Catholic rectory. Some members of the Ascendancy congregation opined that if the Catholics would let their priests marry in the first place they wouldn't have so much trouble.

Patch Munson heard much of this chit-chat going on around him while his Hefty Bag sisters joined in the gossip. Munson didn't know whether the emotion that overcame him was fear or anger, or a little of both. Many times the rumor mill at the church turned out to be malicious gossip. It was an ironic reality that the service-attending congregation could often act in such an un-Christian manner. However in this particular case Patch Munson worried that the rumor mill had it right. He didn't hear any suggestions that this priest, Father Tim Hanlon, was engaged to a black woman, so he was unsure how much people knew. Munson had never paid much attention to this type of gossip in the past. However this time he was directly impacted by the rumors. He was worried that the priest would disregard his vows if he left his ministry. That could mean that Hanlon might go to the authorities and tell them what he knew about the shooting of Aaron Fein. Munson decided that he might have to take matters into his own hands. His wife, Maggie, and his two sisters were leaving that afternoon for a week's vacation at Orange Beach, "down the 'Bama shore."

He never went with them on these vacations because he didn't know how to swim and therefore he didn't like the beach. Now he knew that this respite would provide an opportunity to deal with Hanlon and the black woman.

Priscilla Stengel was once again visiting her father, Frank Malone. She knew that this could be the very last time she ever saw him alive. It was astonishing to see a man whom she had respected throughout her whole life withering away with little meaning left in his existence. The stages of physical deterioration had lasted almost three years but Frank Malone was now in the home stretch. What concerned Priscilla most was that although her father was a lifelong Catholic, he had no desire to see a priest as the end of his life neared. Only the woman from hospice was there with him to offer consolation.

"How are you today, Dad?"

"That's a stupid question, Priscilla. And you're not a stupid girl."

"I was trying to be pleasant."

"All right I understand. But we both know what hospice means. There are only so many days left. I want to make the most of them. I'm glad you came. Did you bring Michael?"

"No."

"It's better this way. He's a good boy. But I hope he remembers what I was like a year ago rather than what I'm like now."

"I think so too. There's something else I wanted to ask you about."

"I think I know what's coming."

"And how would you know that?"

"I don't have much to do around here but think. Thinking isn't always pleasant when you consider what might have been. But when I think about my daughter, Priscilla, all my thoughts are good. And I know how you always think about other people and how you're always wondering about spiritual things. That's why you want me to see a priest before I die. Am I right?"

"I guess there's no fooling you is there?"

"I don't know. Maybe I've been a simple fool for a long time. And then maybe I can look at my life and say it was pretty damn good. But as far as the priest is concerned … I don't want to see a priest. I've done some bad things and I've done some good things. God knows what they are. I'm real sorry for the bad things."

Frank Malone coughed weakly and then continued. "There you go. See, you just heard my confession; and I feel better apologizing to you for the bad things rather than to some young priest, who doesn't speak much English and who has no idea how to comfort a dying man. What do we have at the church now? I think it's a Mexican pastor and an Indian assistant pastor. They can't possibly know what to say to a cancer-ridden crotchety old Irishman like me. I'm just happy you're here Sweetheart. You and Michael are all I have left. I'm happy that I'm leaving a daughter and a grandson behind. Maybe after I'm gone you'll find another man and have another child. Tell them that I love them too. If you love them I will love them too from wherever I am."

"Don't talk that way, Dad."

"What? You don't want me to talk about love?"

"No. You know what I mean. That's not the problem. I mean … don't talk about dying."

"OK. Let's talk about something else. Tell me how your hunt for the Fein killer is going?"

"I have an idea or two. I'm still working on it."

"Well do your old man a favor. When you find this guy, tell him to get himself a good Jew lawyer. There's plenty down here in Florida. He'll figure out some way to get him off. That guy Fein was an animal. The shooter shouldn't be doing jail time for killing a predatory animal."

Priscilla Stengel's views on the topic were not far removed from the sentiments that her father had expressed, but she tried not to be utterly transparent.

"Jesus Christ, Dad … why don't you tell me how you *really* feel on the subject?"

"Let's just say that I don't want Fein as a neighbor in my afterlife."

Patch Munson followed the black woman from her hotel as she drove Tim Hanlon back in the general direction of the Most Holy Tabernacle Catholic Church. Munson was driving his wife's Chevy Equinox rather than his Silverado because he didn't want to risk having the woman seeing his pickup again. They stopped about three miles away and pulled into the parking lot for the Colonial Mall Bel Air, the largest shopping mall in Mobile. They drove through the large lot of the 1.5 million square foot mall until they reached the section outside of Dillard's. Hanlon's Range Rover was parked amidst hundreds of other vehicles, right where Hanlon had dropped it the previous afternoon. Munson could see a small rental car company sticker on the woman's car window, so he assumed that she had come from out of town. This time she didn't have the young boy with her and she and Hanlon had spent a lot more time in her hotel room over the last two days. Munson now believed that this must be the woman who was purported to be Hanlon's fiancé. What he couldn't figure out was why they were sneaking around so much, if everyone knew about them anyway. Then he had another thought. *Maybeh this wudden' his fiancé after all. Maybeh he had hisse'f a fiancé an' a black honey pot t' boot. Jes' what kahnd o priest was this guy, an'way?*

Munson was careful not to get too close to the other cars. He pulled into a vacant spot a couple of rows over but he could still see the rental car and the Range Rover. He watched as Hanlon reached over and kissed his companion on the lips. It was not a familial peck on the cheek, but it stopped short of being a passionate saliva swapper. Regardless it confirmed Munson's opinion that they were lovers of some sort. As Hanlon made his way back into the driver's seat of the Range Rover, Munson made up his mind to follow the woman instead of the priest. It might help him to identify Hanlon's lover. Other than being the most attractive black woman he had ever laid eyes on, Munson had no idea who she was.

❧

"I'll certainly do whatever I can do to help, Detective Kanasani. But I have to tell you that I didn't know Aaron Fein very well. I only met him a couple of times."

"Thank you Professor Richter …"

"Just call me Hawk. Everyone else does …"

"Alright Hawk. I realize that this is a tough topic for you. You're one of the unfortunate few that suffered several losses on the night of the shootings."

"Yes. Now the media has taken to calling it 'Terrifying Thursday.' It was a horrific night."

"I was at home watching TV when I heard the first reports of the shootings. It was just awful. How about yourself?" Kanasani didn't want to sound like a probing cop, so he gently prodded at the professor's activities by disclosing his own location on the night of the shootings.

"I was having dinner at Armani's. My driver came by to pick me up and told me about the atrocities."

"I imagine this must have been shocking to you." Kanasani paused slightly and shifted into the reason for the interview. "Although I have a question or two that may pertain to the Clinton shootings, my purpose here is to investigate the murder of Aaron Fein. We're looking for any and all possible leads. Clinton is dead, but there is still another murderer out there and we want to bring him to justice."

"Why do you feel that there is a tie in between Clinton's rampage and the Fein murder?"

"I don't know that there is one. But I've been in this line of work for a long time and have come to realize that sometimes you just have to go with your gut."

"Not exactly a scientific approach, is it?"

Kanasani ignored the barb and plowed ahead with his questions. "You were one of the original investors in the Fein Center for Women. Am I correct on that?"

"Yes. I believe that's true. Aaron Fein raised money through a group from New York called Golden Bernstein Properties. They did mostly real estate plays but occasionally invested in the underlying businesses of their potential tenants. I was introduced to Gordon Golden at a financial breakfast meeting at the Plaza Hotel in Manhattan and later bought into the FCW, as a limited partner in a business called FGFB Holdings. That business owns two other businesses, one which owns the building itself and another that has ownership of the women's health business. It's not an overly complicated business structure. All together there are a dozen limited partners and our shares of the businesses vary in size. My share is one of the smaller ones."

"Thank you for that background." It was information that Kanasani's team had already uncovered but in an attempt to remain cordial he expressed his gratitude. "Have you had much discussion with the other limited partners since the shooting?"

"I've talked to one or two of the partners that I know personally, but there hasn't been a group conference call yet. However there is a call scheduled for next Thursday. The principal partner on a going forward basis is Amanda Fein. As I understand things, she has basically inherited Aaron's entire estate with the exception of some small bequeaths. Amanda and her attorney are the ones who have orchestrated next week's call."

"Let me switch gears on you for a second. Do you know who Billy Brand is?"

"Sure I do. He's the televangelist from Alabama, who makes a living selling Jesus books and trinkets. He organized a protest against me when I was speaking at the University of South Alabama a couple of years back. I am an outspoken atheist and of course that doesn't sit well with the bible thumping preachers across the South."

"Did anyone tell you that he mentioned you in his sermon yesterday?"

"No. I didn't know that."

"I guess he still bears a grudge because he blames you and the other investors for all of the abortions that continue to be performed at the FCW."

"Are you indicating that this inflammatory rhetoric might cause Fein's killer to strike again and that I could be a target?"

"Precisely. I don't want to alarm you unnecessarily, but I believe that it's appropriate to warn you of the possibilities. And that brings me to another connection. I read through Clinton's manifesto."

"From what I understand, that in itself is quite an accomplishment, Detective Kanasani."

"You've got that right. But anyway are you aware of the fact that Clinton mentions you by name in the manifesto? I guess you're a popular guy, Hawk."

"Yes, I know about it. But trust me I never met this guy in my life. Some reporter called me on the phone about a week ago and asked me a few questions about Fein and Clinton … just the way you're doing. She told me of the reference."

"Do you remember the reporter's name?"

"Yes. It was Priscilla Stengel. She had written a few articles about the Fein Center in the past. But this was the first time that I ever talked to her."

Kanasani jotted a note on his iPad to make certain that he followed up on this revelation and then continued his dialogue with Richter. "I know that this may be stretching things, but if the two crimes committed on Terrifying Thursday were related, this would be my theory. There is some type of anti-abortion conspiracy planned and Clinton and Fein's murderer are somehow connected. The rationale for killing Fein is obvious. But the Clinton slaughter is less understandable. However you yourself taught in the science building at BITSY and lectured on the sixth floor of the building. Is that correct?"

"Yes. So are you saying that I was the original target of Joseph Clinton because of my ownership stake in the FCW and that things just got out of control?"

"That's the theory."

"I don't buy it. Clinton was simply a depraved and unbalanced maniac. That kind of person rarely acts in concert with others. Besides, that manifesto of his is more obsessed with capitalism than with social topics, like abortion. But thanks for the warning nonetheless."

"Even if Clinton wasn't involved with the Fein murder, we still do not have Fein's killer, and we obviously have large groups of people that would like to see the FCW closed. Can I assume from your invest-ment in the FCW that you are a pro-choice advocate?"

"No. I simply was approached with an investment opportunity. That's the rationale for my limited partnership. It is unconnected with my views on the underlying social issue. But yes, I do consider myself pro-choice. But it's not a cause that I would push to the level of advocacy."

"Along those lines, Professor … err … Hawk … do you know of anyone associated with the FCW that might have had a change of heart on the topic over time?"

"I can't think of one off hand. Why do you ask?"

"It's like the ex-smoker thing. Some of the most vehement anti-tobacco people are ex-smokers themselves. Sometimes they knew someone who died from tobacco use, as well. If you translate this to the abortion topic, we may find that some of the biggest pro-life zealots may have once been associated with an abortion clinic. Maybe they even had an abortion personally."

"Now that you mention it, you might want to interview that woman reporter, Priscilla Stengel. It went through my mind when I spoke to her that she once was positive about the Fein Center and her most recent article was far from positive. You always wonder what makes a leopard change its spots." In spite of his leopard comment, Richter knew that his own thoughts on this social issue were still evolving.

Kanasani found Richter's perception to be worthy of note. The physicist was obviously a bright man and in spite of his visual hand-icap he was quite perceptive. Stengel had seen Fein shortly before his death, but the state police had managed to keep that fact out of the press and only a few people who knew about it. Richter was not one of those had this information. Kanasani made another entry about Stengel on his iPad. One more scattered lead to follow up on.

After dropping Tim Hanlon off, Carol Mays started out toward the Mobile Regional Airport, which served both Mobile Alabama and

Pascagoula, Mississippi. She drove for about fifteen minutes and then pulled over to gas up her rental car. Her thoughts were wondrous. She had spent the afternoon making love to the one man who she had been unable to stop thinking about since she was nineteen years old. He was tender in his lovemaking … gentle and caring and yet very strong and physical. When she was in his arms she felt invincible. She dialed his cell phone number but only got his voicemail.

"Hello Tim. It's me. I just wanted to tell you again how wonderful everything was this weekend and how much I love you. We have to trust in God that we are doing the right thing. I'm sure we are. Or God wouldn't have allowed things to go this far … I'm almost at the airport. I'll try you again once I get rid of the car."

What an odd sensation it was for Mays. She had just left her lover and couldn't wait to speak to him again. She was thinking about nothing else, not even about Russell.

The gas station that she pulled into was run by a local convenience market chain with its "Quick Gas, Stop and Hop" store on the same premises. After filling her tank, Mays pulled across the lot and went into the store to purchase an iced tea. At first she didn't notice Patch Munson who was slumped down behind the wheel of the Chevy Equinox that was parked four spaces away. But she noticed him in her rearview mirror just as she was pulling out of the *Stop and Hop*. Mays was instantly angry, but her mood had not allowed her to feel fearful. Over the next few weeks, she would often revisit her feelings at that moment without ever developing an adequate explanation for her actions.

Mays drove up the road about 100 yards and then pulled over on the shoulder to allow the Equinox to pass her. But it didn't.

Patch Munson now realized that the black woman was driving to the airport. He wanted to know who she was and where she was heading. He was afraid that she knew he was following her and he didn't know whether or not Hanlon had discussed his confession with her.

When she pulled over to the side of the road, he knew that she had discovered his tail. He made a quick choice and defining decision. It wasn't the first life altering decision that he had made lately, but it was just as bad as the first one.

When Tim Hanlon arrived back at the rectory, he knew that he was no longer *Father* Tim Hanlon. He was offered some time to clean out his belongings, but nearly everything he owned could fit into his Range Rover. He owned no furniture and his wardrobe was sparse beyond his clerical garb. He had a relatively large collection of woman's jewelry that had belonged to his mother, but that took up little space. The same could be said for the six watches that he had inherited from his father. Hanlon wasn't aware of the exact amount of money that he had in his investment accounts, but he knew it was in excess of $14 million. He remembered that number vaguely from the probate proceedings that took place nine years earlier. His portfolio had been invested in a balanced and non aggressive fashion geared toward preserving the principal. All of his accounts were now handled electronically. Once a year his lawyer and his accountant, two older friends that he had also inherited from his parents, filed his taxes and gave him a thorough written report of his holdings. He never looked at it, even when his advisors asked him whether or not he wanted to make charitable disbursements. He simply instructed them to donate 25% of his annual investment income to the same charities that they themselves endowed.

Hanlon didn't plan on wasting any time at the rectory with prolonged goodbyes. His most recent conversation with the pastor, Father George Goethe, was terse. Goethe had been absolutely horrified when he had learned about Carol Mays and her son Russell. Hanlon merely felt sorry for Goethe, and his lack of understanding. But none of that mattered now. The only thing he could think about was joining Carol and Russ in New York in a few days. After that he would play it one day at a time. Carol had only been gone for half an hour but he missed her already. As he was getting out of his Range Rover to go into the rectory, he left his cell phone in the vehicle. He was four steps away when he heard it ring. By the time he grabbed it, the call had gone to voice mail. He picked up Carol Mays message and decided that he would be in and out of the rectory in time to call her back before she boarded the plane. He felt like he was already flying above the clouds.

Carol Mays couldn't believe that this dreadful looking man had the audacity to pull over behind her on the dirt shoulder of the highway. Her anger spilled over and she got out and walked rapidly back to confront the man behind her. When she got to his driver side window, she suddenly froze. The man had a Colt 38 handgun pointed up from his lap right at her face as he said, "Hush up and do as *Ah* say *iffin yew eveh* want to see *yer* son *alahve* again."

"What are you talking about? Where is Russell? What have you done to him?

"*Jes'* do what *Ah* tell *yew an'* no *one'll git* hurt. *Iffin yew* make one false move *Ah'll* shoot *yew* and we'll shoot Russell also." Munson thought that reusing this woman's son's name would gain him some credibility. He was right.

Carol Mays was paralyzed. She didn't scream or dare do anything that could cause this crazy man to do something terrible. *Where is my son? And what are they doing to him?* These were the only thoughts she had.

"Now *git* back to *yer* car *an'* bring *meh yer* cell phone. Then *git inna* car *an' drahve t'* the airport. Yew can leave *yer* car in the lot, but don't do *no talkin' t'* no one. *Ah'm gunna* follow *yew an'* then *yer'll git* in *mah* car. *Gat* it?"

She walked back to her car, retrieved her cell phone and handed it through the window of the Equinox.

"What have you done with Russell? Why are you doing this?"

"Hush up *an' drahve* to the airport. When *yew git* in here *wit' meh*, we'll talk *'bout yer* boy."

The tiny regional airport was only three miles away and Mays didn't know what to do. However overwhelming fear for her son's safety caused her to comply with the instructions she had been given. She drove shakily to the airport car rental lot and then walked from the lot to the area where the Equinox had pulled over and was waiting. Everything was very compact at the airport and the Equinox was only 50 feet away. When she got up to the car she could see that the scruffy looking man was once again pointing his gun at her. He told her to go back to the car and get her bags as if this had been a last minute thought. Once again she complied with his directive and got both her handbag and her overnight roller bag. When she re-approached the Equinox the weird looking man was still glaring at her as though he were trying to decide what to do next. Finally he told her that he wanted her to drive.

Mays stepped into the driver's seat as her captor climbed over to the passenger side while still keeping the gun trained on her.

Munson acted like he knew what he was doing but it was just a performance. He now had a prisoner but he had no idea what to do with her. All he knew was that he wanted to leave the airport roadside immediately.

"*Jes' drahve,*" he said.

"Where?" she asked.

"Head south *fur* now." They pulled out heading south along County Road 37. Munson's mind was going a mile a minute but every idea he had was a bad one.

When he finished interviewing Hawk Richter, Detective Kanasani had one more interview to complete on the BITSY campus. His partner, Detective Loretta Chambers, had been running down administrative leads. She joined Kanasani for the interview with Melech Katz.

"I know that you've already discussed the Clinton shootings with our colleagues at some length, so we appreciate your willingness to help us out with the Fein investigation also." Kanasani started the interview in his normal non-threatening manner.

"Honestly, I don't know what the right thing to do is anymore. I've tried to be cooperative, but some things start me thinking about stuff I'd rather forget."

"Are you speaking about the Clinton mess? If so let me say that I think your actions were heroic. There was no compelling reason for you to take on a heavily armored assassin and risk your own life the way that you did." Chambers uncharacteristically jumped into the interview. She wanted to express her opinions for personal reasons as well as professional reasons. She had seen some of the debate on TV about Katz' encounter with Joseph Clinton. The idea that some were questioning his heroism was appalling to her. Katz could have easily said that Clinton fired at him first. There was no one else on the rooftop at that point who could have disputed the sequence of events. The fact that Katz stopped further carnage by a mass murderer was all the proof of heroism Chambers needed.

"I'd rather not go back over the rooftop events. You said you wanted to talk about the Fein shooting. I don't know how I can help with that. However I'm willing to try."

"It's certainly a long shot, but we're searching for some synergies between the two events on that awful Thursday evening. We came over to see Professor Richter because he has a financial interest in the Fein Center and of course he lectures here at BITSY. Do you know him?"

"Hawk Richter is very well known, and I have a passing acquaintance with him here on campus. I'm not sure if he knows who I am."

"Everyone knows who you are now, Professor Katz. You're a brave man who risked his life to stop a mass murderer. Let me echo Chamber's sentiments on that matter while I have the chance.

"I guess it's true that people know who I am now. I'm just not comfortable thinking of things that way. I'm normally a more reserved person. Frankly, I'm not what you call a people person. I took the job here at the university to try to get past some of that, but it hasn't worked out that well."

"I'm sorry to hear that." Chambers was angry but not at Katz. Then Kanasani retook the lead on the interview.

"Professor Katz … I am an American Muslim and I am well aware of the hideous events that keep Jews and Muslims at war in the Middle East. Answers are elusive, and I don't pretend to possess one. I know that you served as a field officer in the IDF. I also know that you have your green card and have now established your residency here in the US on your pathway to citizenship. All that matters to me is that you saved many lives when you stopped Joseph Clinton. For some reason it seems that it's heroes like you who are called upon again and again. It's almost as though Allah … or God if you like … calls upon those who are strongest to handle the deepest crises. I hope that you continue your work here at the university. Our young people need role models like you."

Katz simply shrugged his shoulders and glared blankly at first one and then the other of the two detectives. He was thinking about the many lives he had terminated in Gaza. He didn't feel like a hero, and if he was an instrument of God's will, it certainly was bizarre to hear that viewpoint from the voice of an American Muslim. There just had to be a better way. But he didn't know what that was anymore than Kanasani did. He turned his thoughts back to the present and finally said, "So what can I do to help?"

For the next 10 minutes Kanasani, asked Melech Katz more questions about Hawk Richter, about attitudes on campus regarding abortion and whether or not Katz believed there was any remote possibility of a tie in between the two crimes on Terrifying Thursday. He also relayed the fact that Clinton had used the term Murder Incorporated in his manifesto. However no new substantive information emerged from the interview. Kanasani thanked Katz for his time and they left the campus.

"I don't understand why we interviewed Katz. He had nothing whatsoever that he could offer to us with respect to the Fein murder." Loretta Chambers was trying to learn from her mentor, Ismail Kanasani.

"I know. But we were here on campus anyway, and I simply wanted the opportunity to show this guy our support. According to our guys working the BITSY case, Katz has been suffering posttraumatic stress disorder since he left the war zone several years ago. Then that jackass, Brady, up in New York stirs up a controversy and this guy could be suffering a relapse. It just didn't seem fair to me. By the way, I was happy that you led off with your support. It made things easier for me."

"You mean to tell me that you knew he wouldn't be able to offer anything on the Fein matter, and the only reason we interviewed him was to pat him on the back for gunning down Clinton?"

"Yeah, something like that."

"Well maybe we could have gotten lucky and he could have surprised us with some insight that we hadn't thought about."

"Possibly … if you need that for justification …"

"No I don't need it. Katz is a hero. The man took out a domestic terrorist. He should have our support."

"Your OJT is going just fine, Detective Chambers…."

Patch Munson was beside himself with self loathing. He was mentally kicking himself for making multiple reckless decisions. First he foolishly took it upon himself to kill Aaron Fein as retribution for Fein's killing of innocent babies. Then, overcome by guilt, he made asinine decision number two. He confessed the murder to a Catholic priest. Idiotic decision number three was kidnapping the priest's black girl friend, fiancé, or whatever she was. Now he had just made dim-witted decision number four. Having no idea what to do with this woman after he kidnapped her, he brought her home to the residential house on his farm. His wife had already left for the shore with his sisters and the house was empty when they got there. Another disconcerting touch was added to the unfolding drama. Right before they arrived at his house the skies had opened up in a torrential downpour complete with lightning and thunder, just the way it happened on the night he shot Aaron Fein. There was something very eerie about this coincidence that unnerved the chicken farmer.

As he sat across from Mays in the living room of his own house, Patch Munson once again had an attack of the *queasies*. He felt the familiar sinking feeling in his gut. Meanwhile he was terrifying his prisoner while he brandished his unlicensed handgun in her face. She was sitting on his living room couch sobbing noisily and uncontrollably. Every time Munson raised the gun to silence Mays by threatening to shoot her, he realized that he couldn't murder her in cold blood. She wasn't Aaron Fein, and she hadn't done anything wrong enough to warrant such a penalty. He told himself that, *screwin'* a priest *mahght* have been a grievous transgression in the eyes of The Church but it *wudden' lahke* she was *murderin'* babies. He decided to threaten her one more time.

"Stop *cryin'*. Stop *cryin'* or *yew'll neveh* see Russell again."

Carol Mays didn't know what kind of a mad man she was dealing with, but in a bizarre way, the threat to Russell suddenly didn't seem real. The tone of her captor's voice had lost its venomous bite almost as if he was now unsure what he was doing. Normally she might never pick up such a subtle innuendo so quickly, but her mind was totally focused in this moment of extreme danger. Instinctively she stopped her loud crying and lowered her voice to a conversational tone. Intuitively she realized that she needed to gather information rapidly if she was going to survive this ordeal and keep her son safe.

"Please don't hurt my son. Please don't. I'll do whatever you want. Just please don't hurt my son."

"That's *betteh*." Munson didn't know what else to say. However he kept the gun loosely pointed at Mays while he tried to think quickly.

"Tell me you won't hurt Russell. Please, please, just don't hurt my son." Many things went through her mind. Now she thought that it wasn't Tim Hanlon that this mad man was pursuing, after all. The man was actually following Carol Mays! Why? Why? Why? It didn't make any sense. What did he want? Was it money? Was it sex? Was it something else? She determined that she would give him whatever he wanted as long as he didn't hurt her son. She repressed the urge to begin crying again. Then she simply repeated her entreaty. "Please don't hurt Russell."

"*Jes'* hush up. Hush up *an'* let *meh thaank.*" He raised the gun again and pointed it directly at her face. Thirty seconds went by in absolute silence. The gun began to feel heavy and Munson lowered it to his lap again. However he kept it aimed generally at Mays who was sitting about six feet away from him.

Carol Mays was in excellent physical condition. Although she was very light for her height, she had muscles that were nearly invisible but rock hard nonetheless. Her daily workout regimen back in New York was one that kept her body tight, taut, and shapely. But it also allowed her to keep her strength up. She mentally calculated the distance between her captor and herself and she reasoned that she might be able to overwhelm him with some quick movement. The man was heavyset and fleshy looking and she already knew that he moved rather slowly. But again she concluded that she needed information. Finally Munson spoke again.

"*Ah* won't hurt *yer* boy *iffin yew* cooperate." It was a concession of sorts and Mays was tentatively glad to hear it.

"Where is Russell? Can I see him? And what did you do to Jude?"

Munson felt like asking, *"Who is Jude?"* But he knew this would be a tactical mistake so he never asked the question. Instead he re-pointed his weapon and provided no answer to her question. "*Jes'* hush the hell up."

Mays' mind was racing. She could see that her question about Jude had perplexed her captor. *Maybe this oaf is bluffing. Maybe he doesn't have Russell.* Her spirits lifted temporarily. But then she realized that she couldn't take that chance. She still needed to know more. She needed to know for sure that Russell was safe.

Munson's mind was calculating also. *Ah cain't let this woman go. Ah've kidnapped her. An' togetheh, she an' Hanlon alreadeh know too much. If they piece togetheh what they know, Ah'll be arrested fur murder and kidnappin'. Ah've alreadeh killed one person. Ah mahght have to kill another whetheh Ah want to or not.* Even as this logic stream flowed through his mind, Munson again told himself that he couldn't kill the black woman. She simply hadn't committed a capital offense.

"Look *iffin yew* want *t'* see Russell again, it's *goin' t'* take a *lit'le tahme an' yew* need to cooperate." Munson knew that his poker hand didn't even hold two of a kind, but he kept bluffing because the handgun he held in his poker hand was his wild card.

"Whatever you want … just let me see my son."

"Soon *'nough* … now stand up *an'* keep *yer* arms folded *'cross yer titties*." Munson had already stood up and was once again brandishing his weapon. "Now walk into the kitchen *slowleh an' remembeh Ah'm rahght behahnd yew* so keep *yer* arms folded."

Carol Mays didn't feel the hard punch to the back of her neck until she woke up on the kitchen floor, with her hands tightly wired behind her back. She was now lying on her back and her tormentor was straddling her body and sitting on her stomach. He held her head in his hands and was rapidly wrapping duct tape around her face completely covering her mouth. Panic began to set into Mays' brain. She thought she couldn't breathe at all. The splitting headache she experienced allowed her to know that she was still alive. Then she passed out again.

VI

The Bomb Shelter

P atch Munson looked around the main bomb shelter. One of the two fallout shelters on the Munson farm had been left in semi ruin for the last twenty years, but the shelter nearest to the house had been intermittently cared for by Patch Munson and his now deceased father. However the shelter was never meant to serve as a prison and Munson thought that he might have some work to do before he would be able to move his prisoner to this spot. A quick survey of the place led him to consider the fact that it just might have to do. He didn't know how long he would have to keep the black woman in the bomb shelter, because he didn't yet have a plan. *That's mah problem*, he thought. *Ah jes' neveh have a play'un.*

Unlike his son, Junior Munson had a plan for everything before he died. Junior had premeditated everything in life and even bought the family grave sites with enough plots for all of his children and his lone daughter-in-law. He took the same approach to the construction of the bomb shelters. When Junior Munson originally designed the shelter he took in the normal considerations of ventilation; access to deep well water with an appropriate pumping system; access to electricity with a backup generator and storage area for more than six weeks' worth of canned food and bottled water. He also made accommodations for alternative liquid refreshment and a hybrid composting toilet system that used a minimal amount of water, and had an alternative outlet to a nearby deep seated septic system. He added central air-conditioning in the mid-eighties and ran electrical wiring from a small solar energy panel system that also helped power the electricity for the main farmhouse.

The concrete walls to the outer barrier of the shelter were buried between eight and eighteen feet deep below the surface level of the Munson farm. The farm was east and slightly south of the regional airport. The surrounding area had an elevation of almost 180 feet, which was a good bit higher than the 10 feet elevation on Water Street in downtown Mobile. Therefore water seepage at the bottom of the bomb shelter was not a major concern when the shelter was originally constructed. However as a precaution there was a sump pump system that was installed in the shelter that reached another three feet below the thick concrete flooring. The shelter itself was generously spacious as these structures go with more than 350 square feet of floor surface space, partitioned into three separate areas including the 5ft by 5ft makeshift bathroom facility that also housed the sump pump. The walls inside the other two partitions of the shelter were lined with shelving, which for the most part protruded inward between 8 and 18 inches depending upon the wall. This primitive storage facility precluded any large framed paintings, wall mounted lighting or other such decorations. The one exception to this was a built-in locked cabinet that enclosed some of the Munson family's weapons. Just outside of this cabinet there was a cheaply framed picture of Junior Munson and Patch Munson holding hunting rifles. Adjacent to this weapon cabinet were two of the four ventilation passage ways that led up and out into the citrus grove area of the farm.

Over the many years that the bomb shelter had been in existence, it had never been visited by anyone. Patch and Junior Munson had done all of the work on the shelter by themselves with some help from two of the farm hands who had predeceased Junior Munson. Gloria and Marjorie knew about the shelters but had never been in either of them. Maggie Munson also knew about the shelter but had not even discussed it with her husband in more than 10 years. For the most part the shelter had been a private refuge for Patch and Junior Munson. The women of the Munson family knew that the Munson men stored some of their weapons in the shelter. They also imagined that there was an ample store of whiskey in the shelter, but of course, this was never discussed. The Munson women simply knew that the shelter was not a place for them to go for any reason.

There was a second bomb shelter on the farm, and it was not nearly as well appointed. Patch Munson was never quite sure why this other shelter existed at all, but he believed that his father had intended it to be a decoy shelter of some sort. With all of the jabbering that Junior Munson had done in the seventies about the need for protection from a nuclear attack, he needed to have something to show the few curious souls who were intrigued or even mesmerized by his paranoia. The second shelter had been neglected for almost twenty years.

Munson didn't want to leave his prisoner alone in the house for too long. She was securely restrained, and was being watched by Harry who would surely begin to bark if she began to move about vigorously. Still Patch knew he would have to move her soon. He climbed the ladder out of the shelter. Munson had already removed the lock and handle from the underside of the doorway and double-checked and reconfigured the top side handle. Now the door could only be unlocked from the antechamber.

As he stood on top of the concrete ceiling of the bomb shelter, he was still eight feet below the surface level of the farm. He and his father referred to this earthen area as the antechamber to the shelter. He pulled the ladder through the ceiling door of the bomb shelter and shoved it beneath the loose brush in the antechamber that had been pushed between the concrete ceiling of the shelter and the 10 foot long wooden bridge platform at the top of the antechamber near the surface level of the farm. The wooden bridge served as an ersatz lid to the earthen antechamber. Some of the ventilation duct system as well as some heavily sheathed electrical wiring, also snaked its way through this loose eight foot high pile of brush in the antechamber. However the steep makeshift earth and stone stairway was still in good enough shape for Munson to climb up to the top and exit through the four foot by six foot trap door in the bridge. Therefore he didn't need the ladder which was always left in the antechamber. When he got back to the surface, Munson grabbed the rake that had been left nearby and re-covered the wooden bridge and its upper trap door with some of the surrounding brush. Munson and his father had performed this same ritual of obscuring the antechamber and bomb shelter many times over the years. Patch Munson was glad that his father had been a planner.

Tim Hanlon nearly had an accident when he discovered why his calls to Carol Mays had gone unanswered. Getting bad news through the media about someone you love has a certain surreal feel to it. It's as though it's a fictitious story and that if you turn off the media outlet you will close out the story. Now it was Wednesday evening, a little more than 48 hours since he had said goodbye to Carol Mays in the parking lot of the Colonial Mall, back in Mobile. Since then he had driven nearly 1000 miles on his way up north. He was still nearly 200 miles from his ultimate destination in New York City. After hearing the radio news report indicating that "supermodel Carol Mays has been reported missing under suspicious circumstances," Hanlon felt panicky. *What in God's name is going on?*

Hanlon pulled off of Interstate 81 near Martinsburg, West Virginia. He knew he needed to make some phone calls even though he wasn't sure who to call first. He needed to clear his mind in a hurry.

Hanlon traced back over the last 48 hours of relative solitude. On Monday night it took him a little longer than he had planned to get out of the rectory. He had tried to call Mays on her cell phone two or three times before her flight was scheduled to take off, but he only got her voice mail. He checked his phone and saw that four texts on Monday also went unanswered. His original plan had been to drive through Alabama on Monday night and get as far north as he could go. However his late start, his inability to contact Mays and the horrible Alabama storm led to unexpected fatigue. He stopped for the night at a hotel just outside of Birmingham, Alabama. He tried to call Mays one more time before falling asleep. Hanlon got up Tuesday morning and his cell phone battery was totally discharged. He couldn't find his charger right away, so he decided that he would call Mays from the Range Rover once he got back on the road. He was famished however and so he had a huge breakfast before leaving the hotel at about 8:45 AM. All day Tuesday, he drove north along the interstate highway system stopping at Abingdon, Virginia for the night. Tuesday had been a positive day for Hanlon. He was alone with God in a way that he hadn't experienced in some time.

But first his thoughts went back again to Monday. *What a wonderful day!* Monday had been the first day since his ordination that he hadn't said Mass. He also hadn't read the Liturgy of the Hours from his breviary. Monday afternoon with Carol had been exquisite. Later, he didn't think of anything besides leaving Mobile and going to New York to be with his lover and their son.

But then Tuesday was a extraordinary day. He was finally beginning to feel like a lay person. Again there was no Mass and no breviary. But his day was not without prayer. He prayed for understanding of God's will. His worries mounted, however, when his continuous calls to Carol went unanswered as he drove north. He stopped calling at about 10:30 in the morning. He knew that Carol had to be at work after taking Monday off. She was obviously busy. He suddenly thought of himself as a foolish high school boy. It had been less than 24 hours since he had seen his lover and he had called her more than a dozen times. *She loves me, but she has a job and a life beyond the afternoon delight that we shared on Monday. She'll call me when she's free.* His thoughts turned back to God. The rest of the drive on Tuesday he satisfied himself with introspection about his relationship with God. He was convinced that an all knowing and loving God was serving as a "Guiding Hand," as his life was beginning to twist and turn in new directions. Mostly he felt an inner happiness and a sense of excitement. There also was a very slight tinge of trepidation that he thought was probably related to his lack of contact with Mays.

Wednesday was a different day. He tried not to be worried about things. He arranged to rent a storage unit for his belongings in New Jersey. His plan was to stop there and unload on Thursday morning and then head into the city to be with Carol and Russ shortly thereafter. He was also deciding on the fly where he would stay the next two nights and he was making hotel reservations accordingly.

Hanlon kept his mind occupied working these details on the phone as he drove. But he was growing concerned enough to check on Mays' airline flights. She should have boarded in Mobile, and flown to Charlotte, changed planes and then flown back to New York. Both flights had arrived on time, so he presumed that things were okay. That's when he heard the news cast on the radio. He couldn't believe his ears. He had originally planned on making it to New Jersey by Wednesday night, but now as he pulled over in Martinsburg, he was confused. Should he continue on to East Rutherford, New Jersey where he had his hotel reservation and where the self-storage unit was located, or should he turn around and head back toward Mobile for some unknown reason. It was still only 7 PM. He decided to find a hotel right near where he was so that he could make multiple phone calls and gather whatever other information there was on radio, television and the internet. He was scared.

"This is Kenneth Brady and you are watching *The Brady Focus.* Tonight we are following a breaking story involving supermodel Carol Mays. She has been reported missing under suspicious circumstances. Some of you may remember Mays from her appearance in the Sports Illustrated Swimsuit Issue three years back and others may know her from some commercial work she has done as a spokesperson for the The Rhapsody Lifestyle Centers. Ms Mays is well known here in New York throughout the fashion industry. Her good friend and business associate, Jude Royale is with us in the studio tonight to appeal to anyone who might know something about Ms. Mays' disappearance to call the police and offer their input as soon as possible. Good evening Mr. Royale."

"Good evening, Kenneth. I hope that one or more of your viewers may be able to help us out." He sniffled back a tear as he spoke. "I'm very worried about Carol. It is not like her at all to be out of touch with her son. She would have called if she had an emergency and was delayed for some reason. I'm concerned that the only reason she hasn't called is because she can't."

"So let's set the stage for our viewers, Mr. Royale. You're a close personal friend of Ms. Mays and she asked you to watch her son over the last weekend."

"Yes that's right."

"And the reason for Ms. Mays' trip to Alabama was to see an old college friend. She was scheduled to return on Monday night and apparently never made her flight. Is that correct? And also do you know the name of this old college friend?"

"Yes, we now believe that she never left Mobile Alabama on her flight to New York that included a stopover and change of planes in Charlotte. But it took the police 24 hours to categorize this as a missing person case. Somehow or other they originally believed that she had made her flight out of Mobile. Now they are saying she never left Mobile."

"And what about the college friend that she was visiting?"

"Over the past several hours the police have been pursuing that lead vigorously. However for the time being they have asked me not to disclose this person's name. They will probably make that disclosure shortly themselves. I'm trying to cooperate. The police know that I'm reaching out to the media, but I think that they would rather that I waited another 24 hours."

"Is this college friend male or female?"

Royale hesitated and then answered, "Male."

"We know that the police require twenty-four hours before a person can be declared missing. There are reasons for this. Many times there is domestic disharmony, or for one reason or another, the missing person turns up and there is no crime that the police need to be involved in. If the police got involved every time a cheating husband didn't make the family dinner, they'd never get anything done. But you say that this case is different. Explain to us why you believe that Ms. Mays may have been some sort of victim."

"I've known Carol Mays for almost seven years. She is the consummate professional. She takes her work seriously. The only thing more important to Carol than her work is her son, Russ. She had an important meeting with this college friend over the weekend. But she called Russ on Friday night after she reached Mobile. She called again on Saturday and twice on Sunday. She called early Monday morning and said that she would call again when she got to the airport. We never heard from her after that Monday morning call. By 10 PM on Monday night I knew that something must be wrong. I called the police. They said that her cell phone could have died, or something like that could be the cause. They also said that they often found out that some people party too much and others just run into Mr. Right and spend the night. They said it happens all the time."

"I'm sure it does. So let me ask you again, Mr. Royale: Why is Carol Mays different? What makes you believe that she is a victim and not just someone who got her life off track for a couple of days?"

"Carol Mays doesn't do drugs. She has an occasional glass of wine, but I've never seen her have more than two. She is a remarkably centered person, who is responsible, reasonable and reliable. The fact that she hasn't called her son tells me an awful lot. I'm sure this is the longest time she has ever gone without speaking to Russ. And Russ has a birthday coming up this weekend. He will be eight years old."

"So let's go back to this male college friend. What is he to Carol Mays? And while you think about how you want to answer that question, ponder this one also. Who is Russ' father? Are we talking about one and the same man?"

"That is one of the leads that the police are looking into right now."

"So is it safe to say that Ms. Mays has not always been the 'responsible, reasonable and reliable' person that you have made her out to be. As I understand it Ms. Mays is an unmarried mother, and has been since the birth of her son. Is that correct?"

"Carol Mays has never married. That's right."

"Listen, Mr. Royale, with all due respect, sir. If you want to help your friend, Ms. Mays, it would be much more beneficial to all involved if you were more forthcoming with what you know and don't know about this case. I understand that this is an open police investigation. But you have millions of viewers watching you at this moment.

Someone out there may be able to help." Brady shook his head from side to side to show his frustration for the benefit of his viewing audience and then added, "We just have another minute and then we have to move on to the other segments of this evening's program. In the last 45 seconds or so tell us what you can about the Mays matter. And by the way, is her son safe and protected at this time?"

"Yes. We have no reason to believe Russ is in any danger. He is being taken care of this evening by his maternal grandfather who arrived in New York this afternoon. None of us have heard from Carol since Monday. I will also tell you that you're correct in assuming that Russ' father is someone the police are looking to speak with. As I understand it he is also missing."

"The name ... Mr. Royale ... the name. You want to help your friend Carol, don't you?" Brady made one last appeal to get a scoop. Royale bit at his upper lip with his lower teeth and then gave Brady more than he expected.

"He is a Catholic priest by the name of Tim Hanlon."

Tim Hanlon checked into the hotel and immediately called Mays cell phone three more times. Her voice mail was at capacity and he was unable to leave a message. Mays had not given him a phone number for Jude Royale, but when he put his phone down to turn on the television, it rang and the name on the viewer indicated that the caller was the pastor, Father Goethe, calling from Mobile. He didn't want to deal with that man right now so he let the message go to cover. He wondered which police department would be covering Mays disappearance and who he might call to see if he could help out.

Next he fired up in his laptop and put in the name Carol Mays and there were several brand new posts citing her disappearance. The oldest "disappearance" entry had been posted only two hours earlier. The most recent post was two minutes old. It said that police in Alabama were trying to locate a "person of interest," who is rumored to be a Catholic priest. There was an 800 number offered for anyone who had information about Mays to call. Hanlon was shaking. He was very concerned about his lover. He remembered that she had been alarmed by the man at Oak Mountain State Park. She believed that this man had been following them. Could this man possibly have harmed Carol? Was he the same person that had killed Aaron Fein? What would his motive be for harming Carol? He didn't have ready answers for these questions. He felt sick and panic stricken. Hanlon picked up his phone and called the 800 number.

"*Hatline. Cain Ah* have *yer* name *an'* the location *yer callin'* from.*"* The male voice was firm and attentive.

"This is Tim Hanlon and I'm calling about the disappearance of Carol Mays."

"Hey, Father Hanlon. We've been *hopin'* that *yew'd* call. *Cain yew* give us *yer* location please?" The firm voice of the hotline sounded very business-like. It was also obvious that the hotline voice knew that he was a priest and probably knew that he had been with Carol Mays on Monday.

"I'm in West Virginia, I think." His voice was tentative shaky and scared. "What has happened to Carol?"

"We were *hopin'* that *yew* could tell us *'bout* that, Father Hanlon. Where in West Virginia are *yew at?* Are *yew* alone?"

"I want to know what has happened to Carol. By the way, who am I talking to?"

"This is Officer Bubba Looney *wit'* the Mobile *Po'lice. Yer* call *t'* our 800 *hatline* service came *t'mah* desk *'cause Ah'm runnin' wit'* the MPR on Carol Mays." The voice began to sound slightly more genial now that the police officer had identified himself. But Hanlon missed the exaggerated air of self-importance that went along with it. "Please answer the question *'bout* where *yer* at, Father Hanlon." Bubba Looney was fighting off the remnants of a hangover that made long conversations difficult. But now he was much more interested in the fact that he was talking to the person that everyone else was trying to find.

"I'm in a Best Western Hotel right off Interstate 81 just over the border in West Virginia. Now please what can you tell me about Carol?"

"As *Ah* said, *Ah'm runnin' wit'* the *missin'* person's report. It was *fahled* by a man up in New York who was *watchin'* Mays' kid. We've been *thaankin'* that *yew* may have seen her this past *Mundeh*. That so, Father Hanlon?"

"Yes, I spent most of the day with Carol on Monday." Hanlon was uncomfortable with the fact that the police officer kept calling him Father Hanlon and knew that his answers to these questions were probably going to make him even less comfortable with that salutation. "I last saw her at the Colonial Mall. She dropped me off at my car and then she left for the airport."

"What did *y'all* do *durin'* the day on *Mondeh*?"

Carol Mays was still befuddled, but she was slightly less concerned that her captor was ready to kill her at a moment's notice. She also felt vaguely more secure about the safety of her son. However she was acutely aware that the tenuous stability of her imprisonment could shift rapidly. She believed that she was located in a hallway on an upper floor of the house that she had been brought to on Monday night, but she couldn't be sure of that. Her hands were now handcuffed in front of her, and her feet were shackled together, but this facet of her bondage had been getting progressively less onerous over the two days of her capture. Monday night her hands had been tightly wired behind her back. Sometime on Tuesday morning, her dumpy looking jailer showed up again and removed the wire binding after he had replaced it with handcuffs that appeared to be brand new, as the silvery sheen of the metal was unmarked. On Wednesday morning, the man observed that his captive was in severe pain and had passed in and out of consciousness on several occasions. He accommodated her discomfort slightly by moving the handcuffs to the front of her body. He had also cut a small feeding hole in the tape that was wrapped around her face. This also enabled her to breathe more easily, but she was still not able to talk. He warned her not to remove the tape now that her hands were in front of her body. If she did so he would redo the tape and cuff her behind her back once again.

"Do *yew* need to use the bathroom?" It was a bizarre question, that probably only came about because her captor could smell the urine spillage that had already occurred. He had obviously not thought about that aspect of the imprisonment. Mays was sitting on the floor up against one wall, and her legs were not only shackled together at the ankles but heavily wrapped in a tow chain that had two separate padlocks to make mobility nearly impossible, especially in her weakened state. Part of the chain was wrapped around the top stairway post in the hallway. The stairway led to the room where she was originally held before she was knocked unconscious.

Mays didn't know how long she had been in captivity. But she could recall that twice she had been offered liquid refreshment through a straw that was inserted through the tape around her mouth. The first time it was just water, and the second time it was chicken soup and water. She had nothing substantial to eat, but she consumed as much of the soup and water as her subjugator would allow realizing that she would eventually need as much strength as she could muster. The drinking had led to a urinary release sometime during her second day of captivity. Fortunately she had felt no urge to defecate, as she had been literally scared shitless.

After these thoughts ran rapidly through her mind, she nodded her head in the affirmative to her captor's inquiry.

Munson stared at Mays for about a minute or so trying to think through the logistics of the liberty he was about to offer. He had his handgun nearby at all times, more as a show of force than in expectation of use. He had made so many bad decisions lately that now he wanted to be more deliberate in his thought process. Finally he decided to remove enough of the tape on Mays' face, to allow her to talk. Besides the need to remedy the immediate hygienic issue, he needed to know much more about his captive in a hurry. He was certain that someone would soon start looking for her. He also worried that with all of the stormy weather, his wife and sisters might leave the shore earlier than planned.

"Alright. Here's what we are *gunna* do. *Ah'm gunna he'p yew git* to the bathroom *an' Ah'm gunna* take *sem o* the tape from *'round yer* mouth. *Iffin ya* yell or even talk *'bove* a *whispeh, Ah'm gunna* whip *yew wit'* this gun *'til yew* hush up *fur* good. *Yew git* it?"

She nodded her head again in affirmation. Then Munson used a pocket knife to cut some of the tape from near her mouth, so that she could now stretch her mouth open all the way. A guttural noise that sounded like, "euhnneuh" came forth from her mouth and lungs as she was able to breathe in deeper and stretch her mouth somewhat normally for the first time in nearly 48 hours.

"*Yew* need to go *rahght* away?"

"Yes." It was her first word in day and a half.

"First *Ah* need *t'* know *sem* more *'bout yew* than *Ah alreadeh* do." Munson was determined not to let her know how little he knew about her. "*Ah* want *yew* to tell *meh yer* whole name *'cludin' yer* middle name *an' aneh* aliases *yew* have *eveh* used. *An' Ah* want the same *info'mation fur yer* son. *Ah* also want *t'* know what *yer* relationship is *wit'* the priest, that guy Hanlon. And then *Ah* have *sem* more questions."

Mays mind was calculating. *Doesn't this man know who I am? Is he some religious zealot who is worried that I'm stealing Tim away from The Church? What should I tell him and what should I hold back?* She wanted to think about her answer.

"I promise I will tell you everything you want to know. But can I please use the bathroom first? I need to go urgently."

Munson didn't have the fortitude to suppress her request. He was also surprised by her use of the word "urgently" and the general tone and inflection of her voice. It was a southern accent, but a refined one of some sort, not a southern Alabama accent, an educated tone maybe. *Damn*, he thought, *Ah went an' caught meh an uppity niggeh.* He also had a logistical problem. He allowed the bathroom issue to take precedence over his request for immediate answers to his questions. Mays was still wearing the khaki shorts and black t-top from Monday night. But her clothes were stained with sweat and urine.

"*Ah'm gunna* undo the leg chains but we're *gunna* keep *yer* ankle bracelets in place. Then let's walk *o'er* to the bathroom. *Ah 'm fixin' t'* let *yew* go in there *bah yerse'f*, but *yew hafta* leave the door open. *Ah* won't be *lookin'* or *nuthin.'* But *Ah ain't takin' no* chances *neitheh. Yew jes'* do *yer* business and *git* back out here on the floor. We *togetheh* on that?" He started removing the chains before she answered, slightly showing signs of weakness.

"Yes, all right. But can't we close the door, just for a minute." She wanted to see if she could push him for continuous concessions.

"No." He stopped unraveling the chains and looked at her.

"Okay. Just hurry." She continued to give directions in an attempt to take control.

The ensuing trip to the restroom was a relief for Mays for a few different reasons. However in her weakened condition she wasn't processing intellectually the way she wanted to, while she was gaining a modicum of physical relief. The agreed upon "minute" stretched to almost five minutes before Munson's patience ran thin.

"*Yew* done in there yet?"

"Yes." She almost complained about having to redress with her damp shorts, but she worried that the options were few and less appealing. She redressed herself and walked back into the hallway and sat down once again with the same questions running through her mind. *What kind of man is this? What does he want? Does he really have Russell? What does he intend to do with me?* Her captor made no immediate attempt to rewrap her legs with the tow chain.

"Now answer *mah* questions."

"My name is Carol Mays."

"What else?"

"What do you mean?"

"Don't play stupid. What *'bout* the priest?"

"Tim Hanlon is a friend of mine."

"What *kahnd* of friend."

"Just a casual friend … We've known each other for a while. There's nothing personal between us. As you know, he's a priest."

"Tell the truth and shame the devil," Munson snarled the snarky southern expression meaning, *"You're lying."*

"What's your name? I told you mine."

"*Ah'll* ask the questions. *Yew jes'* give the answers."

"Look I'm under your control. If you don't want to tell me your name, then what do you want me to call you?" She was emboldened by the fact that her captor was even debating any of this with her. Surprisingly she was making some progress.

"*Jes'* call *meh*, Patch. Almost *ever'un* calls *meh* Patch."

"What do you want from me, Patch? What've I done to you?"

"*Ah* said that *Ah'm askin'* the questions. Now *yew* best start *tellin' meh* the truth *'bout* Hanlon. And remember, we *gat yer* kid. Now *Ah* know that *yew* been *hidin'* out *wit'* Hanlon *so's* folks won't know he's been *screwin'* a darkie, when he *ain't s'posed t'* be *screwin' no one*." Munson tried to get tougher and ironically he wanted her to make a confession.

"So now tell *meh*, where *'xactly* do *yew* live and where were *yew* headin'* on the plane?"

It was becoming more apparent that this man, Patch, was bluffing about having her son. He didn't even know she was from New York. But she still couldn't take any chances. She confirmed what he already knew hoping that his reaction would reveal more about his motives.

"You're right. Tim Hanlon and I are lovers. He recently confessed this fact to the bishop and he will be leaving the priesthood. There does that satisfy your curiosity? But tell me why that concerns you, Patch?"

Munson knew that he would never answer this question. Besides why was she still asking questions?

"*Ah ain't goin'* there."

"What do I have to do to have you set me free and release my son? I don't know what you want from me."

"*Yew cain* start *bah tellin' meh ever'thaan' yew cain 'bout yer lahfe. Ah'll decahde* when *t'* cut *yew* off. *Iffin yew* do a good *'nuff* job in *tellin' yer storeh, Ah'll thaank 'bout tellin' yew* what we're *gunna* do next."

Mays assumed that Patch was not going to be satisfied with just a minimal amount of information, so she decided to comply with his demands, while trying to avoid divulging information that might put her son in danger. But Mays also realized that her captor was making up the rules as he went along.

"I'm 29 years old and I work in New York City. I grew up outside of Birmingham and went to college at Auburn. After I graduated, I moved to New York and began my modeling career."

"That's it? That's the best *yew cain* do?"

"What do you want from me?"

"What *'bout* the kid? What about Russell? Were *yew* married? Are *yew* married now?"

"I've never been married. Tell me about you, Patch. Are you married? Where is your wife?"

"*Yew* don't need *t'* know *'bout meh an' yew* don't need *t'* know *'bout* Maggie. *B'sahdes yew've* seen me *b'faw. Rahght?*"

"Yes you followed me. Why did you follow me?"

"*Ah wudden' followin' yew. Ah* was *followin'* Hanlon."

"Why?"

"*Ah ain't sayin' nuthin' 'bout* that."

"Then why isn't he sitting here in chains instead of me?"

"*Yew* ask too *maneh dang* questions. We're *gunna* stop *talkin'* now *'cause* we're *gunna* move somewhere else. Don't do *nuthin'* stupid when we're *movin'* or *Ah'm gunna* split your skull open." The talk was tough but the tone was tentative.

At least the next part of Munson's plan had been thought through over the past day and a half. He didn't have all of the details down perfectly yet, but he knew that he had to get this woman out of the house and into the fallout shelter. When the ceiling door was shut the bomb shelter was almost soundproof. However Munson worried that his prisoner might be heard if she yelled up through the duct system that egressed in the citrus grove. Now that he had reconfigured the trap door handle, he felt confident that he could lock the room from the outside and leave her inside without worrying that anyone would find her. He'd figure out what to do after that.

"Can you at least tell me what you have done with my son?"

"Well, first *ya hafta* tell *meh* where *yew thaank* he is. Where *didja* see *'im* last?"

Mays recognized this as a dangerous yet promising question. If Russell was still safe with Jude back in New York, then his ongoing security might be compromised by answering the question truthfully. However if she gave a plausible answer she might be able to determine whether or not this Patch person held her son.

"Well Patch, you know that I left Russell with one of my girlfriends up in New York."

After her answer Munson sat silently in deep thought. *Damn! This woman's kid was in New York! She must wonder how Ah gat her kid from up there.* Munson thought back to their conversation from Monday night in the living room. He remembered that this Mays woman had mentioned someone by the name of Jude. He didn't know whether it was a man's name or a woman's name. He didn't know anyone named Jude. It was probably some stupid Yankee name. Then he remembered the Beatles song, "Hey Jude." He thought; *Paul McCartney ain't a faggot ... though yew neveh cain tell 'bout them Brits ... so he musta been singin' that song to a woman.* He decided to answer on a hunch.

"We snatched Russell when *yer* pal Jude *wudden' watchin'*. Now we *gat 'im an'* we're *gunna* keep *'im 'til yew* give us what we want." For all of his tough talk, Patch Munson was confusing himself more by the moment. He had absolutely no idea what he was going to do with this woman and he didn't know what he wanted her to do. But he knew she would ask. He had been hinting that he had accomplices but his inconsistency with this ruse probably made it difficult for Mays to believe. Then he had the same thought that had haunted him for the last few weeks; *how the fuck did Ah git mahse'f in this mess?*

Carol Mays was worried once again. She didn't remember using Jude's name on Monday night, and so she believed that her ruse about a girlfriend apparently had no meaning to this ugly man who was staring at her. But he had given her some hope that she could somehow earn her freedom. She repeated her oft-asked question, "What do you want me to do?"

"*Ah'll* let *yew* know when *Ah decahde.*" It was a stupid confusing answer that perplexed both of them. Then he had another thought about how to get her out of the house and into the bomb shelter. "*Ah* want *yew* to come *wit' meh* to a place *outsahde* the house. Don't do *anythaan'* stupid. Then *yew cain* see Russell."

Julianne Carson was back in Tampa. This time she was staying in the Bayshore Boulevard residence of Hawk Richter. His 120 year old home was directly across from Hillsborough Bay in South Tampa, Florida. It had been substantially rebuilt after the disastrous no-name hurricane of 1921, and had been renovated many times since. This was a common theme for the homes along the boulevard. The homeowners along Bayshore Boulevard included prominent residents of the area, and there were numerous historic houses, in some cases sitting side by side. On one side of the long curving boulevard an architecturally eclectic group of million dollar homes faced the open bay. Across the boulevard an unbroken 4.5 mile walkway, believed to be the work's longest continuous sidewalk, mirrored the arch of the boulevard and separated the roadway from the seawall and the water's edge. The view was spectacular and in spite of the occasional flooding, the homes along the boulevard were still considered trendy and the real estate was still coveted property.

Julianne planned to spend another week's vacation with Richter and then to stay in Tampa the following week while she worked her Florida accounts. After that she intended to return home to California. But she purposely left herself uncommitted to the plan. This was the new Julianne; the lady who could act spontaneously. Over the last few months she had promised herself that she would be more open to the opportunities that life offered her, and she was trying to make good on that promise. Sitting on the south porch of the house, looking at Hillsborough Bay with her laptop open and the news scrolling onto the screen, she felt Hawk Richter shuffle up behind her.

"Did you hear the news? Carol Mays has gone missing and they suspect foul play."

"Who is Carol Mays and what do you mean by foul play?"

"You don't know who Carol Mays is? I thought you knew everything." Julianne stood up and moved beside Richter and tugged gently around his right arm with both of her own arms in a manner that let him know she was teasing.

"Who is she? Someone from pop culture? I am singularly uninterested in that nonsense."

"She's a supermodel in New York. And the news is saying that she may have been kidnapped or worse?"

"What do mean by worse? Killed?"

"Yes, maybe. That would certainly be awful. She is such a nice person."

"You talk as if you know her."

"No. I don't know her. But I've seen her on TV a few times. She is a very spiritual person."

"What is it with you and people that you think are spiritual?"

"I happen to think spirituality is an important part of life. Anyway, Carol Mays collaborated with another writer a couple of years ago and wrote a book about the compatibility of yoga and Christianity."

"Did you read the book?"

"No I haven't read it yet. But it's on my list. And I did see her being interviewed about the book on *Good Morning, America.* She just seems like my kind of woman. She is into Christian meditation and she takes yoga classes several times a week."

"Probably takes the yoga classes as a prerequisite for her employment. Modeling can be very grueling on the body."

"Probably is. But I wish you could see this woman's body. It is gorgeous."

"Bring her around sometime. I'd be happy to give her a feel."

"This isn't funny." Julianne laughed anyway. "It sounds like Carol Mays is in trouble."

"And tell me again why this is so disturbing to you. You said that you don't know her."

"Well I've never met her. But I believe that we have a spiritual connection. I even keep her picture on my refrigerator at home."

"What's that all about?"

"She's a kindred spirit. I have two women's pictures on my refrigerator … both beautiful people. I have a picture of Carol Mays and a picture of Gina Struben. Now don't tell me you don't know who she is."

"No. I know who Struben is. She's the lead singer of the Lay D's. Everyone's heard of her."

"Trust me, most people know who Carol Mays is also."

"You still haven't explained why you have two women's pictures on your refrigerator."

"I just have a connection with these women. They radiate beauty, sophistication and common sense, all at the same time. I relate to their aura, that's all."

"There you go with that word, 'aura' again. I can't measure an aura. Now, can I?"

"That depends." She reached up and kissed him on the cheek. "For a smart man, you've got a lot to learn. Let's go for a walk." Richter and Carson were still dressed in workout attire from their earlier workout at their respective clubs. They had coordinated their workouts to return home before showering because Julianne wanted to walk along the sidewalk by the Bay even if it didn't stop raining. It had been raining all morning and the last few raindrops were bouncing off the street pavement in a light steam, as the sun started to boldly emerge from behind the thinning clouds.

Once they crossed the boulevard to the sidewalk along the Bay, they began to walk at a casual pace with Richter holding on to Julianne's arm for visual support as they avoided the rollerbladers, joggers and cyclers who shared the pavement with them. They also needed to be mindful of the scattered puddles along the way.

About a mile into their walk, Richter couldn't resist going back to their earlier discussion. "You said that you somehow relate to this Mays' woman's aura, and then you told me I had a lot to learn. But you stopped right there. Is that the best you can do to explain what this aura stuff is all about?"

"I'm sure you know that an aura is an energy field that surrounds each of us. But it is not usually something that can be seen, even by those of us who are sighted."

"Yes I have heard these unsubstantiated claims before. But in terms of today's physics, if you can't see it, hear it, smell it, touch it, taste it, or in some way, measure it, it doesn't exist. Therefore to call it an energy field is inappropriate."

"That's rather myopic thinking, even for a blind man. What about odorless gases, like carbon monoxide? You can't smell or see them. They don't usually make a noise, and you wouldn't normally taste or touch them. But carbon monoxide, for example, has been known to kill people in some instances."

"Yes. Of course these things exist but they can be *measured*. Measurement is the key. Just because the human sensory system cannot pick these things up without tools, doesn't mean that they don't exist. That's why we have science to help our minds move beyond our senses. But I have never heard any scientific proof of the measurement of these so-called auras. In fact this aura concept seems to mean different things to different people. I'm not sure whether this is a semantic problem or if reality distortion is taking place."

"Why are you always so cynical? Can you just trust, even a little bit?"

"As a matter of fact, no I can't. It's not in my nature."

"Alright I'll accept that for now. But let me say something about the connection of my aura to the auras of other people …most specifically, my connection to the aura of Carol Mays. When I first heard this morning that she may have been kidnapped or killed, I knew right away that she was still alive. But I also had a premonition that she is in grave danger. Now I fear that the danger is growing."

"Are these simply unsubstantiated hunches or do you have something more to offer in support?"

"As I said earlier our auras overlap. Carol Mays has a very expansive aura. Look at all the attention she has generated already. My own aura is limited but it is expanding somewhat and we overlap not only with our auras but with our experiences. The experience part might be what you would find to be more germane."

"What experiences do you have in common?"

"We are close in age, both single women. And we are both seekers. She is very big into yoga, as I am. Her spiritual journey has taken her through examinations of eastern and western philosophies and religions. I have gone through some of those same explorations myself. Carol Mays is educated and honest and sincere. And I like to think of myself in those terms as well. Also she is a spokesperson for The Rhapsody Lifestyle Centers, where I'm a member."

"And what about all of the differences? Don't they diminish your aura overlap? You're a white Californian businesswoman. She is a black woman from the Deep South who makes her living by utilizing her physical assets rather than her intellectual acumen. I don't know anything about her other than what you've told me, but I get a different feeling about her than you do. My guess is that's she's dead. How do you explain all of that?"

"Apparently you have no aura overlap with Carol Mays. Remember less than an hour ago, you didn't even know who she was. I wouldn't expect you to have any connection to her aura whatsoever. So your guess that she is dead is well … just a guess."

"You know this all sounds like parapsychological babble to me. Even this whole realm of spiritual thinking that includes various depictions of auras is grossly imprecise and unscientific.

"But that's your problem, Hawk. Science is your God. Science is only a guidepost to me. And, for that matter, science can sometimes be imprecise, even misleading."

"So what you're saying is that science is my crutch and spirituality is yours?" The computer saleswoman and the blind scientist had now stopped walking all together. Julianne fought the urge to feel frustrated or angry. She wanted to teach the teacher. But she knew that an emotional response was not the way to do that. She answered him evenly as she guided his arm to turn around and begin the walk back toward his house.

"No, not at all. But I think that your cynicism is getting in the way of your self-education. It's very unscientific to reject the spirituality of others without proof of its irrelevance." She emphasized the word, "unscientific," so that she could play the game on his home field.

"You know, Julianne … this is what I enjoy most about your company … you are learning to delight in being controversial and argumentative."

Julianne continued to control her impulse to get angry. Her experience told her that it would be unwise to let anger control her reactions. Still it was obvious to her that Hawk Richter was completely misreading her ardor. She simply waited for him to further delineate his perspective.

"Regardless of your belief that I am cynical, I would say that I am merely skeptical. It's not like I haven't done any investigation into the matter of auras. I know that some of religions of India and other Asian countries utilize physical depictions of auras in their idolatry. They assign meaning to the rainbow of colors that make up an aura. And I've read all about the Buddha's aura of enlightenment. And all of this is a very nice fictional tapestry. But I don't believe it's any different from the Irish leprechaun looking for the pot of gold at the end of the rainbow."

Julianne had reached her limit of frustration especially with Richter's choice of words. She felt that he was purposefully demeaning both organized religion and spirituality by calling them "idolatry" and a "fictional tapestry." She was about to counter his comments about the leprechaun, when she actually saw the rainbow. There it was, the largest most beautiful rainbow she had ever seen, stretching from Hillsborough Bay out toward the distant Tampa skyline.

"Hawk, there it is … a sign from the universe that's about as timely and beautiful as anything I've ever seen." Then she remembered that Hawk Richter was incapable of seeing rainbows.

Priscilla Stengel was praying to God to spare her father for a while longer. At least that's what she said aloud. His breathing was shallow. She stared down at his motionless body and thought of all the things that she wanted to say to him. He was still alive, but he wasn't going to get any better. She wasn't sure why she was praying for more longevity for Frank Malone. When he was awake he was in significant pain, and the last 48 hours were a real struggle. Priscilla wondered why a merciful God would allow people to endure such suffering.

Priscilla thought back on the teachings about Jesus that she had learned in grammar school. Somehow they had made sense at the time but now these teachings didn't seem reasonable. Why would God allow his Son, Jesus, to suffer and die on the cross? How exactly, did that save our souls? So much of this now seemed like a rote memory exercise. Yet she was taught these beliefs and the accompanying prayers by her parents. She wondered if Frank Malone still believed them, or if he had rejected them in his final days. And even though he was still alive there was no way that she could ask him these questions. Even if he awakened for a moment or two, would this be the appropriate conversation to have? On one hand she didn't want to upset him and cause his health to further deteriorate. On the other hand, she wondered what could be more important in his final hours than a discussion about God and the afterlife. Wasn't every other line of conversation insignificant in comparison? And what about her own dark secret? Was there any viable reason for her to tell her father that she had done something every bit as evil as what Aaron Fein had done? Did he have a right to know this before he died? She thought not. Her own penance was to bear this guilt alone. But she knew that she would find a way to forgive herself. She also knew that she would work to make changes so that others would not feel her guilt and pain.

Priscilla took a deep breath, stood up and went into the kitchen to put on a pot of coffee. She putted around looking for filters in an aimless sort of way, until she found them right under her nose on the end of the counter. Everything was where it was supposed to be, but her reverie was causing some of the simple symmetries of life to seem scrambled. As she began brewing the coffee, her daydreaming drifted to her son, Michael. She loved him dearly but his affliction was something that saddened her more than anything else. He was such a wonderful person, but so many people who interacted with him treated him as though his autistic condition was more important than his humanity. She knew that one of the few exceptions to this was her father who loved Michael unconditionally. She wasn't sure how she would go about telling Michael about her father when he was gone.

Priscilla went back to her father's bedside and saw his eyelids fluttering as though he were trying to open them. She reached out and held his hand.

"Dad, I love you. Michael loves you too. We're both going to make you proud of us." She thought she felt a slight warm pressure on her hand in answer to her statement. Then the warmth began to fade and he was gone.

It was a lot of driving for one week. Tim Hanlon was exhausted as he drove back down to Alabama. He had been visited briefly by the West Virginia State Police at his hotel room on Wednesday night, but told them little other than the fact that he was headed back to Alabama. Once they had ascertained that Carol Mays was not with Hanlon, there was little that the police could do other than to follow Hanlon as he headed back south and out of the state. Besides this was not their case. It was rapidly gaining national attention, but the FBI had not stepped into the case yet as it was not officially a kidnapping or an interstate crime. At this juncture, it was still a missing person case, and Hanlon was merely a person of interest.

Thursday morning things became interesting. After getting practically no sleep, Hanlon forced down two cups of coffee before leaving Martinsburg and heading south. Even as he left the front door of the hotel three reporters tried to ambush him with questions. Four more reporters were waiting near his vehicle. And this was West Virginia, not New York City. The moment his Range Rover left the hotel parking lot, he could hear helicopters circling above him. Overnight the story had hit the newswires and Tim Hanlon's name had become well known. The overhead choppers were not police helicopters but rather news helicopters. They had decided to follow his every movement. The scenario was reminiscent of the time when the choppers had followed OJ Simpson after he became the prime suspect in the murder of Nicole Brown Simpson. The difference was that in the Mays matter there was no body and no hard evidence of homicide. Nevertheless the media was having a field day with its speculation and coverage. A white Catholic priest fathering a child with a black supermodel and preparing to leave the priesthood was just too much for the media to resist. Everyone prejudged Tim Hanlon. They were sure he had killed Carol Mays and had dumped the body somewhere between Alabama and West Virginia. The Catholic Church had refused to make any statement in the matter, and considered the Hanlon issue an internal affair. However a rumor surfaced that Hanlon was on leave from his duties as a cleric, but The Church had yet to confirm or deny this rumor.

Hanlon was grateful for the Bluetooth hands free phone facility in his Range Rover because he was able to make calls while moving without risking a nuisance stop by the police. At first he stuck to the speed limit but after the first 100 miles he just drove at his normal 75 to 80 mph pace. He tried to reach Carol Mays several more times and then called the Alabama State Police at the agreed upon time of 1 PM to give them a progress report on his travels. He spoke again to Officer Bubba Looney and told him that he should be back in the Mobile area by late afternoon the following day as he planned to stop somewhere enroute to spend the night.

Looney didn't grill him about Mays. He wanted to get him back to Alabama first, but the detective was surprised that Hanlon had many questions for him with respect to the progress of their search for Mays. Obviously he was unaware that the FBI had just taken the lead on the case. Hanlon asked if Looney had heard from Mays' parents, indicating that he had heard on the radio that they were watching his son, Russ. Looney also had a sense that there was little or no relationship between Hanlon and the supermodels' parents. Another intriguing occurrence was the fact that Hanlon asked for the cell phone numbers for Jude Royale and for Lawson Mays. Apparently he didn't have either of these numbers. Looney gave him the numbers and also agreed that he would call him if he had any breaking news before they met in person the following afternoon. Both men made an effort to keep their telephone conversation as cordial as possible. Hanlon wanted help. Looney wanted a pinch.

After getting these numbers Hanlon first called Lawson Mays. The phone was answered but no voice spoke right away.

"Reverend Mays. This is Tim Hanlon." Again the greeting was silence. But a television in the background signaled that a connection had been established.

"Reverend Mays, are you with Russ?"

"*Doncha* dare talk *t' meh 'bout mah* grandson! *An'* what've *yew* done *wit' mah daughteh*?"

"Please, Reverend Mays. I know what the media are saying. I've been listening to these reports all morning, and I can hear all of these people in helicopters above me, every few miles I drive. Please understand that I'm extremely upset about Carol. I have no idea where she is. Whenever she shows up I'm sure there will be a logical explanation for everything. But right now I can't imagine what that explanation could be. I ... I ... I love Carol. What else can I say?"

"*Yew didden'* love her *'nough t'* stand *bah* her the last eight *yeahs*. *Yew* shirked *yer responsibiliteh t'* both *mah daughteh an' t'yer* own son. Now *yew* have *apparentleh* taken Carol against her will. *Ah* demand *t'* know where she is." Mays stopped talking abruptly, because his fears and his anxieties outweighed his anger and he quickly realized that he would learn nothing new by chastising Tim Hanlon.

"Reverend Mays, please listen to me. We don't know one another, so this is very hard on both of us. But please accept the fact that I know nothing whatsoever about where Carol is at this very moment and I'm terribly troubled over that fact. There is a lot of ground that we will have to cover whenever Carol comes back. But I'm hoping that what Carol told me about speaking with you is true."

"What do *yew* mean *bah* that?" Try as he might, Lawson Mays could not control his angry interruption. "Are *yew* now *accusin'* Carol *o lyin' t' yew 'bout semthaan'*?"

"No not at all. Carol told me that she spoke to you and Mrs. Mays about the renewal of our relationship. She also told me that you knew that she and Russ came to see me 10 days ago and that Carol came back down to Mobile this weekend. We even discussed coming to see you and Mrs. Mays before the end of the month. Can I at least assume that all of this is accurate?"

"*Ah* knew *nuthin' 'bout aneh play'un*s *fur y'all t'* come *t'* Bermin'hayum t'* see us." By omission, Reverend Mays confirmed the other details. "Where are *yew* now?" Mays thought it best to learn whatever he could.

"I'm alone driving along Interstate 81 just into northeastern Tennessee on my way to Alabama. I'm meeting with the State Police tomorrow afternoon. I've been in touch with them since I first learned of Carol's disappearance last night. How about you? Where are you? Are you with Russ? Please at least tell me that Russ is safe."

"Russ is safe."

"When and where can I see him?" There was no answer. The phone just went dead.

Hanlon tried to call right back. Dropped cell phone connections were not at all unusual. The phone rang several times and then went to voice mail. Hanlon tried three more times before he concluded that the disconnect was intentional.

For Hanlon there was a surreal feeling on the trip back to Alabama. He was listening to radio news stations that were not only reporting on the speculative kidnapping of Carol Mays, but they were also reporting on the whereabouts of Tim Hanlon's Range Rover even as he was moving. Occasionally another driver would pass him and stare at him in hatred. On at least one occasion this feeling was accompanied by a digital salute from an elderly woman in a Buick.

After his failed attempts to reconnect with Lawson Mays, Hanlon dialed the number he had been given for Jude Royale.

"Jude Royale. Who's calling please?" The voice sounded both effeminate and wary.

"Hello, Jude. This is Tim Hanlon. I'd like to talk with you if I could."

"I know about you through Carol. Can you tell me where she is? Please tell me if you know." Royale was trying not to sound overly accusatory.

"I need help Jude. I'll tell you everything I know. But I don't know where Carol is and I'm scared to death about it." Hanlon's voice was finally breaking. He didn't know where to turn for help. He knew that he was grasping for something he would have a hard time reaching.

Fortuitously Jude Royale was suffering the exact same emotions that Hanlon was feeling. He too was desperately seeking information on the whereabouts of Carol Mays. He decided to try to believe Hanlon.

"Look Tim … err … Father Hanlon … or whatever you want me to call you. Let's try to get off on the right foot. Then let's just decide for now that I believe everything that you're going to tell me … one hundred percent of it … Then maybe we can compare notes and see if we can come up with a possible reason for Carol's disappearance. Every minute with no news is very scary to me."

"Thank you for that, Jude. Carol told me about you as well. I know she trusts you. She said that you have been her best friend in New York for several years and that she recently confided in you about her relationship with me."

"Did she tell you that I was cynical about her having a relationship with a priest?"

"Yes, as a matter of fact, she did. But please understand that our connection started before I became a priest. I never knew about Russ until Carol recently told me that I had a son."

"Hadn't you been following her career at all? I know that she was always guarded in her professional approach to her private life. There was almost never any mention of her son. I only remember two media references to Russ. So I guess you missed those allusions in the press?"

"After I became a priest I still had strong feelings for Carol, but because of my vow of celibacy, I avoided reading about her. Sure I heard some things. And yes, I saw the Sports Illustrated photos. But you're right I missed all the references to her private life. I guess that was because I didn't want to hear things that I couldn't deal with personally."

"She told me that she was the one who re-contacted you and not the other way around."

"Yes, that's true."

"Is that why you're leaving the priesthood?"

"I'm not sure I know how to answer that. I was already having reservations about certain issues. When Carol came back into my life, I took it as a sign that God had other plans for me. Now, I don't know what to think."

"Is it true that when she left you, she was heading to the airport and was unconcerned that anyone might want to harm her?"

Hanlon was hesitant. He still had to resolve the issue of the man that Mays saw near Double Oak Lake in Oak Mountain State Park. Mays believed this was the same man that she had seen leaving the confessional at the church. Hanlon planned to tell the police about a man following him from Mobile to the park. But he wouldn't tell them about the confession. He wanted to pray over this whole situation, but now he was being confronted with a logical question before he had time to evaluate the circumstances. He decided to deceive Royale without telling an outright lie.

"I don't know who interfered with Carol's plans to fly back to New York. She was very happy when she left me heading to the airport. After that I don't know much more than you do.

"But there's something else I want to ask you about, Jude. Carol told me that Russ was staying with you until she got back to New York. Is Russ still with you? Or has he been taken by his grandparents? That's what they're saying on the news."

"Russ was here until his grandfather came to get him last night. Lawson Mays said that he was taking Russ back to Alabama. Russ seemed comfortable with his grandfather, and so I thought it was the right thing to do. I will tell you this much, however. I believe that Lawson Mays will do anything he can to keep you from seeing his grandson. Whatever it is between you and Lawson Mays, I hope it has nothing to do with Carol's disappearance."

"Reverend Mays has never forgiven me for my relationship with his daughter. Carol told me that her father has always known that Russ was my son. But even before that miracle occurred, Lawson despised me because he correctly assumed that I was responsible for Carol's conversion from his Southern Baptist congregation to the Catholic faith."

"Well, you may be interested to know that Carol has always been faithful to her adopted Catholic religion, as long as I've known her. I knew that this was a bone of contention between Carol and her father in the past, but I never knew how this all came about until she recently told me about you. It was hard for Carol because she also loves her father very much."

"Actually I just spoke to him briefly."

"Then you must have known that he had Russ. Right?"

"As I said before, I heard that on the radio about an hour ago, and Lawson Mays didn't confirm it, but he did say that he knew that Russ was safe. For now, that's all that's important. So thanks for validating that information for me."

"Everything you're saying makes sense. Carol is too independent thinking to allow her father to dictate what she does with her life. But she is also a spiritual woman and a considerate person. I can't understand how she could just vanish like this with so many people worrying about her. That's what has me most concerned."

"I share that concern, Jude. That's why I'm asking for your continued support in helping me find Carol. I'll do what I can to patch up things with Reverend Mays, if he'll let me. We all have the same short term wish … to find Carol."

"You mean to find Carol … alive."

"Yes." Hearing these last few words from Royale caused Hanlon's stomach to flip-flop. Exasperating the feeling was the continuous drumming noise of helicopter blades circling above him. He hurriedly ended the call, "Goodbye and thank you." Then he started crying unabashedly as he continued driving back towards Alabama. Meanwhile the "Eye in the Sky" watched with interest.

At first Carol Mays was petrified by her descent down through the earthen antechamber and then down the ladder into the cement bomb shelter. Then she was flabbergasted by the conditions that she found in this subterranean apartment. And that was exactly what it looked like to her, a small apartment. There were two couches in the middle of the largest room that appeared to be pull-out beds as well. The décor was bizarre. All of the 10 ft high walls were lined with shelving, but the room was clearly intended for occupation and not just storage. She remembered when she first moved to New York City, she paid more than $2000 a month for a basement studio apartment on the lower east side. This quick flash back caused her to be more amazed than frightened. However she was still a captive and her hands were still handcuffed in front of her body and her ankles were still loosely shackled together. The only food that Mays had eaten during her captivity, were two chocolate bars that were given to her by her burly new acquaintance. She wondered if she was starting to hallucinate. *What in God's name was the purpose of this underground dwelling?* She was still frightened about the whereabouts of Russell, but somehow she was not physically afraid of this man who called himself Patch. He had already had ample time to kill her or to sexually molest her or to physically violate her in any way that he wanted. And although he frequently threatened her, he didn't seem inclined to inflict further physical harm. Her neck was still sore from where he rabbit-punched her and knocked her unconscious when they were still in the farmhouse. However since that time he had talked tough but had not hurt her at all. Mays had the distinct impression that he didn't know what to do with her. But she still had no idea about his motivation, and that uncertainty worried her most.

Now alone in her new underground home, Mays hadn't seen Patch Munson in more than 12 hours. The bomb shelter was unique in that there was ample lighting and adequate air conditioning and ventilation. There were four eight inch openings in the ceiling located across from the trap door. These openings appeared to be the mechanism for air exchange through some external duct system. Periodically Mays tried to yell up into duct work in the hopes that someone might hear her, but this was an exhausting effort that yielded no apparent results.

Although the shelter was not stocked with food there was a small refrigerator right next to the small alcove that contained the composting toilet. Munson had put about two dozen one liter sized bottles of water in the refrigerator and indicated that she was free to drink it. Mays had learned Patch Munson's last name by removing the picture of Patch and Junior Munson from its frame and discovering an inscription on the rear of the photo that gave their names. She correctly assumed that Junior Munson was Patch's father. However, she had no idea whether this man was dead or alive. Still she figured that now she at least had some information to utilize when she next encountered Munson. At that moment a bigger concern was if and when that next encounter would occur.

While she was in just that reverie, Carol Mays began to hear a scratching noise coming from the antechamber above the ceiling of the bomb shelter. She could also hear the lethargic growling of Munson's dog, Harry. After two minutes of scraping, she saw the ceiling door swing open above her and then the ladder slid down through the opening. Very nimbly Harry poked his snout through the ceiling, then took two steps down on the slightly angled ladder and deftly jumped into the main room of the underground dwelling. Ten seconds later the corpulent body of Patch Munson passed through the opening and backed down the ladder. He was carrying a brown paper bag that appeared to have some kind of food in it.

In spite of the heat above the surface, Munson was dressed in his usual attire of coveralls and a light flannel shirt. He had an earthy odor about him but it was not hopelessly offensive. He was perspiring slightly and seemed somewhat befuddled. Then again this was how he always seemed to Mays.

"*Ah* brought *yew sum'thaan' t'* eat." Munson put a brown paper bag on a small wooden table that was beside one of the two fold out couches that faced each other in the main room. Both Munson and Mays remained standing, facing each other with the five foot length of the couches separating them.

"Thank you Mr. Munson. I appreciate that." She began by being deferential.

"How did *yew* know *mah* name?"

Mays fully expected the question. She answered it in a straight forward manner, hoping to get an additional confirmation in the process. She was still in the data gathering mode.

"I saw it on the back of the picture of you and your father." She nodded in the direction of the framed photo which she had reassembled and replaced in its position on the rear shelving.

"*Whah wuz yew nosin' 'round?*"

"You haven't told me much. You promised me that I would see Russell, and you haven't kept your promise. I'm just looking to see how I can convince you to let me leave here and go join Russell."

"*Ah cain't* let that happen."

"Why not?"

"*Ah jes' cain't.* That's all."

"But why can't I see Russell? Why am I here? What can I do for you so that I can see my son again?" She knew that she sounded like a broken record. But she also believed that unyielding persistence had a way of working sometimes. Therefore her determined questioning remained absolutely obdurate.

"*Yew* ask too *maneh dang* questions." Munson and Harry seemed to growl in unison. However it was Harry that made the only follow up motion. He trotted between the couches and over to the side of the room where Mays stood. Harry put his front paws up near her legs and began sniffing at her crotch. She gently tried to push him away, but the hound was somewhat insistent in its own quest for olfactory information. Finally Munson addressed the dog. "Down *Harreh. Git o'er* here *yew* mangy mutt." The dog understood the tone of voice and waddled back over to Munson's side.

Mays was happy to have the dog's snout out of her crotch, but she was unsettled by the conversation that seemed to be going nowhere. And the dog wasn't the only one whose sense of smell had been aroused. Mays caught the smell of oily fried food coming from the brown paper bag. It was around noon on Thursday and she hadn't eaten a meal since Monday.

"I'm very hungry. Can I have something to eat?"

"*Ah* told *yew. Ah* brought *yew sem* food. It's in the bag. Eat it. *Ah'll brang yew sem* more *tomorrah.* So eat *s'much* as *yew* want." The change in the direction of their conversation was temporarily helpful to both of them.

"Can you take off the handcuffs so that I can eat properly?"

Munson considered this request for a moment and then said, "Sit down on the couch."

When Mays had complied Munson moved the brown bag from the table to a spot on the couch next to her. Then he took out a small key ring from his pocket and unlocked and removed her handcuffs. Mays felt extremely weak and suddenly her stomach began to have sharp pains of hunger, triggered by the scent of greasy food. She opened the bag and found several pieces of fried chicken and some hushpuppies that had been purchased at a local eatery. There was also a half pound container of cole slaw, and a plastic fork and spoon. Mays had not eaten fried food in many years. She was surprised at how intense her craving became. She began devouring the food as soon as her hands were free.

Munson watched as Mays eagerly ate the food that he had given her. When she tried to ask him another question, he simply said, "Hush up and eat."

Mays needed her strength so she did as she was told. Meanwhile Munson observed her silently. When she was finished eating Munson told her to put her hands together again so that he could reapply the handcuffs.

Mays decided to continue to press on lesser issues. After Munson put the handcuffs back in place, Mays complained that she had been wearing the same clothing since Monday.

"My suitcase was in the back of your car but I haven't seen it since we came here. Can you at least bring that to me so that I can change my clothes? Is that too much to ask, Patch?" Mays decided to try to relate to this ogre on a first name basis. She was willing to try anything to see what would work.

"*Ah'll thaank 'bout* it." Munson eyed her suspiciously. He had a sinking feeling of hopelessness. He had this woman locked away on his property and he still couldn't figure out what to do with her. There was no solution presenting itself at this time so he said nothing more.

Finally not knowing what else to do, he walked over to the ladder. He then tilted the ladder slightly and motioned for Harry to jump up on it. He made this motion three or four times before Harry got around to obeying his master's command. Once the hound finally scurried up through the ceiling door, Patch Munson followed and pulled the ladder back up through the trap door and Carol Mays was once again alone in the bomb shelter.

For the second time this month Billy Brand had the opportunity to speak with the state police. First it was Detective Ismail Kanasani of the Florida State Police. Now it was Officer Bubba Looney of the Mobile PD. The subject matter was no longer the Fein murder. It was now the presumed kidnapping of Carol Mays. Brand was aware of the fact that the FBI had now begun its own investigation, but he also knew how territorial the local police could be.

"*Ah'm* interested in your *o-pinions 'bout* Father Tim Hanlon." Bubba Looney towered over Billy Brand. The detective looked more like a rancher than a cop, but his coarse lack of concern for personal hygiene would set him apart from any specific group of people other than barroom drunks. His breath seemed to be permanently stained with the odor of an overnight alcoholic binge.

"*Ah* don't know Tim Hanlon real well, but we've spent *sem tahme togetheh* at a few *communiteh* conferences. *Ah lahke* Tim. *Ah* respect his faith *an' spiritualiteh an' Ah* know that he's incapable of *doin' an'thaan' t'* hurt Carol Mays. What else would *yew lahke t'* know?"

"Well that's a *pertty* strong *openin'* statement of support. Do *yew* know Carol Mays as well? *Ah* mean … do *yew* know her beyond what *ever 'un* else knows *'bout* her?"

"As a *matteh o* fact, *Ah've* met her once or *twahce* in the past. Her *daddeh*, Lawson Mays, is a Baptist minister up in *Bermin'hayum*. *Ah've* known him since *Ah* was knee-high *t'* a grasshopper. He was *vereh* supportive of *mah* own *daddeh* when he started his *ministreh*. They have been *friendleh eveh* since. Lawson *retahred* from active *min'streh 'bout fahve* years ago but *mah daddeh* still stays in touch *wit'* him. In fact *Daddeh* reached out *t'* Lawson earlier *t'day t'* express his prayerful support *fur* Carol's safe return."

"Did he talk to *'im?*"

"*Ah* don't believe he did. But *sum'un* told *'im* that Lawson went up *t'* New York *t'* git his grandson. *B'sahdes, Daddeh* don't do much *talkin'* these days. He does more *furgettin'* than he does *talkin.'* He's *gat Alzhahmeh's an'* it's *comin'* on faster *'an* a *lightnin'* bolt *sneakin'* up on an *ole* magnolia tree."

"*Yew* know we've talked *t'* Hanlon a whole lot *jes'* this afternoon. He *didden' bring no attorneh, neither.* He claimed he *didden'* need one *b'cause* he *ain't* done *nuthin'* wrong. Said he wanted to do *ever'thaan'* he could to *he'p* the search *fur* Mays. Hanlon has a *storylahne fur* his activities from *Mundeh rahght* through *t'* this minute. It all sounds *kinda* true but *rahght* now we're short on evidence that will *verifah* all *o* his *tahmeline.* He admits *t' seein'* Mays as late as 3:30 PM on *Mundeh, an'* we *ain't gat no one else lahned* up that has seen or heard from her since that *tahme.* So we keep *lookin'* at Hanlon. *An'* we're *trahin' t' fahnd* people, *otheh* than his *parishionehs* who know *'im.* The *parishionehs* that we've talked *t's'far* are shocked *bah* what they're *hearin'* in the *meed'yer.* A lot *o 'em* refuse *t'* believe that Hanlon *cuddah* hurt Mays."

"*Ah* don't believe it *eitheh. Afteh* people *git oveh* the shock *o* hea-rin' that he had a child out *o* wedlock, they'll come *'round t' realizin'* that Tim Hanlon is not a *vah'lent* man. *Vah'olatin'* a debatable Church commitment *t' chastiteh, an' vah'olatin' 'nother* human *bein'* are two separate *thaangs. S'far's Ah* know Tim *dudden'* have a *vah'lent* bone in his body. The *onleh* 'V' word that *Ah* would use *t' descrahbe* Father Hanlon is *victim.*"

"*Yew* know that's the way he came *'cross t' meh* also. But he still *mahght* know more *'bout* Carol Mays' disappearance than he's *tellin'* us *s'far.* An hour *afteh* he left the station we *gat* a call from Bodean Bickforth IV, *sayin'* that *he's* now *representin'* Hanlon and that all communication should now go through *'im.* This is *afteh* Hanlon talked *t'* us all *afteh'noon wit'* no counsel. Go *fig'yeh.*"

"Bo Bickforth is a big *tahme attorneh.* Tim must be *payin'* a big *tahme* bill. *An'way, Ah'm* glad to see that Father Hanlon is *gettin'* sem legal support. He'll need it *jes' t'* keep the *meed'yer* at bay." Billy Brand caught himself in mid thought. He didn't want to spend any more time on that topic until he elicited whatever it was that Bubba Looney wanted from this visit. "So how *cain Ah he'p yew* in all *o* this?"

"*Ah* was *wonderin'* whether *yew mahght* be able *t'* talk *t'* Hanlon ... *clergeh'man t' clergeh'man* so *t'* speak *an'* see *iffin yew cain't he'p* us get *t'* the bottom *o* this *mystereh* disappearance. Would *yew mahnd givin' 'im* a call?"

"*Yer askin' meh t'* intervene in a *po'lice* investigation, *b'cause yer* suspect has lawyered up? That *dudden'* seem *quahte* ethical to *meh. An'* if *Ah* told *yew anythaan' o* substance that *mahght* impugn Tim Hanlon, *yew'd probableh* have *sem difficulteh usin'* that in court."

"*Ah'm* not *askin' yew t'* tell *meh an'thaan'* at all ... unless *yew* feel a need to. But if *yew truleh* believe Hanlon is innocent ... *an' Ah* sense that *yew* do ... then *maybeh yew mahght* be able *t'* discover *sum'thaan'* that will *he'p* us clear his name *an' fahnd* Carol Mays."

Looney then played the last card he had in his hand. "*Ah've* heard *yew* preach *'bout rahghteousness an'* the need *fur* the *rahghteous t'* be hands-on. That's *whah Ah* felt that *yew mahght he'p* us out. So, will *yew* call *'im*? Will *yew* reach out *t' he'p* a fellow *clergeh'man*?"

"Well *Ah thaank Ah* may have beaten *y'all* to the punch on this one; *Ah* put in a call to Father Hanlon earlier this afternoon. *Ah diddin'* talk *t' 'im*; *jes'* left a message of support on his cell phone."

"*Yew* did? *Whah*?"

"*Ah've* seen the television stories *lahke ever'un* else. People are *convictin' 'im* of *kidnappin'* or worse *mainleh b'cause* he had a *chahld* out of wedlock. How *crazeh* is that? *Ah* thought that the man could use a *li'l* support. From what *Ah un'erstand* he's not *lahkely t' git* that support from Lawson Mays. It's such a shame. They're both good men."

"So *yew* believe that Hanlon *dudden'* know where Mays *mahght* be? Am *Ah* correct in that conclusion? Then would *yew* care *t'* venture a guess as *t'* what happened *t'* the woman?"

"*Ah'm* a preacher not a *po'liceman*. So in this case *yer* guess is a more educated one than *mah* own *mahght* be." He hesitated as though he had more to say and Looney jumped at the opportunity to press on.

"But …?"

"But *yew mahght* want *t'* look at who else *mahght* be upset *wit'* Carol Mays *fur showin'* up in Mobile."

"Are you *sayin'* the *Cat'lick* clergy *mahght* be involved?"

"No … although *anythaan'* is possible. *Howeveh,* when *yer talkin' wit'* those *parishionehs y'all mahght* want *t'* see which *o 'em mahght* be *fahred* up *angreh 'bout* their priest *havin'* a baby, *'specialleh wit'* a black woman. We both know that racism is still *alahve* here in *Al'bama.*"

"Lots of folks are *jes'* as prejudiced against the papists as they are against the Negroes."

"That *dudden'* stop *'em* from *bein'* prejudiced *'gainst* one *'nother.*"

"That's *certainleh* true."

"*Ah'll* tell *yew* this much. In *mah ministreh Ah* often run across folks who say stupid *thaangs … maybeh* even do stupid *thaangs … 'cause* they believe that it's God's will. This is one *o* the toughest *thaangs* that *Ah* have *t'* deal *wit'*. On one hand, *Ah'm preachin' 'bout rahghteousness an'* proactive opposition *t'* evil, *an'* on the *otheh* hand *Ah've gat t'* make sure that the opposition is peaceful opposition. My *Daddeh* always preached more *simpleh*. He *jes* says that 'two wrongs don't make a *rahght*.' But *Ah'm* still *learnin'* how *t' lahght* a *fahre un'er* the faithful *wit'out incineratin'* the faith. *Yew mahght* say that *evereh* once in a *whahle* Billy Brand has a Billy Joel moment *an' Ah* want *t' hahde* behind the disclaimer that: 'We *didden'* start the *fahre*. It was *alwehs burnin.'* But *Ah* know that *dawg* won't hunt and those lyrics don't play well here in *Al'bama.*"

VII

"The Tale of Patch and Harry"

Priscilla Stengel sat in the front pew of the Catholic Church. Three feet away in an oak casket, the body of her father, Frank Malone, was in motionless final repose. Sitting next to her on her left was her nine year old son, Michael. An additional 43 mourners were scattered around the church, mostly neighbors and fellow parishioners. There were no extended Malone or Stengel family members in the church. Her father had lived in the city of Winston, Florida, for more than forty years and Priscilla had lived here her whole life. Eleven years earlier her father had walked her down the aisle of this same church.

Priscilla had done all of her crying over the last forty eight hours. She sat tearlessly and listened as Father Bijoy Bandopadhyay began speaking to the congregation about a man he had never formally met.

"*Ve* are *gattered* here today, not *een* sorrow, but *een* celebration of the life of Frank Malone. He *vus owa fadda* or *owa brudda* or *owa* friend. But he *vus elso vun* of God's children. Today the Lord has come to take Frank home to his *heawenly revurd*."

Suddenly it all seemed so absurdly humorous to Priscilla, and she gagged in an attempt to stifle a guffaw. She nearly burst out laughing, but was able to bury her face in her hands to avoid the seeming impropriety of such a reaction. When her body shook others around her thought she was shaking with grief over the loss of her father. Some of the neighbors fended off their own tears of sorrow in would-be empathy. However the harder she tried to hold back her laughter, the more her body convulsed and the more those around her looked on with sad and sullen eyes, miscalculating the young woman's grief. Meanwhile the Indian priest rambled on.

"*Dee* Lord *verks een* mysterious *vays* …"

Priscilla finally forced herself to get it together and brought her sorrow back to the surface allowing her bizarre attack of the sillies to subside. She stared at the priest who was now doing everything he could to make eye contact with her as he eulogized her father, but she no longer heard anything he was saying. Whereas a few days earlier it had bothered Priscilla that her father hadn't embraced his spirituality in his final hours, she no longer cared about this now that he was gone. She remembered him as a wonderful man. A loving God could not possibly punish a man who had always tried his best to help others.

"*Ve* know *dat* in his own *vary* Frank Malone has left the *world* a *beta* place …"

Father Bandopadhyay began winding down but Priscilla would have been satisfied if he spoke for hours. She wasn't listening to him. She was contentedly listening to the voices that told her that she needed to get on with her life. She knew that there was more to spirituality than the rubrics and regimens of organized religion. She had read a good deal on the topic, but found some of the literature devoid of true meaning as well. She rejected the secret of the attraction theory that held that simply being open to the universe could bring good and bad things her way through a kind of active visualization. Her desire to be a best-selling novelist had not been realized and her life had been filled with sadness ever since she ended her first pregnancy. Her husband had died. Her mother had died. And now her father had died. Certainly she wouldn't have intentionally – or for that matter unintentionally – done anything to "attract" such disappointments. She had worked hard to think positively but she knew that periodically anger and venom overcame her efforts to find fulfillment.

She knew that she had once made a major mistake. But this realization had nothing to do with the concept of sin. It had everything to do with the concept of fairness. How could she possibly deprive another human being of the right to live? More importantly how could she do this to her own child? She made a promise to God and to her unborn child. She was going to make the most out of her life going forward and she was going to ensure that Michael had a great life ahead as well. Then she would see her unborn child in heaven.

As Priscilla was thinking about these things, her son, Michael began to speak out over the last few words of Father Bandopadhyay's tribute to Frank Malone. Michael's garbled words were accompanied by rapid movement as he attempted to scale the front of the pew and run onto the altar. Priscilla quickly grabbed her son around the waist and avoided disruption. As she held on to her son, she realized that Michael was her one lasting source of joy. She didn't understand all the directions that Michael was being pulled in, but she understood that his energy and vitality were her inspiration to look forward instead of dwelling on the past. Maybe it wasn't fiction that she was being called to write after all. Maybe non-fiction was her calling. Maybe she would solve the mystery of the killing of Aaron Fein and write a book about that. Then maybe she would write a book about the spiritual powers of autistic children. And then … suddenly she had inspirations to write several other books on multiple other subjects as well.

"*Ve* have all been blessed to have Frank Malone *een* of our lives, but *ve* must now allow Frank to return to *owa heawenly* Father, so that he can enjoy *ewerlasting* salvation."

Priscilla glanced over at her father's casket in the aisle and talked to his soul, "*I'll make you proud of me yet. I promise I will.*" The unspoken thought was quite clearly delivered, and her father's answer resonated inside her brain with equal clarity. "*Of course you will Priscilla. Of course you will.*"

Tim Hanlon didn't know what direction to turn in. Regardless of his portfolio wealth, he was a poor man living out of a hotel room where he wasn't exactly welcomed in the first place. During the past two weeks, former parishioners deliberately walked on the opposite side of the street when they saw him in town. Mobile was a city of nearly 200,000 people, and was the third largest city in the state of Alabama. However it maintained a small town feel along the perimeter of the metropolitan area. The population was nearly 48% African-American, and about 44% non-Hispanic White American. Prejudice and racial intolerance were always looming just below the surface, the way they did in many American cities in the South. However interracial harmony was gaining momentum and several religious leaders were at the forefront of that momentum.

A few days earlier Hanlon had received a kind call from Reverend Billy Brand. Brand said that the media's treatment of Hanlon was shameful. He said that he was embarrassed that some members of his own congregation had added ugly accusations. Brand told Hanlon that he was welcome to live in his rectory until the hoopla died down and Mays was found. It was a completely unexpected act of kindness on Brand's part. Hanlon was unsure about how to react. Brand became ever more assertive in his offer until Hanlon agreed to move to one of the Brand family's guest rooms while things got sorted out.

Then speaking through his attorney, Tim Hanlon offered a $100,000.00 reward for information leading to the safe return of Carol Mays. This maneuver caused some unwanted attention to be focused on Hanlon's personal finances. People began to ask questions about Hanlon's personal wealth and the role it may have played in Mays' disappearance. However there were no ransom requests and no credible claims of meaningful information. The bounty did have the effect of generating several declarations of possible Mays sightings around Mobile as well as six or seven cities around the country. None of these claims were realistic.

"How are *yew feelin' t'day*, Father Hanlon? Bessie will be *bringin'* breakfast into the *dinin'* room in *'bout fahve* minutes."

"You and Billy have been so gracious to me, Sarah Anne. I can't thank you enough. I'm not sure where my spirits would be if it weren't for you two."

Sarah Anne averted her eyes for a second as her husband, Billy, entered the room and took up the conversation in mid stride. "It is our absolute *duteh t' he'p* those in need *o* our assistance. *Maneh tahmes* we are able *t' he'p* folks *wit' sem* material *thaan's*, as well as *wit' sem* spiritual *guahdance*. But when Sarah Anne *an' Ah* witnessed what the media was *trahin' t'* do *t'* a good man *lahke yew*, we knew that the best *he'p* we could offer was our friendship."

"It is much appreciated. At times like this you find out who your true friends are. It can be eye opening."

"*Yer* circumstances are *diff'ent 'an* most. *Yer* a man of the cloth. People have *diff'ent* expectations of *yew*. If *yew* fail them in *aneh o* these expectations they're *lahkely t'* be *hardeh* on *yew* than they would be on *themse'ves*. Actually they expect less from *themse'ves*. *Idden* that *sump'an'* else?"

"Yes. But in some ways I blame myself for that reaction. I've been so caught up in my ministry as a priest that I haven't held on to the friendships that I had from my youth. In many ways I've been living life with blinders on."

"Well *yer* not *originalleh* from *Al'bama*, are *yew*?" Sarah Anne asked the question as she and Billy and Hanlon were now all seated together in the dining room. Bessie brought in pre-plated breakfast and put it in front of them.

"No I was born in Connecticut, right outside of New York City. My father worked on Wall Street and my mother was a real estate broker. Both of my parents were the only children in their respective families and they both hoped to have a larger family themselves. But I was an only child. My parents had a difficult time conceiving. By the time I was ready for high school, both of my parents had retired from their respective jobs, and they moved to Atlanta. They were trying to adopt another child and were open enough with me to discuss some of the process. This is one of the reasons why they were so disturbed by the astounding number of abortions in the United States. They tried to adopt an American baby, but there were none to be had. They died in a plane crash in Ethiopia trying to adopt an African baby. I was 15 years old at the time.

"That's *terr'ble. Yew musta* been devastated." Sarah Anne was empathetic.

Billy Brand chimed in also. "It's also *terr'ble* that they had such a difficult *tahme findin'* an American *chahld* to adopt. *Maneh* pre-born American children who *cudda* been a *brotheh* or *sisteh* to *yew* were *simpleh a'borted*."

"That's exactly right. Believe me I've thought about that a thousand times since then. But what is sadly ironic about this is something I read on the internet this morning."

"*Ah* was *hopin' yew* weren't *readin' sem o* that *slan'drous* rubbish. God save the souls of those who publish such salacious litter. *Ah* share *yer* pain as *Ah* have also been *victimahzed bah sem o* these anonymous blog-posters in the past."

"Well I could ignore it, but I feel like I need to know it exists in order to counteract the hideous allegations. And the one reference that I read this morning, involves you both so I feel that I should bring it to your attention. He took out his iPhone, pushed a few buttons and handed it to Brand to read:

> *"Things keep getting stranger in Mobile Alabama. Timothy Hanlon, the priest suspected of kidnapping his one time girlfriend, Carol Mays, has now taken up residence with televangelist Billy Brand and his wife Sarah Ann Brand in their Mobile mansion. Are the Brands looking to expand the franchise? What do they have planned next; a reality TV show? After the introduction of the Billy Brand Bobblehead last year, I guess anything is possible.*
>
> *"But there is a more macabre and ironic aspect of the fact that the Brands now feature the wealthy priest as a house guest. Brand has long been the lead anti-abortion spokesperson for the South and that image has served the coffers of his ministry quite well. But the information that has*

surfaced so far gives no indication that Hanlon shares Brand's views. Although he is a Catholic priest ... and we fully recognize the Catholic Church's stance on abortion ... no one can seem to recall a sermon that Hanlon preached condemning abortion. In fact there is no record of him attending any anti-abortion rallies or speaking out in public on the topic. Could it be because he once wanted a certain someone to have an abortion? Could it be that Carol Mays had her child against the wishes of the young father who was entering the priesthood? That certainly might provide a motive for someone like Hanlon to eliminate the exposure and embarrassment that Mays was about to unleash.

"Yes, these are strange bedfellows indeed: Hanlon and the Brands. I guess we'll all have to stay tuned to their upcoming reality show to find out how this gets sorted out. Meanwhile I guess I can expect to get blasted by Brand in his weekly sermon this Sunday. Now whose reality is that?"

Billy handed the phone to Sarah Ann and waited for her to read the article as well. Then he turned to Hanlon and said; "*Ah* hadn't seen this particular *postin'* yet, although *Ah* did read a few others. *Ah certainleh* hope that our offer of sanctuary *t' yew* here in our home is not *causin' yew* even more discomfort. We *git* our own fair share of negative *publiciteh* on a regular basis. But we are also blessed with *maneh* waves of support and affirmation from our *worldwahde* congregation. On balance our message is confirmed much more *frequentleh* than it is *criticahzed*."

"No please don't worry about me. I just don't want your ministry to suffer because you are supporting me. And as you know, we do share the same views on the horrors of abortion."

"We don't *worreh 'bout* cheap shots *lahke* this. The man is *obviousleh hopin'* that *Ah* will condemn his post *vereh specificalleh* in *mah Sundeh* sermon, *an'* then his blog or *postin'* or *whateveh* it is … will *simpleh* start *trendin'* … *an' maybeh* go *vahral* … *an'* then he will have served his own purpose. *Ah* won't let that happen, but *Ah* will send a message, *wit' yer* permission, *'bout* all such despicable *slandeh*."

Nineteen days is a long time for a child to wait for Christmas. It is an eternity for a prisoner to wait for her release. Carol Mays now knew that that was exactly what she was "a prisoner." She was reasonably certain that Patch Munson had no immediate plan to kill her and he had practically confirmed for her the fact that he didn't have Russell. But she didn't know these things with absolute certainty, and she still couldn't figure out why Munson had kidnapped her. She had a wild notion about the rationale for her abduction, but she couldn't be sure that her mind wasn't just playing games with her.

Her theory was that she was being held as a hostage in order to coerce Tim Hanlon to do something. She knew that Patch Munson had come out of Hanlon's confessional at The Most Holy Tabernacle Church when she first saw him. That indicated that something might have been said in confession that worried Munson. You never knew about these kind of things. After all she herself had acted rather bizarrely in that same confessional.

She theorized that Munson probably confessed something to Hanlon and then had second thoughts about the security of the confessional. This meant that whatever Munson confessed was a major crime, a bank robbery, an aggravated assault possibly even a murder. If he was willing to kidnap her, he could be capable of even more sinister actions. Munson was probably afraid that Hanlon would go to the police with this knowledge. Her theory seemed to make some sense. But the strange part was that Munson had not yet queried her about what she may or may not have heard from Tim Hanlon. This made her worry that Munson was somehow attempting to coerce Hanlon to stay silent. She wondered if Munson had talked to Hanlon about her. She asked herself; *Am I not only a prisoner but actually a hostage of some sort?* But the question that Mays couldn't answer was why Munson didn't just kidnap Hanlon, instead of kidnapping her. The only answer she could come up with was that Munson must believe that Hanlon had told her some details from his confession. At this point all of this was simply theoretical. But now she intended to have a conversation with Munson. At the same time she wondered what was going on in the outside world. People must be searching for her. She worried about the most important men in her life. She worried about Russell. *Was he truly safe somewhere away from this fiend?* She worried about Tim. *Could Tim also have been kidnapped ... or worse yet, killed?* And she worried about her father, Lawson Mays. *What must he be going through?*

Mays had now been alone in the bomb shelter for more than twenty-two hours but she had no perspective about time. For once in her life she wished that she had worn a watch. Patch Munson had taken her iPhone on the roadside outside of the airport and since that time she was left guessing at the time of day. Lately she wasn't even sure of the day of the week, although for some odd reason she had a perception it was a Thursday or a Friday. Although the bomb shelter was air conditioned and the two couches doubled as fold out beds, these amenities provided physical comfort but no emotional or intellectual relief. Mays passed the time between Munson's visits by exercising as best she could with the encumbrance of padlocked leg irons. After the first few days she also made a point of meditating for at least two hours whenever she woke up each morning. Munson had come down into the shelter daily and brought her food, but he had steadfastly refused to discuss the rationale for her captivity. Mays was determined to change that the next time she saw him.

Patch Munson was more worried than ever. The search for Carol Mays was a national news story but attention was centered on Mobile, Alabama, where she was last seen. Munson was particularly concerned about the scrutiny on Tim Hanlon. He was afraid that Hanlon would crack. He was relieved that he had never let Hanlon see him. It was growing increasingly difficult to watch the news shows that were still reporting on bits and pieces of the investigation. A spokeswoman for the Mobile Police Department had made a statement that the likelihood of finding Carol Mays alive was decreasing with every passing day.

Munson had several ancillary issues to deal with as well. His wife, Maggie, had returned from her week at the beach with Munson's two sisters, and was nosier than ever. She noticed that her husband's trips out to his ridiculous underground fortress were more frequent than in times past, and she had begun to ask questions that she had never posed before. Munson backed her off by relating fictitious tales of numerous mice and rats running amuck in the bomb shelter. Patch Munson knew that these stories would be enough to discourage the possibility of Maggie going near the shelter.

However the most pressing problem that Munson faced was his own guilt. He had trapped this woman in a subterranean prison and there was no apparent way of setting her free. She knew where she was and she knew who he was. To set her free was tantamount to signing his own prison sentence. All kinds of crazy ideas went through his head. He couldn't kill her. She had done nothing wrong. He tried to rationalize that she may have done enough wrong things to justify her imprisonment but couldn't quite get there. He remembered that his buddy, Bubba Looney had joked that he "*sem'tahmes* ticketed *niggehs fur drivin' whahle bein'* black." But he told himself that Looney was a racist and that Patch Munson was an unbiased God-fearing Christian.

One of the more bizarre thoughts was that entered Munson's mind was that, as an act of kindness, maybe he should kidnap Tim Hanlon also. Then Hanlon and Mays could live together in the bomb shelter. Yeah, that would be fair, he thought. Then he thought about the atrocious litany of bad decisions he had made lately. First he decided to kill Aaron Fein, the baby killer. Then he decided to confess this killing to Father Hanlon, the Catholic priest. This led him to following the priest, which in turn led him to kidnapping the priest's girlfriend, Carol Mays, who he subsequently learned was a famous fashion model. Now could he actually be thinking about kidnapping Hanlon as well? Munson quickly discarded this idea, and was proud of himself for making better decisions lately.

Julianne Carson rolled off the top of her lover, Hawk Richter. She was fascinated by his physical prowess. At times she was unsure what was more passionate, their lovemaking or their ongoing debate about spirituality. However at the moment she wasn't concerned about spirituality; she was simply staring at Richter's face which manifest a confident, but sightless smile. Julianne now sat upright and naked next to him with her totally spent body delightfully drenched in perspiration. She had never before experienced four orgasms in one morning and felt stupid for even counting. Everything was so spontaneous with Richter that she was able to just go with the flow, not knowing, or for that matter caring, whether she would ever get out of his bed. He was so innovative in his physicality that she wondered why he was so stubborn in his spirituality. Then she dismissed the thought. She remembered that she wanted to be living "in the moment." She wondered whether that meant that she savored her sexual exploits with Richter or whether she simply took pleasure in her own sexual adventurousness. Either way her red faced orgasms were a wonderful part of her new spiritual mantra of worshipping the here and now.

"So what is going through your mind, may I ask?" Richter moved only his lips as he spoke. But after he asked the question he folded both of his hands behind his head and on top of his pillow. He was rapidly becoming more alert.

"I wasn't on any particular wavelength at the moment but now that you ask, I guess I'm beginning to grow curious about the extent of my stay here in Tampa. I hadn't intended it to be ten days long."

"Eleven days but who's counting?"

"Do we need a break?"

"Ah ha, let's hide behind collectivisms. You didn't ask whether *you* or *I* need a break, but left the nonspecific *"we"* hanging in the air so that the decision would be totally mine. How clever of you!"

"Come on Hawk. I don't want to get into intellectual sparring with you this early in the morning. It can get quite tiresome."

"You need to exercise your mind as well as your body, my dear Julianne." With that he reached blindly for her well-toned torso. She stood up quickly and avoided his grasp, and then walked naked out of the bedroom, down the stairs and toward the kitchen, where her laptop sat on top of the center island. Within minutes a more modestly attired Hawk Richter came down the stairs, bare-chested and bare-footed, but wearing his briefs. He held his cane as a safety tool but didn't probe with it because of his familiarity with the environment. He followed the tapping of the keyboard sounds into the kitchen and walked up to where Julianne was seated on a stool at the center island.

"Did I say something to offend you, my dear Julianne?"

"No not at all, I just figured I would take your advice and exercise my mind. I'm reading the news off the internet, because you don't have a newspaper delivered here."

"So what's in today's news."

"There's political unrest in Greece; another suicide bomber in Israel; a sad story about the ongoing suffering in Haiti and an uplifting story about a couple that were remarried after being divorced for 31 years. Anything you want me to read?"

Richter put his hands on her shoulders and changed the subject. "Do you enjoy cavorting around the house naked? Can't people see in my windows?"

"You'd have to be a contortionist to see into the middle of your kitchen from anywhere other than on a ladder between your house and the place next door. That's what's nice about having to walk up ten steps to get into the house. You have sunshine when it's sunny and privacy even when it's not."

"Does that mean it's alright to make love right here on the center island?" He moved his hands down to cover both of her breasts. His hands were warm so she allowed them to rest as cup holders. But for the moment she had no amorous intentions.

"No, I'm exercising my mind. Remember?"

"I never said that you had to exercise your mind to the exclusion of your body." He hugged her closer to him and she leaned her head backwards away from the laptop and against his chest.

Julianne's thoughts went back to the spontaneity that was so much a part of her relationship with Richter. At the same time she could feel his interest rising. But as she suppressed the urge to let physical impulsiveness rule the entire morning, she noticed two other news items of interest. One noted that a group of Chinese scientists were proclaiming that the life on earth would end before the year 2060 due to a worldwide drought and famine. The second article stated that the FBI believed that hopes of finding Carol Mays alive were "very fleeting."

"Here's something you might find interesting. There's another prognostication for the end of the world."

"And exactly what does that mean?"

"It means that all forms of life that exist on planet earth as we know them today will perish in less than fifty years. More personally it means that I won't live into my eighties and you won't live into your nineties."

"Does that bother you?"

"Of course it does. I want to live a good long life. What are you saying … it doesn't bother you?"

"I haven't heard this thesis and it's not on my list for any time soon. But as for living into my nineties, I'm not sure I want to live that long. And why do *you* worry about this? Don't you want to move on to your heavenly afterlife?" His question was dripping with sarcasm, but Julianne wasn't ready to rehash this debate.

"How about this other story? Why is the FBI ready to give up on finding Carol Mays?"

"Is that what it says?"

"No … but to insinuate that she is probably dead … that's a horrible thing to do."

"Why is that?"

"Because she is alive. I can feel her karma and I still sense her aura overlap with mine. If you'd been following this story at all, you'd know that Jude Royale, Carol's friend up in New York, is telling people that Carol felt her own karma and was following her own intuitive guiding path when she went down to Alabama and sought out Tim Hanlon. Apparently Hanlon's own karma led him out of the priesthood and back into Carol's arms, but along the way someone else interfered with the process. Royale believes that some people in Mobile know more about this than they're letting on."

"And who would that someone else be?"

"I have no idea. But whenever I think about this I can sense Carol Mays trying to escape from somewhere or from someone. I can almost hear her cry for help."

"That's very bizarre, Julianne. You've never even met this woman."

"Don't you ever hear voices talking to you?" Carson was now growing angry with Richter and even though they were both nakedly clutching each other in Richter's kitchen, she stepped the conversation up a notch. "After your wife died, didn't you ever feel that she was trying to talk to you? Didn't you ever hear her voice? Don't you ever hear her, even now?"

"No … not exactly." Richter wasn't being entirely truthful. He turned around and felt his way back toward the stairs. This time he used his cane as for some reason he felt less sure of what was in his path.

Before he began his daily descent into the bomb shelter, Patch Munson had made up his mind that he was going to tell Carol Mays the rationale for her captivity. He wanted her to help him determine an ongoing course of action. He didn't realize that Mays also had an agenda for this day's encounter, and that the upcoming dialogue would be more direct than any discussion they had pursued thus far. As usual Harry scrambled down the ladder first with two steps and a jump. Munson followed carrying the daily rations that he was providing to Mays.

"How *yew feelin' t'day?*"

"Could be better."

"*Ah* brought *yew sem* food."

"Thanks. When am I getting out of here?"

Munson was familiar with this question from Mays. But now he was determined to treat it differently. He wasn't going to snap back at her or tell her to "hush up." He didn't answer her immediately but instead moved slowly towards the refrigerator to put the food inside the appliance.

"*Whah* don't we *jes'* set down here *an'* have a *lit'le* chat?"

"There's only one thing I want to talk about. When am I getting out of this dungeon?"

"*Yew* mean *yew* don't *wanna* talk *'bout* Russell?"

Mays recognized this as the same approach that Munson had taken in the past. Whenever he was unsure how to proceed he brought Russell's name into the discussion. Previously he had correctly assumed that this would keep Mays at bay because she wouldn't risk endangering her son. But Mays knew that it was time to get past those scare tactics and find a way to convince Munson to set her loose.

"No, I don't want to talk about Russell right now, other than when you'll let me go see him." Having rebutted his inquiry, she pressed on. "If you're afraid that Tim Hanlon told me what he told you in the confessional, you shouldn't be. He never told me anything." She watched his face for a reaction and could only discern a more attentive demeanor, which didn't tell her much. She needed to get him to talk about it more. What she didn't realize is that Munson had come to the bomb shelter with the intention of telling her plenty, but with no intention whatsoever of setting her free.

"That *dudden'* matter much, one way or *'nother*. Once *Ah gat yew* in here, *Ah cain't* let *yew* go." This reality had hit Mays many times during the past nineteen days. And yet she knew there was a just and reasonable side to Munson buried under his cowhide exterior. After all, he brought her food almost every day that she'd been there. He brought her suitcase into the shelter after her third day of captivity, and he never made any attempt to physically or sexually abuse her. On the other hand, he had only unshackled her ankles a few times to allow her to use the toilet chamber to change her clothes, and then each time he re-shackled her legs. And the damn dog, Harry, didn't seem to like her much at all. He growled even while he went through his annoying daily routine of sticking his cold nose between her legs, while she constantly pushed him away.

"Sure you can. I won't tell anyone. I'll pretend I had amnesia or something." She desperately hoped that Munson was a bigger fool than he had already demonstrated himself to be. But it was Mays who was becoming delusional with desperation.

"No we *cain't* do *nuthin' lahke* that. But we *cain* talk *'bout whah yer* here, *iffin yew'd lahke.*" Mays was surprised to hear this. It was a major concession. But she worried that it might have a more portentous meaning. Maybe he was going to sadistically tell her why she was there and then kill her to keep her from telling anyone else. This sudden panic stricken thought passed quickly as she decided that knowledge was power and she should look to gather whatever information she could possible acquire. Besides if he planned on killing her he would already have done so.

"Fine. So tell me why I'm here."

"*Yer* here *'cause yer* priest friend knows too much *'bout* me. He knows *Ah* killed *sum'un. Ah* thought *maybeh yew* knew that too. Now, *Ah* know *yew* know that, *b'cause Ah jes'* told *yew.*" This was an ominous statement even though it wasn't said in a menacing manner.

"Why are you telling me this now?"

"*Ah* don't know."

"What do you mean, you don't know? You must have a reason for telling me. I'm not in a position where I'm about to tell anyone about it, but I still don't understand why you want to tell me something like this."

"*B'cause, jes' b'cause.*"

"Because what?"

"*B'cause Ah* was *thaankin'* that *maybeh yew* had *sem* crazy-ass *ahdea o* how we *cain git outta* this mess. *Ah'll* tell *yew* straight up, that *Ah ain't fixin' t'*kill *yew no* more. *Yew ain't* done *nuthin' t'*deserve it … *'course*, *yew trah an'* escape … now that's *'nother matteh.*"

"So when are you going to tell me that my son, Russell, is not in any real danger? Let's get past that hurdle. I don't deserve to worry about him. I understand that you just used that tactic to lure me here. Right?"

"Well, *maybeh* that's true *an' maybeh* it *idden.*"

Mays was growing increasingly confident that her son was unharmed. A few days earlier, Munson told Mays that her disappearance was a big story on the news. He didn't say anything about the disappearance of her son. Munson had also told her that the media was hounding Tim Hanlon because he was the last person who had seen Mays two weeks earlier. Again when he relayed this tidbit of information, Munson didn't say anything about Russell. Nevertheless Mays was still squeamish about the possibility that her son was also being held hostage somewhere. She didn't know how to evaluate this possibility because she didn't know enough about what Munson was hiding. She decided to try to develop more information by playing along with Munson's silly games.

"Alright Patch, you want me to help you find a solution for our problem? Then you have to give me more details. Who was it that you killed? Was it your wife or some family member?"

"*Course* not … Munsons don't go *'round killin'* their own kin. The man *Ah* killed deserved *t' dah.* He was evil. Even *Billeh* Brand said that he was worse *'an* Hitler."

Carol Mays remembered the news from last month. When the abortion doctor from Tampa was murdered, the Jewish Defense League had made a big stink about certain southern Christian preachers who made anti-Semitic remarks that were capable of inspiring acts of violence. One of the examples used was Billy Brand's comment that Fein was "akin to Adolf Hitler in his widespread slaughter of human life." *Was Munson telling her that he shot Aaron Fein in Tampa? Wow, no wonder he's so confused.*

"Are you telling me that you murdered Aaron Fein?" She just blurted out the question. There was no reason for guessing any more.

"*Ah didden' murdeh* no one, no how. *Ah jes'* executed a man who was a *murdereh hisse'f.* That *aint* what *Ah* call *murdeh. Ah jes'* made sure he *wudden'* be *killin' no* more babies. That's all there is to it."

"And you told this to Father Hanlon in the confessional? Is that what this is all about? You were afraid that he would tell somebody what you told him. Then why on earth would you go to confession in the first place, if you're so afraid that this would happen? I just don't get it."

"*Ah* don't *git* it much *neitheh.* But *Ah* sure went *an' dun* it. *Yew* see *Ah* had this *terr'ble* case of the queasies. *An' Ah didden'* know what *t'* do *'bout* it. *Ah fig'yud* that *iffin Ah* went *an' tole* a *Cat'lick* priest that he couldn't tell *no one.* But after *Ah dun tole 'im ever'thaan',* then *Ah gat 'round t'thaankin'* straight. So *Ah jes' d'sahded* to follow him *fur* a *whahle. An'* what do *Ah* see? *Ah* see this *holeh rolleh* priest is out there *bangin'* a black bunny. *That'd* be *yew, naturalleh.* So *how's* a man *s'posed t'* trust a priest who follows his *peckeh* through *lahfe? Ah fig'yud* he *musta* told *yew* all *'bout* it."

Carol Mays listened closely to Patch Munson's soliloquy. He was even dumber than she had thought. But if she wanted to survive, she knew that she had to humor him. She would have to determine a course of action because he was apparently incapable of creating one himself. She decided to ingratiate herself to her captor. Instead of being a recalcitrant prisoner, she would play the role of confidante and hope that Munson would allow her more latitude.

"Let's come back to that business about shooting Aaron Fein, a little later. You're right. He was an evil man. But first tell me some more about you."

"*Whatcha lahke t'* know?"

"Where did the name Patch come from?"

"Patch *ain't mah* real name."

"Then what is your real name?"

"*Harreh.*"

"Harry? You mean like the dog over there? You named your dog after yourself and then gave yourself a new name?"

"Not *'xactly.*"

"So explain to me how you got the name Patch."

"Simple *'nough.*"

"I'm listening. I guess you could say I have all day."

"Well when *Ah* was a young *un,* people called *meh Harreh,* or *mostleh* they called *meh Lit'le Harreh.* See … *mah fatheh* was named *Harreh* also. *'Cept* folks *neveh* called him *Harreh.* They called him Junior, *'cause mah fatheh*'s *fatheh* was also named *Harreh. An'* people *did* call *'im Harreh.*"

Mays was astounded that she could follow this crazy drivel. But she managed to find all of the poppycock, fascinating.

"So in essence then, you are Harold Munson III."

"No … *Harreh* Munson III. There *ain't never been no* 'Harolds' in the Munson clan. *Bah* the way *s'cuse meh fur usin'* the word clan. *Ah'm meanin'* a 'C' clan, not a 'K' klan. Hope we're straight on that. *Ah mahght* not be the smartest man in *all o 'Al'bama* but *Ah ain't no* racist *neitheh.*"

"OK. So you are Harry Munson III and when you were growing up they called you 'Little Harry.' But you still haven't explained where the name 'Patch' comes from."

"One of *a good ole boys* who *Ah* did my *schoolin'* with, Bubba Looney, *decahded Ah* was too big to be called *'Lit'le Harreh.'* That was back in 1983. *Ah* was built then *kinda lahke Ah* am now. *An'* then, *mah* sister Gloria was *clamorin' fur* one of *them* new dolls that *wuz* all the rage at the *tahme.* And then, damned if Bubba Looney didn't go *an'* name *meh afteh* one *o* them damn dolls."

"I don't remember. 1983 was well before I was born. So what sort of doll did he name you after?"

"*Them dang* Cabbage Patch dolls … he said *theh* looked *jes' lahke meh.* Then people *jes' dun* left off the cabbage part …though Bubba still uses it once in a *whahle* … And then *b'faw* long *eveh'un* was *callin' meh* Patch. *Ah* even started *introducin' mahse'f* as Patch *an' Ah* been Patch *eveh* since. But *Ah* still *lahked* the name *Harreh … seein's* how *Ah* had that one *fur* a while also ... *so's* when *mah* old *dawg dahed an' Ah gat meh* a new *dawg, Ah* went *an'* called *'im Harreh*. So there *yew* have it. That there's the tale of Patch and *Harreh*."

Mays was more than a little bit flabbergasted by the "Tale of Patch and Harry," but she wanted to move on. Now that she had Munson in a convivial condition, she wanted to see if she couldn't extract more concessions. If she couldn't secure her release right away, at least she could try to make her environment slightly more humane and livable.

"Patch, you know I haven't bathed in more than two weeks. Do you think we could go back to the big house for a spell so I could take a shower? We could do it when no one's around."

"That *ain't gunna* happen, not *aneh tahme* soon *an'way*." His response had a vague sense of weakening resolve, and Mays decided to push on.

"Listen Patch, I feel disgusting. The only water down here is the small amount that flushes in the composting toilet and whatever trickle I can get from the one spigot that's next to it."

"*Yew gat drinkin'* water in the fridge *an' Ah jes'* brought *yew 'nother* gallon *t'day. An'* there *ain't nuthin'* wrong *wit'* the spigot water *an'way*. It comes up from the well."

"But there's no place to shower at all. What do you expect me to do?"

Yew'll jes' have to take a sponge bath. *Ah'll* bring *yew sem* towels *tomorrah*."

"No. I want to go to the house to take a shower. Then you can bring me back here."

"*Ah alreadeh* said that *ain't happenin'* ... *yer jes' stayin'* here."

"How am I even going to take a sponge bath with all of these chains on me?"

"Simple. *Yew jes'* wash down *s'far's* possible, then *yew* wash up *s'far's* possible, then *yew* wash Possible."

"That's not funny, Patch. But speaking of Possible, I have another issue. I'm going to get my period soon and I don't have any tampons. Could you at least bring me some tampons tomorrow?"

Carol Mays watched Munson's face curl up in scarlet consternation as though he had never heard of such a thing before. She was glad she made him squirm. She would bet that he had never purchased any female personal hygiene products in his life, and she could see that he was terrorized by the thought of going to the local convenience store to do so now.

"Do *them thaangs* come in *diff'ent sahzes an'* stuff ... or *don't it* much *matteh*?"

"Not different sizes, but just get extra absorbent. Or for that matter, anything is better than nothing." Mays knew that she had Munson where she wanted him for the moment. He was discussing things that he never in a million years wanted to discuss and he knew that it was his own fault.

Mays could feel Munson's guilt without hearing another word from him. However he managed to say "*Ah'll* see what *Ah cain* do."

Melech Katz finally surrendered to Abe Elowitz' many attempts to get him to attend his group psychotherapy session. The session took place on a Saturday afternoon. That had been the consensus of the participants, who worked during the week and had social plans for their Saturday nights. Elowitz' group had been meeting together bi-weekly for more than four months. Katz was the only new member of the group and two others had moved on. Not everybody in the group was very vocal, but Katz did get a chance to hear a bit about everybody. There were two people that interested Katz more than the others. Priscilla Stengel was a young woman who had a handicapped child; had just lost her father; had lost her husband in a car accident; and was still suffering from significant guilt over having had an abortion many years earlier. He was amazed that she had managed to keep her sanity and actually exhibit an upbeat attitude.

The other person that interested Katz was a man about his age who had the most common name in the phone book, John Smith. Smith was an ex-Marine corporal who had served a tour of duty in

Iraq and another tour in Afghanistan. Smith didn't relate well to the other members of the psychotherapy group. During the session itself he never spoke unless someone asked him a direct question. However at the conclusion of the session, Smith came over to Katz and shook his hand.

"I was glad that you shot that scum bag on the rooftop at BITSY. I'm amazed that there are so many assholes in the world. Thanks for taking one of them out."

"It certainly felt like the right thing to do at the time. But it was reminiscent of events in Gaza. It almost felt like someone else was pulling the trigger."

"I understand. Some days I feel like I've never left Afghanistan. You'd think that when you wake up and realize that you're home in the United States, that you would feel good about that … but sometimes I feel like I'd be better off back in the combat theater. At least in Afghanistan, there was always another Marine who had your back."

"I know the feeling. But I don't like coming to a session like this and explaining it to anyone else." Katz looked at the ex-corporal and realized that he was *still* a Marine.

"When my company was in Afghanistan there were plenty of days when it was either kill or be killed. Honestly some days I didn't care which it was."

"War can be very dehumanizing."

"Only if you let it … The saving grace was the fact that you always wanted to save the ass of the Marine next to you."

"But that's not much grace at all."

"It is what it is. The old adage 'there's no atheists in foxholes,' is not meant as humor. If God determined that I needed to be in Iraq or Afghanistan, so be it. I did my best to save my fellow Marines and support my country. If I ended up taking one for the team, then I would just reach the Pearly Gates earlier than I had originally planned."

"War is hell." Katz opted for a cliché because it fit.

"Sometimes being back in the human race is worse."

"I know that feeling too. But it can't be right.

"We'll see sooner or later, I guess. Meanwhile thanks for taking out that scumbag Clinton." John Smith reached out and shook hands with Katz for a second time and then walked toward the door. Katz started to follow him out the door, when he spotted Priscilla Stengel waiting near Dr. Elowitz' conference room.

"I was sorry to hear about your father. Did I hear correctly that he just died this week?"

"Just buried him yesterday. Thank you for your condolences. I miss him already but in some ways I feel like he's still here with us. The only reason I came this afternoon was that I felt like he was telling me to come here. The sessions have been helpful to me over the last few months. I know that you're new to our group. But we all knew about you, coming in tonight. I'm glad you decided to become part of our group."

There was something about Priscilla Stengel that was appealing to Melech Katz. She was not attractive physically, and she was a few years older than him, but she had a quality about her that indicated that she knew who she was and where she was going. At this stage of his life, Katz found those qualities appealing. Maybe this group psychotherapy might work out after all. He wanted to go out and have a few drinks and think things through. He decided to invite Stengel to join him.

"Thanks, I think it might help. Can I offer to buy you a drink?"

"You can certainly offer and I'd probably accept at another time, but right now I have a private session coming up with Dr. Elowitz. I'm just waiting for him to finish up.

"All right another time then."

"Sounds promising." As Katz smiled and departed, Priscilla Stengel felt better about herself. She had interested someone. That hadn't happened a lot lately. Not only that, the guy was a very hunky Mediterranean with great dark eyes. Maybe things were turning in a new direction for her. Then she waited for her session with Elowitz to begin. This could be a crucial step for her new plan.

Patch Munson sat in the parlor of the old farm house and watched the news along with his wife. Maggie Munson was fascinated by the story of Carol Mays, the missing model. But she also noticed that whenever a news clip appeared on the TV about Mays, her husband would grab the remote and do one of two things. He would either increase the volume indicating this was something that he wanted to hear or he would quickly change the channel as though this was something he had already heard and didn't want to discuss with his wife. This was one of the station switching times and Patch Munson quickly changed the channel.

"Leave that on, Patch. *Ah wanna* see what *ther'all sayin' 'bout* that actress *ladeh*."

"She *ain't no* actress. She's a model. *B'sahdes*, who cares what those reporters say. Woman's *more 'an lahkely* dead, *an'how*." He stood up quickly and threw the remote back on the couch. "*Ah'm headin' oveh t'* Dumbarton's … *meetin'* up *wit'* Bubba *an' maybeh sem othehs. Ain't gettin'* home *earleh* … so don't be *waitin'* up or *nuthin'* …"

Maggie Munson was surprised by her husband's disclosure. She knew that he went to Dumbarton's Pub when he went out with his buddies on a Saturday night, but he never came right out and said as much. She also knew that he wasn't drinking Dr Pepper when he went to Dumbarton's, but they never discussed it. *At least he ain't fixin' t' go t' the strip bars oveh on Wilson Avenue,* she thought. But then again Maggie didn't like it when he hung out with Bubba Looney, *That man is trouble lookin' t' happen.* As the front door swung closed behind him, Maggie said a prayer for her husband's safe keeping. She had an odd feeling he needed it.

After finally leaving Richter's Bayshore Boulevard residence, the place that Julianne Carson had begun referring to as their "love shack," Richter and Carson spent the rest of Saturday on various errands, including a trip up north of the city to the BITSY campus.

Richter wanted to speak with the dean about his upcoming sabbatical. His ongoing discussions with Julianne helped him recognize that he was working too hard on the teaching phases of his life and not balancing this with the learning aspects of his life. He needed to take a break from the classroom and the public speaking circuit.

Following their stopover at BITSY they drove over to Ybor City for some light shopping at Centro Ybor. They stopped at a cigar store on 7th Avenue, where Richter purchased his preferred smokes. They then went into a trendy corner bistro, sat at the bar and ordered some drinks. Shortly after they sat down, Julianne saw a familiar face glaring at them. She recognized Melech Katz from the recent television footage covering the events of Terrifying Thursday. He was drinking alone at the far end of the bar, and from general appearances he may have been there for some time.

"Someone is staring at you." She barely got the words out to tell Richter when Katz got up and walked over to where they were sitting.

Katz had been winding down in the bar since leaving the group psychotherapy session. Since coming to the United States, he had become an avid baseball fan and so he managed to pass the time alone at the bistro watching the ball game between the Baltimore Orioles and the Tampa Bay Rays. He thought it was interesting how much better the Rays had played since they changed their name from the *Devil* Rays. However those passing thoughts disappeared when he spotted Richter coming into the bar accompanied by an attractive woman. Uncharacteristically he decided to approach the couple.

"Hawk Richter? Hi, it's Mel Katz. We've met a few times at BITSY,"

"Sure, sure, Mel, how are you doing?"

"I'm doing alright. I don't mean to interrupt, but I just wanted to say hello for a second or two." He stood next to Julianne as he spoke and at first looked past her at Richter. But the alcohol got the better of discretion and he began looking directly at Julianne Carson as he continued talking. Richter, however, assumed Katz was conversing with him.

"People are still talking about your courageous act of heroism. My kudos to you."

"Well, it hasn't all been pleasant. I've garnered some criticism as well. But I'd rather not talk about me. I have something that I want to say that involves you directly."

Julianne could smell the alcohol on Katz' breath, but she thought the young professor had the most beautiful shy smile she had ever seen. Even with droopy eyelids he still was a gorgeous hunk of a man. He had pearl white teeth, dimpled cheeks and a cleft chin. His eyes were dark and penetrating. He had a chiseled body that was quite visible in the tight t-shirt that he was wearing. And he was still looking at her, even as he spoke to Richter. She felt pretty special now getting the attention of two interesting men. Nevertheless she also had a feeling that Katz might want a private moment to discuss something with Richter. She sensed that it wasn't something academic.

"Why don't I make a trip to the ladies room so you two can talk?" She didn't wait for an answer but simply picked up her pocketbook and left the bar area.

"She's a nice looking woman, Hawk."

"I'll take your word for it,"

"I didn't mean to interrupt like this but I wanted to mention to you that a couple of detectives from the Florida State Police came to talk to me about Aaron Fein's killing. They said that they were trying to see if it was linked somehow to the BITSY murders. They also asked me if I knew you."

"Detective Kanasani?"

"Yes. You know him?"

"Sort of. It is surprising that he would interview you about Aaron Fein's murder. Kanasani came to see me about Fein because I'm an investor in the FCW, but I don't know why he would interview you. There's nothing linking Fein's murder and the BITSY murders. But I'll say this. Kanasani worried me when he said that they had no solid leads on the Fein murder. He followed by saying that I could also be a target of some anti-abortion nutcase. So anyway what exactly did he ask about me?"

"He asked me how well I knew you; whether or not I liked you; what kind of a person you were; whether you had made any outspoken statements about abortion on campus; and who among the faculty members knew you better than I did."

"So what did you tell him?"

"That there wasn't much to say …after all this is already the longest conversation we've ever had."

Richter laughed at Katz' friendly candor. "Well I appreciate you going out of your way to say hello and tell me about Kanasani. Was there anything else that he said that you think I should know?"

"No, nothing really, except for the fact that he was genuinely concerned for your safety. He said that some Alabama televangelist had linked your name with Aaron Fein, and was agitating to eliminate the Fein Center entirely. But that just sounds a lot like what he told you anyway. I didn't think Kanasani was such a bad guy."

Julianne Carson was coming back to the bar area from the ladies room and smiled as she approached the two professors.

"Did you take care of your business? Or do you need a few more minutes?"

"We're fine Julianne. You know, I don't think that I introduced you two before. Julianne this is Mel Katz. Mel … Julianne Carson. By the way Mel would you care to join us for dinner? We're just waiting for a table. I could easily tell them to make it three." Richter was being polite but he didn't want his offer to be accepted.

Katz started to feel uncomfortable and courteously declined. Julianne was slightly disappointed. She liked the idea of a threesome for dinner. She also briefly pleasured herself with thoughts of where such an evening might lead. She reminded herself that she was now the new Julianne, the woman who was eternally living in the moment.

Meanwhile Katz noticed Julianne's brief blushing and felt a clicking connection with her. But as attractive as Julianne was to Katz, he didn't want to pursue the connection any further. He already had enough complications in his life.

A few moments later Katz said goodbye and left the bar. After the younger professor was gone, Richter turned his shaded unseeing eyes toward Julianne and said, "I might want to make a trip up to Mobile to talk to that Billy Brand character."

"You know … somehow I knew this was coming," Julianne replied."

"Really, what was it this time? Your intuition? Your aura? Your karma? The guiding hand or some other mystical nonsense? Richter was obviously annoyed but he didn't know exactly why. He only knew that he wanted to go to Mobile to persuade Brand to leave his name out of his sermons.

"Touchy, touchy … now aren't we?" Julianne chided Richter in a teasing way but also grabbed his arm affectionately to show her support. "I just think that there's a lot going on up in Mobile these days."

Bubba Looney referred to himself as "a redneck's redneck." He loved his country music, his whiskey and his women, in that order. He was often accused of being a blowhard by some of his cronies, because his stories of manly exploits were frequently over inflated. But as a hard drinking Alabama boy, with the right connections to the other good-ole-boys in the city of Mobile, he had somehow managed to make it to detective. This was in spite of the fact that he had been hauled in by other cops on four different occasions when he was much too drunk to drive. He was never charged even once. Looney also had a problem with binge drinking that caused him to go on four and five day benders and occasionally miss work. These days were written off as sick time by his boss who was another one of Looney's drinking buddies. Recently though Looney's boozing was getting out of hand and other cops were less inclined to go out on the town with him. But Bubba Looney could usually count on his farmer buddy, Patch Munson, for a night of ear twisting and elbow-bending. They were in the midst of that routine on Saturday night when Bubba decided to kick it up a notch by doing shots with his beers. Munson was sluggish for most of the night, and Bubba was ready to start howling at the moon.

"*Yew* see where that *Cat'lick* preacher put out a big-ass *bounteh t' fahnd* his *niggeh* girlfriend. What a joke! *Yew cain onleh* collect the *moneh iffin* this black bimbo shows up *alahve*. *Ever 'un* knows that this Hanlon guy, this *Cat'lick* priest, killed her *an'* dumped her black ass *semwhere*. She'll show up sooner or later but when she does no one's *gunna* be *collectin'* no reward, *b'cause* she's *gunna* be deader than dirt." Bubba Looney put his arm around Patch Munson and added, "*yew slowin'* down on *meh*? If *yew cain't* run *wit'* the big *dawgs*, stay on the porch."

Looney was firing down shots of bourbon with draft chasers and Patch Munson was having a hard time keeping pace with his buddy. There were about a dozen other patrons in Dumbarton's Pub but none of them paid much attention to the conversation between Munson and Looney.

"*Sumptin' Ah wanna esk yew 'bout*, Bubba, *yew* know, '*bout* that Mays case."

"Go *'head*, shoot."

"*Iffin y'all* knew where this Mays woman was at, and *yew* set her free unharmed … is it still *kidnappin'*? *Yew thaank* the law would show *clemenceh fur* the kidnapper if he undid the *kidnappin' wit'* no harm done *t'* the woman?"

"Depends."

"On what?"

"First … on *whatcha* mean *bah* 'no harm.' Second, that *ain't gunna* happen, *'cause ever 'un's watchin'* this priest *lahke* a hawk. *Iffin* he *jes'* kidnapped her, then where'd he stash her, *an'* how's he *feedin'* her?"

"What if the priest didn't do it? What if *'nother* person snatched Mays?"

"What *fur*?"

"Damned if *Ah* know … but *jes'* say he did. *An'* then he lets her go … is that still *kidnappin'*?"

"Well this is still *Al'bama*. But this Mays woman is *sem kinda* famous. *Iffin 'nother niggeh* snatched her, it may not be as big a deal, *dependin'* of course, on what Mays has to say. But *iffin* a white guy did it, we could have *ourse 'ves* a wholesale race riot. That's *whah* we *gat* so much anger *buildin'* up here *alreadeh*. Hanlon's a white guy *an'* a *Cat'lick* priest."

Looney stopped for a moment in thought. Then he added, "Least he *ain't* a faggot. That *woulda* made *thaangs* even crazier than they *alreadeh is*. *Maneh* of *them Cat'lick* priests are faggots, you know. But this Hanlon guy appears *t'lahke pusseh*. *B'sahdes*, *whah* are *yew askin' meh* all this stuff? *Yew* had too much *hootch?*

"Look Bubba, *Ah ain't drank nearleh s'much* as *yew*. But *Ah gotta* trust *sum'un. Yew an' meh* go back a long way. Remember when *yer* truck *mirreh* hit the *preacheh*." Munson referenced the time shortly after they graduated high school when Looney ran over Billy Brand. It was clear and evident collateral for any disclosures of his own that he chose to make. "*Ah been keepin'* that there secret *fur maneh yeahs*. Now *Ah gat meh sump'in' Ah* need *yer he'p wit'*. Let's go *fur* a *rahde*."

"*Aw rahght*, let *meh* take a piss first."

Munson went and started his Silverado. Minutes later Looney came out of Dumbarton's Pub and jumped in the passenger seat. They headed back towards Munson's farm.

Patch Munson didn't often visit the bomb shelter late at night. At first he had some difficulty locating it in the darkness, because he and Bubba Looney were totally smashed. Normally he knew his property like the back of his hand. There was no real problem, however, because while the two good-ole-boys stumbled around waving a flashlight along the ground, Harry sprinted ahead to the edge of the citrus grove, and barked around the edges of the loose foliage that covered the wooden bridge that lidded the earthen antechamber above the bomb shelter.

When Looney and Munson caught up with Harry, Bubba Looney became even more surprised by the sophistication of the concealment of the fallout shelter. It was close up near the citrus tree line, but ten feet away from the post fence that outlined the residential section. It was more than 200 yards from the dirt road that ran behind the citrus grove at the north end of the farm where the chicken houses were located. It was plainly intended not to be near anything else on the property.

"*Yew* are one crazy-ass redneck, Munson. *Ah* have no idea what *y'all* built down *un'er* the ground here, but it sure as hell is in the middle *o* nowhere."

"No it *ain't*. Look back there," he said pointing back past the magnolia trees to the farmhouse which had two or three recognition lights on inside the house. We *ain't* more *'an* 400 yards from the house, *jes' seems furtha*."

Munson picked up the rake that had been left in the area for years with one function in mind and he began taking away some of the loose leaves, sticks and grass that covered the wooden bridge platform, just below the surface level. He cleared away enough brush to uncover the upper trap door portal which opened to the earthen stairway. The stairway, in turn, led into the antechamber above the concrete ceiling of the bomb shelter. Meanwhile Looney held the flashlight and stared down in amazement. He rubbed his eyes a couple of times in disbelief. He couldn't fathom how Patch Munson had kept this underground construction secret for all these years. He was about to find out that Munson had an even bigger secret awaiting them below.

Munson opened the upper trap door and climbed down the earth and stone stairway into the antechamber, with Looney and Harry following behind him. Mays had been sleeping when she began to hear a feint but familiar scraping sound above her. Because of the extensive soundproofing of the underground bomb shelter, she never heard Munson's approach until he started removing the brushwood from atop of the ceiling door. However this time things were different. It was night time. Munson hadn't been out to the shelter at night since he brought her there. When the lower trap door leading from the antechamber to the bomb shelter was opened, she was both startled and frightened to see that Munson had brought someone with him.

Bubba Looney was a much bigger man than Patch Munson. While Munson was an obese 270 pounds, he was only 5' 10" tall. Looney was 6'4" tall and a few pounds lighter than Munson. They were both physically menacing in their own way, but Looney radiated a cruel meanness that emanated from an animalistic hunger that couldn't be easily sated.

Munson's threatening appearance was mostly a function of his ogre-like head and facial features. But once people got to know Munson, his ugliness was no longer that intimidating. Carol Mays had been growing less fearful of Patch Munson with every ensuing encounter. He talked tough, but somewhere within his make-up there was a sense of fairness, possibly even compassion. He had settled into a routine of sorts, arriving at approximately the same time each day. Munson had become almost predictable – until this first nighttime visit. The routine had been broken, and Mays' first glance at Munson's drunken companion induced sheer terror. Bubba Looney was moving a flashlight around the chamber in awe. His facial features were silhouetted by the glow. Mays barely even noticed Harry as he did his usual bothersome sniffing routine that Looney was now spotlighting with his flashlight. But she was terrified when she heard Looney half-growl, half-drool in a dogged drunken tone, "Well, will *yew lookit* that? *Harreh*'s *gat* his snout in *'er* snatch, Patch!"

Munson was inebriated to the point that he had difficulty responding to Looney's inane alliterative pronouncement. He just yelled at the dog, "*git o'er* here, *Harreh*." The dog danced back toward where Munson was standing near the ladder, while Looney advanced past the fold out sofa bed and toward the petrified prisoner.

"Holy shit, Munson, you *gat yerse'f yer* own *fuckin' niggeh* whore. How long you been *holdin'* out on *meh*?" Looney thought for a moment and then his eyes opened wide and he asked, "*Yew gat aneh* more o 'em? She the *onleh* one down here?" Looney began shining the flashlight quickly around the bomb shelter and was startled to the point of being spooked when in the next instant the whole room was lit up as Patch Munson threw the light switch in the corner. Cognition came to Looney, seconds after the lights went on. He realized quickly

that it was just the three of them in the chamber. He glared at a trem-
bling and shackled Carol Mays.

"You're Hanlon's whore. Carol Mays, *rahght*?" Then he turned to
Munson and said, "Cabbage Patch, *yew* dumb *fuckeh*, *yew* done *sem
amazin'leh* stupid shit in *yer lahfe*, but this here takes the cake." He
began laughing heartily with a sinister twist while Munson looked on
in a befuddled manner. Mays stared in absolute abject horror!

Looney tried to balance several impulsive reactions. He could
turn in his dim-witted friend and become a hero of sorts. But he also
thought that maybe he would work some kind of deal with Munson
so that they could collect the $100,000 reward. As a police officer, he
wasn't directly eligible for the reward money. He wondered how he
could have his pie and eat it also. He laughed heartily once again. It
was obvious to all three of them that the next move was Looney's.

In Tampa, Priscilla Stengel was rapidly developing a whole new
vigor about her writing. She now saw some significant synergies
between her work as a freelance investigative reporter and her aspirations to write a full length book. And to do the work appropriately as
a columnist she needed to follow her investigative instincts. She went
back over the particulars of the night of the Aaron Fein shooting. For
several weeks now the final few moments of her conversation with
Fein had been haunting her. But she was even more spooked by the
thought that Fein's killer may have been in the building at the same
time that she was there. And then there was a matter of the pickup
truck that cut her off as she was following Fein out of the executive
parking lot. The police seemed to have a lot of interest in that angle.
That thought had led her to seek assistance from Abe Elowitz, her
psychotherapist who had once before helped her understand some of
the ruminations of her own mind through hypnosis.

The police had asked her to collaborate with their hypnotist but she
refused because she had no way of controlling the process. Besides
they had treated her more like a suspect than a witness.

Elowitz was more than just a psychotherapist for Stengel. He served as her spiritual therapist as well. She had been going to him for a number of years and he helped her to relax and meditate with pre-hypnotic techniques. But as a trained psychiatrist he was also adept at inducing hypnotic trances. She met with him right after the group therapy session and went right to work on her hypnosis. In the process she recalled that the license plate on the pickup truck was an Alabama license plate, and that it contained three specific letters – MVN – although she couldn't recall the accompanying numbers on the plate. She later learned that plates with these three letters were normally assigned to vehicles in the Mobile, Alabama area. She didn't know if this had any significance but she decided to follow up on the lead and see where it led.

Bubba Looney leered at Carol Mays and then grabbed at her as though she were a defenseless shackled animal that would submit to whatever taunting or torture he decided to create. She launched her body backward, away from his clutching advances. Mays was now fully awake, conscious and extremely frightened. This was an aberration with respect to the way events had unfolded over the previous nineteen days. She was suddenly very conscious of her vulnerability. She was wearing the same shorts that Munson had allowed her to change into three days earlier and she was wearing a sleeveless t-shirt which she had put on each evening as a night shirt. She reached down and grabbed a sheet off of the bedding and protectively clutched it to her chest for a second before Looney reached out and ripped it away from her. The big man then backed off for a second and laughed while still staring at Mays. Then noting that her ankles were shackled, he said to Munson. "*Thaank yew betteh git meh* the key *t' them* ankle *ahrons.*"

"*Whah?*"

"*Yew* know damn well *whah.*"

"*Yew* don't need *t'* be *messin' wit'* her Bubba. *Yew jes' gat t' he'p* me *fig'yeh* what *t'* do *wit'* her."

Looney looked slightly annoyed and then asked Munson: "What've *yew* been *doin' wit'* this *darkie? Yew* been *screwin'* her in this *fuckin'* dungeon *whahle eveh'un else's lookin' eveh'where fur* her? Huh, that *'bout rahght?* Well now that *yew* shared *yer lit'le* secret *wit' meh, Ah* guess *Ah'll* take *mah* share *o* the chocolate too, *whilst* we *fig'yeh* out where *t'* dump her black ass once *an' fur* all." He began to loosen his belt buckle and lowered his jeans down around his knees in an instant.

"No. Don't hurt her. She *ain't dun nuthin'* wrong – yet."

Looney began laughing again. "Cabbage Patch, *yew* ignorant asshole, *yew ain't gat no* choice. People are *lookin'* all *oveh fur* this *niggeh. Yew an' meh* go back a long ways, so *Ah'll he'p yew fig'yeh* this out … but first *Ah'm gunna* get *meh* a piece *o* this dark meat." With his boots still on his feet and his jeans down around his ankles, Looney sat down on the sofa bed and began to unlace his boots. Mays was suddenly overcome with anger that was stronger than her fear. She took two quick shackled steps and launched her body on top of Looney chains and all, while simultaneously head-butting him squarely in the face. Looney roared in pain as blood splattered from his nose. Mays attempted to sink her teeth into Looney's juggler vein. He yanked her off his body with both of his hands and arms and threw her across the room like a toy doll. Looney stumbled to his feet and yanked his unbuckled jeans back up around his hips while Munson tried to grab him to break up the melee.

"Calm down Bubba. We *gotta thaank sensibleh*. Don't hurt the girl. *Ah* told *yew*; she *ain't dun nuthin'* wrong. *An' so's y'know, Ah ain't* touched her *none neitheh. Ah jes'* been *keepin'* an eye on her here, *so's Ah cain fig'yah* out what *t'* do next." Meanwhile Harry began barking in frenzied confusion. The hound was temporarily unsure of how to intervene.

Looney was angry beyond control. He paid no attention to Patch Munson and simply pushed him out of the way and then advanced on Carol Mays once again. He was now furious at Munson as well as at Mays. He carefully avoided her swinging arms as he moved closer.

He then lashed her across the face with the back of his right hand and trapped her against the wall with his body. He tried to put his left forearm across her throat as he reached down with his right hand and ripped off most of her night shirt with three successive yanking strokes. Mays spit blood from inside her mouth as she struggled to breathe. Then she slumped to a seated position on the floor and against the wall under the force of Looney's overpowering strength. Looney was in the process of dropping his jeans once again when he heard the most outlandish words come from behind him.

"Leave her alone, Bubba, or *Ah'm gunna* shoot *yew*!" When Looney turned around he saw his drunken friend Patch Munson pointing a shaking gun at his head. Looney was one hundred percent sure that Munson was never going to shoot him. However he was annoyed with Munson for interrupting his desire to teach Mays a lesson. Looney looked quickly at the black woman still seated against the wall with both fettered legs stretched out in front of her and gasping for breath. He turned away from her slowly and started walking back across the room toward Munson.

"Cabbage Patch, *yew* stupid, drunken, *niggeh-lovin'* son of a bitch … *Ah* don't know where *yer* sick-ass *mahnd* has gone, but *Ah* also know that *yew ain't gunna* shoot *yer lahfe-long* friend *jes' 'cause* he wants *t' git a lit'le* black ass. Give me that *fuckin'* gun *b'faw yew* hurt *yerse'f.*" As he said this Harry began to bark furiously, and began jumping up on Looney who pushed the dog away forcefully. Looney began carefully moving past the opened sofa bed but kept his eyes on Munson.

"Don't come *aneh closeh*, Bubba. We *cain* talk from here. We *gat t'* talk *'bout* this mess. But *Ah* don't want *t'* make it *aneh* worse *'an* it is."

"Don't be such a cabbage-headed *fuckin'* fool, Patch. *Yew cain* do *betteh 'an* this here darkie. *Yew* may have gotten whipped *wit'* the *ugleh* stick a few *tahmes*, but *yer* still a good-ole- boy, *an'* a *fahne* redneck too. *Yew don't* need *t'* be *protectin' no niggeh*s. He reached out quickly and put both hands on the barrel of the Colt .38 Super. Simultaneously Harry jumped back at Looney but too late to make a difference. Looney's quick yank on the gun startled the drunken chicken farmer and Munson's finger tightened around the trigger. The gun discharged its bullet directly into Bubba Looney's chest.

The shooting of Bubba Looney took place at approximately five minutes before midnight on Saturday night. Munson and Mays unsuccessfully attempted to revive the police detective and he died twenty minutes after he was shot. There was excessive blood across the floor of the bomb shelter. Then after Looney bled out and died his bladder and bowels emptied in short order and there were bodily fluids everywhere. Munson whimpered in pain and agony as though he had shot himself and Carol Mays worried that his subsequent panic-like breathing might lead to a horrific outcome. All the while Harry intermittently barked, growled and whimpered not unlike the reaction of his master. Mays needed to keep Munson calm and rational and tried to do so by agreeing to help him get rid of the body with a promise not to tell anyone what had happened. They both knew that this was a porous promise. Mays also worried that her incarceration would now last even longer. They hadn't said more than a few words to each other while they were trying to revive Looney. Meanwhile Mays eyed the location of Munson's Colt .38 Super, which was never out of Munson's reach. Looney's body had bounced off the sofa bed and onto the floor when he was shot, and the bedding was drenched.

Finally Patch stood up and aimed the gun at his terrorized captive. She was mortally afraid that he would shoot again. At first he said nothing. It was slightly reminiscent of the original night of her captivity, except now there was a dead body between them.

"This *neveh wuddah* happened *iffin yewd'a* stayed away from that *gawd-damned* priest."

"Don't blame me Patch."

"Damn it girl. Bubba's now on his way *t'* the promised land," he whimpered, "*an' Ah dun sent 'im* there."

"Bubba Looney is now on his way to *hell*, and no one could deserve the trip more." She waited for that to sink in and then asked in a conspiratorial tone, "So how're we going to get him out of here?" His answer gave her chills.

"*We ain't.*"

Munson began to back away toward the ladder with Harry circling around next to him. With his left hand he lifted the ladder a foot or so. It was Harry's signal to begin climbing out.

"No Patch, you can't leave him here with me."

"The hell *Ah cain't.*" Then, he added, "*Ah'll* be back *tomorrah an'* then we'll *jes' fig'yeh* out what *t'* do then." He kept the gun pointed at the battered torso of Carol Mays and she tried to rush at him shackles and all but fell flat on her face and then stopped when she heard the trigger cock. "*Ah* said *Ah'll* be back." With that Munson ascended the ladder into the antechamber, removed the ladder and closed the ceiling door behind him.

Sunday brought an intermittent sunshine on a beautiful Southern Alabama morning. The throngs of worshipers that flocked into the halls of the Christian Ascendancy Community Church were buzzing about what Billy might say about harboring the much maligned Catholic priest, Father Tim Hanlon. Billy didn't disappoint them. The sermon was about "forgiveness" or what Billy Brand called: "*furgiveness.*" The topic was posted on the billboard outside the church and also on the church website so that the extended congregation would have an early inkling about the subject matter.

The church was packed although many in the congregation were not happy with Billy Brand's decision. In the middle of the church Patch Munson sat next to his wife Maggie. Up in the choir Munson's two rotund sisters sat in their black Hefty Bag dresses.

Each of the Munsons had something different going through their mind. Maggie was worried about her husband's mental health. He had become more distant than ever over the last several weeks and she was clueless as to why. She had no idea what he had been up to last night, but he didn't come into the house until 2 AM and then he spent more than a half hour in the shower, before coming to bed and never touching her at all. He was out of bed and wandering around the house less than two hours later.

Meanwhile Munson's two sisters were bumping their way into position in the choir, more concerned about the fact that Lorileen Ashton's dress was showing too much cleavage … *"Ah'd ratheh be buried in a croaker sack,"* … than they were about what Billy Brand was going to say about Tim Hanlon.

For now Patch Munson was praying for a plan to help him achieve *earthly* salvation. He wasn't ready yet to face the afterlife; he just wanted to be secure here on earth. He knew that he couldn't trick God, but a plan like that was hatching inside his skull anyway. A hammering headache helped remind him of the awful activities of the last ten hours.

As they all waited for the preliminary prayers to be completed leading up to the sermon, Patch Munson once again recounted the mounting pile of mistakes that he had made in the last three weeks.

Mistake number one: he decided to be Aaron Fein's executioner. Mistake number two: he never discarded the unregistered Colt 38 Super. Mistake number three: he tried to purge the queasies by confessing his transgression to a Catholic priest. Mistake number four: he followed the priest and consequently found out about his girlfriend. Mistake number five: he kidnapped the girlfriend who turned out to be fashion model Carol Mays. Mistake number six: he held Mays prisoner in the family bomb shelter. Mistake number seven; he got drunk with Bubba Looney and told him about Mays. Mistake number eight: he shot and killed Bubba Looney. Mistake number nine: Looney's *dead* body was still in the bomb shelter. And finally mistake number 10: Carol Mays *live* body was still in the same fallout shelter. It may have been a sunny Alabama Sunday morning for most of the churchgoers. But Patch Munson felt that there was a perpetual cloud over his head.

Before he went to the pulpit to deliver his remarks Reverend Brand had some thoughts of his own. He wondered how Tim Hanlon was doing back in the rectory. *Would Hanlon watch the services on TV as he said he would; and would he appear at the brief fellowship reception in the courtyard after services as he said he might? And finally how would the planned reconciliation meeting go between Hanlon and Lawson Mays that evening.* At first Brand didn't have answers to these questions but when he prayed in silence, God answered him in positive manner on all three questions, and that energized him as he started his sermon.

"*T'day* we're *gunna* talk *'bout 'furgiveness.'* Yes, *fur-give-ness.*" He paused between each syllable, delivering a part of the word to a third of his audience at a time. As he gestured with an open right palm to the left, then to the center and then to the right, of the congregation, his eyes danced along the same path. He magically made eye contact with every man, woman and child seated in front of him. He then used his hand to rapidly draw an open circle in the air in front of him as if he lassoed in his title word and captured his congregation along with it. Enchantingly, eight words into his sermon, Billy Brand had garnered the total attention of the assembled Christian worshipers by simply saying the words slowly and then gesticulating with rapid fanfare. His television crew knew him well and had captured the relevant angles of his eyes in a close cropped video that sent a similar signal to the expansive multi-media audience. And once Billy had captured his congregation he never let them go.

"Now *jes'* what do *y'all* believe we mean *bah furgiveness*? *Iffin* a man breaks a bond or a contract *wit' y'all*, do *y'all* go *an'* say '*mah* neighbor is a no good reprobate?' When the *wahfe* sees the husband return home *afteh* a *nahght* out *wit'* the boys *an'* he's *higheh* than a Georgia pine, does she throw him out *lahke* an *egg-sucking dawg*? *An'* what *iffin* the next *tahme* he gets back *drunker than Cooter Brown;* does she *furgive 'im 'nother tahme*? *An'* then on still *'nother* day, he comes home again *lookin lahke wobbly plaster. An'* so now the *wahfe* is *thaankin';* What *t'* do? What *t'* do? Is there *aneh* room still *fur fur-giveness*? Well here's what the *bahble* says *'bout* that. *Ah'm quotin'* from Matthew 18:21– 22;

*'Then came Peter t' him, and said, Lord, how
oft shall mah brother sin against meh, an' Ah
still furgive him? Till seven tahmes? Jesus saith
unto him, Ah say unto thee, not just until seven
tahmes: but, until seventy tahmes seven.'*

"So *sem* folks are now *thaankin'* 'wow *Ah gat me* 487 more *tahmes*
out *wit'* the boys." The preacher stopped and canvassed the eyes in the
church once again from left to right. This time he had a slight frozen smile, and it evoked a chuckle or two from the crowd before he
completed the eye sweep and unexpectedly thundered rapidly, "No
damn no! The Lord *furgives* ... but he *dudden'* condone. A sin is still a
sin. Every single transgression against a *wahfe*, a husband, a neighbor
or even a stranger is a transgression against *Almahghteh* God." Then
he slowed down and added softly, "But in his infinite goodness, God
furgives our sins, *an'* in the Lord's Prayer we ask God *t' furgive* our
trespasses in the same way that we *furgive* those who trespass against
us. So then *iffin* we sin *seventeh tahmes* seven *an'* ask *fur furgiveness*
than we must also *furgive seventeh tahmes* seven."

Billy Brand changed the pace of his remarks the way a tennis
player takes pace off the ball to deceive his opponent, and he effectively kept his audience off balance. But they loved it. He continued.

"In his most courageous act of *furgiveness,* Jesus *furgave* those
who put him *t'* death. *Ah* quote from Luke 23:34:

'And Jesus said ... Father, *furgive* them, *fur* they know not what
they do. ... and they cast lots to *divahde* his garments.'

"What great love ... His *fahnest* hour of *furgiveness* ... *Cain* we
furgive lahke Jesus? Well we better *b'cause* in Matthew 6:14 – 15
Jesus says,

"If *yew furgive* those who sin against *yew*, *yer heavenleh* Father
will *furgive y'all*. But if *yew* refuse to *furgive* others, *yer* Father will
not *furgive yer* sins."

"So now what does this mean *fur y'all*? *Ah'll* tell *yew* what
it means. It means *y'all* have hope. We can hope that *sum'un* who
we've wrongly prejudged will have that *Christ-lahke* love in his heart

to *furgive* us, even as we spread harsh accusations and rumors *oveh an' oveh, maybeh* even seven *tahmes seventeh*. But there's one other part of *furgiveness* that we need to remember. It is this: we must seek *furgiveness* by *acknowledgin'* our *wrongdoin'*. We must be *sorreh* in order to be *furgiven*.

"Now *sem* of *y'all* know that Sarah Anne *an' Ah* have extended our home *fur* the use of Father Tim Hanlon, *an' sem* of *y'all mahght* be *thaankin'* the priest has done *sum'thaan' graveleh* wrong. Who are we *t'*prejudge *sum'un*! The *vereh* man who suffers most from the disappearance of a loved one should be *sum'un* we seek *t'*help *an'* not *t'*hurt. *Ah* ask *y'all t'*pray *wit' meh fur* the safe return of Carol Mays. *An'* we should also pray ... the seven *tahmes seventeh* of us ... who have wagged our tongues in disparagement, that we be *furgiven bah* a good man such as Father Tim Hanlon."

When he stepped down from the pulpit there was an unusual buzz in the congregation. They all wanted to know how Billy Brand could be so sure of his footing. What did he know that they didn't know? How did he know that Father Tim Hanlon was an innocent man? Billy Brand had only one answer that he offered only to himself: *The Lord told me so.*

The fellowship reception after services at the Christian Ascendancy Community Church generally drew about 250 people or about half of those who had attended the services at the large church. The only refreshments that were served were a watery juice punch, two mammoth baskets of fruit and multiple sheets of a rather plain crumb cake. The crowds varied somewhat but about eighty of the people were regulars. Billy Brand himself didn't go to the reception every Sunday but he appeared briefly on most Sundays. Sarah Anne hosted the reception, and Bessie and other members of the house staff served and cleaned up. Brand wanted the congregation to spend the time with one another rather than listen to him continue to talk after services. He knew that after about fifteen minutes, only the most fervent of his followers would still be at fellowship and that was when he would usually stop by.

When Billy Brand walked into the courtyard on this Sunday morning, he was accompanied by Tim Hanlon. He spotted Sarah Anne on the opposite side of the courtyard and smiled and touched his fingers to his lips, blowing her a kiss. A few members of the congregation greeted both Brand and Hanlon in a gracious and supportive manner while others shied away from contact. In spite of Patch Munson's request to leave soon after services, the Munson sisters, Gloria and Marjorie, were immovably planted near the paver stoned walkway to the courtyard, like centurions posted abreast the Apian Way. Maggie Munson was engaged in gossip with her two rotund sisters-in-law. Patch Munson was standing behind them and was now trying to move out of the path of the two oncoming preachers. As he backed away from the Munson women he bumped into Billy Brand's father, the bewildered Reverend Will Brand, nearly sending the elder minister sprawling. The ensuing commotion brought the Brand and Munson families all together quickly, as Patch Munson tried to make quick quiet apologies.

Billy Brand took control of the situation and said to Tim Hanlon, "*Ah'd lahke yew* to meet the Munson family. They have been faithful members of our congregation *fur maneh* years." When Tim Hanlon shook hands with Patch Munson, he noticed the man was sweating profusely and had great difficulty making eye contact. Munson also didn't say a word. Hanlon assumed that this particular parishioner was probably not one of his sympathizers. But he also felt that there was something about Patch Munson that was unnerving. The Munson sisters however were gracious and extended their wishes for the safe return of Tim Hanlon's "friend."

When the Brands moved on to converse with other members of the congregation, Patch Munson left the courtyard and waited in his Silverado with Harry, until Maggie joined him for the short ride home. Gradually the crowd dispersed and the preachers all returned to the rectory.

About an hour later Tim Hanlon was reading a newspaper in the parlor of the rectory. Billy Brand came into the room to ask him how he was feeling.

"*Ah* guess this *mahght* not qualify as a typical *Sundeh fur yew*. Personally *Ah* usually enjoy *sem* solitude on *Sundeh aftehnoon* when services are *oveh*. If *Ah* don't take a nap, *Ah usualleh jes'* do *sem readin'*. But *Ah* wanted *t'* stop *bah t'* see how *yer doin' an' t'* make sure *yer feelin'* okay. *Ah* hope that our services weren't too *trahin' fur yew* given the circumstances."

"No, just the opposite … it was helpful to get out and meet some people. I felt that it went well. I just hope that I didn't cause any discomfort."

"There was only one person that *Ah* felt acted a *lit'le* strange toward *yew*."

"The Munson fellow?"

"Yup, Patch Munson. Patch *idden* the most sociable guy *t'* begin *wit'*. But once people get to know him, they *lahke* him. He's always been a bit on the sullen side. *Yew* know the *tahpe*, quiet, but not *unfriendleh. Howeveh t'day* he seemed jumpy *'bout som'thaan'*. *Ah'd* say he looked *lahke* a long-tailed cat in a room full of *rockin'* chairs."

"Really? I just thought he was one of those who believed I had something to do with Carol's disappearance."

"If Patch Munson thought *yew* had *sum'thaan' t'* do *wit'* Carol's disappearance, *he'd a tole yew* so. No, *Ah'd jes'* say that he was wound up *tahghter* than an eight day clock. *Ah* have no *ahdea* why. *Maybeh Ah'll* stop *bah sem'tahme* soon *an'* see how *thaangs* are *goin'* out on the Munson farm. *Meanwhahle Ah jes'* heard from Lawson Mays. He says he should be here by 7:30 *t'night. Yew* ought *t' git sem* rest between now *an'* then. *Ah'm lookin' furward t' helpin' t' git thaangs* back on the straight *an' narrah 'tween y'all*."

Patch Munson had the upper hand in making a deal with Carol Mays, but whether he could enforce the bargain once it was made was another matter altogether. It was shortly past 7 PM on Sunday evening when Patch and Harry returned to the bomb shelter. He found Carol Mays in a near state of shock.

For several hours Mays had been considering the possibility that she had been buried alive with an already reeking corpse. The bomb shelter had suddenly grown much much smaller. Because of the "amenities" of air conditioning, reasonable bedding and adequate food, she had not previously considered her prison to be her tomb. But that had all changed in the last 18 hours. She was now living with a corpse, and it was beginning to stink to high heaven, or stink like hell, or just plain reek. She didn't need to make a distinction. The horrible part was that the rancid odor was getting stronger by the hour. She had begun to wonder if a person could die from stench alone.

So many thoughts had gone through Mays mind during her first nineteen days of captivity. But the twentieth day was different.

During the first nineteen days she had continuously thought about what she would do when she escaped. She had pined for her son Russell, especially on his birthday which she missed, and for her lover, Tim Hanlon. She also had time to think about God and prayed that her conviction that there was a God was accurate and that He would soon set her free. This imprisonment was merely some way of testing her faith, and she was up to the challenge. She would be able to somehow convince the confused chicken farmer to set her free. But all of these thoughts and notions changed on the twentieth day, the day on which she had acquired a roommate … a dead roommate … a stinking dead roommate at that.

"*Ah* told *yew Ah* was *comin'* back." As soon as she had heard the overhead scratching Mays had experienced some psychological relief but once she heard Patch Munson's voice her relief was immediately replaced with raging anger.

"You bastard! You left me alone to rot along with your friend's carcass. What kind of animal are you? You're less human than Harry." As soon as she said that, Harry rushed over and began sniffing and licking at her feet, which Mays found to be much preferable to Harry's customary sniffing and licking arena. Neither Munson nor Mays was inclined to further assess Harry's opinion on the matter. Then suddenly all three live animals became more acutely aware of the god-awful stench emanating from the lifeless stiffening pile of flesh formerly known as Bubba Looney.

Munson never got around to answering Mays question. Decisions needed to be made immediately. Mays wondered why it took so long to get to "immediately."

Each of the men came to the meeting with a different perspective. Tim Hanlon was grateful to Billy Brand for mediating the encounter. He was also happy to be doing something that didn't require his attorney Bodean Bickforth IV, to be present. Lawson Mays wanted information. He wanted to look Hanlon in the eye and try to understand what made this man tick. He also went to the meeting with a nagging sense of guilt that he couldn't shake. For the better part of two weeks he had done an awful lot to make Tim Hanlon's life miserable. More recently his prayerful introspection was causing him to think differently. Billy Brand went to the meeting because he believed that God had directed him to do so.

One of the more remarkable features of the meeting of the three Christian leaders was that they had managed to meet without being overwhelmed by the media. After all the attention that the Carol Mays affair had attracted over the past fortnight, Brand had suggested that they meet in the business offices of the Christian Ascendancy Community Church and they did so without any media distractions.

When Lawson Mays first laid eyes on Tim Hanlon, his anger receded. One of the many skills that are acquired over time by religious ministers is an ability to sense the good and the evil in people. The moment he was in the same room with Tim Hanlon, Reverend Mays understood that Hanlon couldn't hurt his daughter. Hanlon was simply not a violent man. For sure, there were things that he didn't like about the Catholic priest, but he immediately concluded that he would need to collaborate with him in order to find his daughter. Still the meeting took on a relatively formal tone in an informal setting.

"If *Ah* may *Ah* would *lahke* to pray at the outset that we have come together in the presence of God *t'* ask *fur* His *he'p* in *findin'* Carol Mays. We have agreed *t'* suspend whatever *diff'ences an' dis'greements* we may have in order that the Lord may *he'p* us *wit'* this *vereh* specific prayer *an'* supplication: the safe return of his daughter Carol *t'* the presence *o* those who love her."

"Amen." Lawson Mays added emphatically.

"Amen." Tim Hanlon echoed in a quieter, reverent tone.

"Tim, *Ah* know this is painful, but *neveh'theless necessareh*. Would *yew mahnd walkin'* us through what happened *jes' b'faw* Carol disappeared?" Billy Brand had warned Hanlon in advance that this was the best way to proceed, and Hanlon had given his opening statement some thought before he made it.

"I don't mind, Billy. I have covered some of these details several times before. I have spoken with each of you separately as well as with the police. But in the hope that we can wring out even one more idea about where Carol might be, I'll go through it again."

Lawson Mays nodded his head and the black man's graying eyebrows came together as he listened intently to each word as Hanlon spoke.

"We spent the weekend together and Carol was very helpful to me in dealing with my decision to leave my ministry. She never judged me. She never pushed me in one direction or the other, but she was supportive and happy about my decision.

"I met with the bishop's office on Saturday and was relieved of my responsibility to offer Mass on Sunday at Most Holy Tabernacle but Carol and I did attend morning services at The Immaculate Conception Basilica on Sunday. I didn't return to the rectory after meeting with the diocesan officials. Carol and I went to the Colonial Mall but we had two cars, so I left my car at the mall and then we went back downtown for dinner. We stayed at the Radisson Admiral Semmes Hotel, on Government Street. We spent some time talking about what our lives were all about and how happy I was to find out about Russ."

Hanlon took a deep breath and permitted himself a slight smile of reflective remembrance. Then he added, "You just never know what God has in store for you. I was amazed at how happy I was about Russ, but at the same time I was saddened by how much of his life I had already missed."

"What had *yew an'* Carol *d'sahded t'* do? Were *yew play'unin'* on *livin'* together? *Gettin'* married? *Goin' yer* separate ways? What were *yer play'uns?*" Lawson Mays tried hard to keep the sarcasm out of his voice. Both Hanlon and Brand ignored any unintended innuendo and Hanlon tried to answer the older preacher's questions.

"We realized that we never stopped loving one another. We decided that we would take up our relationship from the point where we left it eight years ago. Then we would see where that took us."

"But there's an eight year old boy in that equation now. He *jes'* had his *birt'deh* last week."

"Yes, a wonderful gift from God. I'm sure that our gift, Russ, will guide many of our decisions in the future. The first of those decisions was that I planned on moving to New York."

"So then *yew* have *d'sahded t'* leave the priesthood *fur* good?"

"I have already resigned my ministry." The conversation was rapidly becoming a two way dialogue, between Mays and Hanlon. Billy Brand respectfully waited to interject any thoughts or questions he might have.

"*Mah* daughter is a *vereh* strong woman. *Ah* was not *happeh* when she *d'sahded t'* become a *Cat'lick* but *Ah* was even more *unhappeh* 'bout her choice of profession. *Ah didden' thaank* that it was possible to live a virtuous and respectable *lahfe* in that *envahr'ment. Ah* believe that she has opened *mah* eyes a *lit'le* 'bout those views. Although *Ah* still see that *settin'* as a sin-laden sump, Carol has persuaded me that the fashion industry is not *entahrely* immoral. *Maneh* of the men and women that she has met are virtuous individuals who do *maneh* good *thaangs* with the economic wherewithal that they generate. Even that *homosex'yal* person, Jude Royale, has *sem redeemin'* qualities. *Howeveh* these folks often *carreh themse'ves* in a *mannah* that is reprehensible and undermines human *digniteh*. What're *yer o-pinions* on that?"

Billy Brand was amazed. The conversation had quickly gone from a discussion among three ministers in an attempt to decipher Carol's possible whereabouts to a discussion between a potential father-in-law and son-in-law, wherein the former queries the latter about his opinions and intentions. He wouldn't have been surprised if any minute now Hanlon asked Mays for his daughter's hand in marriage. Brand felt like he wasn't even there.

"You said that Carol is a very strong person. This is certainly evident. She chose the fashion industry, knowing that she could work within it and not be consumed by it. By all measures, she has been quite successful. But, in my recent discussions with Carol, she told me that her days in the industry are numbered and she was looking forward to the next phase of her life. I'm not in a position to criticize what goes on in any industry. There are obviously immoral practices in every industry. They just differ in nature and notoriety. However, I was happy to hear that Carol was ready to move on and do new things with her life." Hanlon had deftly avoided commenting on homosexuality because his views differed from those of the other two ministers and now was not the time to hash out these differences.

There was about fifteen seconds of silence that felt much longer to all three in the room. Billy Brand felt that it might be time to redirect the conversation to the last day that Carol was seen. He knew that he had to be sensitive about the fact that Hanlon had spent the weekend sleeping with Mays' daughter. Brand was glad that the conversation to this point had been civil, but he knew that it could change easily. He tried to move the discussion to the point when Carol Mays and Tim Hanlon parted company.

"Tim, when Carol left *yew* at the mall on that *Mundeh*, what was her mood? Was she fearful *o an'one* or *an'thaan'*? Could *yew* tell us *agin 'bout* the man that *yew* said she was worried *'bout*?"

Hanlon was finding it difficult to keep his emotions in check. This was the hardest of all topics for him to discuss. Over the past two weeks, he had been criticized by some for "creating a red herring" by talking about Carol's fears of the man she had seen in Oak Mountain State Park. Although this disclosure was made discreetly to the FBI and to Lawson Mays, he had also recently confided in Billy Brand. Fortunately the details of his disclosure had not leaked to the media. Most news outlets had simply indicated that the FBI was searching for information leading to an additional person of interest beyond Tim

Hanlon. However the rumor mill had started that this person of interest was a figment of the imagination of Tim Hanlon.

"When Carol brought Russ to meet me, we went to Oak Mountain State Park. That's about 30 miles south of where you live, Reverend Mays. We talked about many things and even discussed driving to your place and talking to you, but we didn't think any of us were ready for that at that point. So we just enjoyed the day at the park. But at one point Carol went to the bathroom area and saw someone that she believed might be following us. She said that she had seen the same man outside of The Most Holy Tabernacle Church a week earlier. Carol also said that the man had a gun and that she saw it. She said that he was driving a silver-colored pickup truck and he had some kind of hound with him. She described him as about her height, but with a very large head, a thick body and heavy legs. That's what I remember from her description. I don't remember her estimating an age, but she also didn't say he was young or old. She did say that he was very creepy and he obviously scared her. But I never saw him myself and as far as I know Carol didn't see him again after that encounter."

"What *'xactly* did *yew* do *'bout* this?" Reverend Mays was incredulous on the one hand that Tim Hanlon would do nothing at all about such a threat if he thought it was real. On the other hand he thought that Hanlon came across as being honest in his recanting of this story. It was the second time he had heard it and it just seemed to be honest. Hanlon certainly wanted the authorities to follow up on this angle now that Carol had disappeared.

"At first I told Carol that many men carry guns in the South. I didn't want her to be afraid. When we didn't see this ogre or his truck again, we thought that whoever might have been following us had been scared off. Then after Carol disappeared I relayed all of this information to the police and then to the FBI."

"And what have they told *yew* *'bout* their progress *wit'* this *info'mation*?'

"Not very much at all. They've asked me to give them these details on several different occasions. Frankly I feel that they still wanted to implicate me in some way. Have they told you much about their progress?"

"They've covered this same *info'mation wit' meh an'* asked lots *o otheh* questions *'bout* who else *mahght* want *t'* harm Carol. They also asked *meh* multiple *tahmes* what *Ah* knew *'bout yew an' 'bout yer* involvement *wit' mah* daughter. *Ah* told *'em ever'thaan'* that *Ah* knew which *wudden'* much."

Reverend Mays stopped at that point and redirected the discussion to one specific anxiety. "The authorities *gat* one problem *'bout yer* story… far as *Ah cain* tell … *an'* it's the same *worreh Ah* have. *Whah* won't *yew* submit *t'* a *lah-detecteh* test?"

Tim Hanlon was holding back on one additional piece of information that he had only hinted at when he spoke with the police. He strongly suspected that the man who Mays had spotted in the park had also killed Aaron Fein. But then he had no clear proof that this individual had anything to do with Mays disappearance. There was no ransom note, no communication of any sort from any kidnapper. What he told the authorities was that he thought the man in the silver-colored pickup might have been following him and not Carol. He said that it might have something to do with the man's confession. That was as specific as he allowed himself to get and he never mentioned Aaron Fein. This was the reason that he had hired Bodean Bickforth IV to protect him from lie detector tests and ongoing inquiries from the police and the FBI. Even though he no longer was administering the sacraments, he was still a Catholic, and while ministering as a priest he had heard the confession of a murderer. He was well aware that Canon 983 forbade him to betray a penitent in word or innuendo. Accordingly the sacramental seal of confession was inviolable.

"I won't take a lie detector test because I would be in danger of violating Catholic Canon 983 by further discussing the man Carol was concerned about. I didn't hurt Carol or take Carol against her will. I don't know who did or exactly why they may have done so. As much as I love Carol, I just can't say any more about my decision than that."

Billy Brand and Lawson Mays looked back and forth at one another. They both knew what was going on and they silently asked themselves the same question; *what had Tim Hanlon heard in the confessional?* Brand was further amazed with what Lawson Mays then said to Tim Hanlon.

"Reverend Hanlon, *Ah* know that Reverend Brand has offered *yew* the *hospitaliteh o* his home *fur temporareh housin'*, but *yer* son … *mah* grandson … is now *livin'* in *Bermin'hayum*. Why don't *yew* come up *an'* live *wit'* us *fur* a *whahle*. We all know that this situation *wit'* Carol is in God's hands. He'll let us know His will soon *'nough*."

The deal was that Mays would help Munson chain up Looney's stiffening carcass so that the 250 pound body could be hauled up through the two trap doors. Munson had driven his Silverado out to the edge of the antechamber a half hour earlier, and he brought tow chains and padlocks to make the removal. He needed Mays to ensure that the hardening remains of Bubba Looney could be held upright against the ladder in order to be extracted from the bomb shelter to the antechamber and then from the antechamber to the surface. This process required a deal between Mays and Munson and it was struck. Munson agreed to move Mays from the shelter to another location as soon as he had disposed of Bubba Looney's body. In return Mays agreed to hold up and guide the smelly body against the ladder while Munson and his Silverado hauled the body out. She also agreed to stay silent throughout the process and recognized that Munson would shoot her if she broke her end of the agreement. And while this verbal contract seemed plausible enough, the practicality of the endeavor broke down quickly. Limbs from Looney's leaden remains kept getting stuck in the ladder. Mays quickly became nauseous. After three or four minutes of uncontrollable dry heave vomiting she was simply too weak to effectuate her end of the agreement.

By 8:30 PM, Patch Munson was ready to acknowledge the hopelessness of an easy extraction of Bubba Looney. He decided that because he would be unable to remove Mohammed from the mountain that he would have to dump the mountain on Mohammed. Even as he was making this decision he could smell the strong foul stench of rotting meat as rigor mortis had entered every muscle in Looney's body which began to take on a luminous purplish hue. He called down to Mays and told her to throw up the handcuffs that were on the floor below. After she did so he instructed her to climb up the ladder and out of the bomb shelter. She was weakened and still ankle-shackled but this call of reprieve gave her new energy. She pushed the cooling malodorous flesh pile away from the ladder and carefully climbed up through the ceiling of the bomb shelter and into the earthen antechamber, eight feet below the surface level of the farm. Even in the damp darkening night, she quickly found the earthen stairs that would take her from the antechamber to the surface. As soon as she got to the surface she made a grave mistake. She let out a long loud guttural cry of "*H...eell...ppp*!!!"

For the second time in twenty days, Munson rabbit punched her in the back of the neck. She went down in a heap. As she felt herself beginning to black out, she also felt her mouth being re-wrapped with duct tape. This time the wrapping also crudely covered her eyes and only a small aperture in the two inch tape around her nose allowed her to breathe. She passed out and when she awoke she immediately wished she hadn't.

VIII

Spontaneous Combustion

Officer Bubba Looney never showed up for work on Monday morning, but he wasn't considered a missing person. The chief of detectives Vance Hillyear had been down this road before with Looney. He assumed that Looney was once again out on a boozing binge. Hillyear was more than a little bit annoyed this time, and he was contemplating what discipline he could enact on his subordinate. Hillyear and Looney went back a ways together and had always covered one another's back, but lately Hillyear began to feel that Looney was taking advantage of their friendship. Looney hadn't returned his phone calls nor had he left a message. Hillyear was feeling stupid for allowing Looney to poke around in the Carol Mays missing person case. The FBI was running with this now and wasn't sharing much with the police in Mobile. Nevertheless the local press continued to see if they could source information from the Mobile police detectives. The efforts of Bubba Looney were solo endeavors to turn up some meaningful information that might allow the city police to upstage the FBI. Looney always was a loose cannon and so Hillyear thought that there was little to lose in allowing Looney to continue poking around in the investigation. If anyone got disciplined it would be Looney and not Hillyear.

Hillyear's annoyance continued to grow throughout the day when he was unable to reach Looney by phone no one answered the door at his apartment. He left one additional message on Looney's cell phone.

"*Gad* damn it, Bubba, *yew* stupid redneck, *git* rid of whatever bimbo *yer shackin'* up *wit' an'* git *yer* sorry ass into work. *Iffin Ah* don't hear from *yew inna* next *twenteh-faw* hours, *Ah ain't gunna coveh yer sorreh* ass *aneh longeh.*"

Bobby Joe, the foreman of the Munson chicken farm, was mesmerized by what he saw. Rarely did Patch Munson ever do any work around the chicken farm. Any exertion of effort that Munson offered for farm matters always involved the citrus grove and the orchard farming. He didn't even do much of that.

Normally Munson would walk out to the chicken farm about once a week and ask some innocuous questions. He rarely drove out to the farm, always preferring to stretch his legs and meander out along with Harry. But here it was early on a Monday morning, and Patch Munson had driven out to the chicken farm in his Silverado. He had come up along the dirt road on the interior of the Munson property and turned into a small lot adjacent to the number six chicken grow-out house. Then he had proceeded to get behind the wheel of the front loading John Deere 420 Tractor. He wheeled it over to the nearby piles of chicken dung. As Munson took his first large scoop of the chicken dung and dumped it into the adjacent manure truck, Bobby Joe could no longer contain his curiosity.

"Top *o* the *mornin'* Patch. What's *goin'* on? *Didden'* hear *nuthin'* from *y'all 'bout movin' no* chicken shit. Or did we miss *sump'in?'*

Munson was a man on a mission. He had thought about what he was going to say to Bobby Joe, for most of the morning, but never came up with an adequate answer, so he just decided to go ahead and move the dung without explanation. Bobby Joe was his employee. He didn't owe him any answers for anything. If Bobby Joe questioned him, he would think of something to say right there on the spot and Bobby Joe would just have to accept his answer regardless. Now that moment of truth had arrived.

"No, *yew ain't* missed *nuthin'. Ah'm jes' gunna* move *sem* of the chicken shit to the back *o* the residential property. That's all."

"Geez Patch, *we'd a dun* that *fur yew*. We *cain* still do it now. *Whah* don't *yew* hop on down *an'* let *meh git sem o* the boys *o'er* here *an' git* their shit *togetheh*." He laughed mindlessly at his spontaneous construction of an idiomatic pun, although he would never have described it as such.

"No, *Ah'm jes' gunna* do it *mahse'f*. *'Sides Ah* need the *exercahse*."

Bobby Joe was growing even more stupefied. Was this Munson's idea of exercise? What had gotten into Patch lately? Even with his occasional *belly full o moonshine an' brain full o bees,* Munson was never one to work out life's frustrations by doing farm work. However he could see the resolve on Munson's face and decided that he would stand ready to help if needed but that he wouldn't press Munson on what he was up to.

When Munson finally had a full load in the manure dumpster, he got into the truck and drove it down the dirt road, past the citrus grove and beyond the picket fence to the property at the rear of the residential acreage. He then drove across the farm lawn to the site of the main bomb shelter, which over the last 30 hours or so had served as the tomb of Bubba Looney. Munson knew that he had to act fast as there was already a rancid smell emanating from the shelter. He also knew that he didn't have enough chicken dung to fill the shelter but that if he kept the lower trap door shut he had enough to fill the 800 cubic feet of the antechamber between the ceiling of the shelter and the surface of the farm. The difficulty that he was going to have was getting the dung through the four foot by six foot upper trap door in the 10 foot long wooden bridge platform at the surface level of the farm. He also knew that he would need to dump a whole lot more chicken dung down through the four separate outlets to the ventilation duct system that opened near the edge of the citrus grove. He realized that he needed to take care of the duct system ventilation first because that was where the smell of the Looney cadaver was beginning to waft to the surface most prominently.

Over the next four hours Munson drove back and forth from the chicken farm to the bomb shelter and citrus grove and dumped and shoveled manure into the pathways to the underground refuge, first closing off the ventilation ducts and then piling the manure into the antechamber above the bomb shelter.

Meanwhile Bobby Joe and another of the workers watched in utter amazement as they saw Munson fill up the manure dumpster for the fourth consecutive time. Although Bobby Joe viewed this from a distance of about one hundred feet, he could smell Munson, whose boots as well as the legs to his coveralls were covered in chicken crap. There was also a small trail of heat smoke that snaked behind the truck. Bobby Joe knew that Munson had already moved a larger volume of the fowl feces than he could possibly need for lawn and garden fertilizer. Curiosity finally got the best of him and he decided to follow Munson at a distance in one of the other farm vehicles. He watched as Munson drove up near the section of the residential property that was near the picket fence at the edge of the citrus grove. He could also see a slight coil of smoke rising from the area where Munson was dumping the manure. He knew that it was dangerous to pile that much manure in one spot. Bobby Joe knew about the bomb shelter's existence, but he had never told Munson that he knew about it. It was apparent to the other farm worker that there must be a hole in the ground near the site because there was no big above ground pile or piles of manure that could be seen. Bobby Joe also noticed that Munson's dog, Harry, was now running in circles, another 100 feet past the dung dumping spot as though he didn't want to go near it.

Bobby Joe wondered if Patch Munson knew what the hell he was doing. Then suddenly he recognized that his boss was even dumber than he thought. Within a minute after Munson dumped his last load on top of the already smoking chicken shit, spontaneous combustion took place from the rising heat that was generated in the decomposing dung. Bobby Joe couldn't believe his eyes. Flames rose nearly seven feet in the air. Patch Munson quickly drove the truck to safety 50 feet away from the inferno of poultry poop and then got out of truck and stared in horror and amazement at the reeking smoke that was rising twenty feet above the flames. Harry howled in the distance.

⚜

Both men awakened early on Monday morning for the drive from Mobile to Birmingham. Lawson Mays and Tim Hanlon took separate vehicles. Hanlon left an hour after Mays but they arrived at Mays' Birmingham residence within minutes of one another and around noontime. They made an agreement; initially Hanlon would stay for about a week and then they would decide how to proceed from there. A lot would depend upon how Russ related to his father.

As soon as Hanlon arrived in Birmingham he was greeted by Ella and Lawson Mays, and by Russ. The moment was even more emotional than their first meeting, less than four weeks earlier. Hanlon wanted to console his son about his missing mother but he didn't want to frighten him any more than he was already frightened. Hanlon was appreciative that Lawson and Ella Mays had not poisoned Russ' mind against him. But the young boy still knew that some people believed that his father had something to do with his mother's absence.

Hanlon wanted to run over to Russ and wrap his arms around his son the moment they were in the room together, but he chose a more reserved approach until they could gather an understanding of each other's feelings about the missing woman in their lives.

"Hello Russ. I missed you. I've been trying to find your Mom so that we can all get back together again."

"You should have called me."

It was the first moment of truth, but before he could say anything, Ella Mays intervened.

"*Yer* father did call *yew*, Russell. We *jes'* thought it would be best to wait *'til* he came here *an'* we could all talk *togetheh*. That was *mah* decision."

"But you didn't tell me that, Nanna."

"*Ah* told *yew* we *was* all *buseh trahin' t' fahnd yer* momma. That *'ncluded yer Daddeh* as well. He's *bin buseh lookin' fur yer* momma *jes' lahke* all the rest *o* us."

"Do you know where Mommy is?" The question was clearly directed at Hanlon but didn't sound accusatory.

"I wish I did Russ. I wish I did."

"Mommy didn't come home for my birthday. She was always home for my birthday."

Hanlon was at a loss for a response. The sting of his silence was shared by everyone, but it was also a grim reminder that Carol didn't come home because she simply couldn't come home. Everyone felt that pain, but only Russ could talk.

"I heard Uncle Jude tell someone she might be in heaven. I don't want Mommy to be in heaven."

Tim Hanlon couldn't hold back his emotions any longer. He opened his arms and took a half step toward Russ, and the eight year old looked once quickly at his grandfather as though asking if it were okay, and then walked slowly toward his father's arms. Hanlon hugged his son but still didn't verbally respond to him immediately. Russ raised his arms and allowed himself to be hugged but didn't truly return the embrace.

"Who's going to take care of me?" Russ asked the question into his father's arms, but his grandfather answered the question. "God will take care of us all."

"Even Mommy?

"Even Mommy." This time it was Hanlon who spoke. He did so with conviction.

Another day, another fallout shelter. On the same Monday morning, Carol Mays was devastated to wake up and remember that she had simply been moved to another subterranean chamber. She recalled the events of the night before with regret and apprehension. Patch Munson had picked Mays up and transported his prisoner a short distance to this new location. She was tape-blindfolded at the time and was unaware of the exact location of this new underground enclosure. However she had managed to recover her senses soon after she had been struck by Munson. Once he brought her to this new location he took her out of the truck and removed some of the taping around her eyes so that she could see. Then she was forced to descend shackle-footed into the new shelter at gunpoint. Munson allowed her to remove the remaining tape from her mouth but he re-cuffed her hands in front of her body as an extra precaution against any attempt for escape. She remembered being relieved that he didn't bind her hands behind her back once again.

This bomb shelter was not nearly as big or as well appointed as her last prison. *But at least there are no dead bodies in this one,* she thought ... *for now, anyway.* The access to the second shelter was identical to that of the first bomb shelter, with the same type wooden bridge and earthen antechamber sitting above the fallout shelter. However the second bomb shelter was smaller and more sparsely equipped. There were three bare light bulbs that hung from an electrical strip in the center of the ceiling, ten feet above the concrete floor. These three bulbs provided all the lighting necessary to illuminate Mays' new underground prison cell. The shelter was eight feet wide and about fourteen feet long. Unlike the first bomb shelter, the walls were entirely barren except for a small mounted motor that powered the air exchange system. There was no shelving and no refrigerator. To her dismay a hybrid composting toilet similar to the one in the last bomb shelter didn't appear to be in working order. Next to the toilet there was a sump pump that would remove rising water but the hole was dry and she couldn't tell whether the pump was in working order anyway. A long exposed electrical cord ran along the wall of room from the electrical strip in the ceiling to an exposed make-shift four plug power strip near the toilet and sump pump. A wire on the pump was then plugged into the power strip.

As she looked around this sub-basement level enclosure there was little else to warrant consideration. The ceiling had a locked trap door similar to the other shelter, and there were no furnishings other than a card table and four folding chairs. There was nothing that could possibly serve as bedding and she had spent the previous night uncomfortably attempting to sleep on the cool cement floor. Mays realized that there was nothing left to do but pray. So she prayed.

After Patch Munson, his foreman Bobby Joe and the other two full time chicken farm workers doused the dung heap fire with hundreds of gallons of water from the nearby citrus grove irrigation system, what remained was what Billy Joe referred to as a *"soppin', sinkin'stinkin' pile of shit."* But Billy Joe had no idea what lay below the pile.

Unbeknownst to Munson, Billy Joe had actually been in bomb shelter three years earlier. But he never disclosed that to Munson and he had a good reason not to do so. So he didn't say anything about the lower cement enclosure at this moment either. He also didn't question Munson about the particulars of his morning-long endeavor until after they had completely extinguished the fire. That effort had taken them more than forty five minutes and they were aided by a moderate rain shower that began soaking the field and the workers. When the fire was out and the smoke had settled Bobby Joe stared into the antechamber pit and he couldn't help but think that this was an image of a rainy day in hell. The charred wooden bridge and the surface level trap door had fallen in on top of the now soaking pile of chicken dung. There were some electrical wires visible as well as a tinny reflection from some of the smashed air conditioning duct system. The metal ladder was also partially visible, but the cement ceiling to the bomb shelter below remained covered. However the lower wooden trap door had also been partially incinerated and the liquefying sea of chicken manure was gradually seeping through to the lower enclosure. Patch worried that the bomb shelter would be exposed in a matter of time. Finally Bobby Joe got up the courage to confront his boss.

"Patch what the *fuck* is *goin'* on? What the *fuck* is down in the hole? All *them* wires *an'* tin *an'* wood *an'* whatnot … *iffin yer trahin'* to burn rubbish this is one hell of a way to do it."

Munson had no response at all. He was a man on a mission and he still had much of his mission yet to complete. His inner terrors had confiscated whatever was left of his meager common sense. He knew that in addition to resolving the issues with this site, he also had to resolve the dilemma that awaited him with respect to Carol Mays. Meanwhile Bobby Joe and his two subordinates continued to stare at Patch Munson waiting for an answer to the two questions that Bobby

Joe had posed. The only thing the four men had in common was that they stunk as though they had been smoking cigars amidst two week old refuse in the dumpster of an old age home. If any one of them had vomited the resulting odor would have been an upgrade.

When Munson didn't answer for thirty seconds or so, Bobby Joe had one more question for him; "We *dun?*"

Patch just kept staring down into the hole and could see the *"soppin', sinkin' stinkin' pile of shit"* slowly slipping and slopping down through the hole in the seared lower trap door and into the bomb shelter tomb below.

Bobby Joe repeated his question, "We *dun,* Patch?"

"Yea *go on* back *t'* the chicken houses. *Ah'll* watch *o'er* this crap *an'* make sure it *don't reignahte.*"

"No chance *o* that *hap'nin'* Patch." Bobby Joe stared at Munson as though he were going to try one more time to ask him why he was dumping all of the manure in the hole in the first place, but he could no longer stand the stench and he knew that he smelled pretty awful himself, so he turned to the other two workers and said, "Let's *git.*" Then the rain began to intensify.

After the workers left Patch kept watching the sea of watered down chicken dung that now filled in most of the antechamber. At first he thought the seepage had stopped, but then he could see a five inch eye of depression in the ten foot long, six foot wide dung pile, right about where the lower trap door would be and he realized that there was still a slight downward gravitational tug from this small depression. It was like the neck of an hour glass, and Patch knew that his freedom might well expire when most of the manure fell through the aperture from the antechamber to the bomb shelter. The sands of his life just plain stunk.

On Monday morning when the Mobile Police Department brought Will Brand back to the property of the Christian Ascendancy Community Church, his son, Billy Brand was embarrassed. He didn't know that his father had left his home and was found wandering around in his pajamas in downtown Mobile. The elder preacher's rapid decline was frightening. He had been diagnosed with Alzheimer's less than eighteen months earlier. But the progressively degenerative disease was now moving rapidly. In addition Will Brand was also suffering from an inoperative brain tumor that had caused him to lose a considerable amount of body mass. And now Will's return to the rectory with the police was a humiliating event. Billy Brand was not embarrassed by his father's confusion. He was embarrassed by his own inability to watch over and protect his father from exposure to world at large.

The elder Brand preacher had always been an inspiration to his son. Billy Brand possessed terrific operational skills and talents that helped the Brand ministry spread throughout the country and helped raise tens of millions of dollars for charitable causes. But Billy had continuously strived to emulate his father's capacity to intuitively know the right things to do and say. He also strained to emulate his father's intractable faith.

Will Brand stubbornly adhered to his faith regardless of the challenges in life that tested him. He never exhibited the slightest doubt or reservation about Jesus Christ and his teachings. Meanwhile the younger Brand in his private moments occasionally worried about his own faith. He could never let any of his congregation see this uncertainty and he fought hard to suppress these feelings that occasionally surfaced. Whenever he had substantive questions of faith, he could always turn to his father. Will Brand had always been there for him. He was there for him at the time of the accident in high school. He was there for him when he struggled with the decision to go to divinity school. And he was there for him through the trauma of each of Sarah Anne's three miscarriages. Now he was rapidly slipping away and Billy Brand wanted more than anything to have his father live a healthy life for another decade or two. But that wasn't going to happen no matter how hard Billy prayed for some miraculous recovery and Billy knew this fact intuitively.

Billy felt guilty when he and Sarah Anne hired a fulltime nurse caretaker to watch over his father while the younger couple worked the operational aspects of the ministry. He didn't want to outsource his duty to care for his father, and consequently he frequently sent the nurse home early so his father wouldn't feel that he had abandoned him. This was the first time his father had wandered off after the nurse went home and Billy panicked when he realized that his father had taken his car, even though he hadn't driven a car in almost two years. His sense of panic abated when the police found the car and soon after found the elder minister in downtown Mobile. After the police took Will Brand back home, Billy Brand sat in the family living room with his father and they spoke about the things that were on their minds, even though the conversation occasionally got disjointed. After a while Billy looked at his father and addressed the problem of his errant wanderlust.

"*Daddeh, yew gat t'* make sure that *yew* don't go *wanderin'* off *wit'out* Sarah Anne or *meh bein'* with *yew*." Billy still called his father "Daddy" in their private moments. However his respect for his father transcended even this most important parent/child relationship. His father was his spiritual compass as well.

"*Ah* know, but *Ah furgot.*"

"*Yew cain't furget*, Daddy. We were worried sick *'bout yew*."

"*Nuthin t' worreh 'bout*. The Lord takes care *o His chil'ren*." The younger Brand found the notion of his father as a child hard to fathom, but the more he thought about it, the more it began to make sense to him. *Child is father to the man*, he mused.

"*Ah* guess we're all God's *chil'ren* after all. He loves us when we're young *an'* when we're old, when we're healthy and when we're sick." Even as he said these words Billy Brand thought about what he was truly worried about when his father went downtown. He was afraid that some of the young punks would find him and abuse him or that some of the indigent and forlorn homeless would take advantage of him in some way. But now that his father had said the words about the Lord taking care of his children, he changed his perspective. He simply realized that he was still short of the depth of faith and trust in God that his father was able to conjure up. He changed the topic, hoping that his father would be lucid enough to give him guidance on a matter that had just come about that afternoon.

"Daddy, *Ah* have *sum'thaan'* to ask *yew* '*bout*. This afternoon *Ah gat* a phone call from that atheist professor, Bertrand Richter. He says he wants to come here to Mobile *an'* talk *t' meh* '*bout mah preachin'* on *A-bortion. Ah* asked '*im iffin* they were still *play'unin'* on *openin'* a branch of the *Fahne Cenneh fur* Women in our neck *o* the woods *an'* he said that he *wudden'* sure, but that he wanted *t'* talk *t' meh an'way. Ah* said that when he could tell *meh* that they *wudden' openin'* a *Cenneh* up this way then *Ah'd* talk *t'* '*im*. But now *fur sem* reason *Ah thaank Ah didden'* do the *rahght thaang. Ah'm feelin' lahke* the Lord is *tellin' meh Ah* should *o* handled this in a *diff'ent mannah. Whadayeh thaank Daddeh?"*

"*Lahke yew* said *b'faw*, we're all God's *chil'ren.*"

"Of course, *yer rahght. Ah'll* call '*im* back *an' invahte* '*im* on up.

Julianne Carson had now been living out of Tampa for more than two weeks and had spent only a handful of days in her California office since early July. It was now the first Monday in August and she was grateful that her job was one that she could perform using a virtual office approach. She made three overnight trips during the weekdays to see customers in New York, Atlanta and Washington DC, but on each occasion she travelled back to Tampa on the earliest return flights that she could get. Meanwhile Hawk Richter had been adjusting his schedule somewhat as well. He had been out of Florida only once since Carson had more or less moved in with him. That trip was a short flight over to Houston to speak at an aeronautics convention. That speaking engagement coincided with the days that Julianne Carson had spent up in New York with her clientele, so they both returned to Tampa at about the same time. Although Julianne found her time with Richter to be quite stimulating, she also enjoyed her personal space, and so she was glad that they belonged to separate health clubs.

Julianne Carson's membership in the Rhapsody Lifestyle Centers allowed her to use the facilities at the Tampa Center and it was every bit as nicely appointed as her home center, north of the Silicon Valley in California. When she was in Tampa she was getting up early each day and going right to the Rhapsody Lifestyle Center. These centers provided a soup to nuts approach to health and wellness. There were staff physicians and medical practitioners of every conceivable background and interest. Through the centers' wide network of spiritual gurus, fitness experts, dieticians and personal health coaches the members were able to access Pilates, yoga and dance classes. They could also avail themselves of services like ayurvedic oil baths, Balinese massage, aromatherapy, foot massage, hydrotherapy, hyperbaric oxygen therapy, colonic washout and other treatments. All of these services also linked her medical records to the practitioners at the various centers. Julianne found this membership to be the perfect fit for all of her mind/body/spirit needs. One of the financial backers of these centers was singer Gina Struben, who along with Carol Mays were the two women she admired most.

On this particular Monday Julianne varied her normal routine. She had a series of conference calls that took her into the early afternoon. She missed her normal morning class but joined another yoga session that started around 2 PM. She quickly and effectively got to a comfortable position where her chakras were appropriately aligned with her subtle life wheel. She sensed her throat, heart and solar plexus chakras get to an aligned channel with her brow chakra, her all encompassing third eye chakra. Meanwhile she was very comfortable with her base chakra as well. She managed to get to this energy collection stage of chakra cognition very rapidly. Then as Julianne was approaching a trance-like meditative state, she experienced something she had never quite felt before. She had effectively blotted out the past and future and was breathing effectively in the present. This much she had been able to accomplish many times in the past: getting herself to the here and now. But today was different. Although the time was *now*, the place was somehow *not here*. It wasn't Shambhala either. It was a different place. And it wasn't a nebulous location. It was Mobile, Alabama. She was experiencing a clairvoyant encounter with the spirit of Carol Mays. Julianne suddenly and intuitively knew that Carol Mays was alive and somehow underground near the airport in Mobile, Alabama. She had been following this story closely in the news and the prevailing opinion of the investigators was that Mays was dead. Julianne now knew differently, but she didn't know what to do about it. Recently she had a nebulous connection with the city of Mobile, a city to which she had never travelled. This connection emanated from her discussions with Hawk Richter who had been to Mobile before and wanted to return there to meet Billy Brand. Earlier Richter told her that he had called Brand but had been rebuked and rebuffed by the young preacher, who was vehemently opposed to Richter's financial backing of the Fein Center for Women.

When Julianne finished her class, she was soaking wet and chilled. Her normally animated face wore a strangely blank expression. She had returned from wherever it was that she had been and was just beginning to feel "normal" again. However she didn't *want* to feel normal. She wanted those fleeting moments of connection to return. She couldn't quite get there. At first she thought that she might want to discuss this with Yogi Garish, her Tampa based teacher, but then she thought better of it. She knew that she couldn't bring someone else into the equation. Besides she wasn't looking for an explanation. She was simply looking to reestablish the connection. Julianne went into the locker room, undressed slowly almost meditatively and went into the shower. As the water cascaded over her body the connection returned. There was a spectrum of colors that seemed to emanate from her crown chakra as she allowed the hot shower faucet to pulsate against the top of her head and down over her body. Intuitively she adjusted the water temperature to a cooler flow. Then the connection was visceral and spoke to an almost primeval part of her circle of life. For a very fleeting moment she felt as though her flesh was Carol Mays's flesh. It was an awesome connection of some sort but it departed almost as fast as it had come on. When she got out of the shower she felt astonishingly clean. She had a premonition that she would experience some kind of freedom very soon. She didn't know exactly what that meant. She was already feeling pretty liberated.

Carol Mays' prayers had led her down an intriguing path of empathy. Instead of feeling sorry for herself and angry at her captor, she began to think about what it must be like to be Patch Munson. He was not someone who had received an enormous amount of gifts from God. His large head encased a pitifully ugly face that only a blind mother could find handsome. His physical stature was far from athletic and his personality was one of dimwitted determination. So what was it that someone could possibly find endearing about Patch Munson? Well, he seemed to be a man of his word. He had promised her that there would be repercussions if she tried to escape and had twice knocked her unconscious when she went against his will. However he was in some ways a principled man. He had stopped Bubba Looney from raping her and then ended up shooting his friend in the process. Patch Munson didn't then turn his gun on her. Mays' realized that Munson had ample opportunity to kill her whenever he chose to do so. But for some previously unfathomable reason Munson had spared her. He had even gone so far as to try to make her incarceration tolerable. When Mays' deliberated on these things, she came to a simple conclusion. Eventually Patch Munson was going to set her free. And something in her prayers led her to believe that her freedom would soon be at hand. This reflection was the only way that she could tolerate her current circumstances.

Mays recognized that she had been visited every day of her captivity by Munson. She wondered if he would continue to be so solicitous of her well being. Now that he had moved her to this other second bomb shelter, would he still come by and bring her food. She wondered about other things as well. What was he planning on doing with the body of Bubba Looney? How would he manage to avoid detection for all of his crazy crimes? He could easily be charged with two murders and one kidnapping in the last month alone. *Had he committed other crimes that she didn't know about? Just how crazy was this guy?* As she deliberated on these questions she tried to stop herself from speculating beyond what she already knew. She simply tried to concentrate on how she could make it easier for Patch Munson to come to the conclusion that he should free her immediately.

It was about this time that she began to hear the familiar scratching that signified that Patch and Harry would soon be in her midst. Mays was fearful that things might change for the worse but she didn't know how much worse things could be while she was still alive. She was barely surviving in this new dungeon after being roughly deposited there by Munson. After Bubba Looney had torn off her night shirt on Saturday night, she had made her most recent change of clothes on Sunday while she was waiting for Munson to return. But her current wardrobe of denim shorts and a dirty white t shirt had not ever been cleaned since she was first captured. The same was true of her reused bra and panties. This was now her entire wardrobe. Her black roller luggage bag that held her other clothes as well as her tooth brush and other hygienic products had been left behind in the other fallout shelter. She hadn't been allowed to bathe since her abduction began and this alone was very dehumanizing. She knew that she had to get out.

When the ceiling trap door opened, Mays immediately noticed a foul stench. She wasn't sure what the odor was. However had she known that Patch Munson had spent the last hour bathing she would have been grateful that she hadn't had to put up with the "full monty."

When the dynamic duo of Patch and Harry finally scrambled down the stairs, Mays defensively covered her crotch straight away. And for once the dog kept his distance, albeit with a growl. Mays was scared because Munson had no bag with him. He carried only his gun. The look on his face was one of deranged animation. He was breathing short heavy gulps of air. When Mays realized that Munson was terribly frightened, she began to panic and her plan to reason with Munson suddenly seemed foolish.

"Don't hurt me Patch. Please don't hurt me. You have to let me out of here. I feel like the walls are closing in on me. Please, please." It was at this point that she saw the deranged animation begin to melt away. He stood across from her and the fear began to subside as well. When he spoke it was in a suddenly different tone, a tone of resignation.

"Sit down." He gave the order without raising his voice. She pulled one of the folding chairs away from the table and sat in it. Munson pulled another chair out from the table and sat in it himself.

There was about five feet of open space between where they each sat facing one another. Mays was still cuffed and shackled so Munson didn't worry too much about any sudden movements. "*Ah wanna* talk. *Ah'm thaankin'* that *maybeh yew cain he'p meh* after all."

"Certainly Patch. What do you want me to do?"

"*Ah* want *yew t'* talk *t' meh. Ah* want *yew t' he'p meh* make a *play'un.*"

"I can do that. I can help you make a plan. Do you want to tell someone what you've done?"

"Yes, that's it. But *Ah* don't *wanna* go *t'* jail."

"You need to get a lawyer, Patch. If you don't know any lawyers, I can help you get a good one. I know several excellent attorneys up in New York and I'm sure they can work with the best attorneys in Alabama to see that you get treated fairly. I'll let them know that you shot Looney in self defense and that you also stopped him from raping me."

"Don't know *dat it'ud matteh* much. *Iffin Ah* tell them that *Ah* shot Aaron *Fahne an'* Bubba too, *they's jes' gunna thaank Ah'm* a *homicahdal* mad man." He paused as if he were considering the validity of that self assessment. Then he went one step further. "*An'* what *'bout yer* man *Fatheh* Hanlon. He *ain't gunna* be real *happeh* once he *fahnds* out that *Ah* snatched *yew an'* kept *yew* in *mah* bomb shelters."

"We can handle that too, Patch. Tim won't go to the authorities. If he was going to do that he would've done so already. Besides, I'll tell them that I don't want to press charges. Maybe I'll tell them that I came along willingly. There must be a way we can tell a story that would work. I'll do and say whatever you want but please take me out of here. I can't stand it any longer. This is even worse than the other place. Just get me out of here and I'll make sure nothing bad happens to you."

"*Ah mahght* be dumb, but *Ah'm* not stupid."

"What are you talking about Patch? That's a difference without a distinction."

"Huh?"

"Never mind. Just answer one question for me. When am I getting out of here?"

"Soon."

It was the best one word answer she had heard in quite some time. However she wasn't placated. She knew that this discussion was the only thing standing between her and a rapidly growing feeling of choking claustrophobia. This was a feeling that she hadn't experienced in the other chamber. She knew that she had to cajole the compassionate part of Patch Munson's personality to rise to the rescue and unseat the more sinister aspects of his character that were obviously rooted in fear and stupidity. She also realized that she would need to craft the plan herself and then sell it to Munson. But in order to do so she needed more information and it was difficult doing that when the answers she got from Munson were terse tidbits of trust, and not the kind of information she would need to be able to convince Munson that she was his earnest conspirator and not simply his captive prisoner. Nevertheless she was determined to earn that trust.

"Alright Patch. Please listen to me. I'm going to say a lot of different things. If you disagree stop me. But unless we're both thinking together we're not going to be able to fix our problems." His nod of agreement was all that she needed to see.

"First of all, I need to know who else knows that I'm here. You obviously told your friend Bubba. Does anyone else know or suspect that I'm here?"

"*Ah ain't* told nobody *nuthin'*, but *Ah thaank* that Maggie *mahght* be *thaankin' sump'in's* up. She *jes'* gave *meh* a piece *o* her mind when *Ah jes' gat dun washin'* all the chicken shit *off o meh*." Munson then proceeded to relate the story of his morning activities including his hour long bath and shower. Mays then understood the weird aroma of fowl, smoke and soap that still covered Munson but was not nearly as dense as it had been earlier. Oddly Harry sat in the corner as though he were listening intently to this whole conversation but wanted to disavow any participation in the stinking insanity of the morning. When Munson was through telling his story, Mays had a sense that Munson was in a rare talkative mood and he seemed willing to listen to any plausible plan to change their circumstances. She took a chance and became more aggressive in her questioning and in leading the planning process.

"Okay Patch, so we said we need to get you a lawyer … the right lawyer. So I need to know some more things. Besides your friend, Bubba, and the abortion guy, Fein, have you hurt anyone else?" She purposely left her own predicament out of his list of crimes.

"Not so *fah*." Mays ignored the ominous response. It sounded more like a subliminal threat than an idle intimidation.

"All right we can easily beat the Bubba rap. I'll testify that he was attacking me and that you tried to stop him and that the shooting was accidental."

"No offence meant but no *jureh* is *gunna side wit'* a *cullud* woman who's *sidin' wit'* a *whahte* man *'bout killin' 'nother whahte* man *'specially* when *da* other *whahte* man's a cop." Carol Mays was intrigued by the way Munson thought and realized that there was some truth to his statement. That gave her an idea that she thought she could sell to Munson. She was surprised that she hadn't thought of it sooner.

"So maybe we tell people that I killed Bubba and you could testify that I did it in self defense. We could even tell them that Bubba was the person who kidnapped me in the first place. We could say that Bubba repeatedly raped me and that he told you about it when you both got drunk. Then we could say that you tried to stop him when he brought you to the bomb shelter and that I grabbed the gun and shot him, and that you then brought me here while you thought about what to do next."

Munson brightened at the idea. But he wondered if he could trust Mays. He stared at her and suddenly couldn't believe his good fortune. This woman was awfully smart he thought. Damn, yes. This plan might just work. He continued to stare at his prisoner. Even after three weeks of captivity she still was an attractive looking woman. He noticed that she had long shapely legs. They looked good even in the shackles. Her skin was smooth and even toned. And although she had smudged dirt across her clothes and body from being dragged from shelter to shelter, her natural beauty was still quite evident.

As the first thoughts of relief came with this new plan that Mays had conjured up, Munson could feel the tension resign from his body.

He kept staring at Mays without saying anything. Now he was simply staring at her chest.

"Patch?"

"*Ah'm thaankin' 'bout stuff,* " he finally offered.

But Munson wasn't thinking so much about the proposed plan as he was about his captive. He remembered getting a fleeting glance at her breasts when Bubba Looney ripped her night shirt half off of her body. It was an odd thought process his mind was going through. *Kinda small titties fur a black woman*, he thought. *But pertty titties jes' the same.* Then suddenly Munson felt something that he hadn't been able to conjure up for many months. *Damn, I gat myse'f a woody!*

The incongruity of the whole situation was fascinating to Munson and he wanted to feel happy about his sudden change in fortune but he wasn't sure what to do next. He finally lifted his eyes off Mays' chest and looked her in the eyes. He saw someone he liked. He decided he might be able to trust her also. He reached into the pocket to his coveralls and took out his key ring. Then he stood up and moved over toward Mays.

"Give me your hands."

Mays held up her hands and was surprised and happy to see Munson unlock and remove the cuffs. "Thank you, Patch. Can we undo the leg irons also? Will you let me out of here? We can start working the plan right away. The sooner the better … it will much more believable if we start telling people about everything before Bubba's dead too long."

"Not so fast. *Ah gotta* do *thaangs mah weh.* Step by step. But *Ah'll* tell *yew* this. *Ah lahke* the *play'un.*"

"Please, Patch. Let me out of here. I feel so grubby. I haven't bathed in weeks. Remember what you felt like three hours ago. Think about how I feel after three weeks."

Munson considered her plea with empathy, but he wasn't ready to do anything as dramatic as let her out of the bomb shelter until he had thought through every aspect of the plan another few times. He decided that he could afford a compromise however.

"Stay here, *Harreh.*" He addressed his initial comment to his dog. Then he turned to Mays and said, "Don't do *nuthin'* foolish. *Ah'll* be back in fifteen minutes." He grabbed his gun, went up the ladder and pulled it through the ceiling and reclosed and locked the trap door behind him.

As promised, Munson returned to the shelter quickly. He brought with him a commercial hose that was attached to the irrigation system for the citrus grove, which he had then pulled through the trap door. He also brought a bar of soap. Munson himself was pretty soaked because the weather outside had turned into another torrential downpour. Mays quickly got the idea that Munson was going to allow her to somehow bathe or at least let her clean herself up. She thought that if this were a concession of some sort, she would take each small concession as it came.

"*Ah'm gunna* let *yew* wash *yerse'f* up. This here hose is on extra low. When *yew* turn it on it's *plenneh pow'ful. Yew cain* stand *o'er* the sump pump and let the *wateh* go down in the hole. The pump'll *automaticalleh* turn on *an'* drain the *wateh* out *o* the hole *an'* back *t'* the citrus grove. *Ah* brought *yew sem* soap too. Here catch." He threw her the bar of soap.

"You want me to bathe now? You have to undo the leg irons, or I won't be able to get all of my clothes off." She stopped for a second and then added; "And you don't intend to watch, do you?"

"*Jes'* sit back down *inna* chair *an' Ah'll* let *yew unlaack* the *ahrons.*" He put his key ring on the table so that she could perform her own release while he kept his weapon out of her reach. She did as he asked and quickly removed the irons.

"Okay, let's *git* on *wit'* it. What're *yew waitin' fur. Yew* said *yew* wanted to take a bath. *Git* to it."

It wasn't any sense of modesty that caused Mays to pause. She was dying to clean up as soon as possible. But this was a breakthrough of sorts and she wanted to push Munson as far as she could. She remembered her earlier prayers and the accompanying introspection that she went through. She also remembered thinking that Munson must have a spiritual side to him. He went to church services. She knew that much from what he had told her about the process that led him from Reverend Brand to Father Tim Hanlon. Maybe she could convince him that it was sinful for him to watch her bathe. She wasn't going to waste much time with this idea but thought that it was worth a try. At the same time she worried about the actions that this man might take. After all he had already shot and killed two people.

"You know, Patch, we didn't come up with our plan all by ourselves. God is helping us every step of the way. And we're going to need him to help us the rest of the way as well. And I don't think God wants you to watch me bathe. Do you?"

Whatever perverse reasoning was running through his mind, Patch Munson had been looking forward to just that. He had been thinking about watching Mays strip and take her bath for the past fifteen minutes, ever since he had resurrected his erection. He thought of her in the same terms that he remembered the beautiful young women in the strip joints on Dale Mabry Highway in Tampa. He didn't plan on attacking her. He just wanted to enjoy the view. But now he had second thoughts. Maybe Mays was right. Maybe God was watching over them. He had made so many bad decisions in a row. Maybe it was time to listen to what God was telling him through one of his angels. He just never knew before that God had *black* angels too.

"*Alrahght, Ah'm gunna* wait up in the antechamber *jes'* outside the trap door. *Yew cain* take off *yer* clothes *an'* throw 'em up through the trap door. *Ah ain't gunna looket yew* or *nuthin.'* When *yew* finish *washin' yerse'f* up, *git outta da* way *an' Ah'll jes'* pull *mah* hose up through the open door. *Ah'll* even wash up *yer* clothes *an'* bring 'em back *tomorrah*. That sound *lahke* a good *'nough* deal?"

"Will you promise me that I'll get out tomorrow?"

"That's what *Ah'm thaankin'* now. But *Ah gotta* sleep on it. *Rahght* now *Ah ain't* sure *whetheh Ah* should scratch *mah* watch or wind *mah* butt." With that he moved away from Mays and signaled for Harry to climb the ladder, and they both went up to the antechamber. A few seconds later, Mays took off her tennis shoes and socks and threw them in the corner. Then she threw her shorts, top and underwear up through the ceiling to the antechamber and turned on the hose. Munson quickly retrieved the few items of clothing as visions of a naked Carol Mays danced through his head. Munson mused that Maggie would certainly be in for a big surprise tonight. It probably wouldn't even matter that he still smelled slightly of smoked chicken dung.

Meanwhile down below, Carol Mays caressed her skin with the soap bar. She never believed that a hose bath could feel so exquisite. She stood over the sump pump hole as she washed up and she heard the pump start to crank into gear pumping the water back up through the underground drainage system that led out to the citrus grove. She held the hose on top of her head for a good three minutes with one hand while she washed herself with the soap in her other hand. The feeling of clean water cascading down her body was cleansing in many ways. She felt some of her animosity toward Munson washing away as well. *The man is a simpleton, a buffoon, but he's human. I've got to count on the basic goodness of humans. He'll come through for me. I know he will. I'll get out of this underground horror very soon.* She also had the odd sensation that when she was talking to herself about this, she was actually talking to someone else. Who was it? Was it God? Was it her guardian angel? Was it a spiritual alter ego of some kind? Or was she somehow sending out vibes to Tim and others, telling them that she would soon be free. She wasn't sure what it was. But it clearly was a feeling of shared emancipation.

She continued to hold the hose with its slightly chilling water over her head. She was reminded of her baptism, in her father's Baptist Church at the age of four. Her decision to baptize Russell as a Catholic shortly after birth rather than in her father's church, had been a divisive choice on her part. Now in retrospect she wished she hadn't made that choice. Were these religious practices so different in the long run? These thoughts about her father and about Russell brought tears to her eyes, but they were tears of joy. She couldn't wait to embrace her son, and she felt absolutely positive that she could induce her father, the Reverend Lawson Mays and her lover, Father Tim Hanlon to embrace each other's spirituality. The cleansing properties of water were mystifying, even exhilarating but she finally moved the hose to help scrub other parts of her body. She felt her skin tone returning and her mind rejuvenating along with it.

As she washed the rest of her body she began to think of what a miraculous creation human life was, and how interesting it was that

God had fashioned our bodies as vessels to deliver our spirits along the continuum of time. She also thought about the miraculous way that this was achieved through procreation. What a wonderful circumstance that her spiritual and physical bonding with Tim Hanlon had produced the greatest gift she had ever received: Russell.

She realized that the restorative powers of water were more than symbolic, but she thanked God for every drop of water he put on the earth. With that thought she moved the hose back over her mouth as she craned her neck toward the ceiling and began drinking from Munson's hose. As she held her head up she could see Munson breaking his promise as he played "Peeping Tom" through the trap door. She didn't care. Maybe a little guilt for Munson was a good thing.

When Munson saw Mays looking up at him he pulled back quickly as though he was merely an accidental voyeur. But his heart was beating rapidly as he examined the absolute beauty of his black angel. He also began feeling enormous remorse for ever hurting her. Concurrently he mistook his state of physical arousal for "real true love." He decided to risk taking another peek, and happily noted that Mays eyes were now averted as she was looking down and washing *possible* and her lower extremities. The guilt continued to mount and it began to conflict with his voyeuristic ardor. He pulled back away from the trap door and snapped at Harry as though it were the dog's fault. "*Whadda yew starin' at Harreh?*"

Down below the sump pump basin emptied several times as the flowing water spilled rapidly into the hole. After about the fourth or fifth time the pump made a weird noise and died. Mays simply continued her shower, while the water rose in the basin indicating that surrounding water level was relatively close to the underside of the foundation. None of this mattered much at all to Mays who simply kept luxuriating in the pleasant feeling of fresh clean water. She drank almost a quart of water because she hadn't had anything to eat or drink since Sunday afternoon, almost twenty-four hours earlier. Finally after about fifteen minutes she heard the disembodied voice of Patch Munson call down to her in feigned impatience.

"*Yew dun* down there?" Munson didn't wait for an answer, but simply pulled the hose up through the opening, splattering water all over the bomb shelter as he did so and then splattering a barking Harry before finally turning the hose off after he retrieved it through the ceiling.

"Patch, please bring some food when you come tomorrow. I'm starving." She yelled up at Munson.

The only answer she got was the sound of the trap door closing. The temporary ecstasy of her hose bath was replaced by the realization that she was trapped in her birthday suit in a wet subterranean bomb shelter that suddenly seemed more confining and ominous than ever.

Priscilla Stengel was energized by her date with Melech Katz. They both liked Chinese food so they decided to go to P.F. Chang's at the Westshore Plaza. It was almost forty-five minutes from her home in Winston, Florida, but Priscilla had spent the day downtown, and her son Michael was away for a week at camp. P.F. Chang's wasn't fancy but the food was good and the atmosphere was informal, although somewhat crowded. Both Stengel and Katz were more interested in a mutual friendship than they were in a romantic relationship. The fact that they had met each other at group psychotherapy made it easier for them to have their discussion on topics of mutual interest. They were both surprised to find that they had a mutual acquaintance or two. They both had been interviewed by Detective Ismail Kanasani with respect to the Aaron Fein murder. The subject was of passing interest to Katz but was a mainstream issue for Stengel. In addition Katz had a casual relationship with Hawk Richter, and Stengel had talked to him once on the phone in the course of conducting her own investigative work.

Katz had no real idea why he had asked Stengel to have dinner with him. But he was glad he did. His date with Priscilla Stengel was different. She was several years older than he was. However Stengel had a direction, a desire, and a drive that Katz just couldn't muster in himself.

Her idea of using her investigative reporting skills to solve the mystery of the Fein murder and then put the story into a book was a legitimate aspiration. Katz found himself wishing he had a similar ambition or longing but he had none. He had resolved that helping Stengel with her yearning might be a surrogate of some sort for his own empty wish list.

For Stengel it was slightly different. She felt flattered that a young, good looking guy like Katz would find her personable and attractive enough to ask her out on a date. That hadn't happened in more than a decade. But she was also a realist. So after some trifling chit chat about a couple of the other members of their therapy group, Stengel unabashedly decided to ask a very direct question.

"You probably could have had dinner with almost any woman in Tampa, so why did you choose to have dinner with me?"

"Your question answers itself." He smiled broadly when he gave his answer and this was the first time Priscilla had seen him relax. His smile was just short of intoxicating to her, but she managed to keep her cool and returned his smile.

"What does that mean?"

"It means that I like people who are direct. And I sometimes wish I could be more direct myself. In our sessions with Elowitz you were able to share some of your life experiences pretty freely. I find that difficult to do. But I admire that trait in others. That's why I suggested that we have dinner."

"That's a pretty direct answer." They both laughed easily. Neither of them felt any sensual tension or amorous ardor, although Stengel certainly hadn't ruled out romance entirely. For now they were merely contented with the answers they gave each other. They were simply becoming friends.

"Speaking of being direct, let me go back to our earlier discussion of the Aaron Fein thing. You said that Kanasani originally interviewed you because you were at the FCW on Terrifying Thursday. But of course by now he has vetted you and realizes that you had nothing to do with Fein's murder. So have you heard much from him since the time he came out to your house?

"He's called me a few times. When he interviewed Hawk Richter, Richter told him that I had also called him asking questions, so

Kanasani called me and asked me what I was doing. I explained that I was just doing my job."

"How did he react to that?"

"Surprisingly he was supportive of what I was doing. He asked me to call him if I came up with any insights. He also wanted me to come into Tampa to work with their psychologist to see if they could get me to remember more about my last meeting with Aaron Fein. But I told him that I'd rather not do that. I had my own way of handling that sort of information gathering. Besides, I don't think that Kanasani has ruled me out entirely as a suspect. I have some sources inside the FCW that have told me that Kanasani has continued to drop my name occasionally and has been looking for reactions."

"Kanasani seemed like a nice enough guy. He's probably still suspicious because you haven't been willing to work with him. Maybe you should make a deal to cooperate with him and then you could write the inside story if and when they ever do solve the murder."

"I've thought about it. I might already have some information that could be of interest to Kanasani. Maybe I'll give him a call after all. Thanks for the extra push."

"Glad I could help."

The dinner date went well for both Priscilla Stengel and for Melech Katz. They talked about many personal items that they were adjusting to. Katz wasn't comfortable enough to share details of his involvement in the bloodshed in the Gaza Strip, but he was at least able to tell her that he was somewhat traumatized by all of the killing that he had seen and been a part of. When it looked like the discussion might get more finite on this topic all that Katz offered was that, "I can't understand why anybody's God allows us humans to destroy each other and desecrate our own existence in the process."

"So, is it God's fault, Mel?"

"I don't know. If I'm supposed to have a free will to decide these things, I'm not sure where it went."

"Good evening ladies and gentlemen, I'm Kenneth Brady and you are watching *The Brady Focus*. We are broadcasting from our studios here in New York, and have several stories to report on. Hurricane season is upon us and has been causing havoc across the Caribbean on several island paradises. The latest storm to threaten the United States is Tropical Storm Jesus. As you can imagine there is already a storm about the storm. Although the squall has barely gathered the wind force necessary to be categorized as a named tropical storm, the very name of the storm itself is causing a tempest. And it may end up becoming more than just a tempest in a teapot. We'll get to that in a second.

"The second story of the evening is the reported disappearance of an Alabama police detective by the name of Bubba Looney. The odd and interesting part of this story is that Detective Looney was originally the lead detective on the missing person case involving supermodel, Carol Mays. The FBI has been handling the Mays disappearance, because they fear that it was a kidnapping and because of the fact that the original suspect had been travelling interstate. From what we understand the Mobile Police Department never officially asked for their help. Now one of their own is missing. I wonder if they'll ask for help now. What is really going on in Mobile, Alabama?

"The third story of the evening is also from down south … this time from the state of Florida and the city of Tampa. Last night was the one month anniversary of the terrible shootings in that town on Terrifying Thursday. This morning the district attorney's office announced that they have completed their investigation of Professor Melech Katz' involvement in the shooting of Joseph Clinton and have determined that he will not be charged with any crimes, misdemeanors or misconduct in any way. *The Focus* has surmised that the DA presumed that Katz somehow acted in self-defense when he gunned down the deranged mass murderer. Alright as you know we had Professor Katz on *The Brady Focus* last month and we presented an outlook that proved to be unpopular. In order to be fair to Professor Katz our producers asked him if he would like to come back on *The Focus* tonight and he apparently replied with a cryptic three word answer, starting in 'go' and ending in 'yourselves.' So I guess that will be that. I'll leave it to you viewers to decide: Is he a heartthrob hero or a nervous nellie ex-IDF military man. That's all *The Focus* will have to say on the matter.

"Now back to the lead story of the night, Tropical Storm Jesus. Now to help us decipher what the tumult is all about, we have meteorologist Doctor Bruce Manley on *The Focus* with us. And how are you this evening Dr. Manley?"

"I'm doing quite well thank you, Kenneth."

"Okay now you heard me say at the top of the hour that this business about Hurricane Jesus might be a tempest in a teapot. So I don't want to overstate the implications of the name of the storm. But for our viewers at home could you just tell us exactly how storms get their names in the first place?"

"Sure Kenneth. The agency that's responsible for coming up with names for tropical storms in the Atlantic is the World Meteorological Organization. When a tropical *depression* reaches the stage where it has sustained surface winds of 39 miles per hour it officially becomes a tropical *storm* and is assigned a name. If this storm then grows in intensity and has sustained surface winds of greater than 73 miles per hour it is reclassified as a hurricane and the new hurricane assumes the name that had been given to the tropical storm from which it had morphed."

"Alright then Dr. Manley, backup a step with me if you will. So the hurricanes get their names from the tropical storms with the same names. Got it. Who then selects the names for these tropical storms?"

"As I said Kenneth, the World Meteorological Organization maintains a list of names for the tropical storms. This list contains 21 names for each year, using a sequential alphabetic formula. The letters Q, U X, Y and Z are not used for this list. There are six separate lists consisting of 21 names each. Every six years the list rotates back to the first year's 21 names. These names are set in advance so, for example, you would know that the name of the fifth hurricane in the year 2017 would be Emily."

"This seems like such an unimaginative approach to naming these natural disasters. I'm sure that some of our viewers are amazed at the mundane pseudo-scientific process."

"Well the process for naming these Atlantic storms dates back to 1953, when the National Hurricane Center in Miami, Florida, adopted a process that was used by the military in the Pacific during World War II. At first only women's names were used. But over time the women's movements took umbrage with the fact that such devastating natural phenomena should only bear female names. So in 1979 they started alternating male names into the mix. The National Hurricane Center then turned over the responsibility for maintaining and updating the lists to the World Meteorological Organization."

"Is there a reason why they only made six lists, in essence six years worth of names and then decided that they should recycle the names?"

"There probably is a reason, but I don't know what it is."

"Okay then, before we all get lost in this background trivia, let's get to the issue at hand: Hurricane Jesus. What is all of the fuss really about? This is the 10th tropical storm this year and that should take us up to the letter 'J.' And from what I've been told the name 'Jesus' was *not* anywhere to be found on the master list. Is that right?"

"Yes that's right; the six 'J' names that are on the six different lists are Joyce, Jerry, Josephine, Joaquin, Julia and Jose. There is no Jesus."

"Careful, Dr. Manley … you don't want to be quoted out of context."

Brady had already gone over the time that was originally slotted for this segment but he was having some fun with it. So, much to the chagrin of his producers, he kept rolling with the interview of Dr. Manley.

Meanwhile down in Tampa, Florida, Hawk Richter and Julianne Carson were watching *The Brady Focus* while enjoying a glass of wine. Coincidentally in Mobile, The Reverend Billy Brand and his wife Sarah Ann were also monitoring the show. Back north in New York, Brady continued to question Dr. Manley.

"So Dr. Manley the controversy over Hurricane Jesus is that somehow or other Jesus became a replacement name for one of these 'J' names. Is that right? How does that happen?

"Well first let me tell you that the tropical storm names we are discussing are only for the list of storms originating in the Atlantic. There are separate lists that are also maintained by an international committee of the World Meteorological Organization that handle the nomenclature for storms that originate in the Eastern and Western North Pacific regions. However hurricanes in these other world regions are referred to as cyclones or typhoons."

"Hold on Dr. Manley. That's more information than we need. We're running out of time here. Is the name 'Jesus' on any of these other lists of cyclones, typhoons or other hurricanes?"

"No it is not."

"So then how did this Atlantic Tropical Storm get renamed as Jesus? Who is responsible for this?"

"As I indicated, these lists are *maintained* by the WMO, which is headquartered in Geneva Switzerland. What 'list maintenance' infers is that names are frequently retired from the list when they are especially destructive storms. So there will be no more hurricanes named Hugo, Andrew, Katrina or Irene because of the devastation caused by these storms in '89, '92 '05 and 2011 respectively. There are many retired names besides these however. There are more than 75 retired names in the Atlantic region alone. The retirement is done by a vote of a committee of the WMO. When a name is removed from the list it is replaced by another name starting with the same letter."

"All great trivia, Dr. Manley ... but let me ask the question once again: How did Jesus get its name?"

"Apparently there was an argument or debate over last year's Tropical Storm Joaquin as to whether or not it should have been retired. It wasn't a storm for very long, never even made it to hurricane status, but it did some damage to the home island country of one member of the WMO committee. Because he was rebuked on the retirement request when we got to the tenth storm this year he retaliated by sponsoring some erroneous media releases that referred to this tropical depression as Tropical Storm Jesus. As you can tell I'm using the Hispanic pronunciation, 'Hay-SOOS,' rather than the Anglo-Saxon pronunciation of 'Gee-Zus.' It remains as a tropical storm and has not yet passed the threshold of 74 mph to become Hurricane Jesus. The storm was slow to garner its true name of Tropical Storm Julia because its wind hovered around 37 to 39 mph. So anyway the name Hurricane Jesus slipped out into the public domain even though the name is an imposter."

"Fascinating Dr Manley. And while you may say Hurricane Hay-SOOS, everyone else I hear talking about the storm is very bluntly calling it Hurricane Gee-Zus."

"Remember it's not even a hurricane yet, and its real name is Julia."

"I understand. However across the Bible Belt several Christian preachers are condemning the use of Jesus' name in vain. They are angry about attributing such violence to an all loving God."

"Some are. Some aren't. Some of these preachers are the ones actually propagating the use of the name and using it as a precursor to fire and brimstone retribution for leading immoral lives. This whole fiasco has gotten totally out of control. "

"So we need to wrap this segment up. But before we go, bring us up to date on exactly the current status of Hurricane Jesus."

"At this point, there's not that much to tell. Tropical Storm Julia, AKA Hurricane Jesus, is gathering momentum just off the coast of the island of Barbados, where the Atlantic Ocean meets the Caribbean. It could make landfall in Barbados over the next twelve hours.

"Thank you for that report Dr. Manley, when we come back *The Focus* will be talking with Chief of Detectives Vance Hillyear from Mobile Alabama, about the wild and crazy things that are going on down in that Southern city."

Brady tapped his pencil on his desk in front of him as though he were setting the tempo for the next interview, having already gone over the allotted time on the piece on Hurricane Jesus. After the commercial break he began speaking at a faster pace as he began the interview with his next guest.

"Chief Detective Hillyear, it has now been three full weeks since the disappearance of supermodel Carol Mays. What can you tell us about how the investigation is going?"

"Our department has been *cooperatin' wit'* the *FBah* on this ongoing search *an* although *sem o* the details *o* our investigation are *classifahed an'* restricted, *Ah cain* tell *yew* that we *ain't* received no ransom notes *an'* have no hard evidence of *kidnappin'* or other foul play. We are also *examinin'* the *possibiliteh* that Ms. Mays may have been an accident victim of *sem* sort.

"I assume that your office is coordinating its efforts with the investigative work of the FBI. Is that right?" It was almost as though Brady had not listened to Hillyear make his declaration of cooperation, two seconds earlier.

"You *mahght* say that."

"Was that a yes or a no?"

"Yes."

"Now then, as I understand it, the detective that you had assigned to the Mays investigation was a fellow by the name of Bubba Looney. Do I have the name right?"

In contrast to Brady's rapid fire questions, Hillyear paused before he answered the simplest question. He was peeved that the FBI had somehow leaked Looney's disappearance to the media. They had called looking for Looney at about noon to re-verify and corroborate some minor details of the investigation and instead uncovered the fact that Looney was MIA. They had pushed hard to find him and Hillyear had tried to cover for his buddy until he could no longer do so. He acknowledged that Looney was supposed to have been at work and hadn't yet showed up or called. Hillyear was now worried that when the drunken Looney showed up in the next day or two, the whole department would be ridiculed. And because he had been forced to do the *Brady Focus* interview by the clueless PR department of the mayor's office, the police department could well become the laughing stock of the nation.

"Bubba Looney is one of the men, yes."

"Is it also true that Looney did not show up for work today and that no one has been able to reach him?"

"That's *'bout rahght*."

"Do you suspect foul play?"

"*Ah honestleh dunno.*"

"I'm not asking you what you know. I'm asking you what you think, Detective Hillyear."

"*Ah thaank … Ah dunno.*"

Brady was once again up against a time constraint. He decided that his viewers would have to decide for themselves about how honestly Detective Hillyear was answering his questions.

"Before I let you go Detective Hillyear, could you tell me whether or not Father Tim Hanlon is still a suspect in the disappearance of Carol Mays?"

"All *Ah cain* tell *yew* is that Hanlon is still a person of interest. *Yew* must remember, Mr. Brady, that we're not even sure that a *crahme* has been committed here, so *Ah'd* suggest that *y'all* keep the 'suspect' talk in check."

"Well let's just hope that all of these missing people in a Mobile turn up pretty soon. Can we agree on that much Detective Hillyear?"

"*Ah thaank* so."

When Julianne Carson arrived back at the Westshore Boulevard home of Hawk Richter, she was greeted with a surprising statement from Richter.

"I'm going out of town for a day or so. I'm heading up to Mobile. Billy Brand had a change of heart and he's going to see me after all."

"That's fascinating, Hawk."

"What's fascinating about it? The man hates my guts. I imagine that his change of heart simply means that he wants to chastise me in person. I've taken enough criticism from him in the last couple of years to last a lifetime. First he's on my case because I'm an atheist. Then lately he's been all over me because he thinks I'm pro-abortion, when in reality I'm pro-choice. He obviously can't, or won't, make a distinction between the two."

"If you feel so strongly that he only wants to chastise you, why did you approach him in the first place?"

"I'm not entirely sure, quite frankly. But I felt that there was a small chance that I could get him to see things differently. It's not like I want to be involved in an ongoing public debate with the guy. By the way, where exactly do you stand on all of this? You've skirted the issue when I've brought it up before."

"That's not true. I've told you before that I personally could never have an abortion."

"I realize that you've said that before. That's your choice. But that doesn't answer my question. How do you feel about another woman's right to make a different choice?"

"I'm not sure I want to debate this issue with you right here, right now."

"Well that's the dilemma that I'm facing when I meet Brand in Mobile. He doesn't see any middle ground whatsoever. He doesn't see any reason for any abortion under any circumstances." Richter felt compelled to get Julianne's opinion on the matter, regardless of whether or not he would agree with it."

"What do you want me to say? You have your opinions. And if past precedence has anything to say about it, you will stick to your convictions regardless of how I feel on the matter. You have to admit your positions on issues like this have been pretty intractable in the past."

"I think what I'm saying is my opinions on this topic are evolving. I'm not so sure that I've given this issue as much attention as some other intellectual enigmi."

"This isn't simply an intellectual riddle, Hawk. This is a moral issue. There is a significant difference between those two character-izations. Frankly I have a very difficult time discussing where I stand on this issue myself. My views are not always popular with some of my friends and colleagues."

"Explain." Richter was genuinely curious.

"I feel truly sorry for the rare woman who was victimized by rape or incest. But I also feel sorry for victims of tsunamis, plane crashes, drive-by shootings, and birth defects. And furthermore I feel very sorry for the unborn baby whose life is terminated before it begins. I could just never do that. And frankly, I feel the same way regardless of the way a baby was conceived. It's not the *baby's fault* that he or she was conceived under unlawful or immoral circumstances. And I think it's a mother's duty to bring that baby to term. Yes I realize that there is significant physical and emotional suffering that a prospective mother would go through in these awful circumstances but that pain pales in comparison to the tragedy of the death of a preborn child, who was never given a chance at life."

"So if you feel that strongly about this, how do you feel about my financial investment in the FCW?"

"I told you earlier that I didn't want to debate this. But now that you have insisted on dragging me into this discussion, I will tell you that I don't like it one bit. It demeans you and it disgusts me. There, I've said it."

Richter was stunned by the forcefulness of her reply. However he wanted to hear what she believed and how she felt, because he respected her judgment. When he replied his voice was lacking its usual over-whelming self-confidence. Instead it was edged with a reflective charac-ter normally reserved for Richter's discourse with his fellow scientists.

"I've been thinking more about this lately. I've never believed that anyone had 'a right to life,' because that phrase presupposes that there is an other world existence, a spiritual existence that possibly predates birth and/or postdates death. Some people, apparently including you, Julianne, believe that this spiritual existence can even parallel life and that persons have a right to move from that alternative spiritual exis-tence into and out of life. As you know I don't believe in any of this spiritual world. I just don't. However … having said that … while I might not believe in a 'right to *life*,' I can still believe in a 'right to *live*.' There's a difference. If a human being is living, it's wrong for someone to take that life away."

"So then, to your way of thinking it all comes down to *when* that person is alive. Is that it?"

"In a word, yes. And I confess to not thinking about this more extensively in the past. And I could possibly even agree with your notion that life begins at conception."

"Then how can you accept abortion at any stage of a pregnancy? Doesn't a prenatal child have what you call a 'right to live' as soon as it has been created?"

"Yes. And I've changed my mind, but not completely. I still believe that a woman could legitimately choose her own life over that of her child, if it were obvious that she would die if the child lived."

"I can see the logic to your position. But let me say this. I wouldn't care to know the woman who made that choice. And by the way, that situation is highly theoretical, and makes a mockery of your chosen field of science. There are infinite permutations of probabilities and risks that make a bi-polar scenario, such as whether the mother or the child must die, highly improbable. The physicians should simply do their best to save both the mother and the child and not take the easy way out of such a rare circumstance. In my opinion that scenario is simply created as a political red herring."

"I never realized you felt so strongly on this issue."

"I simply felt that your opinions on the topic were obvious. I didn't think we needed another topic to debate."

"Not very heroic of you. Now is it?"

"So alright I've been chastised. I get it. But enough of this esoteric bullshit … are you going to sell your interest in the FCW or not?"

The question was blunt. Richter had been giving the matter some consideration throughout the day, while he was mentally preparing for his discussion with Billy Brand. He answered Julianne Carson's question in a way that left her thinking about how human Richter was. She was disappointed to learn that he was going to let his ego get in the way of his intellect.

"I don't think it's appropriate for anyone to pressure me into making a portfolio decision based on their own moral convictions. I might decide to divest myself of my interest in the FCW, but I won't be pressured into doing it immediately because of Billy Brand's morals and values."

"What about your own morals and values?"

Richter was not used to losing debates. He knew that Julianne was gaining an edge on him. However he attributed this to the fact that his own position was shifting. He decided to counter her verbal foray with an attempt at humor. "I'm an atheist. Remember? We don't have morals and values."

Julianne played it straight. "You, Hawk Richter, do have morals and values. That's why you're not really an atheist. And don't be so stubborn about it or in your next life you'll come back as a donkey."

All Richter could do was laugh. They both knew that the abortion debate was over for the day and that this round went to Julianne. She walked over to where he was sitting and kissed him on the forehead like he was a little boy. He accepted her gesture graciously because he was already beginning to think about his trip to Mobile. His reflection was interrupted by Julianne's voice as she walked by him.

"By the way, I want to go with you tomorrow when you go up to Mobile. I have something astounding to tell you about." She then proceeded to tell Richter all about her morning meditation session and her clairvoyant encounter with the spirit of Carol Mays up to and including the reconnecting moment in the shower. She finished by declaring, "It was the most awesome experience I've ever had. I was planning on heading up to Mobile even before I came back here. And then to hear that Billy Brand had invited you up there also makes everything that much more amazing."

"I'm not meeting with Brand until tomorrow evening, so I was planning on having my driver, Paul, take me up there in the morning. The weather has been awful with all of these storms circling around. Flights are all backed up and I think it's better just to drive there. You're welcome to come along for the ride, but I want to meet Brand by myself."

"That's fine. I think I'm going to need some time by myself as well."

"What exactly are you planning to do? You don't expect to somehow find this Mays woman, do you?"

"I have no idea. I just need to get closer. That's all."

❧

Maggie Munson was an extremely tolerant woman. From the time she was a little girl her ambitions were narrow and defined. She wanted to meet a nice southern God-fearing Christian man, get married and have a couple children or more. It hadn't quite worked out the way she had it all planned. After marrying Patch Munson, some of her girlfriends were envious. Although Munson was far from the best looking bachelor in Mobile, Maggie wasn't a threat to become Miss Alabama either. Besides Munson came from "good stock," and had a worthwhile occupation, assets and income. He even was a churchgoer.

The part of Maggie's plan that didn't work out so well was her hope for having children. At first, Patch wanted to "hold off *fur a whahle*" in their design to become parents. So they took appropriate precautions to preclude the possibility of conceiving. When *"fur a whahle,"* turned into five years, Maggie became more insistent in her wishes. However by now much of their physical intimacy had fallen by the wayside. They were having sexual relations less than two or three times a year. Her husband used to make fun of some of the local Baptists (*"Yew* know *whah* Baptists *neveh* make love *standin'* up? *'Cause* they're *'fraid sum'un mahght* see *'em, an' thaank* they're *dancin'*) but he had become unimaginative in their sex life and seemed quite incapable of *thaankin'* outside the box. There had been little variation from the missionary position and she guessed that her husband was rapidly becoming as bored with their sex life as she was. The problem then became that he wasn't exactly bored stiff.

Finally with her biological clock ticking and her maternal instincts in high gear, Maggie began asking her husband if they could adopt a child. Patch Munson refused to acquiesce to her plea; he also became even more remote in the bedroom. His fishing trips began to take precedence over his domestic duties as a husband. She began to realize that her husband's "good stock," included some genetic defects that left him "dumber than a box of rocks." He often said that he wanted an heir – probably another in the growing line of Harry Munsons, who took different monikers and left their real names to the dogs. However Patch Munson didn't appreciate that he needed to be home tending to his husbandly duties when she was ovulating, instead of hanging out on a fishing boat with the likes of Bubba Looney. For a few years the debate raged in silence. However it raged nonetheless. A fair amount of the time Maggie enjoyed the company of her sisters-in-law more than she enjoyed the company of her own husband. She didn't interfere with her husband's fishing trips and she didn't interfere with the inane obsession that he shared with his father, Junior Munson, about tending to their ridiculous bomb shelter. She hoped that this particular preoccupation would fade away following the death of Junior Munson but Patch Munson had only become more obsessed with the place lately. However, Maggie had a secret. She had never disclosed that she had actually been inside the crazy subterranean fallout shelter once or twice herself!

Three years earlier while Patch Munson was away on one of his fishing trips with Bubba Looney, Maggie was having an awful time containing her anger and indignation about being neglected. She snuck a few glasses of wine from a secret stash that she had hidden in with the bathroom cleaning materials. Then she had a few more glasses of wine just for courage. In order to dissipate some of her negative emotion she wandered out past the back of the residential property, past the citrus grove and out near the chicken farm. That was the beginning of a short but torrid affair with none other than Bobby Joe, the chicken farm foreman. Maggie even worked up the courage to explore the bomb shelter. She found the key to the trap door on her husband's key chain and made a copy.

Maggie and Bobby Joe laughed and carried on down in the bomb shelter during two of Patch's fishing weekends. So while Patch was off chasing grouper in the gulf, Maggie was being *groped and gitty-up'd* by Bobby Joe on the pull out couches in the fallout shelter. Whenever she thought about those two weekend rendezvous all she could ever do was say *"whew,"* to herself and try not to perspire too profusely from the shear memory of the pulsating, the penetrating and the eventual predicament. The predicament was that *Bobby Joe had gone and knocked her up.*

Maggie Munson remembered her fourteen week pregnancy quite vividly. She never remembered being that scared. She knew that her husband was dumb, but not that dumb. She was afraid to see a doctor and she was afraid not to see one. She never told Bobby Joe about her pregnancy but she broke off the affair. Bobby Joe didn't complain because he didn't want Maggie telling her husband about it. Those fourteen weeks challenged Maggie more than anything ever before in her life. Although there was something liberating about her affair with Bobby Joe, there had also been some self chastisement that went along with it. But the self rebuke was not for having the affair. It was a different regret. If she was going to have an affair, couldn't she have attracted someone better than Bobby Joe? He was not much brighter than her husband Patch, and other than being hung like a Brahma bull, he had little to offer. This was the American South. Where was Rhett Butler when she needed him? She just wanted to hear the words "Frankly, Maggie, I don't give a damn." Then maybe she would be able to get on with her life.

Maggie did eventually move on, but not before she had seriously considered getting an abortion. She couldn't help the feeling. At the time she was very lonely and very scared. She knew that it wasn't Patch's baby; it was Bobby Joe's baby. More importantly it was her baby! Still more essentially it was not an "it." The fetus was a baby! She decided that she couldn't possibly consider aborting her own child. She felt enormous guilt for even considering that option, but finally God decided to take the baby. Maggie had a miscarriage. Maybe there was a reason, but she could never fully understand. However she continued to pray. As family harmony persisted, it appeared that her prayerful petitions for God's forgiveness were met in some ways. In other ways … not so much. She was still a young woman. She might not ever have a child, but she sure wouldn't mind trying. Her short tryst with Bobby Joe had made her pray that Patch might pay more attention to her physical needs. Maybe she could even show him a thing or two that might excite him.

Then on this Monday evening in early August her prayers were answered. It had been a very odd day. Her husband left in the early hours of the morning but she saw him out at the edge of the residential property right near the bomb shelter dumping fowl dung over the area where the shelter was located. She gazed out the farmhouse kitchen window a few times and noticed that her husband had piled so much damn chicken shit in one spot that it had combusted. Then she saw Bobby Joe and the other workers help her husband extinguish the fire. Meanwhile she just watched all of this from the distant kitchen window while discussing it on the phone with her Hefty Bag sisters-in-law. Marjorie and Gloria Munson could see and smell all of the smoke from their house in the nearby housing development, across the state highway and north of the chicken farm. The three women spent the better part of the morning and early afternoon talking on the phone and trying to find out what Patch Munson was up to.

After the fire was doused, things got even weirder. Munson came back to the farmhouse to clean up and Maggie had never smelled anything so awful in all of her life. She insisted that Patch and Harry hose down in the back yard for twenty minutes before even thinking about coming inside. When Munson was finally allowed in his own house, he spent another half an hour cleaning himself with soap, laundry detergent and seven or eight year old cologne. Then when he was finally satisfied that he had rid himself of the putrid stink, he redressed and left the house and got back in his pickup with Harry and left without a word. Maggie had asked him what he was up to four different times and each time Patch had given the same one word reply, "*Nuthin.'*" Maggie saw her husband's Silverado crossing the back lawn, driving past the bomb shelter and out to the westernmost part of the residential acreage. She could see the back end of his truck when it stopped, but she couldn't see Munson.

Maggie was so furious at her pig headed husband that she felt like marching right over to the grow-out houses and renewing her scandalous screwing with Bobby Joe. But then she thought better of it as she realized that Bobby Joe probably smelled every bit as awful as her husband. She continued to fume for a while waiting for her husband to return. The rain seemed interminable. She never remembered such a rainy summer. After a while she saw her husband's truck pull away from the spot where it had been parked for more than an hour and a half. The Silverado drove back past the farmhouse and splashed out onto the state highway. Twenty minutes later, she saw the truck pull back alongside of the house.

And then this was when Maggie's prayers were finally answered. Her husband, Patch Munson showed up and opened the kitchen door. He was silhouetted in the doorway by pounding rain and lightning strikes in the backdrop. He seemed like one of the Magi coming with gifts. Munson brought a bouquet of flowers, a box of candy and a real fine stiffy. For Maggie it was better than gold, frankincense and myrrh.

"Maggie, *Ah thaank Ah* been *neglectin' yew* a bit. *So's Ah gat yew sem* stuff."

It was the most romantic line that Maggie Munson had heard in many years. Her anger dissipated immediately. As soon as she saw the myrrh, she instantly put the gold and frankincense to the side and led her husband by the hand up the stairs and along the hallelujah trail to the bedroom.

Tim Hanlon's son Russ had gone to bed and Ella Mays was upstairs reading. Hanlon was in the parlor of the Mays home, watching the news on TV. When Lawson Mays entered the room he had a very specific conversation that he wanted to have with Tim Hanlon. Hanlon also had something he wanted to tell Mays.

"*Ah* know that *yew* heard *sum'thaan'* in *yer* confessional that *yew* don't *wanna* tell the *po'lice*, but *yew* must also *thaank 'bout* the ramifications *o sayin' nuthin'* at all. Is there *anythaan'* in the confession that *yew* heard that could *he'p* us *fahnd* Carol.

"I have been torn and tormented about this for three weeks. But I have put my faith in God and I firmly believe that He will return Carol to us without the need for my disclosing what I heard in the confessional."

"And what if He *dudden'*?"

"Are you asking me to break my vow? Do you believe that God will answer our prayers if we don't have faith in Him? What would you do if you were in my position?"

"*Ah* don't know the answers *t' aneh o* those questions. But *Ah strongleh* suspect that *Ah mahght* be tempted *t'* tell the *FBah* whatever *Ah* knew *an'* convince *mahse'f* that it was God's will that *Ah* do so."

"Reverend Mays, I know that you're hurting. I know that you're worried sick about Carol. Please understand that I'm also worried sick about her. And I certainly appreciate what you have done for Russ and for me. And that brings me to another matter. I want you to look after Russ a while longer. I thought it was the right thing to do to come up here and see him and I did so. But I feel like somehow I should be back in Mobile. I feel like Carol is down there someplace, and I just don't feel right being up here. I want to go back down there in the morning."

"*Yew jes' gat* here *t' day*. Yew need *t'* spend *sem* more *tahme wit' yer* son. If *yew* have the faith in God *lahke yew jes'* spoke *'bout*, then *yew* know that He'll return Carol *t'* us whether *yer* here in *Bermin'hayum* or back in Mobile. *B'sahdes iffin yer fixin' t'* travel back *t'* Mobile, the Lord went *an'* put some awful weather in *yer* way."

IX

Hurricane Jesus

---

ropical Storm Jesus became Hurricane Jesus in the early hours of Tuesday morning. It whipped across the Florida Keys did some major damage to three bridges connecting the lower Keys and flooded Key West. It was heading in a northwesterly direction as it spun out into the Gulf of Mexico and headed toward the Mexican coastline. It was very fast moving for a hurricane. A few hours later after whirling around chaotically in the Gulf, the hurricane changed directions and began heading in a due north direction toward New Orleans. It was changing course in a relatively unpredictable manner however and it also gathered centrifugal momentum and climbed quickly to a category 3 hurricane with sustained wind gusts in excess of 125 mph.

Carol Mays was an emotional wreck. She was astounded that she was able to sleep at all on Monday night. The specter of her near-term release offered fleeting feelings of euphoria. However the reality of her situation remained extremely grim. She couldn't be sure that she could count on Munson. He had strongly indicated that she would be set free on this day, but he had never made an ironclad promise. She remembered his words exactly:

> *"That's what Ah'm thaankin' now. But Ah gotta sleep on it. Right now Ah ain't sure whether Ah should scratch mah watch or wind mah butt."*

And that was what bothered her. For the most part, Munson seemed to be a man of his word. If he had *promised* her that she would be set her free today, then her chances of being released were good. But the very fact that he had refused to make that promise concerned her. She was worried that there must be a catch of some kind and she didn't know what that catch was. For that matter she didn't even know exactly when she would see Munson again. She was doing a much worse job of tracking time since she was moved to the second bomb shelter. Her initial method of tracking time had been stroking estimated hours on the side of wooden shelving in the first shelter. She had used her belt buckle to do this and then simply recalibrated after visits from Munson as she always made some attempt to estimate the time and the day, from the few words he said.

It had now been a full three weeks since she was originally confined in the first bomb shelter, and a total of 22 days in captivity altogether. Other than clinging to the vague hope that Patch Munson was at heart a decent man, Mays had little to be happy about. She was standing eighteen feet below the surface of the Munson farm, and ten feet below the ceiling of this second bomb shelter. She was also now stark-assed naked because Munson had taken her only clothes while promising to return them washed and dried. She still had her tennis shoes and socks but that wasn't much of a consolation.

Mays tried to approximate the amount of time that the elapsed since Munson's last visit. She had fallen asleep on the clammy cement floor for a period that she estimated to be between three or four hours. She believed that she initially dozed off around 8 PM. Mays might have slept longer except she was awakened by water that had seeped up out of the sump pump basin and under her naked body. She then moved over to sit in one of the folding chairs and leaned her head down on the flimsy card table. The sump pump had stopped working and the water level of the surrounding area began to rise because of the prolonged heavy rainfall. When she first noticed the water she wasn't terribly concerned because it barely covered one end of the slightly uneven floor. However when she was awake for more than an hour she realized that the water was rising, even if it was at a very slow pace. The water now covered the entire floor and was at least an eighth of an inch deep on the side of the shelter that contained the basin. She picked up her tennis shoes and put them on the table. They were important and prized possessions because at that moment they were her *only* possessions period.

Mays then went over to the sump pump which protruded from the basin about six inches above the ground. She played around with it for a few minutes trying to somehow jostle it back into a functioning mode. After fifteen minutes of frustration, she decided to disconnect the extension cord from the pump so that the slowly rising water wouldn't get to the electrical connection and short out the power to the shelter. The one thing that she had been able to count on for the past three weeks was power to the shelters. The fact that both shelters remained illuminated throughout her captivity helped her maintain her sanity. The electrical power had also facilitated the air conditioning in the first shelter and the fan and air exchange system through the air ducts in the second shelter. She constantly worried about losing power, especially when the trap door was shut and Munson was gone. Fortunately the motor for the air exchange system was mounted near the ceiling, and this was also where the two electrical outlets were mounted. Mays was careful to remove the extension cord both from the pump and from the ceiling outlet. Just as she did this one of the three ceiling bulbs blew out.

After another half hour she was splashing in at least a quarter inch of water on every part of the floor. Mays now was legitimately concerned about the time. She guessed that it was somewhere around 2 AM on Tuesday, which meant that she probably wouldn't see Munson for at least another ten to twelve hours. She continued to pray and also to rethink all of the thoughts that she had had for the last three weeks. *Who is taking care of Russell? What has happened to Tim?* Even much less important questions circled through her consciousness. *What does Jude think about everything? How is my agent handling all of my missed engagements?* Then there were other primitive concerns as well. *How are my parents coping with my disappearance? Is anyone still looking for me? Will I ever get out of here? How fast is this water rising?* Another hour went by and the water was still rising. It was rising at a faster rate. There was now an inch and a half of water throughout the shelter. At this rate she could be sitting in as much as two feet of water before Munson returned.

The water was lukewarm as it rose up from under the shelter. Meanwhile Carol Mays had nothing but her thoughts and prayers as well as the table, the four chairs and her tennis shoes to separate her from sheer madness. There weren't even the minor diversions that she had in the other shelter such as the refrigerator and the ability to decide when to eat the paltry food allocations that Munson had brought or when to drink the water that he had allocated. The one saving grace since the beginning of her captivity had been that Munson kept showing up, day after day. When the hours between visits became irregular, Mays felt panic begin to set in, but it always dissipated whenever Munson finally showed up. But she knew that things had definitely changed since she was brought to the second shelter. She was now absolutely famished. She hadn't had anything to eat since right before she was visited in the first shelter by Munson and Looney together, on Saturday night. The only fluids she had consumed was the water that she drank from the hose the day before. She didn't dare drink any of the rising water because it also had enveloped the hybrid toilet which she had attempted to use right after Munson left with her clothes. She had also peed in the sump pump basin herself when she was taking a shower the evening before. There was no way to sum up her circumstances other than to say they were more desperate than ever. She tried to pass more time by assuming that Munson would return soon enough and by guessing what he might bring with him. She remembered asking him for tampons on Saturday afternoon and he hadn't brought them yet. It didn't matter much at this point. She hadn't gotten her period and she didn't feel as though she would be getting it any time soon. Her body had gone into survival mode and had apparently shut down some of its normal functions. What she wanted from Munson was a ladder and permission to leave. Her second most urgent need was food and drink, assuming that Munson would keep his word and return her clothing.

There was one other very important difference in her captivity. For most of the last three weeks her legs had been shackled together and wrapped around whatever object was convenient. She also had to put up with periodic handcuffing depending upon Munson's mood. But when Munson left the last time he left her naked and that meant that she wasn't wearing handcuffs or leg shackles either. These items were sitting in the shallow water on the floor of the shelter and Mays began to wonder how these items might help her escape. She thought more expansively about the ten to twelve hours that she had before Munson would return. She just needed to get her energy up. Maybe if she could somehow get another hour or two of sleep she would feel stronger. Throughout her captivity she had been using meditation techniques to lower her heartbeat and strengthen her personal resolve. However in the last 36 hours her fear had become crippling and her ability to meditate had been subjugated to a terror and dread that only allowed her to think and worry. She put her head down on the table anyway and tried to build her resolve and try to generate a viable escape plan.

This Carson woman must be some kind of saint to put up with Richter's nonsense these last few weeks, thought Paul, as he chauffeured Hawk Richter and Julianne Carson, from Richter's Bayshore Boulevard home in Tampa up along Route 75 on their way to Mobile. *Or maybe she's just a masochist.* Either way, Paul usually found the couple's ongoing intellectual debates and arguments to be particularly jejune, even though he assumed that they believed their discourse to be sophisticated and meaningful. *Mutual mental masturbation ... that's what it is.* Paul knew that there wasn't much that he could do to talk some sense into these people. They were hopelessly caught up in their own bullshit. He also worried that he would have to put up with this pseudo intellectual poppycock all the way to Mobile. *Couldn't they just find a nice music station to listen to on the radio?*

"I don't know why you find spirituality so difficult to understand. If you won't believe in anything unless it can be proven to be true than it's nearly impossible to reach for anything new. That, Hawk, is a classic Catch 22. Science is all about beliefs that morph into theories and experimentation. Why won't you accord spirituality the same latitude? I don't consider myself a card carrying member of any organized religion, but I can grasp elements of many different religions and find relevance. I am a seeker and the religion that most closely aligns with my views is the Sikhism."

"I thought you were doing the Buddhist thing. Isn't that what you spend your time with, Buddhism?"

"It's not just about how I spend my time. It's what I believe."

Paul started worrying. He didn't want to hear the "time," lecture again replete with all of Richter's references to the French Revolutionary Calendar. But Richter took a different path with Julianne and Paul did his best to tune them both out and keep his mind on the road ahead. Meanwhile Julianne continued her explanation.

"I'm not defining myself as a Sikh. I'm not a member of any organized religion. I merely look to find the best in many different spiritual practices. But even though I find great solace in Shambhala Buddhism, it is technically not a theology. It is more akin to a religious philosophy that doesn't embody a notion of God as part of its teachings. And as you know I'm a theist and a creationist. That's where I lose touch with Buddhism. I think I simply need more.

"I believe in a monotheistic supreme being. That is also part of the Sikh teachings. Furthermore Guru Nanak's teachings include a concept that is different from heaven and hell. It is all about an afterlife that is a salvation through a spiritual union with God. There is balance in the Sikh religion and a great deal of optimism. I enjoy that as a spiritual guidepost."

"Alright I'll accept that explanation. But let me cut to the chase on this other issue. So even though you say you're not a Buddhist, you believe that your meditative exercise has led you to some sort of transformational connection to this missing woman Carol Mays. Correct?"

"Yes, absolutely. Otherwise I wouldn't be travelling up to Mobile with you."

"So tell me. Just how does this work?"

"What do you mean?"

"How does this connection take place? Do you feel warmth of some sort? Do you hear voices? Or see visions? How does this connection manifest itself?"

"The connection isn't manifest solely through typical stimulation of the traditional five senses. It is something altogether different. It's difficult to describe."

"Try me. We have about an eight hour ride to Mobile. Despite what you might believe I'm not totally insensitive."

"I never said you were insensitive."

"You didn't have to … I can *sense* it."

"Are you trying to make fun of me?"

"No …of course not. What purpose would that serve?"

As this prattle raged on, Paul began to wish that the car was equipped with one of those glass windows that went up between the seats to preclude the driver from eavesdropping on the conversation of those seated in the back. He didn't want to eavesdrop; he simply wanted to conceal his contempt for this nattering nonsense. But the verbal sparring in the back seat continued nonetheless even as Paul attempted to negotiate safe passage along Route 75.

The driving distance to Mobile, Alabama from Tampa, Florida was 515 miles. They left at 6 AM and the trip would be almost entirely along the interstate highway system. With speed limits of 70 MPH for most of the way, Paul originally believed that he would be able to make the trip in less than eight hours even with two hygiene breaks enroute. But the trip got off to a slow start immediately. Water was already poring across Bayshore Boulevard in the early morning and they left shortly before the electricity went out at 6:30 AM.

As they drove north of Tampa however, traffic slowed to about 50 MPH as the incessant rain and sporadic gusts of wind made for semi-hazardous driving conditions. Along stretches of the interstate there were already some flat standing water puddles. Paul wanted to be sure that Richter's Cadillac XTS didn't hydroplane as he sped through the labyrinth of wet spots, puddles and emerging pools of rain water.

"I'm surprised we're not making better time. There aren't many cars on the road." Julianne didn't say this directly to Paul, but rather indirectly and simultaneously to both Paul and to Richter. It was an undisguised thought simply stated aloud rather than a direct challenge to Paul's skill as a driver. However Paul's patience was growing thin even though they were barely two hours into the trip.

Most sane people have decided to remain home. The driver thought it but didn't say it. Instead the challenge remained uncontested and Hawk Richter changed the topic so that strife between his driver and his lover wouldn't ensue.

"My colleagues believe that global warming is responsible for the increase in storm activity that we are experiencing the last few years. What do you think, Julianne?" The fact that he pronounced her name at the end of his question was both an unintentional acknowledgement that Paul had unwittingly been part of the exchange all along and an attempt to regroup the conversation as a two person dialogue. Paul was not unhappy with this development.

"I'm not sure. But ... remember that internet article ... the one saying that Chinese scientists claimed that life on earth would end before 2060 due to world-wide drought and famine? The article pointed to global warming as the principal culprit."

"Yes, what about it? It seems like there's one of these doomsday prophesies that pop up every other year. Remember the Mayan predictions for 2012? That combined with some bastardization of the predictions of Nostradamus gave everybody a thrill for a while. They made a movie out of it and everything."

"But those weren't spiritual predictions. They weren't biblical references to the Apocalypse or Armageddon. These were predictions rooted in the science of the times. Am I right? And Nostradamus was a scientist was he not?

"Before you made the point about belief systems in science as well as in your spiritual world. This is where they come together. The Mayan predictions were rooted in the nexus of the science of astronomy and the pseudoscience of astrology, which is to say they weren't rooted in science at all.

As far as Nostradamus is concerned he was a 16th Century French apothecary by trade … basically a druggist … maybe you could call him a chemist. But under any of these classifications I wouldn't consider him a scientist. He was reportedly also a medical doctor, who embraced the occult and became a seer … My opinion? I think he was sucking down some of his own medicine. He was probably into hallucinogens way before their time. So … I think he would lean more toward your spirituality than my science."

"Oh really, what about Sigmund Freud? Scientist or Spiritualist?"

"Probably more spiritualist. His scientific methods … or lack thereof … were constantly under critical review. Personally, I don't think of him as one of the great thinkers of history anyway."

"Who then do you think of as the greatest thinkers of all time. I hope that they're not a list of who's who among atheists."

"No not at all … actually most of the world's great polymaths had at one time or another embraced a spiritual side to their musings."

"Excuse my ignorance but what is a 'polymath'?"

In the front seat as he tried to keep his eyes on the road, Paul couldn't help but overhear the ongoing volley. As much as he hated to admit it, he found some of the discussion informative in a way. He simply didn't care much for either of debaters. They both were arrogant and Richter could be outright haughty and condescending upon occasion. He was eavesdropping on the conversation but he was glad that Julianne Carson had asked what a polymath was, because he certainly didn't know and definitely didn't want to ask.

"A polymath is someone who has exhibited great skill and great accomplishments in a number of different fields."

"You mean sort of like a Renaissance Man?"

"Yes that's the general idea. And certainly the Renaissance was one of the greatest eras ever for polymaths. Michelangelo was a sculptor, painter, architect, poet, and engineer. His statue of David, his sculpture of the Pieta and his painting on the Sistine Chapel ceiling are great examples of his artistic diversity as well as his theism. And Leonardo da Vinci was also a painter and sculptor who made important contributions in the fields of engineering, optics, anatomy and hydrodynamics. Another Renaissance man, Roger Bacon, an English Franciscan friar was also a philosopher, theologian and scientist. These were three men of encyclopedic knowledge and understanding, in a word: 'polymaths.'

"But polymaths were prominent well before the Renaissance and lived in many places besides Europe. The Persian poet, Omar Khayyam was also an astronomer, a mathematician, a physician and a physicist. Of course one of the all time most famous polymaths was the Greek Aristotle who excelled as a biologist, a musician and a mathematician, and he is revered as one of the greatest philosophers ever."

"None of those thinkers was an atheist as far as I know. In fact it appears that most of them had direct connections to religions or religious beliefs."

"This may be true, Julianne. But in more recent years the polymath Bertrand Russell was most certainly an avowed atheist. My own parents thought so much of his philosophies that even though they were German they named me after this Brit. He was a logician, a mathematician, a renowned pacifist, a gifted historian, and social activist and an admired philosopher, who won the Nobel Prize in literature."

"That's interesting. If you think so much of Bertrand Russell then why do you call yourself Hawk instead of Bertrand?"

"My parents liked the idea of me being a namesake to Russell, mostly because of his pacifist thinking. I'd just rather have my own name and be who I am."

"Interesting."

"I think not. Regardless, I do have enormous respect for Bertrand Russell. He had great regard for the dignity of human life, which goes to show you that not every atheist is a hedonist. The man lived to be nearly 100 years old and was quite consistent throughout his life in his belief that there was no afterlife or succession of lives in any cyclical reincarnation."

"Are there other atheistic polymaths with similar achievements that come to mind?"

"Well yes as a matter of fact. First there was Karl Marx, who in addition to his work as a political theorist and revolutionary was also an economist and a humanistic sociologist. Marx was famous for describing religion as 'the opiate of the people.' Multi-talented artists, Vincent van Gogh and Pablo Picasso were also atheists, but I wouldn't necessarily classify them as polymaths. Even though Picasso was a sculptor, a painter and a stage designer, his talents remained within the field of art."

Paul kept driving north on I 75. The weather continued to be awful and he was developing a migraine headache but he kept an ear tuned to the conversation in the back seat simply because it had now become a fascinating distraction. However he found it difficult to keep up with the dialog. No sooner would he be digesting some commentary about Bertrand Russell than he had to readjust to Richter's thoughts and comments on other famous polymaths. At least he now knew what a polymath was.

"You know, Julianne there have been some great American poly-maths over the past two hundred years as well. Ben Franklin comes to mind as one of the more prolific ones. He was a printer by trade, but also an author and an inventor, a statesman and a diplomat. It's almost hard to believe that the same guy who invented the lightning rod, bifocals and the Franklin stove was also the principal author of the Declaration of Independence and a theoretical physicist, a politi-cian and even a postmaster. Where did people like Franklin find the time to master so many interests and pursuits?"

"I give up. I have enough trouble keeping up with simple changes in computer system designs. It makes me feel somewhat inferior just to think of the vast talent of some of these people. It seems like you have quite a collection of personal heroes among your polymath pals."

"I'm not done yet. Two other American polymaths that I admire come to mind: Frank Lloyd Wright, the architect was also an interior designer, a writer and an educator. And finally Steve Jobs who was not only a successful serial entrepreneur, but was also a world class designer, inventor and movie producer. Jobs was also somewhat like you in that he was a seeker. He spent time in India trying to find his spiritual compass. From what I've read, I don't know that he ever found it."

"Yes. I've heard some of the same things about Jobs. But sometimes you have to realize that the search is its own reward. And that's why I have my own favorite polymath, the Dalai Lama. He does as much to bridge the gap between spirituality and science as anyone now living. He has made an ardent case for their co-existence. He has referred to Buddhism as both a religion and as a science of the mind. He also is an avid student of cosmology, psychology, neurobiology and physics."

"Watch out! Watch out" Paul shouted but it was just after the collision.

Richter was about to respond to Julianne's comments about the Dalai Lama when he was jolted by the impact of another vehicle that sideswiped their Cadillac XTS. Fortunately it was a side by side impact and not a head on or perpendicular crash. The other vehicle was a small car trying to pass them but instead it hydroplaned through one of the ever increasing water pools and smacked into the side of the XTS. They were not that far into their journey at this point. They were just north of the city of Alachua. They were also very near an exit ramp so both vehicles pulled off to the side of the road after driving halfway up the ramp. Fortunately no one was physically hurt. However Paul was so incensed about the pointlessness of the accident that his migraine headache intensified. He wondered why all of these polymaths could do so many things well and yet God didn't give the other driver the simple ability to do one thing well: drive intelligently.

The agreement between Priscilla Stengel and Detective Ismail Kanasani provided some immediate results on one front. Kanasani had been clinging to the hope that the silver truck that Stengel had seen near the FCW on Terrifying Thursday was a legitimate lead. She had originally told him that it was a silver pickup with out of state plates. However there were more than eleven million silver colored pickup trucks in the forty-nine states outside of Florida. Now that Stengel was able to provide additional specifics Kanasani's hopefulness was reinvigorated.

Stengel's assertion that the plates were from Alabama narrowed the number down to less than 212,000 pickup trucks. Then when she identified the truck as a Silverado the number shrank to 34,000 of these silver-colored vehicles registered in "The Heart of Dixie." When she was able to identify three of the letters on the plate as being MVN, the number was now down to 452, and of these about half were registered to addresses in and around the city of Mobile.

This last fact grabbed Kanasani's attention because the South's most outspoken opponent of abortion, the Reverend Billy Brand lived and worked in Mobile. Kanasani had instinctually interviewed the preacher just two weeks earlier and came away convinced that Brand could easily have incited someone to kill Aaron Fein. However his initial reflections on that were that the shooter could have heard Brand on television and still be local to the Tampa area. Now he wanted to explore the real possibility of the gunman coming from the Mobile area, possibly even being a member of the Christian Ascendancy Community Church congregation.

After receiving the call from Priscilla Stengel the night before, Kanasani went right to work on his computer. Even though he worked until 2 AM, he made certain that he was ready to meet with Stengel bright and early Tuesday morning. Stengel was able to provide two additional facts about the pickup truck. The first fact was that the man in the pickup truck had been accompanied by a mixed breed dog with floppy ears like a Bassett Hound. The second fact was that there was a small NRA sticker on the left side of the truck's rear bumper.

Kanasani was sitting in his office discussing these details at 8 AM on Tuesday morning with Detective Loretta Chambers, while Priscilla

Stengel was in the next room working with a police artist and trying to sketch a facial resemblance to the man in the pickup. They were working as quickly as they could. If this were truly a valid lead they wanted to run with it immediately.

"What caused her change of heart?"

"You're not going to believe this. She had a dinner date last night with none other than our friend, Mel Katz."

"I didn't know they knew one another."

"Neither did I. But remember we spoke to both of them, and apparently Katz figured that out and encouraged Stengel to cooperate with us. So I guess our off-the-cuff interview with Katz paid off after all. Amazing, a good will gesture turns into a good break for us."

"My Mom always said that 'Everything happens for a reason.' There might be something to that after all."

"Yes Loretta." Kanasani smiled in a teasing way but was upbeat.

"What blows my mind is those two being out on a dinner date. She looks like she could be his mother."

"Well that's pretty catty don't you think. She's probably only eight or nine years older than him. Although I will admit that she has had a tough go of things and it shows."

"Yea, but Katz is drop dead gorgeous. If I wasn't married I'd let him park his loafers under my footboard."

"See you just never know about these things."

The two detectives had their chit-chat interrupted by the police artist who showed them the preliminary drawing he had made after working with Stengel for a half an hour. The drawing included only shoulders and a head shot because that was all Stengel had seen.

Kanasani looked at it quickly and said, "Can we do any better than this? Looks like a freaking cabbage patch doll … big round head, narrow eyes and a tiny mouth … only thing is cabbage patch dolls are cute and lovable … we can't have a cute and lovable killer … now can we?"

"I think it's a damn good likeness." Priscilla Stengel had now followed the sketch artist into the room. "Remember I never said he looked like a killer. I just said he looked stupid. Besides who knows if he had anything to do with Fein's murder."

The phone rang and Kanasani grabbed it out of sheer reflex once he saw that it was from the Mobile Police Department. He began writing things down on his yellow legal pad in a rapid scrawl. The others in the room watched him and listened to one side of the conversation.

"Really? That was pretty fast, Chief Hillyear. Yea? Is that right? Great …that narrows it down significantly."

"Uh huh. Yea, she's in here with us now. We should have a drawing ready in less than a half hour."

"Yeah, I saw that last night on *The Brady Focus* … you guys have your hands full … people dropping out of sight left and right and all that …"

"Yeah … uh huh …"

"Wait … go back … say that name, again. … wow …"

Kanasani stopped scribbling notes on the yellow pad and grabbed an Alabama DMV report that he had just printed five minutes earlier. He quickly found the name he was looking for and then he hit the speakerphone so the others in the room could hear both sides of the rest of the conversation

"Does this guy Patch Munson have a brother named Harry?" Kanasani was getting excited that they may be on to a rock solid lead after all.

"*Nah*, but *Ah* know this guy through his friendship *wit'* Looney. He *ain't gunna* hurt *any'un. An' far's Ah* know he *ain't gat* no brothers *neitheh*. But now that *yew* mention it, Patch Munson has a *dawg* named *Harreh … neveh* goes *no* place *wit'out 'im*."

"I know you guys up there in the Yellowhammer State do things differently from us down here in the Sunshine State, but I figure you still don't license pickup trucks to dogs." Both police detectives laughed in friendly rivalry.

"*Y'all ain't gat* much sunshine lately down there in *yer* Sunshine State. Now do *yew? Ah* guess *Ah'd* let that go *iffin yew* could *jes'* keep *yer weatheh* down there. *An'way, Ah* guess *yer tellin'* me that *y'all* found a person by the name of *Harreh* Munson who drives … what was it again … a silver colored Chevy Silverado?"

"Exactly, it's right here on the DMV report. Technically the color is listed as *Silver-Ice*."

"Well would *y'all sen'* it *rahght* up here. That there's *vereh 'ntres-tin'*. Course we *gat* a few questions *fur* Patch *aneh'how, seein' as …* *lahke Ah* told *yew jes' b'faw…* he's one *o* the last boys *t'* see Bubba Looney. *'Parently* they *wuz* out *boozin' t'getheh* on *Sat'day nahght.* *So's Ah* guess *Ah'm gunna git meh* out *t'* the Munson farm *sem tahme t'day t'* talk *t'ole* Patch. That is *'nless* Bubba *gits* his *fool' se'f* back *'n* office *'fore* then."

"If you can wait a few hours, I'll go with you. I'll chopper up there right away and I'll bring this report and the drawing with me."

"Couldn't hurt *none, Ah* guess. *Yew cain* come on up if *yew lahke. Person'leh, Ah ain't gat* no qualms *wit'* it. But *Ah cain't* make no promises *neitheh. Jes'* let *meh* ask *'round* a bit … *neveh* know … *sem o* the powers that be *'round* here don't *lahke* it much when *otheh* PD's go *pokin'* in our pot."

"Well we certainly could use your help," Kanasani said patroniz-ingly. "We've got an unsolved murder on our hands and that alone is reason enough for us to go up to your good city. I know that you've got some ongoing high profile missing persons investigations and I prom-ise we won't interfere and that we'll cooperate in any way we can."

"*Lahke Ah* said, come on up and we'll see how *thaangs* go. Okay *wit' y'all? Bah* the *weh* Detective Kanasani, what kind of name is that anyhow? *Yew I'talian?*

"No, American."

"*Alrahght* good. We *gat sem I'talians* here in Mobile, but *'most* all *o 'em* are *Cat'licks.* Not *that Ah gat anythaan' 'gainst Cat'licks* mind *yew.* It's *jes'* that *thaangs* will be *easieh b'cause yer 'Merican. So's Ah gat* it straight when *Ah* tell the Chief, what's *yer* first name Detective Kanasani?"

"Ismail."

"Ismail? *Yer* a Jew?" The Alabama detective sounded more per-plexed than alarmed.

Around the room in Tampa office of the Florida State Police, Kanasani, Chambers, Stengel and the sketch artist looked at one another in amazement. Kanasani cut off the call without answering the inane inquiry. He then said to Chambers, "Call and get us a chopper. Don't give them too much information. Blame it on me. Just tell them that we need it to catch the killer. I'll take whatever heat comes down later."

"I'm going with you." Stengel made a statement. She didn't want to make a request.

"You can't go with us. You're a civilian."

"I'm not just a civilian. I'm a witness."

Kanasani thought about it for a second and realized that Stengel was more of a suspect than a witness. But she also seemed to be a good luck charm.

"You can ride up with us, but you have to stay out of the way. I don't know when we'll be back or whether I'll be able to take you back with us. By the way, don't you have a kid to take care of?"

"He's at camp for a week."

The phone rang again. Kanasani looked at the incoming number and turned to the sketch artist and said, "Answer it and tell him that the Muslim Detective Ismail Kanasani left two minutes ago and is on his way to Mobile."

⚜

Melech Katz checked his iPhone and looked again at the string of texts he had sent and received from Priscilla Stengel since the previous night.

Priscilla:	11:54 PM Thnx 4 din din. Had a grt time. ☺
Melech:	11:55 PM U R welcome. Had a grt time 2. ☺
Priscilla:	11:55 PM BTW took your suggestion & ☎Kanasani.
Melech:	11:55 PM Gd move.
Priscilla:	11:56 PM He seemed real happy. ☺
Melech:	11:56 PM Not surprised.
Priscilla:	11:56 PM Wants me 2 come in 1st thing in AM.
Melech:	11:57 PM U going 2 go?
Priscilla:	11:57 PM Yes. He said I'll get inside scoop in return, just like u said.
Melech:	11:58 PM Sounds like good deal 2 me.

Priscilla: 11:58 PM Wants me in at crack of dawn. ☹

Melech: 11:59 PM Go 4 it !!!

Priscilla: 11:59 PM Intend 2

Melech: 11:59 PM Keep me posted.

Priscilla: 12:00 AM Will do. Thnx again 4 din din & Gd nite. bests. ☺

Melech: 12:01 AM Good Night.

There was a long pause between texts but Katz was the one who restarted the texting in the morning. He was curious about what information the police were trying to elicit from Priscilla. He was worried that he might have unwittingly encouraged her to walk into a bad situation. Katz wasn't a very trusting soul lately. He thought he had done the right thing on the rooftop by shooting Clinton and the next thing he knew he was being criticized by some sleazy media types. He was forced to get an attorney to make sure things went his way but he was blessed by the fact that he had several attorneys that were willing to take his case pro bono. Still he didn't want to cause any similar hardship for Priscilla Stengel. She was a nice lady. He liked her a lot. They had some things in common.

Melech: 7:07 AM U up yet?

Priscilla: 7:10 AM Just arrived at FSPD.

Melech: 7:11 AM What will u be doing there?

Priscilla: 7:11 AM Not entirely sure. Got some info they'd like me 2 share.

Melech: 7:12 AM U going 2 get an attorney?

Priscilla: 7:12 AM Don't need 1.

Melech: 7:12 AM Didn't think I needed attorney either 4 a while. Doesn't hurt.

Priscilla: 7:12 AM Hurts plenty in the pocketbook.

Melech: 7:12 AM If u need it, I might be able to get u some help, possibly pro bono.

Priscilla: 7:13 AM Got 2 go. Working with their sketch artist.

Melech: 7:14 AM OK keep me posted.

Priscilla: 7:14 AM Will do.

There was another lengthy hiatus in the text stream until Priscilla started it up again after her meeting with Kanasani, Chambers and the sketch artist. She was glad she had someone to open up to.

Priscilla: 9:06 AM U won't believe this. I'm ✈ 2 Mobile Al in a PD chopper.
Melech: 9:06 AM ?????????
Priscilla: 9:07 AM My ideas r panning out. ☺
Melech: 9:07 AM What's in Mobile? Weather's crazy u know. ☹
Priscilla: 9:07 AM Possible suspect in Fein murder.
Melech: 9:09 AM Really !!!! Y R U telling me? BTW Thnx 4 the trust.
Priscilla: 9:09 AM Got 2 trust somebody. May help me verify things down the line.
Melech: 9:10 AM ✓ Good thinking. Will save our txt exchange.
Priscilla: 9:13 AM Sorry, GTG.✋. Will check in later.
Melech: 9:13 AM Still choppering to Mobile?
Priscilla: 9:14 AM So far, yes. GTG.✋ Later.

Katz wondered how he might be able to help Stengel. He was glad that she was at least suspicious of the police department's motives. It was hard to trust anyone these days. He was pleased that Priscilla trusted him. He determined that he would watch her back no matter what. But he was also curious about what information Stengel had that would cause such rapid fire deployment of police activity even in the face of a coming hurricane.

Maggie Munson had a terrible nightmare or was it simply a terrible premonition. Her husband was sleeping soundly next to her. His snoring was calmer and more rhythmical than it had been in weeks. For that matter she had been sleeping soundly herself until the nightmare. She was now wide awake and sitting on the edge of the bed. She reminisced about the last twelve hours. Patch had been acting weirdly for weeks now. *What happened yesterday that changed things so suddenly?* She wasn't complaining about the ending. It was the best sex that she had experienced since their honeymoon in New Orleans ... better even than the giddy-up sex that she had with Bobby Joe in the fallout shelter.

That thought then brought about another set of thoughts and questions. *Why had Patch been burning up his beloved bomb shelter in the first place? Had he somehow discovered that she and Bobby Joe had used it as a love shack a few years back?* No, that was highly unlikely. Bobby Joe was right there helping Patch. They must have been trying to hide something. *But what?* It must have been something awfully important for Patch to make that decision.

Maggie continued to mull it over as she returned to dwelling once again on the earlier sexual awakening of her husband. *What brought that on?* He barely said anything to her after he extinguished the chicken-shit fire and washed and cleaned himself up. *And then why in hell did he go back into the torrential storm? What was he doing parked at the northwestern edge, out near the citrus grove fence?* Maggie remembered that Patch had been parked out there for nearly 90 minutes, although she never saw him out near the truck. *Wasn't that where the other bomb shelter was located?* That had been the speculation of Marjorie and Gloria, Patch's sisters. None of the Munson women had ever been in the second shelter, and Maggie wasn't certain it truly existed. Of course, Maggie couldn't tell her sisters-in-law about her visits to the first shelter either. But she had listened with interest to their speculation on the phone about that second shelter. Then there was still more questions. *What was Patch doing in the second shelter? Was he down there alone?* As far as Maggie knew Patch always went to the bomb shelter alone or with his father, and his father was now gone. Then again she wondered if that was just her belief and that maybe Patch had used the bomb shelters for the same purpose that she and Bobby Joe had used it. Her own guilt drove her personal suspicions. And it drove still more questions. *Why did Patch drive down to the florist to get her flowers and candy? And why was he so horny?* All of this speculation brought her back to "the nightmare" that still seemed more like an evil premonition and woke her out of a sound sleep.

Right before Maggie woke up to all of this questioning and speculation, she had experienced a vivid nightmare about being trapped naked in the bomb shelter after being left there by Bobby Joe. Patch had apparently found out about the affair and plowed her under with a huge pile of chicken shit, which then caught fire and became her entry to hell. Even with this vivid dream of hell fire, she could hear God's charge to his angels to bring on the forgiving graces of rainfall. Although she was sleeping in a deep REM stage, it didn't produce the normal paradox of encephalic conflict between mental excitement and muscular immobility. Instead her subconscious nightmare caused her to physically roll around and moan slightly while perspiring heavily. Meanwhile her half-conscious self could hear the howling and splattering of the winds and rainfall outside her bedroom window.

Maggie's nightmare escalated to open warfare between the light blue-winged angels of heaven striking open huge gray clouds full of rain by pointing lightning bolts in their direction, and the horned and red-caped forces of Satan redirecting the lightning remnants toward trees and houses. People all ran out of their burning houses naked and in all different directions. Some fell into numerous smoldering and fiery pits, while others were swooped up by thousands of angels that filled the skies.

Maggie could see all of the Brands, first Will and Ellen Brand and then Billy and Sarah Ann, being swept up quickly. It was odd to see their skinny tushies naked, but up they went toward heaven. She saw her obese husband – still proudly sporting his short, thick erection – get swooped up by two angels, who dropped him twice before finally getting him under control and whisking him away. To her subconscious consternation she also saw Lorileen Ashton in her low cut cleavage-exposing dress getting swept up by angels as well. She seemed to be the only earthling wearing any clothing whatsoever. Marjorie Munson was being swept up but Gloria Munson had tripped into one of the burning pits. It was the first time ever that Maggie could remember the sisters being separated and Maggie's subconscious served up a quick gruesome picture of horned and red-caped Bobby Joe doing Gloria doggy-style down in one of the now numerous fiery pits. That image almost woke her up and she tried hard to awaken but couldn't get there, as the terrifying dream thundered along.

Maggie saw a host of public figures that she had recently seen on the news crossing the stage of her dream. Even in her sleep Maggie felt guilty as her subconscious mind couldn't help but focus on the genitalia of these various characters as they ran around naked in the backyard of her mind. Bubba Looney had a huge penis but tiny testicles. He fell into a fiery pit. The missing black model, Carol Mays, was also naked, but her nipples and pubic area were somehow airbrushed out of her dream and remained unexposed. She looked like a neutered black Barbie Doll as she was swooped heavenly by a black angel.

Father Tim Hanlon had a long and large, but flaccid penis as he ran past one fiery pit after another looking for something or someone. His feet were being bombarded by sparks coming out of the pits, but when one of his bare feet caught fire, a small cloud opened and a pee-stream of rain pissed down on his leg and temporarily extinguished his pain. But no angel came by to swoop him up just yet, and the fiery pits kept sending out their flaming invitations. Hanlon kept darting from pit to pit but he was slowing down.

Meanwhile Maggie observed Aaron Fein somehow crawling out of one of the pits and starting to grab at the ankles of several lovely naked young women from the church congregation. When Fein finally crawled to the surface, Maggie could see that his penis was diseased, disfigured and dripping with puss. Maggie gagged even in her dream, as she couldn't shake the vision of this miscreant, now on all fours like a diseased dog, but still grabbing and clinging to ankles. Then to her surprise the two angels who had been carrying Patch accidently dropped him on top of Fein and knocked him unconscious back into the pit, thereby freeing the ankles of nubile lasses that Fein had ensnared. When Patch's legs also caught fire, the angels seemed annoyed but splashed out the flames nonetheless. Patch was now trying to cover his erection with both of his hands. He lumbered away from the pit that had recaptured Fein, and the angels picked him up once again. They tried to elevate but the burden of Patch Munson's ample girth was just too much for the willowy winged ones and they ended up accidentally dropping him once again. This time he tumbled back into his own bomb shelter full of fiery chicken shit, and plopped down right next to Maggie. That was when she awakened. However just before she reached consciousness, she did notice that Patch's stubby penis was still hard.

Tim Hanlon was feeling sick to his stomach. So many things were on his mind. However the utmost concern that controlled all of his other anxieties was distress about Carol Mays. A month earlier he would never have thought his life would be on such public display. And he didn't care at all about the negative publicity that he continued to receive from the media or about the pariah treatment he was receiving from the Catholic Church. However he did think that it was odd that the hierarchy of The Church often moved quickly to transfer and assist homosexual pedophile priests, while they treated adult heterosexual transgressions in a manner that seemed more cavalier than Christian. But that was not his immediate concern. He cared only about specific important people in his life, predominantly Carol and now Russ. He also was grateful to Lawson and Ella Mays as well as Billy and Sarah Anne Brand. He had no other family. Yes, he had initially received words of support from former parishioners, but he had not heard from any of these folks in more than a week. Much of the time he was alone with his own thoughts and prayers and this condition had lingered over the last several weeks during which he had spent an inordinate amount of time driving alone in his Range Rover. He had driven almost 4000 miles in the last month, and he was once again on the road back to Mobile from Birmingham.

With all of the possibilities concerning Carol Mays' wellbeing crossing his consciousness on a moment to moment basis, Hanlon was exasperated with his own ineptitude. Nearly three hours into his drive back to Mobile on Tuesday morning, he made a decision. He hoped it was what God wanted. He decided to give the FBI more information than he had in the past. He had a cell phone number for Agent Fran Church and he dialed it.

"Fran Church … oh hello Father Hanlon." Her phone displayed his name but she still sounded surprised to hear from him.

"I have some additional thoughts that may or may not be important in finding Carol."

"Yes. Tell me."

"The person who Carol believed was following us may also have something to do with the murder of Aaron Fein.

"That's the abortion guy in Tampa. Right?"

"Yes."

"How would Carol Mays be connected with Aaron Fein? Did she know him? Or ever even meet him?

"Not to my knowledge … she doesn't know that the person who was following us could possibly be connected to Aaron Fein. For now you can just consider it a hunch … but a somewhat educated hunch?"

Fran Church was a quick study. She knew where this discussion might go, and she decided to take it right there immediately.

"Did this person who was following you come to see you in the confessional, Father Hanlon?

There was dead silence on the other side of the phone.

"Father Hanlon?"

"Yes." He meant to imply; *yes I'm here*.

Fran Church assumed that he was replying positively to her inquiry about the confessional.

"Did this person say that he had killed Aaron Fein?"

Again there was dead silence on the phone and once again Church was the first to break the silence.

"Father Hanlon?"

"Yes."

The second time the delayed response took on a different connotation. Agent Church simply went right after Hanlon

"Look Father Hanlon if this is a game that we're playing, God knows the game. Why don't you just tell me what you want to tell me and let God decide if you have done the right thing or not.

"I'm sorry Agent Church that's all I want to say." He hung up the cell phone and didn't answer either of Church's two subsequent attempts to reconnect. However he continued to drive through the thickening rainfall in the direction of Mobile.

❧❦❧

This was early in the season to get as far down in the alphabet as Hurricane Jesus (a/k/a Julia). Remarkably Jesus was the fifth of the ten named tropical storms that had already made it to hurricane status. Hurricane Colin had battered the Bahamas and scooted up the east coast of the United States making landfall in North Carolina. The other three hurricanes, Danielle, Earl and Hermine all circled through the Gulf of Mexico and made landfall along the shores of Galveston and Corpus Christie in Texas as well as Morgan City in south central Louisiana.

Although Tropical Storm Ian had never made it to hurricane stature, its slow moving and unusual path up the western shore of Florida drenched Clearwater, Panama City and Pensacola before spilling out of Florida and into Mobile, Alabama and continuing on to Biloxi Mississippi. The wide corridor of rain from Ian was still hovering over these final two cities, even as Hurricane Jesus gained its momentum. At 11:30 AM, the National Hurricane Center upgraded Hurricane Jesus (nee Julia) to a category four hurricane and also announced that its course had veered further to the east and was now expected to make landfall somewhere between Biloxi and Pensacola at about 7 PM that evening. Speculation was increasing that Hurricane Jesus would be the most powerful hurricane ever to make landfall in that area.

Patch Munson had hoped to get out of bed and start his day before Maggie awakened. It didn't happen that way. However he dressed quickly while his wife was in the shower and went out to his car to retrieve the few items of clothing that he had taken from Carol Mays. He made it in and out of the pouring rain without getting soaked although he had to listen to Harry howl in complaint on a leash in his doghouse. Harry didn't like thunder at all and the night before was replete with a full eight hours of heavenly fireworks. Munson had never before used the washer and dryer that were in the first floor laundry room. If things needed cleaning, that was Maggie's work. He decided to hand wash the four pieces of clothing that he had received from Mays, and he simply used a bar of rough hand soap to do it. He scrubbed the t-shirt, denim shorts and underwear for almost five full minutes at the scrub sink in the laundry and kept sniffing his work until he was satisfied that they smelled more like soap than sweat. He then hand wrung the water out of the clothing as best he could. However even if it weren't raining cats and dogs outside, he still wouldn't have been able to hang Mays' clothes out on a line, so he decided that he would throw them in the dryer and see how fast they could dry. He was happy to find out that the dryer wasn't complicated … just throw the clothes in, push the on button and wait for results. But what he wasn't happy to hear were the footsteps in the hallway as Maggie approached from behind him, totally mystified by the fact that her husband seemed to be doing laundry.

"Patch, *wudda yew doin'*?"

"*Laundreh.*"

"Huh?"

"*Laundreh.*"

"*Yew neveh* did *no laundreh b'faw.*"

"Lately *Ah dun sem thaangs Ah ain't neveh dun b'faw.*"

Maggie was now right next to Patch. They were both staring down at the spinning dryer.

"*Ah cudda dun laundreh fur yew* Patch. So *whah yew doin'* it *yerse'f? Yew gat sum'thaan'yew* don't want *meh t'* see?" With that she went to reach past her husband and open the dryer door. But Munson blocked his wife's attempt with an ominous glare.

"Let it be, Maggie, *jes'* let it be."

"*Whah* should *Ah* let it be? *Iffin yew ain't gat nuthin' t'hahde*, then *whah* should *Ah* let it be?"

"*Cuz Ah* said so."

Maggie turned around and stomped off in the direction of the kitchen with a plan in mind. In less than five minutes she had heated up some grits for her husband but flavored them with lots of sugar to hide the fact that she had laced his grits with an ample dose of a strong laxative that she had been using for her own irregularity. When she called Munson in for breakfast she could still hear the dryer in the distance but acted as though it was the farthest thing from her mind. Another ten minutes went by before Patch Munson made a hurried rush toward the bathroom which was next to the laundry area. As soon as Maggie realized that her husband was safely ensconced in the crapper, she quietly snuck by into the laundry room and opened the dryer. Meanwhile when Patch heard the dryer stop, he simply remained on the throne not knowing exactly when to abdicate.

Still naked, still frightened and still counting on a man who had recently shot and killed two people, Carol Mays was worried about her own delirium. *Was she in fact still sane?*

Mays' attempts at a breakout plan had been futile. After some heavy meditation had led to another forty-five minutes of shut eye, Mays made her most serious attempt at escaping. She dressed in the only clothing that she owned at the moment, her tennis shoes, and stood on top of the flimsy card table. Her hopes had been that the trap door in the ceiling had seen better days and was starting to rot. However the planning of Junior Munson had included thick solid wooden doors in the bomb cellar ceilings. Patch Munson had removed the hardware on the underside of the trap door so that Mays had nothing she could latch onto. She was left with the option of trying to splinter the wood by swinging the heavy buckle of the ankle irons and smashing it into the trap door. She could just about hit it by standing on her toes on the table and swinging the ankle irons by their chain. After three different assaults on the door left barely a chip or two in the portal, Mays realized that her arms were getting exhausted much faster than she was able to wear a significant dent in the door. Finally one of the fragile legs of the table buckled, throwing the naked Mays into the water that was now more than two feet deep and rising at an ever accelerating rate. When she picked herself up out of the water she was satisfied to notice that she hadn't done any significant damage to the table. One of the legs had merely folded under during her assault on the trap door. She figured that she would wait a few minutes, catch her breath and recapture her strength and then attack the door again.

That was a half hour earlier and now Mays was now standing in water that came up above her knees. She had lost her ability to calculate time completely, but her wild estimate was that it wasn't yet noontime.

"*An'* how do *Ah* know that*?*" She asked herself this question out loud because over the last several hours she said everything to herself out loud. It somehow made her feel that she wasn't entirely alone. She thought for a second and then answered herself out loud as she had been doing. She was also vaguely aware that the Alabama accent that she had worked so hard to neutralize was now slipping back into her diction.

"*Yew* don't know. That's *jes'* it. *Yew* have no clue what *tahme* it is. *An' yew* have no *ahdea* what's *goin' t'* happen next."

Patch Munson had retrieved Carol Mays clothing from the garbage where Maggie had thrown the four items before stomping back up to her bedroom, an hour earlier. He knew that he had a lot to explain to his wife but that infidelity was not one of his recent transgressions. Normally, he would have just left things unsaid until he was ready to deal with them, but he had a weird notion that this time things might be different. He ripped off a sizable piece of the brown paper shopping bag that he had gotten from the drug store the night before when he purchased the flowers and the candy for Maggie and the tampons … which were still in the Silverado … for Carol Mays. He searched around for a pen but couldn't find one right away. Instead he was able to retrieve a laundry marker from down the hallway. Then he scrawled his short note to his wife.

> *Dear Maggie, The clothes you found are not*
> *what you think. You are my only woman. I just*
> *got me in some dumb trouble and I'm fixin to fix*

it presently. I'll explain later. I'm sorry if I got
you all tangled up in my mess. But you are my
one and only. Love, Patch.

He scribbled his note hastily and misspelled every other word, but he felt some momentary relief when he finished writing it. He left the note on the kitchen counter, took Mays' mostly dry clothing and went out the back door and over to where he had parked the Silverado in the driveway. After throwing Mays' clothes behind the driver seat, he walked over in the rain and unleashed his hound. Harry promptly hopped up and into the Silverado through the passenger side door the moment Patch opened it.

Munson drove out through the rain even as a burst of sunshine tried to emerge in the sky over northern Mobile. But as Mother Nature struggled to provide a short interlude of sunshine, the earth below the Silverado's tire wheels was completely drenched. Munson's recent forays back and forth to the fallout shelter had left multiple sets of tire tracks in the rapidly eroding country lawn grass.

Munson got out of his vehicle right near the first bomb shelter and peered into the still stinking sink hole. Over night the rain had washed a good deal of the manure down from the remains of the antechamber and through the crevice in the scorched trap door. The door itself was now about fifty percent visible and although it had two huge gashes in it, it appeared that it might still be sturdy enough to tolerate some weight without caving in entirely. Munson knew that this was a situation that he would need to rectify sooner rather than later. He realized that the chicken-shit fix was a terrible idea and so he needed to think long and hard so that he could do it right this time. After some deliberation he conjured up a two step remedy. He would drive through the citrus grove and gather some small and medium sized tree limbs that he could use to refill the antechamber. This would obscure the lower trap door once again and provide some structure for part two of his plan which was simply to wait until the rain stopped completely and then dump about ten yards of cement into the antechamber hole on top of the branches. When that hardened he wouldn't have to worry about the leaky trap door any more. Then after the cement cured, he would cover the remaining depth with dirt and soil and then reseed the whole surface.

Munson turned to his hound and said, *"Ah thaank we gat us a play'un, Harreh. Ole* Bubba should be *happeh* that *wur gunna* be *buryin' 'im lahke a gawd-damn E-gyptian* king. *Onleh thaang* is, Bubba's tomb is *gunna* be *un'ergroun'* not *lahke them E-gyptian peer'mids."*

Munson then proceeded to drive through the citrus grove picking up loose limbs and branches. The interval of bright sunshine was delusionary. The radio in the Silverado kept interrupting the country music with sporadic static and warnings of the coming of Hurricane Jesus. But the sun stayed out for more than an hour and a half, while Munson and Harry kept dumping more loose tree limbs and brushwood into the pit that once was the bomb shelter antechamber. Finally around noontime with the sun still shining brightly, a heavily perspiring Munson and his now mangy-looking mutt stood looking over the mass of wood in the smelly pit. That's when the sky began to sprinkle rain down on Patch and Harry. The farmer turned to his dog and remarked about the sunshower, *"Lookit' Harreh,* the devil's *beatin* his *wahfe."* Harry simply growled in agreement and they both got back into the pickup.

Munson was satisfied that his fill-in effort for the first bomb shelter was a moderate success. But he knew that he had a much bigger challenge ahead in the second shelter, and he had yet to decide how to deal with it. If he freed Mays, he wouldn't need to bring her food. For that matter he probably didn't need to give her the tampons that were behind his seat either. *But Ah cain't jes' let 'er go, he mused.*

Then Munson turned toward Harry again and said, "Let's go *git sem* chow, *Harreh. 'At's* what *wull* do. Then *maybeh* we *cain* talk *wit'* Mays *'bout gettin'* us a good Jew *law'yeh so's* we *cain* tell *whah* we *dun ever'thaan'* that we *dun.* On second thought, *maybeh wull jes'* get *ourse'ves* a good redneck *law'yeh, seein's* how we *alreadeh 'liminated* a Jew when we *wuz* in *Tamper. Ah* doubt we *cain fahnd* us a Bernstein or a Cohen that'd be *happeh wit'* us *fur bumpin'* off Aaron *Fahne.*

Harry just glowered at his master as if to say, *"What's this 'we' shit?"*

Commandeering a helicopter for the excursion up to Alabama had proven to be more difficult than Ismail Kanasani had anticipated. His partner Loretta Chambers had been unable to swing the deal and so Kanasani had to call in a number of favors to get a pilot and a chopper. There was more than a little red tape involved. The department only had three Bell 407 helicopters hangered in the Tampa area. These were usually used for aerial surveillance and traffic patrol around the city of Tampa. They were not normally used to transport personnel to distant locations. Taking one of these choppers out of the state of Florida was unheard of. The Bell 407 was a single-engine helicopter that could accommodate six passengers, in addition to the pilot. It had a flight time ceiling of 3.5 hours and a top speed of about 140 mph. Kanasani had used this chopper before in an investigation while searching the Florida coastline for a small yacht in a drug related murder several years earlier. He didn't believe in misusing the assets of the department but he also believed that he should make full use of the tools that he had at his disposal.

One of the main reasons that Kanasani and Chambers had such difficulty getting a pilot and a chopper was the weather. It wasn't a performance problem with the Bell 407, which featured a four blade main rotor and a vigorous Rolls-Royce/Allison turboshaft. The weather problem was related to alternative use for the asset. Typically tropical storms and hurricanes caused a certain amount of danger and destruction to the lands they visited. The administrative management of the Police Department wanted to ensure that all the helicopters were available if needed when the storm center passed Tampa. These realities caused a time consuming negotiation within the department that involved department heads, meteorologists and the detective bureau. Finally around 10:30 AM a compromise was reached. Kanasani and his partner were allowed to use one of the Bell 407 choppers to fly as far as Pensacola. This way the chopper would still be in the state if it was needed back at home and the department could avoid any media inquiries about an AWOL chopper during a weather related emergency. Kanasani never mentioned that he had an additional passenger in Priscilla Stengel. But he was beginning to worry about what he told her and didn't tell her. He noticed that she was taking pictures with her iPhone and that she seemed to be texting or playing games with it also. He resolved to be careful with what he disclosed to her. He was playing his instincts and he would have a hard time winning a debate if one arose. He knew that the pilot wouldn't ask any questions but would simply assume permission for a civilian passenger had been granted.

Just before they lifted off Priscilla had another text exchange with Melech Katz.

Priscilla: 10:58 AM About ready to lift off in chopper from Tampa
Melech: 10:58 AM Still heading 2 Mobile?
Priscilla: 10:59 AM ✈ 2 Pensacola; then Rental car 2 Mobile.
Melech: 11:00 AM Wacko plan !!! Heard about Jesus?
Priscilla: 11:00 AM ☦ ?
Melech: 11:00 AM Ha Ha!!! No Hurricane Jesus?
Priscilla: 11:00 AM Same thing.
Melech: 11:00 AM Don't go getting all spiritual and stuff on me.
Priscilla: 11:01 AM No time 2 argue. Remember the name Patch Munson. Just in case.
Melech: 11:01 AM In case what?
Priscilla: 11:01 AM Boarding. 👋 GTG txt later. ☺

The chopper lifted off from Tampa just after 11 AM and headed out across the Gulf of Mexico. The expected flight time should have been slightly less than three hours to Pensacola, but because of the intermittent high winds, the pilot decided to hug the coastline in a broad arc rather than flying in a direct northwesterly straight line 330 air miles across the northern part of the Gulf. This plan added about twenty-five minutes and fifty-five miles to their itinerary and just about maxed out the range of the chopper.

The moment they were airborne, the wind picked up and the aircraft began getting jostled about. The cabin itself was airtight and permitted easy conversation, but the air bumps that greeted the initial part of the flight kept the early conversation focused on the weather rather than the mission. Finally when their stomachs were able to achieve some semblance of equilibrium the conversation moved to the task at hand.

"I certainly hope that we aren't chasing phantoms. This is a hell of an effort to follow up on the notion that we *may* have a lead on a man who *may* have been the driver that cut off Priscilla here, and who *may* have been following Aaron Fein on the night he was killed and who *may* or *may not* know something about the murder. That's a lot of *may's* to knit together for a legitimate break to come about."

For the first time in their professional relationship, Loretta Chambers, expressed some doubt on the wisdom of her mentor Ismail Kanasani. As soon as she articulated her thoughts, she realized how unprofessional she sounded. She realized immediately that if she had these doubts she should have stated them earlier. By not doing so she was as much as admitting that she was being led around by the nose earlier. However Kanasani took this minor critique in stride.

"None of us would be on this flight if we weren't able to eliminate some of those maybes. Trust me this fellow Patch Munson is the guy who Priscilla saw outside the Fein Center. So we're left with the maybes of whether or not he knew anything about the murder."

"How can you be so sure that Munson was the guy?"

"You guys only heard half the conversation back in the office before I put the speaker on. The guy we spoke to up here in Alabama said that they were going to go out to talk to this character Patch Munson, because he was out drinking with Munson at some place called Dumbarton's Pub. He also said ... now get this ... that Looney sometimes called him Cabbage Patch Munson!" He turned in his seat and faced Chambers who was beside him. She looked surprised.

"Why didn't you tell me that earlier?" As soon as she asked the question a strong gust of Gulf wind lifted the helicopter about eight feet in the air and then dropped it back down four seconds later. They all left their stomachs at the higher altitude but Kanasani recovered first and answered the question.

"I was planning on it, but I wanted to make sure we could get this chopper. So while you were trying to get us hooked up with the aviation department, I was trying to pull up this guy's picture from the Alabama DMV. I was hoping to show his picture to Priscilla. But after I got the printout earlier this morning, their computer went down. However I'm sure we'll get to see this guy in a few hours anyway. But for now I think you'd agree there can only be one Cabbage Patch Munson."

Hawk Richter's driver, Paul, was more upset with Julianne Carson than he was with Hawk Richter. Julianne had been the one who brushed off the minor side swiping accident as "a trivial distraction" and insisted that they continue their journey. They had heard the radio reports of flooding throughout the Florida Panhandle, and they had seen some of it with their own eyes. The driving was slower than they had projected and they had unanticipated twenty minute stop after being sideswiped. However they still made it up to Interstate Route 10 by 9:50 AM. But then the weather turned even stormier and it took another two hours to reach Tallahassee.

By noon, they had debated the wisdom of continuing their trip more than a half dozen times. However each time they prepared to stop there was a short interval of calm and even sporadic sunshine. Although it never lasted more than 20 minutes or so, for better or for worse they just kept on going – mostly at Julianne's urging. *What is it with this woman?* Paul wondered. *She has no clue how she intends to find a person that the police and FBI haven't been able to find for three weeks. Is she a psychotic nut?*

After Tallahassee they still had more than 200 miles to travel to get to the Florida, Alabama border. The reports on the radio indicated that the western panhandle was still wrestling with the slow moving remnants of Tropical Storm Ian and that Hurricane Jesus had changed course and was now bearing down on the Mississippi-Alabama coastline and could hit square into the Mobile Bay area. For the umpteenth time Paul suggested that they find a hotel and stop for the night because there was no way that Reverend Billy Brand would be able to see them anyway. Richter seemed amenable to the idea but the zany woman sitting next to him kept talking about how important it was to get to Mobile before they stopped so that they could find Carol Mays. This made no sense to Paul but Richter had so far allowed Mays' sentiments to prevail and they had pressed ahead after only a ten minute rest stop in Tallahassee.

By 3 PM they had travelled beyond Pensacola and crossed over the border into Alabama. The campus of The Christian Ascendancy Community Church was located several miles north of downtown Mobile. They still had more than an hour ride to get up near the church but they didn't as yet have a hotel room. Meanwhile the road conditions were now more hazardous than ever.

When their chopper finally landed in Pensacola, Priscilla Stengel and Loretta Chambers were green at the gills from the harrowing flight. Ismail Kanasani was also contented to finally be back on firm ground, or at least on soggy, somewhat firm ground. When he turned his cell phone back on he noticed that there were five calls waiting for him including one from someone named Agent Fran Church. He checked his watch. It was now 2:45 PM. He walked into the small terminal and began returning his calls while Chambers and Stengel went to the rental car area. Fifteen minutes later they were driving out into the torrential downpour on their way to Mobile.

Sitting in the rear of the car Priscilla checked her iPhone and saw that she had several additional texts from Melech Katz.

Melech: 11:15 AM Can't believe u r ✈ up there in a chopper. ☹ Be safe.
Melech: 11:55 AM Just wondering: Munson = suspect?

Melech: 11:55 AM Might be a gd idea 2 take lots of pix with ur iPhone.

Melech: 11:55 AM BTW How about a follow up dinner when u get back? ☺

The last text made Priscilla smile. But she thought she'd wait a while to return his texts. She would certainly enjoy another dinner with Katz. As crazy as things were going at just this moment, she was happy. Right now she wanted to make it up to Mobile safely and get a leg up on her story. Then when she returned home, she wanted to get her personal life back in shape. All kinds of resolutions went through her mind. She was going to join a gym to lose weight. She was going to start pilates classes. She was going to straighten out her spiritual life. She thought that she now also had two men in her life, her wonderful son Michael, and her new friend and text buddy Melech Katz. Then she felt a little silly for having these thoughts. Still it was fun to be a little silly. She hadn't been silly in some time.

Carol Mays believed her heart couldn't beat any faster. The water level inside the bomb shelter was now above her waist. She thought for sure that Patch Munson would have returned by now. She examined the folding card table that had previously buckled under her when she was attempting to escape and noticed that the leg had folded but it had not broken. The four folding chairs seemed to be sturdier than the table, but even if she put two chairs next to one another so that she could stand with one foot on each of them, they could easily fold if she shifted her weight or moved her feet too suddenly. Besides, the seating surface of the chairs was only eighteen inches off the ground, whereas the table surface was ten inches higher than that. And to further complicate her calculations, the table was now completely immersed in the rising water and only three or four inches of the chair backs rose above the water level.

The lighting in the bomb chamber now came from only two bulbs, but it reflected off the rising water to provide an eerie illumination to the shrinking area above the water level. The water itself was relatively clear and Mays was still able to see the hand and leg irons on the floor of the shelter, but the lighting gave them a refracted look of movement as she peered down toward them trying to plan another attempt at banging through the ceiling door. She ducked down neck deep, retrieved the irons and put them on top of the submerged table.

Mays summoned all of the energy that she had left and climbed on top of the table once again. She swung the heavy ankle irons at the trap door three or four times in succession and finally made a five inch by three inch splinter in the thick wooden door. She reached up with her bare hand and yanked at the split in the wood and managed to rip down a ruler length piece of the door. The splinter was about a quarter inch thick at the largest end.

"That's a start." Mays said aloud in naked euphoria. She went back and swung the leg irons even harder. A lateral four inch chip broke free. She swung again quickly but missed the area of the door that had splintered and did little damage to the portal. She swung at the door another half dozen times in quick succession, but the overhead position of the door and her own ebbing strength made each successive swing less impactful. She also noticed that her right hand was beginning to bleed from where she had forcefully grabbed at the splintering wood. She fought off her frustration and gathered her strength once again believing that one mighty blow might do more damage than the succession of lesser blows that she had just delivered. She bent her knees slightly in the hope of getting additional torque added to her swing at the trap door, and then with a violent grunt she swung the leg irons with all of her might at the wooden door. However the change in position of her knees also altered her aim. She swung and missed and began to topple toward the water once again. In order to try to catch herself she let go of the leg irons momentarily. It was a big mistake. The irons smashed into and through the nearby remaining two light bulbs sending a shower of sparks down over the rising water. Carol Mays saw only the beginning of the four second spark shower, because she plunged headfirst into the water. When she resurfaced the bomb shelter was in total darkness.

Patch Munson was unaware of how popular he had suddenly become. An ever growing number of people wanted to speak with him. However for various reasons they had not yet come to question the farmer. Billy Brand had been worried that something might be wrong in the Munson household ever since Sunday fellowship, but he had not yet gotten around to making a call on the Munsons. Detective Vance Hillyear wanted to talk to Munson about what he might know of the whereabouts of Bubba Looney. However Hillyear was still back at the police station answering questions from the mayor's staff, while fielding inquiries from the FBI and from the Florida State Police. He was about to head out to the Munson farm when the weather got so bad that he began worrying more about his own home and family than he did about Patch Munson and Bubba Looney. Then there was FBI Agent Fran Church who wanted to know what, if anything, Munson knew about the disappearance of Carol Mays and possibly about the murder of Aaron Fein. There was also Detective Kanasani of the Florida State PD, who wanted to know what Munson was doing outside of the FCW on Terrifying Thursday. Finally there was Carol Mays, who was waiting for Munson to return to the bomb shelter to set her free.

Meanwhile Munson battled the reinvigorated storm as he determined what to do next. He decided that he would talk it over with Harry.

"*Ah guess* we ought *t' git sum'thaan' t'* eat *b'faw* we head back *t'* talk *wit'* the *cullud* woman. *Wuddaya thaank, Harreh?*" The dog understood what "*sum'thaan' t'* eat" meant and hung his tongue out in salivary concurrence.

Munson talked to the dog in a manner that hid the way he felt about Carol Mays. He didn't want Harry to perceive any weakness on his part. He called Mays "the *cullud* woman," rather than referring to her by name for just this reason. But he was deluding only himself. Harry had witnessed how Munson had elected to save Mays at the cost of the life of Bubba Looney. The dog wasn't fooled by any false show of toughness.

"*An' Ah reckon* we ought *t' braang somthaan' fur* her also. How *'bout MaacDonald*'s?" He got a single bark from the dog who recognized the word "*MaacDonald*'s," and considered a Big Mac and fries a rare treat offered by Munson only when he wanted the dog to be docile.

They drove through the take-out window at McDonald's and Munson ordered three Big Macs four large fries and two super sized cokes. The girl at the window handed Munson a Styrofoam tray with the two cokes standing at stiff-stuck top heavy attention. The weight was slightly lopsided and when Munson tried to reel the tray in from the pouring rain, one of the cokes toppled loose and the contents were dumped entirely in his lap. Meanwhile the girl at the window was attempting to hand through the remainder of Munson's order. The normal white and red McDonald paper bag was enclosed inside a plastic bag for protection against the elements. The girl knew Munson as he was a regular customer and immediately tried to remedy the spill.

"That's *alrahght*, Mr. Munson. *Ah'll jes' git yew 'nother* coke. She didn't seem to understand that the real problem was that syrupy soft drink was now soaking Munson's nether regions and Harry had begun to lap at the liquid, thereby endangering the remainder of the order to say nothing of the aforementioned nether regions. Munson pushed the dog away semi-violently and attempted to restore order. Finally they started back to the farm and Munson began to share the fourth order of fries with the hound.

Patch Munson and Harry arrived back at the farm at almost exactly 3 PM. The rain was now pelting down hard and the wind had once again picked up substantially. Munson was feeling awfully wet inside the truck from his spilled coke and he was still not sure exactly what would transpire once he got out to the bomb shelter. He cursed himself once again for not having a strategy. The closest he could come to a true plan was the idea that he would go down into the shelter and have his Big Mac meal with his prisoner and with Harry. Then the three of them would decide exactly what to do. Munson paused in the driveway for a moment or two, and then began driving out over the shredded lawn tracks that led up to the first bomb shelter. He decided to cut across on an angle toward the second shelter rather than turn at first shelter. The lawn was already such a mess that it no longer mattered to him. He drove on this angle route for nearly 300 yards. The lawn was now softer than ever and the wheels to Munson's Silverado began to spin and sling grass and mud in all different directions. His Silverado 1500 was not equipped with four-wheel drive and when he was halfway to the second shelter, the truck got stuck in the mud.

Maggie Munson was watching her husband's mud-slinging adventure through the kitchen window. It was a good distance to the spot where her husband appeared to be stuck in the mud. But she could still see his truck throwing mud without moving some 300 yards in the distance. *The man's a simple fool*, she thought to herself. *What else is new?* Once again she looked at his apology/love note scrawled in laundry marker on the scrap of shopping bag. *Ah thaank Patch may be stuck in more ways than one.* After that final thought, she did what she usually did when she was frustrated with her husband; she called her Hefty Bag sisters-in-law to complain.

On the road to Mobile, Ismail Kanasani gave Loretta Chambers and Priscilla Stengel some of the details of his brief conversation with Agent Fran Church. They both agreed that speaking to Munson sooner rather than later was a good idea. Church said that she had set up a face to face meeting with Tim Hanlon for 4 PM and that she wanted to have that discussion before talking to Munson. Kanasani also related how Church listened with great interest to what he told her about Munson, the silver-ice colored Chevy Silverado and the ongoing investigation into the murder of Aaron Fein.

"Did you agree that you would wait to see Munson until after she spoke to Hanlon?"

"I made no such promise. Then again she didn't make any promises either. I think we're on our own as far as the Fibbies are concerned.

I'm not even sure that her meeting with Hanlon is legit. The Fibbies have been known to use decoys in the past to make sure they're out in front of everything. I guess we'll see soon enough. I also tried to get in touch with the Mobile PD and I was unable to get Hillyear to answer my call. At this point, I'm not going to hold my breath and wait for those folks either. From what the desk sergeant told me over the phone, the department was pretty tied up responding to flooding problems. Apparently there are numerous roads washed out. Downtown is already a mess and they're worried about looting."

"I say we just head out to the Munson farm and see what happens from there." Priscilla Stengel was sitting in the back seat, and she knew that she would have to take a back seat in whatever would transpire out at the Munson residence. However that didn't mean that she couldn't express her opinion.

"I think we ought to secure a place to stay first. Rooms may be at a premium once Jesus comes calling." Loretta Chambers expressed what she thought would be the most reasonable idea.

"Well I have another surprise for you ladies on that front. One of the other calls that I made while you were getting the car was to Reverend Billy Brand. I met him a couple of weeks back when I came up here to ask him about his sermons and some of his radical anti-abortion rhetoric. I told him that we had a new clue that led us right back up here to Alabama. I didn't mention Munson by name …just told him we'd like to talk. I did mention that I was travelling with two women and he was pretty surprised by my sense of urgency, given the current weather conditions. He said that if we were determined to make it up to Mobile that we were more than welcome to stay in guest rooms he had right there at the rectory."

"I hope you said yes."

"I did. I think it might be a good idea to see if he knows Munson before we go out to question him. I didn't mention Munson to Brand because I wanted to do that face-to-face."

"Do you trust him?"

"Yes. I might not agree with how Brand says and does things, but I'm thoroughly convinced that his motives are methodically rooted in his ministry. He is a man who scrupulously preaches only what he truly believes. You can learn much more from a man like that when you're talking face-to-face than talking on the phone. If he knows Munson, it could be a big help."

They drove along in silence for a while and Priscilla decided that she could now update her text exchange with Katz.

Priscilla:	2:44 PM Yes. Would enjoy doing dinner again when I return. ☺
Melech:	2:44 PM Where R U?
Priscilla:	2:44 PM Between Pensacola and Mobile.
Melech:	2:45 PM What's weather like?
Priscilla:	2:46 PM God awful.
Melech:	2:46 PM What about Munson? Suspect?
Priscilla:	2:46 PM Yes. Mobile chicken farmer. Was in Tampa on TT.
Melech:	2:46 PM You saw him?
Priscilla:	2:47 PM I think so. Looks that way. Will let u know when I c him.
Melech:	2:47 PM Wow !!
Priscilla:	2:48 PM Want 2 know what else is wild?
Melech:	2:48 PM Shoot.
Priscilla:	2:48 PM Looks like we'll be staying at home of Rev Billy Brand tonight.
Melech:	2:48 PM The ✝ televangelist guy?
Priscilla:	2:49 PM None other.
Melech:	2:49 PM How did that come about?
Priscilla:	2:49 PM Long story. Apparently Kanasani knows him.
Melech:	2:49 PM Thought Kanasani was a Muslim?
Priscilla:	2:49 PM He is. Doesn't matter. He still knows Brand. GTG. 🖐
Melech:	2:50 PM Remember lots of pix.
Priscilla:	2:50 PM ✓ Got it. Remember I'm a reporter. Not stupid. ☺ Will get pix.

Melech: 2:51 PM GTG. Txt later?
Priscilla: 2:51 PM Will do. Bests.

When she finished texting Katz, Stengel pulled a small mirror out of her pocketbook and surveyed her face and hair. I've got some work to do, she thought.

Hawk Richter and Julianne Carson had continued their incessant debate on the correct lens through which the world should be viewed to the everlasting frustration of Richter's driver. Paul had quit trying to get Richter and Carson to stop for the night before they got to Mobile and the three of them had finally agreed to get two rooms at the Hampton Inn out near the airport. To get there they had to pass right through the outskirts of the city of Mobile. It made no real sense to Paul. But the agreed upon location for their choice of hotel had two advantages. The hotel was located in the general vicinity of the area where Carol Mays' rental car was found shortly after her disappearance and it was also only seven miles away from the campus of the Christian Ascendancy Community Church.

Paul was being paid well by Richter and he realized that part of his job was listening to endless lectures on myriad topics by the blind professor. That part was acceptable. He had been chauffeuring Richter for more than three years now and knew what to expect from him and how to tune him out from time to time. But his new girlfriend, Julianne Carson was another trip altogether.

Julianne unnerved Paul. She was always talking about different theologies and sometimes bizarre religious and spiritual practices. But for whatever reason Richter seemed to find her interesting, or at least amusing. That must be it he thought. Richter found her amusing. He wondered if that amusement translated to the bedroom. *Carson's not a bad looking woman. She has great legs, and a decent ass. Her face is pretty but not beautiful. She's probably into kinky sex*, he guessed. *That's why Richter likes her.* But there was something about Julianne Carson that Paul didn't like and he couldn't quite put a finger on it. Maybe it was her annoying habit of never talking directly to him. Rather she would say things that she wanted Paul to hear, but she would address them to Richter.

As they were finally getting close to the hotel she said to Richter, "Maybe you should tell Paul to be ready to go on a moment's notice. We can't be sure exactly when another clue from Carol will come about."

Richter didn't answer her and that made Paul happy. Paul didn't answer her either because the request wasn't made of him directly. It had been a long trip. The trip that was supposed to be made leisurely in eight hours had taken eleven agonizing hours and by the time they pulled up in front of the hotel Paul's nerves were shot. As he opened the driver's side front door the wind nearly ripped it off its hinges. Richter and Julianne climbed out of the rear seat and the wind knocked Richter's omnipresent sunglasses away from his eyes, but the professor quickly caught them while they were still on his face and he rapidly repositioned them. Julianne then steered the scientist in the direction of the front door, while Paul closed the doors behind them.

"Welcome to Mobile," he heard someone say as he followed Richter and Julianne into the lobby. The wind howled behind them.

After sitting in his Silverado for almost half an hour, Munson decided he couldn't wait any longer for the rain to stop. It showed no sign of letting up. His pants were soaked and he had already shared one of the Big Macs and another box of fries with Harry. He didn't want to eat the other burgers or the other fries until he got into the dry comfort of the bomb shelter. He made a decision. He was already pretty wet from the spilled coke; he wasn't going to worry about getting any wetter. He wanted to bring the lunch, the dry clothes and Mays' tampons with him but he realized that he couldn't manage it all. He decided that they wouldn't need the cokes. They were too cumbersome to carry anyway. He stuffed Mays clothing and tampons inside his shirt so that they would have the best chance of staying dry. He considered his options for a few more seconds and then said to his hound:

"*Yew gunna* stay put, *Harreh. Cain't* have *yew sniffin'* at the *cullud* girl when she *ain't gat* no clothes on. *Ah'll* be back soon, *probableh wit'* the girl."

Then he grabbed the plastic McDonalds bag and got out of the truck. Before leaving he reached behind the seat and grabbed the _{Colt} .38 Super that he still had not discarded. Then he began to walk the remaining 300 yards to the shelter. When he arrived at top of the bomb shelter ten minutes later, he was soaked to the bone.

From the kitchen window of the main house, Maggie was able to observe most of her husband's movements. She was now using a pair of his hunting binoculars that she had retrieved from the bedroom. But as Munson got closer to the bomb shelter it was hard for his wife to see his exact movements because they were partially obscured by nearby trees and further clouded by the blowing rain. Maggie was now more worried than ever. Once again she got on the phone and called her Hefty Bag sisters in law.

Carol Mays was totally in the dark. She never fathomed that she would ever experience anything as frightening as her current predicament. It took her nearly five complete minutes to fully comprehend what she had done. After breaking the two light bulbs and plunging into the water, she had resurfaced to a new world, a world that was both pitch dark and envelopingly wet. For the first minute her mind could grasp nothing but these two sensory perceptions. Then she began to feel odd about her nakedness. She was still wearing her tennis shoes and soaking wet socks but she was otherwise nude. Her mind started playing games with her about this very fact. She had come into the world bear naked. Was she now getting ready to leave the world bear naked as well? No! She thought emphatically. I'm not bear naked. That separated her human species from the nakedness of the bear. Her feet coverings were suddenly more important than ever. Not only were they able to help her navigate better than she might without them, but also they represented a philosophical barrier between life and death as well as between humans and other animal species. Once Carol Mays grasped this simple reality, she knew that the next best thing she could do now was to pray. This would further separate her from the bear. So she immediately said a prayer of thanks for her tennis shoes. It was straight forward and without pretense: *Thank you Jesus Christ for the gift of my tennis shoes.* This prayer was the start of her recovery.

The light in the darkness was not visible but it was palpable nonetheless. After the initial panic and the ensuing prayer of thanksgiving, Mays continued to pursue her contemplative prayers in the wet darkness. *Dear God, I don't know why I'm being tested but if it's your will, I accept the challenge and I accept the outcome.* As she prayed she began to find some direction. She had been standing in water that was now beyond her hips and effectively up to her midsection. The water level was showing no sign of receding. But Mays subconscious self began to direct her actions as she prayed. She felt around in the darkness and found the submerged card table. She reached under the water and made sure that all four of the spindly legs of the table were locked in place as securely as possible under the circumstances. Then she found one of the four metal chairs and placed it on top of the table and centered it as well as she possibly could. She also lined up two of the other chairs near the table to use as stepping stones as needed. The difficulty that she had was not knowing whether or not the table was now centered directly under the trap door or not. She didn't know how much its position might have switched under the duress of her attempts with the leg irons to crack the door. She located the leg irons as well as the handcuffs and moved them over near the table but left them on the floor to avoid unbalancing the table.

Mays was well aware that as the water rose in the bomb shelter she might need to get up on the table, but she also avoided doing so any earlier than necessary. Therefore once she had the few potentially usable items relocated to the best possible position, she simply sat down on one of the spare chairs right next to the table. While in this seated position the water level came up over the top of her breasts to just below her collarbone. She realized that she was not in a position where she would be able to slouch at all. Once she settled into her seat she resumed her prayers. She prayed that if her hours left on earth were running out, that her son Russell and his father, Tim, be afforded a long and happy life together. She also prayed for understanding among the men who were important in her life, including not only her son, her lover, and her father, but also including Patch Munson. Mays had come to understand Munson as a misguided soul, who must have believed in some bizarre way that he was doing the work of the Lord. For all she knew maybe Munson was truly an instrument of God's will. She didn't think of God as vengeful in any way. That was not the God that she knew, loved and trusted. So she was perplexed by the possibility that Munson could be carrying out His will. She prayed that she would gain some understanding of these things in her own final hours that she was now resigned to acknowledging. She was surprised at her own acceptance of the imminence of death, but she still believed that it was her duty to cling to life until her last breath. This paradox quickly became her last struggle. When it became too stressful to keep her chin out of the water, she used her chair as a step to get to a standing position on the table and then carefully reseated herself in the chair that she had earlier placed on top of the table. When reseated, the water level once again sank below her breasts which now seemed to be floating gently on top of the water that was already eighteen inches above the table surface. She was sitting in just this position when she heard the rustling noise above her. *Was Munson coming back after all?* She uttered one more prayer to God: "*Hurreh Jesus, hurreh.*"

Reverend Billy Brand was most famous as a televangelist, whose influence spread throughout the South. His services were occasionally picked up as a curiosity by some of the media types up north. He was well known to millions of people in different states, but in

Southern Alabama, in the northern area of the city of Mobile, Billy was revered as a local Protestant Pastor. In and around Mobile, Billy still made occasional vocational visits to the homes of members of his local congregation. When he was once asked by a New York talk show host why he did this he replied; "*Whah* does Dr. *Ahz* still do heart surgery?"

So it wasn't unusual for Billy Brand to take a phone call from a member of his local congregation. And this particular phone call was coming from someone who sang in the choir. He was however surprised by the urgency in the voice of Gloria Munson.

"*Yew gotta he'p* us out Reverend *Billeh*. Maggie's worried that my fool *brotheh* Patch is *jes' 'bout t'* do *sum'thaan'* real dumb, *an'* she has no *ideah* what that *sum'thaan'* is. He drove out *t'* the middle *o* the farm *an' gat* out in the *pourin'* rain. Maggie says he's *gat* a gun *wit' 'im an'* he started *walkin'* out in the middle *o* the dang storm, *payin'* no mind *whatsoeveh t'* the elements."

"*Ah* thought that Patch *mahght* have been *actin'* a bit odd on *Sundeh* at the fellowship. Have Patch *an'* Maggie been *havin'* problems? *Whah idden* she *callin' meh, herse'f?*" Brand immediately felt some personal guilt for not following up on his instincts earlier. He knew that those instincts were instilled by God.

"*Ah* don't know *'xactleh*, but *Ah* do know that Maggie don't often *git* this upset *wit' nuthin'* that *mah puddin'-headed* brother does. *An'* this *tahme* she has *sum'thaan'* else *t' worreh 'bout.*"

"*Whadda* that be?"

"Patch may go lots *o* places *wit'out* his *wahfe*, Maggie, but he *neveh* goes *nowhere wit'out Harreh*. Maggie said that, "This *tahme* he left *Harreh* in the pickup *an'* he *hisse'f* has been *out an' 'bout* in this awful storm *fur* more than half an hour."

Brand looked at his watch. It was 3:45 PM. He had only one other meeting scheduled for the day and that was at 7 PM with Bertrand Richter. He hadn't yet heard from Richter about any possible change in plan, but he felt that it was highly likely that Richter would cancel given the weather. The only other potential impediment was the fact that he had invited the detective from Florida and two of his cronies to stay at his house. Brand didn't know whether they would show up either, but he figured he could just ask Sarah Anne to greet them if they arrived before he returned from the Munson farm.

"*Alrahght Glor'yeh. Ah'll* take a *rahde* out *t'* the farm *an'* see *iffin Ah cain offeh aneh he'p t'* Maggie *an'* Patch." He paused and then added, *"Jes'gimme* a few minutes *t'* work out *sem* logistics *wit'* Sarah Anne." What he didn't know was that at that moment Sarah Anne was on the phone talking with Tim Hanlon, whom she had also invited to spend the night, and he too was nearing the church rectory.

The Tombigbee River is a 200 mile long tributary of the Mobile River. Starting in eastern Mississippi, it is joined with the Alabama River about 30 miles north of Mobile where the confluence forms the Mobile River. The Mobile River spills into Mobile Bay which then flows south to the Gulf of Mexico. The southward flowing Tombigbee's watershed covers a large part of the rural northeastern Mississippi and western Alabama. By 4:15 PM on Tuesday, following a battering by Tropical Storm Ian and shortly before the arrival of Hurricane Jesus, the Tombigbee River overflowed its banks, flooding large areas of the rural plain and soaking the low hills northwest of the city. Rising water began to wash out roadways throughout the region. Even at the more elevated spots out near the Mobile Regional Airport standing water rendered the road shoulders useless. The Mobile Airport had already been closed since early morning and during the next several hours the larger airports from the Florida Panhandle straight across to New Orleans were temporarily closing, in anticipation of the arrival of Hurricane Jesus. In the most recent weather reports Jesus had ascended to a Category 5 Hurricane. They now indicated that the rapidly moving storm would make landfall just west of Mobile Bay. These meteorological estimates had also moved up the estimated time for the coming of Jesus to 5:30 PM.

A few minutes after they checked into their respective rooms at the hotel, Hawk Richter and Julianne Carson took their leave from Richter's driver, Paul. Richter had told Paul to get some rest because he would need him to drive him over to the Christian Ascendancy Community Church for his 7 PM meeting with Reverend Billy Brand. That set of instructions was not what bothered Paul. What bothered him was the fact that Julianne Carson had told him that she might need him earlier than that because she wanted to see what she could do about locating Carol Mays. *Yes that woman is a total psycho,* he thought, *and I'll be damned if I'm going to let some psycho risk her life along with mine by venturing out in this weather on some spiritual séance.*

By the time Patch Munson arrived at the wooden bridge that covered the antechamber to the second bomb shelter, much of the bridge was already exposed because the light brush had been partially washed away and partially blown away by the heavy rains and high winds respectively. In the past this might have provided a minor restoration problem, but now Munson was happy that some of his ground work had already been done. He quickly whisked away the remaining loose soil and brush in an effort to rapidly gain access to the dry antechamber. Even as he was doing so the rain kept pelting down and the winds were now ferocious. In the distance he heard a loud crack that he at first believed to be an enormous thunder clap. But as his eyes followed where his ears led them, he saw that one of the huge magnolia trees was literally splintered in half by some combination of lightning and wind. If there indeed had been an accompanying thunder clap, it was highly incidental. Munson quickly descended to the antechamber level above the trap door to the bomb shelter. In his haste he didn't close the upper trap door above him. He was simply dying to dry out. When he yanked open the lower trap door, he realized that wasn't going to happen.

The encounter had not gone the way any of them had planned. Just as Reverend Billy Brand was getting into his metallic white Ford F250 pickup, Ismail Kanasani and his two female passengers pulled into his driveway. The conversation between Brand and Kanasani was brief and to the point. Because of the hard driving rain the conversation took place on the front seat in the cab of the F250. Kanasani had immediately asked if Brand knew Cabbage Patch Munson and Brand acknowledged that he knew the family and corrected Kanasani by telling him that Patch Munson never used "Cabbage" as part of his name although he had once heard Bubba Looney refer to him by this moniker.

After explaining that he was just now heading to the Munson farm to speak with Patch Munson and his wife, Maggie, Brand requested that he be allowed to speak with Munson before Kanasani interviewed him. Kanasani refused to back down. He indicated that although he was grateful to Brand for his offer of hospitality, he thought it would be best to get his own accommodations and still talk to Munson immediately. The outcome of this quick exchange was that they agreed that they would all ride out to the farm together and Brand did not rescind his offer of hospitality. Brand offered to take everyone in his vehicle because they might need its four wheel drive capability. But Kanasani wanted more freedom than that arrangement might allow so he decided to simply follow the preacher's truck.

Priscilla began texting rapidly to Melech Katz. She sent him several pictures via text message. There were pictures of trees twisting in the wind and of small light objects flying through the air. One picture showed three light plastic garbage can covers flying six feet off the ground like mega-sized Frisbees. She also sent pictures of Reverend Brand and Kanasani talking inside Kanasani's car and several pictures of the rain pelting sideways against the walls of the Christian Ascendancy Community Church. Some of the pictures were clearer than others but they all told a story of emerging hazards. Finally she got a text back from Katz.

Melech: 4:52 PM Great Pix!!! Looks like things r wild up there.
Priscilla: 4:52 PM Even wilder than U could possibly believe. Heading 2 C Munson.
Melech: 4:53 PM B careful & send more pix. I'm saving them.
Priscilla: 4:53 PM Good. Thnx. More later. ☺

Five minutes after Kanasani, Chambers and Stengel left for the Munson farm with Billy Brand in his white Ford F250 pickup, Tim Hanlon arrived at the rectory of the Christian Ascendancy Community Church in his black Range Rover. He was fatigued and frazzled from his harrowing trip south from Birmingham in the pouring rain. Upon his arrival he was greeted by Sarah Anne Brand.

"Afternoon …Tim … horrible weather … *idden* it? *Billeh jes'* left *headin'* out to the Munson farm? How was *yer* trip?"

"The weather was awful. But I just couldn't stay up there right now." I have this feeling that Carol will be found soon."

"*Yew* know *yer* welcome here, *any tahme.* But y*ew shudda* waited *'til* the storm passes through. It's dangerous out there *rahght* now. *Ah'm* not sure what in the Lord's name *Billeh* is *doin'* out there *eitheh.*"

"Billy's not home? Is everything alright?"

"*Ah thaank* so. But he *jes'* wanted to go out to see the Munsons. Don't ask me *whah.* Then *jes' 'bout* when he was *fixin' t'* head out there, *stormeh weatheh an' all*, the *Floor'da po'lice arrahve* and they *decahded* to go out there *wiffim.*"

"The Munsons are the people that we met at the fellowship on Sunday. Aren't they?"

"That's *'em.*"

"How do I get to the Munson's place?"

There were so many things happening in Julianne Carson life lately that it was impossible to think that things were still getting more startling by the hour. They went to their room and looked out the window at the furious storm winds. Mother Nature was screaming. And this was only the preamble. Hurricane Jesus was on the way. Hawk Richter could not see the trees blowing outside the window but he had already felt the wind force when he nearly lost his sunglasses on the way into the hotel.

"Open the window so I can hear the wind," he requested.

Julianne did as he asked and opened the window.

"This is sort of like the night we had dinner at Armani's," Richter posited.

"You mean the lightning, the thunder and the rain?"

"Yes, but I don't remember hearing the wind howling like that … not even out on the veranda."

"The night at Armani's was Terrifying Thursday. But for a while it was very tranquil out there on the veranda. Things certainly can change fast. I enjoyed that evening but I wanted a different ending."

"We should just recreate the ending here and now." He tucked at the belt buckle around his pants as he spoke.

The temptation for Julianne to take Richter up on his offer was compelling. However her desire to meditate and to relocate the vivid feelings of aura intersection with Carol Mays was even stronger. It was only yesterday in Tampa when she had experienced her distinctive clairvoyant encounter with the spirit of Carol Mays. She recalled her invigorating shower experience and wanted to emotionally revisit the feeling of near perfect chakra alignment that had led to her contemplative speculation about the intersection of her own life wheel with that of Carol Mays. Her difficulty was that she had no idea how to locate Mays and she was merely following what she recently had been referring to as her "pathway to the present." It was all part of her desire to live in the here and now. And although she didn't know where to find Carol Mays, she did know how to please Hawk Richter. And she certainly was not opposed to some mid afternoon passion. So she began silently unbuttoning her blouse.

"I didn't hear a response," Richter said as he unzipped his pants and removed them by sitting down backwards on the bed. Meanwhile the wind continued to howl outside the open window. Finally Julianne hit a note of compromise in her conflicting desires. She moved closer to Richter and stood where he could reach out and touch her anywhere he wished. As his hands moved inside her blouse and up across her now bare stomach, she laid out the plan.

"Why don't you call Billy Brand and see if your meeting is still on for tonight or if you can move it to tomorrow? Then we'll decide how to ride out the storm."

"I think we'll be riding out the storm right here in the room and I can think of many interesting ways to do just that." When he felt Julianne pull back slightly, he added, "but give me my phone and I'll call him if it makes you happy."

Julianne backed away from Richter and then retrieved his cell phone and handed it to him as he still sat on edge of the bed. Richter used the voice activation selection on his smart phone to get the appropriate number dialed for the rectory. When his call went to voice mail he simply left his message.

"Hello, this is Hawk Richter. We have a meeting scheduled for 7 PM this evening and I'm already in Mobile, staying out at the Hampton Inn out near the airport. Given the weather situation, I assume that we will want to move our meeting to tomorrow. Can you please give me a call back to confirm a timeframe?" He then left his cell phone number and handed the phone back to Julianne and said, "Satisfied? Now are you ready to ride out the storm?"

Lately Julianne had opted to be completely uninhibited in her search for sexual gratification. This had led to a more vigorous physicality in each and every sexual encounter and it had simply grown more prominent in her relationship with Richter. But her physical coupling with Richter did not always match the imaginative cravings that drove Julianne's seeking. She was every bit as much a seeker in her sexual desires as she was in her metaphysical pursuits, her intellectual curiosities and her spiritual quests. Therefore her uninhibited attitude rendered her guiltless about the fact that her physical copulation with Hawk Richter was accompanied by her fantasies. And her current fantasy was about pleasuring Melech Katz, the man that she had recently met in the bistro in Ybor City section of Tampa. Meanwhile, Richter was blissfully unaware that he was serving as a dildo surrogate for his fellow professor.

Less than a minute after they had satisfied each other, Hawk Richter and Julianne Carson were laying side by side, both waiting for their respiration rates to return to a somewhat normal rhythm. Richter's cell phone rang and Julianne handed it to him accidentally hitting the speaker phone button in the process.

"Hello." Richter was still breathing heavily and one word was about all that he could muster at the moment.

"Hello Professor Richter? This is Sarah Anne Brand."

"Yes, hello Mrs. Brand."

"Ah'm returnin' yer call *t' Billeh. Ah* don't *thaank* that he'll be able *t'* return *yer* call *'til* the *mornin' b'cause* he's out at the Munson farm *wit' sem po'lice* detectives from down *yer* way in *Tamper*.

"Alright, that's fine. I just didn't want to head out in the storm. I'd appreciate it if he could just give me a call in the morning. Is everything ok? This is a crazy time to be outside. What brings the Florida police up this way if I might ask?"

Sarah Anne Brand may have seemed simple minded to those who didn't know better. In reality she was a bright intelligent lady who knew how to present an unsophisticated, even childlike façade. But right now she was worried. She returned Richter's call because she sensed some synergy in the fact that Richter was from Tampa, just as the police were from Tampa. She wanted to get a feel for what was happening without appearing overly concerned. She was native to Southern Alabama and simply didn't trust folks from places as far away as Tampa. But she knew that she might have to give a little information to get a little in return, so she gambled that there was a connection between Richter and the Florida detectives, both appearing in Mobile on the same day.

"Ah'm not sure *'bout* that; but it seems *ever'un* is interested in *gettin'* out *t'* see the Munsons in an awful *hurreh*. Father Hanlon *jes'* arrived here a few minutes back. That's *whah Ah* missed *yer* call *comin'* in. He *didden'* stay but a minute *an'* then he went out *t'* the farm also.

So now do *yew* want *t* 'tell *meh* what *yew thaank's happenin'* out there that has *ever'un* so *fahred* up in the middle *o* a *hurr'cane?*"

"I'm sorry Mrs. Brand. I don't know what's going on. I simply came up here to discuss some differences of opinion that I have with your husband. They don't involve the police as far as I know. And I have no idea who the Munsons are."

Richter's brain was processing the fact that Detective Ismail Kanasani was the guy who came to see him at BITSY and warned him about a potential aftermath to the Fein shooting. They had also discussed Billy Brand's sermons at the time. Now Sarah Anne Brand was telling him that Kanasani was a house guest. Obviously there was more to learn, and he was genuinely concerned. Meanwhile Richter was still breathing quite rapidly following his sexual encounter with Julianne and so his answer to the preacher's wife came out in a staccato like rush.

Sarah Anne Brand misinterpreted Richter breathless reply as potentially a disingenuous answer, so decided not to ask any more questions or provide any more information, and simply ended the call with a polite goodbye. "All *rahght* then Professor Richter, *Ah'll* tell *Billeh* we spoke *an' Ah'll* ask *'im t'*call *yew* in the *mornin'. Bah* now."

Julianne had heard every word of the short conversation and she was much more attuned to the fact that Tim Hanlon was heading out to the Munson farm than she was to the disclosure that the Florida detectives were also on their way there. Once again she could feel the intersection of her aura with that of Carol Mays. She jumped up from the bedside, went into the bathroom for a ninety second shower and came back out dressed in jeans and a t-shirt. She just looked at Richter still lying in the bed and said, "I'm going to borrow your car for a couple of hours." She really didn't want Richter to come along with her so she was content that he gave her a haphazard hand gesture as she made her pronouncement but didn't verbalize an objection. Julianne noticed that Richter was still breathing shortly and but she didn't notice that he was now perspiring more heavily than he had been when she got up. When she bent over to kiss him goodbye she understood his lack of protest to be benign acceptance. She quickly closed the door behind her before Richter could change his mind and marched down the hallway to get the keys from Richter's driver, Paul.

Five minutes after Julianne left him, Bertrand "Hawk" Richter got out of the bed and took two steps toward the bathroom and felt a strangulating tightening in his chest. "Oh my God," he said. He had often used this phrase in mock dismay when teasing some of his colleagues. This time his humor had expired. On his third step he collapsed dead from a massive heart attack. By this time Julianne had acquired the keys from Paul; had managed to get directions to the Munson farm from the front desk clerk who knew the family and had set out on her way in the driving rain. When Richter's life expired she didn't feel his aura.

Carol Mays looked up and couldn't believe her eyes. Whereas everyone else in Mobile saw darkness, dampness and dread, Carol saw light and lightness; brightness and brilliance. There was fresh air and maybe a fresh start. God was answering her prayers. He had sent Patch Munson to save her. She felt that she was being reborn. It was almost to the point that she felt like kicking off her tennis shoes so that she could bask in the total nakedness of her rebirth. That last thought brought a wave of reality across her consciousness, and her toes tightened as her body clung to its only apparel.

"Patch, *yew* came back ...*jes'* in *tahme*." Mays voice was loud and clear and had all of its original Alabama accented roots.

Munson was confused, concerned and frightened. The apparition staring up at him was not the one he expected. He gaped down at the exposed black supermodel virtually floating on top of five feet of water. As he gawked downward from the antechamber he felt an unbalancing tug of blackness, darkness and a foreboding nadir. There was almost no visibility below the water line in the bomb shelter, and his black angel was calling his name. In an accented voice that sounded a lot like his own accent, she again called out to him. "Patch *Ah* want *yew t'* pull *meh* up."

Munson dropped to his knees above the trap door. He was now that much closer to Mays, and he could see that she had somehow stabilized her body in the water below, but she was too close to him to be standing on the floor of the bomb shelter. It was all extremely eerie and then the scenario got even more electric as several successive lightning bolts lit up the sky above him. It was an odd sensory experience in another way because he could hear the roar of the wind but because he was kneeling eight feet below the surface, the air around him was relatively still even while some loose foliage floated down around him. At the same time the rain pelted his already soaked body, and raindrops fell from his huge head and face like teardrops sweating off an ice sculpture of some humanoid. Munson was breathing heavily and had his mouth ajar as he gasped and dripped perspiration and raindrops. Then finally the real tears came too. He began to sob uncontrollably on his knees.

"Put *yer laddeh inna* hole, Patch. Put *yer laddeh inna* hole." The trap door in the ceiling was ten feet above the shelter floor. The table top was 28 inches off the floor, and Mays was 5'9" tall. She was able to reach another 18 inches over her head and therefore was almost able to reach out and touch Munson as he knelt. However in the darkness she had not been able to put the table directly under the trap door and so she wasn't standing directly under the opening. She knew that if she got down and repositioned the table and then put a chair on top of the table and stood on top of the chair, she would actually be able to get her fingertips above the ceiling. She was that close. But now the water in the bomb shelter was almost six feet deep. Mays could no longer stand on the shelter floor without holding her breath under the water. For the past forty-five minutes she was not able to sit in the chair that she had placed on top of the table and stay above the water line. So before the miraculous appearance of Patch Munson, she had simply been standing on the table getting ready to move up to standing on the chair on top of the table. But the plan was changing.

"Put *yer laddeh inna* hole." She repeated her plea even though Munson was now sobbing openly, and had not responded to her previous request. Meanwhile the rain from the darkened sky was splashing down through the opening, causing Mays to wonder how fast this additional water was helping to fill up the bomb shelter.

Munson suddenly stood up and looked away from Mays and pulled her clothes out from under his shirt. "*Ah* cleaned *yer* clothes *an' trahed t' git 'em* back here *drahed.* But they *ain't drah.*"

"*Jes'* leave *'em* there and *git yer laddeh*, Patch."

Munson did what he was told and got the ladder and started to drop it into the hole. But he let go too loosely and the bottom of the ladder began to float slightly and then came down heavily on the edge of the folding table. Mays attempted to move over from her position on the table in order to guide the ladder to the floor. However in doing so, she displaced the weight balance on the table and one of the legs folded under once again and she began to splash around wildly trying to catch her balance. Then she fell hard against the ladder and the top of ladder hit Munson's shins forcefully knocking him off balance and into the trap door opening. Munson caught himself at first with one leg in and one leg out of the space between the ceiling and the rising water. As he struggled with his own weight, thunder and lightning once again energized the heavens above him.

Carol Mays' naked body was again fully immersed in the water, and the ladder had fallen into the shelter and was quickly submerged. As Mays bobbed up to the surface her first vision was the briefly illuminated spectacle of one of Patch Munson's bulbous legs and his hind quarters looming over the water as he tried to pull himself back through the trap door opening to the surface of the antechamber. For a few seconds wet earth, small loose stones and pelting rain careened down through the hole. Mays quickly understood that Munson didn't have the arm strength to keep his plunging body mass from yielding to gravity so she swam away from his sorry sagging ass to avoid the inevitable human landslide. In less than ten seconds Munson's hold on the upper world gave way and he plunged into the water filled bomb shelter ass first but not without a last desperate grab at the upper surface. In doing so he unwittingly whipped the trap door back over the opening. The light and lightness as well as the brightness and brilliance that Carol Mays had seen and felt amidst the storm skies were all gone. It was 5 PM. Hurricane Jesus had arrived early.

At different moments in time the brain responds to different sensory perceptions in its ability to make sense of the occurrences. The *visual onslaught* on Carol Mays' brain that had included the lightning, the hulking humanoid carcass of Patch Munson and the darkening of her anticipated aperture to freedom was shut down completely. It was immediately replaced by an *auditory onslaught* on her brain. Thunder replaced the lightning. The loud petrified groan/moan/roar that emanated from the human avalanche replaced the hulking carcass. And the slam shutting boom of the trap door coupled with an enormous plop splash replaced the vision of the darkening aperture. The next sound Mays heard in the pitch darkness was a half gargled cry; "*He'p Ah caint* swim!!!*" This was followed by the sound of much frantic splashing.

Billy Brand drove slowly out to the Munson farm. The wind was now very severe and he drove at a no more than 25 miles per hour. Not only was the weather now totally out of control, but also Brand needed time to think through what might happen out at the Munson farm. He was now aware that the detectives from Florida believed that Patch Munson might somehow be involved in the murder of Aaron Fein. He knew that they only wanted to ask questions but they were certainly exhibiting a great deal of urgency in the matter. Brand didn't believe that Munson was involved in the demise of Aaron Fein. He had never heard Munson utter a single word in support of the Right-to-Life movement or opposed to abortion, even though he hoped that Munson and others felt that way. What concerned Brand terribly was that Munson or any other member of his congregation might misconstrue his message in a way that led to murder. He thought that his message was clear: stop the institutional murderous spree of abortions and bring down the institutions. Let God deal with the sinners, if the state wouldn't do so. He never intended to cause physical harm to any of the sinners themselves. That was the Lord's work.

But as Billy drove out to the farm he began to recognize that there was a distinct possibility that he had incited the shooting of Aaron Fein. Brand began to feel a guilt that he had never before felt. He started to think about Aaron Fein in a human context and he wondered why he hadn't thought about him that way in the past. It was not his job to pass judgment on human beings. It was his job to lead other human beings to salvation. He wondered how his Heavenly Father would judge his failings, and he also wondered what his earthly father, Will Brand, might counsel him to do as he faced the dilemma of saving both the soul and the freedom of Patch Munson. Once again he wished that he had made a more earnest attempt at reaching out to Aaron Fein before he died. He consoled himself with the fact that he hadn't made that same mistake again. This time he had reached out to Hawk Richter and invited him to the Christian Ascendancy Community Church to discuss their differences.

Billy Brand was not able to come to a resolute course of action before arriving in front of the Munson farmhouse. He slowly made a turn into the driveway and was immediately followed onto the property by two other vehicles. They were greeted by a large section of rooftop shingles that was blown from the top of the farmhouse and crashed across the front hood of Billy Brand's Ford pickup before continuing across the property, smashing into a tree and splitting into several smaller pieces. The madness of Hurricane Jesus had arrived full strength.

Tim Hanlon raced toward the Munson farm. Twice his Range Rover went into hydroplane lock down to secure four wheel stability. He could feel it, though he couldn't quite describe it. He knew that

Carol was going to be found. *What trauma had she suffered?* He worried if it would be the same Carol. This had been the worst three weeks of his life and they had followed the best three weeks of his life. The sum of the six weeks was that he was at a loss to find himself spiritually. He had never felt needy before in his life. Now he needed Carol. He also needed God. He was speeding toward some place simply known as the Munson farm and he hoped to find both of them there.

The directions that he had been given by Sarah Anne said that he was to go past five lights and a two lane street called Cotton Knot Way. Then it was the first driveway on the right. He wasn't sure he had counted the lights correctly and he began to worry that he had passed the farm. He had been driving for nearly fifteen minutes, and he hadn't passed a single car. There was windblown rubbish littering the roadway as he continued on his quest. Five miles into the ride he had to avoid an abandoned bicycle that had blown across the road, and then he had to swerve around a fence post and a wire grid of some kind that had also made its way onto the road. Part of the wire grid got stuck under his Range Rover and he dragged it for more than 500 feet before it shook loose and blew away. He was starting to understand that his pace was maniacal when he felt the awesome power of a wind gust hit the side of the Range Rover. That slowed him back down to about 35 MPH. Then suddenly up in front of him he saw Billy Brand's pickup with a new model sedan following close behind it. Brand and the other driver were driving much slower than Hanlon, and he came up behind them quickly, just as they passed Cotton Knot Way. Hanlon saw the other two vehicles put on their right turn signals and he did the same. In another 200 feet they all pulled into the driveway adjacent to the Munson farmhouse. Just as he was pulling up behind Brand he saw the roof shingle segment fly in front of him and smash off of Brand's pickup. He said a quick prayer aloud inside his vehicle, "Please God keep us all safe from earthly harm while we attempt to fulfill your will, and please grant us the wisdom to discern the course of action that will lead to that fulfillment."

Julianne Carson had been brusque at the doorway to Paul's hotel room. After banging on the door for a full minute she had finally awakened the weary driver from his deep sleep. With an air of total control and conviction she induced the driver to turn over the keys to Hawk Richter's Cadillac XTS at the doorway and she never looked back. After getting directions to the Munson farm, she headed in that direction immediately.

Julianne arrived in the driveway to the Munson household only to see several other occupied vehicles had already converged on the farm. Billy Brand's white Ford F250 was in the driveway as was Tim Hanlon's black Range Rover and Maggie Munson's scarlet metallic Chevy Equinox. There also was the grey colored sedan that had been driven to the farm by Ismail Kanasani. However Julianne had no way of knowing whose vehicles these were; how they got there, when they arrived or who drove them there. She had never met any of the people who were connected to these vehicles, and she knew that none of them would have any idea who she was. She also didn't know why there were so many people sitting inside these vehicles, other than the possibility that they were somehow trying to escape from the elements of the storm, and the strong probability that they had been attracted to this venue by the strong aura of Carol Mays. Julianne knew for certain that that was why she was there. She wondered if the others knew the real reason that they were there. She was now totally convinced that Carol Mays was somewhere close by.

After Carson pulled into the driveway behind these other vehicles she looked out over the property. In the distance she could see trees swinging violently in the heavy winds, and above the howl she could hear several loud snapping noises as branches were snapped from tree trunks. She could see one massive branch leaning against the trunk of a magnolia tree close to the rear of the house. The tree trunk was also split about twenty feet above the ground and a four foot long sear mark indicated that the tree probably had been struck by lightning. She remained behind the wheel of the Cadillac for a few minutes simply staring out across the rear property. Far out across the lawn she could see another vehicle. She stared out at Munson's Silverado and wondered what the truck was doing in the middle of the lawn in the middle of a hurricane.

Paul couldn't get back to sleep after being awakened by Julianne. He was exhausted by the harrowing drive up from Tampa. On one hand he was dog-tired; on the other hand he was still wired from the trip. He knew that he had just had a nap but he was unsure of its duration. Finally after about five minutes of rolling around in bed, he looked at the clock on the table and noticed that it was still only 4:45 PM. He was now wide awake and he began to think about what had just transpired. Julianne Carson had come banging on his door for the keys to Richter's car. In his half conscious state of mind, he had simply surrendered the keys without asking if Richter had approved her request. Now he started to wonder how this had come about. Something didn't seem right. Maybe Julianne and Richter had another argument. Maybe they had a falling out. Maybe he should find out. He picked up the phone and dialed the extension for Richter's room. There was no answer. Maybe Richter went with Julianne after all. But if that were the case why didn't Richter ask him to drive them. He had already told him to be at the ready for a possible trip to meet Billy Brand.

Finally Paul got out of bed and looked out the window of the hotel room and saw that the rain was streaking sideways across the window, trees were bent in submission to the roaring wind and articles of debris and tree limbs were being blown about in chaotic swirls. Now wide awake he wondered why in hell that crazy woman would want to be out driving in the middle of a hurricane. He dressed quickly and walked out of Room 317 and down the hall. He knocked on the door to Room 305. When Richter didn't answer Paul began to worry. He called the front desk and asked them to send security up to the third floor. On a hunch he persuaded the security manager to open the door to the room saying that he believed that Hawk Richter may be gravely ill. After several more knocks went unanswered, the security manager opened the door and they came across the naked body of Hawk Richter lying face down on the middle of the floor.

"Damn! What happened here?" The security manager looked to Paul for an answer. Paul was already on his knees searching for a pulse. Then he just looked up and said: "He's dead. Apparently that bitch just fucked him to death. She left here less than twenty minutes ago."

The security manager was already on the phone calling 911 and asking for an ambulance and the police to be sent out to the hotel.

"You can skip the ambulance, "said Paul. "He isn't coming back."

Carol Mays moved rapidly and instinctively in the dark wet nadir. She dived to the floor of the bomb shelter, quickly located the ladder, grabbed a rung and resurfaced immediately, only to be accidently smacked on the side of the head by a thrashing Patch Munson, who was whirling around near the water's surface. Furiously splashing for his life, Munson had no idea what was passing near him when Mays attempted to raise the 12 foot long ladder in the direction of the ceiling, but he grabbed at it anyway.

Mays was trying desperately to avoid becoming disoriented. Her objective was clear she needed to poke the ladder up into the closed trap door. She knew that it was unlocked but she could only guess how heavy it might be. In the pitch darkness she also had lost perspective of where exactly in the ceiling surface the trap door was located. She knew that her efforts would be further complicated by the fact she could no longer stand on the floor of the bomb shelter and keep her head above the water. She quickly decided on an alternative interim measure and tried to jam the ladder between two of the walls. She calculated that the ladder was a good bit longer than the 8 foot width of the room and was obviously shorter than the length of the room because it had sunk to the floor when it fell through the hole. She didn't have time to do the geometry in her head but hurriedly managed to jam the ladder against the floor and leaned it against the wall on the other side. She quickly climbed on the makeshift stairway and kept her head above the water while she reached out for the gurgling man nearby. When Patch Munson found her arm he nearly yanked her off the ladder in desperation, but Mays managed to pull him alongside the ladder while he continued to splash loudly in the darkness with his other arm.

"Patch, Patch … calm down … hold on here." She brought his hand to the ladder and his other hand quickly followed suit as he was now able to keep his head above the water line, even though he was still spitting and gasping water that he had nearly aspirated.

Munson couldn't talk but he heard his black angel speaking to him in the darkness. "*Jes'* hold onto the *laddeh* Patch, while *Ah fahnd* the door in the ceiling." He did as he was told with his heart pounding like a jackhammer. He waited for what seemed like an eternity, for her next words, and when he didn't hear them right away he started to understand what eternity might really mean.

Carol Mays mind was spinning through alternatives faster than she could decide on their relative merit. She had her full body resting against the ladder that was leaning between the walls. She reached up and could feel the ceiling but what she felt was cement. She was desperately hoping to feel wood. She tried to do some naked calculations. She knew the water was rising but she also recognized her body was now higher than it was when she had been standing on the table. That was a good sign. She worried about the weight of Patch Munson if he somehow managed to swing his whole body on top of the ladder. Although she could see nothing at all, her mind presented a vivid picture of her predicament. She recalled that twice the old wooden ladder had groaned under Munson's weight on the occasions that he and Harry had visited her in the bomb shelter. She fretted that the cumulative weight of her body and Munson's might overburden the waterlogged ladder. As long as parts of their bodies remained buoyed by the water this might be less concerning, but she didn't want to take any unnecessary chances. She knew that Munson had been wearing his usual boots, coveralls and long sleeved flannel shirt and knew that these had now taken on additional water weight.

Patch Munson didn't quite understand the directive from his black angel but she had saved him from drowning so that when he heard her voice he began to heed her directive.

"Hold on *wit'* one hand *an' git* undressed *wit'* the *uddeh.* Let *yer* clothes sink to the floor. *Git yer* boots off *an'* then *ever 'thaan'* else goes *'cept yer uneh'shawts.*"

Munson was again surprised to hear the change in Mays' accent, and he was somewhat fixated on this difference while he undid his clothes and allowed them to float down to the floor. He felt lighter but he was relieved when he was able to return both hands to the ladder.

As Munson was undressing, Mays found a profound eureka moment. God was answering her quick prayer. In the abysmal darkness her fingers found wood. The trap door was several feet to the right of her position on the ladder, but there was no doubt about it, it was definitely wood. She began thinking rapidly once again. She did not have enough leverage to open the door with the ladder positioned almost three feet away from being directly under the trap door. She decided that she would go under the water and reposition the ladder, realizing that this would be that much more difficult with Munson hanging on to the side of it. Munson still hadn't said a word but she could hear his heavy labored breathing quite clearly. For a brief moment she wished that she hadn't reached out to him when he was nearly drowning, but then she quickly purged the thought. Everything was in God's hands. Of that much she was certain. She took a deep breath and submerged herself below the water until she stepped off the ladder onto the floor and pushed it in the darkness for what she believed to be two or three feet. Then she re-climbed the ladder. The first thing she noticed when she got above the water level was that Munson was once again sobbing, "*Ah'm sorreh. Ah'm so sorreh.*" She didn't know who was meant to be the recipient of the apology but she hoped that it was God. She didn't want to be collateral damage in the vengeance of the Lord.

After scrambling back up the ladder, Mays was much more attuned to the geometry of her dilemma. She knew from calculations that she had made during her stay that the ceiling was ten feet high. The ladder had protruded an additional two feet when Munson had used it for entry and exit, but it was now leaning across an eight-foot wide water filled room. That meant that the top of the ladder was leaning against the far wall about 14 inches below the ceiling. When she stood on the third to last rung of the ladder, she was directly below the trap door and about three and a half feet from the ceiling. Once the water level passed below her chest as she climbed the ladder, she put her hands over her head anticipating that her palms would touch wood. It was a magnificent feeling when they did so once again, and it took Carol Mays less than a second to shove the trap door skyward. It snapped over and open with a loud emphatic thud. Mays took one more step up the ladder and leveraged her body up through the hole with a quick "muscle-up" motion. She stood in the antechamber on top of the bomb shelter ceiling, still eight feet below the farm surface, attired only in her tennis shoes. She suddenly noticed her nakedness. Right next to where she stood were several items. In addition to her clothing there was a large bag of food from McDonalds. She quickly slipped into her panties and denim shorts and pulled her t-top over her head, without bothering to put her bra on first. Then she noticed two other items. One was a box of tampons and the other was Munson's Colt .38 Super.

The convergence of seekers in the living room of the Munson farmhouse was nothing short of anarchic. Maggie Munson, who had opened her front door of her home to all of the other seekers, was seeking a rationale for her husband's sudden apparent madness. Ismail Kanasani and Loretta Chambers were seeking to find the whereabouts of Patch Munson so they could ask him why he was in Tampa on Terrifying Thursday. Billy Brand was seeking forgiveness and he wasn't quite sure where to look for it. Priscilla Stengel was seeking to find a solution to the murder of Aaron Fein so that she could clear her own name and simultaneously weave an interesting needlepoint of the story behind the abortionist's demise. Tim Hanlon was seeking to find his lover and the mother of his child. And all of these people were seeking to find out who this other woman in the room, Julianne Carson, was and what she was doing in Mobile claiming that she had an aura overlap with Carol Mays. Julianne's simple explanation was that she was a seeker and that the Guiding Hand had led her there.

Meanwhile no one was in-charge.

Kanasani and Chambers had no police jurisdiction in Alabama and recognized that they were guests on private property merely hoping to advance the progress of their investigation.

Billy Brand had temporarily lost his stature and swagger as he was provisionally blaming himself for the possibility that he had provoked a murder.

Tim Hanlon was likewise feeling sheepish about the fact that he should have done more, and done it sooner to help Munson, if indeed Munson was Aaron Fein's killer. He had simply trusted in God to show him the way. He didn't feel like God was telling him to lead the charge right now, but he felt that God would soon be answering his prayers anyway. He knew it was time to be a humble follower. If he maintained his humility God would give him his reward.

Priscilla Stengel was certainly not in charge. She felt as though she were merely the scribe in the passionate story that she saw unfolding.

Julianne Carson had already proclaimed that she was following the Guiding Hand, who she believed would continue to lead them in the right direction.

That left Maggie Munson to take the initiative to determine the next course of action as the seekers all gathered in her living room. She had a sudden urge to punt on these responsibilities and call her Hefty Bag sisters-in-law to ask for guidance but then she remembered the advice that her father had once given her "Think twice. Then you'll be the genius in the family." She decided to tell the others what they should do.

"*Y'all arrahved* here *'bout* the same *tahme lookin' fur mah* Patch. *Ah thaank* he went *an'* lost his *mahnd, mahnd yew. Howev'eh iffin yew* look out the back way, *yew cain* see his truck parked *rahght* smack dab in the middle *o* the lawn *'bout* 300 yards out *t'* the northwest. Looks *lahke* he was *headin' fur* the citrus grove. *Ah ain't* seen him in *nearleh* an hour an' a half, since he *gat* out *o* his truck. *Ah trahed callin'* his phone but he *gat* it turned off. *Ah'm* plenty worried *'bout* Patch *an' Ah thaank sem o* us ought *t'* go out back *an'* see *iffin* he needs *he'p.*"

That was Maggie Munson's entire leadership statement, but before anyone replied, the loud ring of Billy Brand's cell phone startled everyone simultaneously.

"Hello Sarah Anne. *Ever 'thaan' alrahght?*"

"*Billeh, yew gat* to come home *rahght* now. It's *yer* Daddy, Reverend Will." Billy listened and choked back his emotions. He was just about to ask for a better explanation of her statement, a word or two that might indicate that his father had a problem but that it wasn't a grave issue. That's when the loud crash came right through the kitchen and the wall between the living room and the kitchen collapsed under the weight of the newly fallen magnolia tree. The heating oil tank that led into the basement burner was ruptured as well and oil simultaneously spilled just outside of the rear kitchen door. Miraculously none of the seven people standing in the living room was trapped by the collapsing wall and they all scrambled for relative safety through the front door of the house, just before the sparks in the kitchen ignited the heating oil that was leaking from the tank into what was left of the kitchen that now had massive segments of an uprooted magnolia tree planted across its width and through to the living room.

Sarah Anne Brand could hear the colossal commotion on the other end of the phone and then the line went dead. Billy was now out in the elements and kept calling his wife's name into the dead cell phone air. Then he looked up and saw part of the problem. A cell tower that was across the street and a few hundred feet down the road had several antenna arms loosely dangling from their support poles. Almost as soon as he noticed this predicament, an enormous gust of wind accompanied by a shearing metal sound punctuated the rip through of the now detached cell tower parts as they penetrated the roof of the nearest house on the highway.

The seven folks who had been inside the Munson house moved in unison in the direction of the five vehicles that had been parked next to the now burning farm house. The driveway was partially blockaded by some burning wood that had already broken away from the farm house. Straight ahead was the wide relatively flat country lawn of the residential section of the farm. There were tire grooves leading right off the end of the driveway and out into the yard and it would normally have seemed to be the logical escape route but the lawn was so soaked now that it was a near certainty that only the two vehicles with four wheel drive would be able to get a significant distance away from the house before getting stuck in the mud. Richter's Cadillac was also equipped with all wheel drive but it was lower to the ground than the two pickups and certainly ran a risk of getting stuck as well.

Billy Brand wanted to return to the church, but he was unsure what God wanted him to do. Maggie played the role of the Lord's emissary,

"*Whah* don't go back *t'* the church. Reverend Will needs *yew an'* so does Sarah Anne. There may be *otheh* parishioners that need *yer he'p* also."

"You'll need *mah* truck *t'* get out *'cross* the lawn. *Maybeh* we could *jes'* switch our cars. *Yew* take *mah* truck *an' Ah'll* take *yer* Equinox."

The bargain was struck in less than a minute. Billy quickly swerved around the burning debris in the driveway and headed out on to the state road in the direction of his church. Maggie let Kanasani drive Brand's Ford pickup and they abandoned the rented sedan. Munson's house was rapidly engulfed in flames so they moved quickly.

Once Billy Brand left, the other six members of this odd assemblage regrouped. The three engines started and the imperiled vehicles started out across the lawn. Julianne was driving Richter's Cadillac and got stuck about two hundred feet out. The Ford pickup was out in front of them but Tim Hanlon waited in his range Rover while Julianne opened the door to the Cadillac to exit. As soon as she opened it six inches the wind whipped it open all the way and the door strained mightily against it hinges causing the car to tilt violently in the eight inch deep mud. The wind also blew Julianne away from the car with a force that she had never before felt in her life. She fell to the ground and was covered with mud just as a loud crash behind signaled that the backbone framework of the farmhouse had collapsed. In the distance sirens could be heard, but there was chaos everywhere, not just at the Munson farm. That's when they all heard the distinctive loud popping noise of five gunshots in quick succession. The sound appeared to be coming from someplace directly ahead of them. Somehow Julianne managed to get back to her feet and fight her way against the wind gusts to get into the passenger side of Hanlon's Range Rover. She jumped in and Hanlon drove toward the Ford in front of them, which had stopped beside Munson's abandoned Silverado.

Patch Munson hung onto the side of the ladder and looked up through trap door entranceway. It had only been a few minutes since he had fallen through that opening but they seemed like the longest few minutes of his life. He was amazed at how easily Carol Mays had pulled herself to freedom and he was fearful that she might simply flip the door shut over him and throw him into darkness once again. He also knew that if she wanted to, she could simply pick up his gun and shoot him. She could easily justify doing so. But he realized that she had already saved him and did so at her own peril. He could only hope that she wouldn't have a change of heart now that she had achieved her own freedom. Energized by seeing Mays escape, Munson splashed his way on to the ladder which he could now see clearly. Although the storm clouds darkened the sky and the trap door was not wide, the difference in lighting was significant. This was no longer total darkness.

After Mays finished dressing she picked up Munson's Colt and held it for a few seconds. She had no intention of using it, but she wanted to make sure that Munson couldn't get it either. She then had to make an important decision. Would she help Munson get out of the bomb shelter or would she simply scramble up the last few steps of earth and stone to reach the farm surface. Meanwhile there was a good deal of fresh branches, twigs and loose earth that had blown into the antechamber where she was standing. The rain had abated only slightly and the wind was still howling. The lightning and thunder still sparked and crackled above her.

If Munson had been able to swim, it would have been easy for him to get off the ladder and poke it up through the opening in the ceiling. He was certainly aware of this, having gone up and down this ladder several times in the last two days alone. But he was scared to death to loosen the ladder from its locked in position against the wall because if the ladder fell to the floor again he knew he would drown. So he thought that he would exit the same way that Mays had accomplished her exodus. Munson ascended to the third step from the top of the ladder. If he took another step higher he wouldn't have been directly under the opening. Still on the third rung his body protruded through the now open trap door. He was able to reach through with both his arms and the top of his shoulders. His arm pits remained agonizingly just below the ceiling. However whereas Carol Mays was able to quickly pull her light frame through the hole, Munson was attempting to haul his 270 pound body up without the requisite arm strength. When he tried the first time he was able to move up about three inches but his feet simultaneously lost contact with the ladder rung and that brought on a wave of anxiety that nullified his advancement. He allowed his feet to return onto the ladder rung, as his arms and shoulders yielded the meager progress they had made.

Mays could hear the effect of the winds on the surface of the farm, but she didn't feel the wind directly because she was still eight feet below the surface. Although it was only 5:20 PM the sky had darkened with the storm. In contrast to her subterranean existence over the past three weeks, the remaining daylight was brilliant. However Mays had no true idea of the time of day nor was she knowledgeable about the severity of the weather on the ground above her. Her first inclination was to clamber up the stone and earth steps immediately and let Munson fend for himself. He was currently steadily balanced on the ladder with an open passageway to gain his freedom. In a worst case scenario he should be able to balance on the ladder until the water rose further and buoyed his body so that he could eventually splash up through the opening. However suddenly Munson's footing gave way and he accidently kicked over the ladder in a clumsy second effort to extricate himself from the bomb shelter.

"Aaagh, " was all Munson could say as he tried to hold up his body with his arms and shoulders above the ceiling breach, but his entire lower body dangling below. His feet reached into the top of the rising water and Mays noticed that Munson was exerting maximum effort to splash and try to find the ladder again with his feet. Mays however could see past Munson that the ladder had slid several feet away along the wall and she knew that his feet wouldn't be able to make contact with the ladder unless he released his position. She knew right then that he wouldn't be able to get out without help. She knew that he would die and so she made a decision that she later found difficult to believe she had made. She picked up his Colt .38 Super and fired 5 shots emptying the rounds that were left in gun's chamber.

Tim Hanlon pulled his Range Rover up alongside the Ford F250, which had stopped near Munson's Silverado. He rolled down his window in spite of the torrential downpour and howling wind. Kanasani also lowered the window to the Ford pickup in anticipation of listening to what Hanlon wanted to say.

"That sounded like gunshots a couple of minutes ago. It definitely wasn't thunder. What do you think?"

"Yeah. I'd say gunshots. Sounded like they were coming from the edge of the citrus grove. Mrs. Munson has identified this truck as her husband's vehicle. There's a dog inside the truck also. Mrs. Munson says that the dog's name is Harry. Maybe Harry knows where Munson is, so we're going to let him out and see where he heads. I should warn you that we have good reason to believe that Mr. Munson may well be armed and dangerous when we find him, so if you'd like to hang back here that's fine with me."

Kanasani didn't mention the fact that they were now quite certain that Munson had been in Tampa on Terrifying Thursday because his license plate contained the letters MVN. That much they already knew from the DMV report, but the corroborating evidence was the NRA sticker on the rear bumper right where Priscilla had said it would be when they discussed her recall of the situation earlier that morning.

Standing on the floor of the antechamber, Carol Mays had fired the last five rounds of Munson's Colt .38 through the open upper trap door and into the air above her. Then she had simply reached past Munson's hairy outstretched arms and shoulders and dropped the gun into the rising water of the bomb shelter. Once she had taken care of the weapon, she continued the execution of the remarkable decision that she had made.

"Patch, *yer gunna* need *he'p gettin'* out *o* there." She suddenly noticed her own Alabama accent and then studiously purged it in her next few sentences. Her freedom was apparently returning in bits and pieces.

"I'm going to crawl past you and slip back into the water so that I can reposition the ladder again. In order to do that I'll need you to stay off the ladder. If you fall back in, grab for the ladder and hold on to the side like you did before. But don't get on the ladder until I tell you that it's okay. That way I can move the ladder up through the trap door space. Then we'll both be able to climb out without a problem. You got all of that?"

Munson stared up at his black angel and just nodded his concurrence. He was having great difficulty hanging on through the ceiling. Mays began to worry that Munson's normally Spartan cognitive abilities had been further diminished and marginalized by his fright. She looked over his massive but fleshy bare back and shoulders and noticed that his whole body was very hairy. Every other time she had seen him, he had been wearing coveralls but now he was only wearing his briefs, which just broke the water line in the bomb shelter below. Munson's massive face and head were now a deep reddening color from the effort he was expending and Mays thought that Munson looked like a weak gorilla. She dared not allow herself to conjecture about the "missing link." In reality she had no time to think at all. She knew that rapid action was required if she was going to accomplish her mission. She dropped to her knees and crawled over above the two feet of open space behind Munson's back and arms and stared down into the darkening hole. Then she took a deep breath and plunged head first past Munson and into the water below.

Munson's mind was processing everything that Mays had said perfectly. Although he was scared to death, and his arm strength was ebbing rapidly, he put his trust in his black angel.

Carol Mays found the ladder quickly and grabbed it with both hands. However the process of getting the ladder back up through the ceiling doorway was not nearly as simple as she envisioned it would be. Because Munson's hulking body was still blocking off about half of the opening and his lower torso was dangling down several feet into the bomb shelter, Mays was forced to bring the top of the ladder down toward the floor in order to move it past Munson. This maneuver was further complicated by some obstacles that were still on the floor of the bomb shelter including four folding chairs, a partially collapsed table and the leg irons and hand cuffs. Although the rising water was murky but somewhat clear, the amount of light that was now coming into the bomb shelter was inadequate because of the storm and because Munson's body blocked off a good portion of the opening to the sky.

Although she worried somewhat about the cleanliness of the water in the bomb shelter, Carol Mays still needed to keep her eyes open in order to be able to accomplish anything at all. She was swimming underwater and carting the ladder along with her. She nearly had the top of the ladder past Munson's feet when the bottom of the ladder got tangled up in the objects below. Carol had been holding her breath for a while and now needed to resurface in order to refill her lungs with comparatively clean air. She managed to do this without letting go of her grip on the top rung of the ladder. However no sooner had she surfaced then she heard Patch Munson's sorrowful moan.

"Lord *he'p meh. Ah'm fallin'. Hurreh,* Lord *hurreh.*"

As soon as he uttered these words they could both hear barking at the farm surface. Munson's hound had misinterpreted his plea and thought that Munson was calling him by name: "*Harreh,* Lord *Harreh.*"

In the following instant Munson's arms slipped and he lost his grip on the hatchway and splashed back into the water yanking the ladder from Mays' grip and sinking it further below the surface where it once again lodged itself between the walls. Munson fell with his back on top of the ladder and he got his right foot lodged between two of the ladder rungs causing his head to be trapped just below the water line. He tried to pry his right foot loose by moving his left foot in behind it but Patch Munson ended up getting both feet trapped together tightly between two ladder rungs as he flailed wildly with his naked hairy arms stretched out to either side.

As soon as she recovered from the jolt of losing her grip on the ladder, Carol came to the realization that Patch Munson was drowning. She immediately dove under the water to see if she could either move Munson's body or move the ladder in the direction of the ceiling hole. She felt much weaker because her arm had been wrenched wickedly in her attempt to hold onto the ladder when Munson fell on it. Nevertheless she dove three separate times in an attempt to save her former jailer but she was unable to budge the ladder or loosen Munson's feet. When she surfaced after her third try she again heard the dog bark.

First she looked down and saw the last bubbles of air escape from Munson's open mouth. Then she looked up and saw the glorious face of Tim Hanlon. She tried to reach up to him with both her arms while treading water with her feet but she couldn't reach him right away. When her arms went down to the water line again, she saw Hanlon quickly dropping to his knees and reaching down into the opening with his massive hands. She grabbed for his forearms. Hanlon locked his hands around her forearms and lifted her enough so that he could firmly reposition his grip at her armpits. Then he rapidly pulled her upward, while getting up to one knee and then quickly standing and pulling Carol from the abyss in one long continuous motion. Mays slight body rapidly hissed up through the water like a missile being launched out of a submarine and the concerned exultation that covered Hanlon's face led to a fiery warm embrace. Almost instantly there were two more people standing in the antechamber to the bomb shelter. While Tim Hanlon wrapped his arms around Carol, she kissed him quickly and then immediately looked past him and saw Ismail Kanasani's attempt to reach down and grab Munson and the ladder. But the distance was too great.

"How long has he been under?" he asked.

"A few minutes," Carol answered. Kanasani didn't hesitate. He handed his weapon to Loretta Chambers who was at his side and plunged into the water.

It took another four minutes to get Munson and the ladder up out of the bomb shelter to a leaning position in the antechamber. He had already drowned. There was no hope of revival.

An eerie disquieting stillness was taking place on the surface of the farm just above the antechamber, as the eye of the Hurricane Jesus was passing over the farm and nearby northern sections of Mobile. Meanwhile Maggie Munson stood on the bridge at the farm's surface. She had not wanted to descend into the bomb shelter. She had self-programmed her mind to think of these things as sinful bordellos and places of ill repute. Julianne Carson stood next to her looking for rainbows, and some kind of sign. She was thrilled that Carol Mays had been saved by her own aura and she couldn't wait to meet her in person. Priscilla Stengel was the third woman on the bridge. She was busily snapping pictures with her iPhone. She no longer had live texting capability because the local cell tower had now crashed along with all of its antenna supports. Electricity was also out. But during this transitory lull in the mayhem the sky took on the natural late afternoon luminance of a mid-summer day. However signs of pandemonium were everywhere around them. In the distance the Munson residence had burned to the ground. The citrus grove had lost almost thirty trees to uprooting and splitting. Beyond the citrus farm, four of the six chicken houses had been completely destroyed; the roofs blown off; the walls crashed down and the chickens scattering widely. Almost all of these scenes were captured by the camera in Priscilla's iPhone.

Billy Brand's Ford pickup and Tim Hanlon's Range Rover were parked about twenty feet from the bridge above the antechamber. Ninety-five percent of the destruction around them had taken place in less than fifteen minutes, and during that same fifteen minutes, Carol Mays had twice climbed to her freedom; the oddball posse of seekers had converged on the bomb shelter and Patch Munson had surrendered his life in a watery grave.

Maggie Munson peered down into the antechamber but she could not bring herself to cry. She recalled her last contact with her husband with ambivalence. She had enjoyed a night time of conjugal excitement, but the next day had so far been the most confounding day of her life. Her connubial joy had been displaced by the realization that her husband had truly gone mad. And now he was dead. She had no idea why he had kidnapped Carol Mays, but she felt that the evidence that she could see from the bridge seemed to indicate that her husband and Mays had utilized the bomb shelter in the same way that she had used it to entertain Billy Joe. She saw that her husband was only wearing his undershorts and it appeared that Mays was not yet fully dressed either. She recognized the bra that was on the floor below was the same one that she had found in the dryer earlier in the day. She sighed heavily but didn't cry. She would probably not even have offered up a sigh if she knew about Bubba Looney and Aaron Fein. But those facts had not come to light just yet.

Ismail Kanasani had now taken charge. After a futile attempt to resuscitate Patch Munson and other futile attempts to call for help, he accepted his duty as the leader to do what he could to protect those around him. He recognized that they had just been through some incredible fury on the part of Hurricane Jesus. Now that things were suddenly calm he correctly surmised that they had previously passed through the most ferocious part of the storm … the eye wall … and that they were now sitting in the deceptive calm of the eye of Hurricane Jesus. He knew from his police survival training courses that this meant that they would soon be passing through the eye wall a second time as the cyclone eye passed over and the most devastating winds of the eyewall revisited the farm and the surrounding territory. From the wreckage he had witnessed earlier he believed that the antechamber in which he was now standing, eight feet below the farm surface, might well be the safest place to wait out the storm. But first he had work to do. He climbed up the earth and stone stairway to the wooden bridge above the subterranean alcove. Carol Mays, Tim Hanlon, and finally Loretta Chambers in that order followed up the stairs and through the trap door on the wooden surface bridge. Kanasani walked over to Maggie Munson first and told her what she already knew.

"I'm sorry, Mrs. Munson, but your husband is dead."

"God save his soul." Maggie Munson looked heavenward, refusing to make eye contact with anyone around her. She was also starting to feel victimized in some way by one or two of the people around her, but when these feelings surfaced she quickly repressed them. Billy Brand had taught her to be non-judgmental and even though he wasn't there right now in person, his aura pervaded her thought process.

When Carol Mays got to the farm surface, she felt enormous relief. She was a free woman at last. Although she was soaked to the bone and still had large rivulets of water dropping from her matted hair, the feeling of freedom was absolutely exhilarating. She wondered why she had taken her freedom for granted in the past. She looked around her and didn't notice the devastation as much as she sensed the smell of citrus fruit, the warmth of the overhead sun and the comforting touch of Tim Hanlon, who had his arms around her shoulders.

As Mays continued to look around her, her eyes met the smiling stare of Julianne Carson. Julianne seemed to be searching Mays eyes for something. Neither woman could get a handle on what was happening, but both felt a connection. Mays acted first and spoke right into the face that was staring at her.

"Hi I'm Carol. We've met before I know. But I'm sorry I can't recall when."

"It's alright. We can talk about it later. My name is Julianne. I don't recall meeting in person until now."

Mays was perplexed at first but allowed her puzzlement to pass as Julianne lowered her gaze. Mays attributed her uncertainty to the confusion of the moment, encoding her feeling of connectedness as some sort of déjà vu. Julianne simply realized that this exact moment was not the time for an intense discussion of aura overlap.

"The storm isn't over," proclaimed Detective Kanasani. We need to get shelter from the next wave." Even as he made this proclamation they all began to feel fat heavy raindrops, and the sky began to re-darken. They all looked to the south and saw a clearly defined gray line heading their way. It was a funnel shaped cloud, but much larger at the base than a traditional tornado. "I think we all should go back down the first flight of stairs and do so quickly.

"I'm never going back down there again." Carol Mays voice was demonstrative and clear. "Tim, that's your car isn't it?" She pointed at his Range Rover.

"Yes," he said. "Let's go."

The wind came as suddenly as it had departed twenty minutes earlier. Mays and Hanlon barely made it to the Range Rover before the wind attacked the farm. Meanwhile Loretta Chambers, Priscilla Stengel, Julianne Carson and a reluctant Maggie Munson followed Ismail Kanasani down into the antechamber. When they arrived back on the floor of the antechamber, they had effectively escaped the surface wind on the farm, but a new peril had emerged as the water level from below had risen to the top of the bomb shelter and trickled out across the antechamber floor. It now began rising much faster than a trickle.

The Rev. Billy had a sense of foreboding as he drove back to the Christian Ascendancy Church rectory. Sarah Anne was never one to interrupt his ministry for anything other than the most important issues. Routine household difficulties did not fit into this category. Minor illnesses were also overlooked while the congregation's shepherd tended to his sheep. For these reasons Billy Brand was preparing himself for the worst.

Even though the roads were much more treacherous on the way back to the church than they had been on the way out, Brand was driving much more rapidly in this homeward direction. At first he had to avoid all kinds of obstacles that were blowing across the state highway. But about halfway to the church the wind subsided and the sky became much clearer. Billy Brand realized that the eye of Hurricane Jesus was now upon him and he took advantage of the calm weather to scoot on home as fast as he could get there. When Sarah Anne met him at the front door to the rectory he knew in advance what she was about to tell him. It was all in her eyes. But he waited for her to utter the words anyway.

"God has taken *yer* father, *Billeh*. Reverend Will has gone on to his *heavenleh* reward."

Billy Brand's shoulders slumped in recognition of the inevitable. Then he silently prayed to God; *Lord give me the strength to be half the leader that my father has been to his congregation. Please forgive him his few trespasses and allow him to work with me as my inspiration to become more Christ-like in my ministry.* Then he decided to save his own confession for a later moment of contemplation. Then he went to his room and indulged himself in a moment of humanity and cried like a baby.

The backside of the eyewall of Hurricane Jesus reached what was left of the Munson farm within a minute of the time it took for Hanlon and Mays to climb into the Range Rover, while the others returned to the antechamber of the bomb shelter. Hanlon drove his vehicle another hundred feet away from the shelter and stopped. He merely wanted to put some more distance between their position and the fallen trees in the citrus grove. Now there was the additional hazard of broken pieces of the wooden post and rail fence that were taking to the air in unison with the anti-gravitational ferocity of the storm.

Events had unfolded so rapidly that Hanlon and Mays had exchanged very few words since he had pulled her from the water filled bomb shelter, choosing instead to communicate through embrace and eye contact. They both knew that there was a lot yet to talk about, but that now it was still survival time. The couple watched in awe from the front seat of the Range Rover as a large segment of fence post took to the air right near where they had just been parked and smashed through the front windshield of Billy Brand's Ford F250.

Down on the floor of the antechamber, the water rose rapidly from the bomb shelter below. Almost instantly there was eight inches of water covering the feet of the five living occupants of the antechamber. The antechamber was crowded with previously placed foliage that encased some of the wiring and venting system from the shelter below. After extracting the body of Patch Munson, Kanasani had closed the trap door leading to the lower room. That had offered them some additional standing room but did little to stop the rising tide from simply seeping its way around the trap door boards. Meanwhile debris continued to sporadically blow into the antechamber from the farm above them.

The body of Patch Munson still had its swollen feet stuck in the ladder and his lifeless arms were spread on either side. The ladder and Munson were both now stuck together and leaning on a sixty degree angle against the far wall of the antechamber over some of the foliage. Maggie Munson approached her husband's body but merely stared from a distance of three feet. Finally she turned around and faced Julianne Carson and asked her bluntly. "Who are you?"

Although most of their attention was captivated by the danger that surrounded them, Kanasani, Chambers and Stengel also were interested in the answer that Julianne Carson might provide. The others had at least marginally identified themselves to Maggie Munson and their reasons for being out at the farm. Julianne Carson had seemed to appear out of nowhere and for no apparent reason.

"My name is Julianne Carson. I came here to do what I could to help save Carol Mays. Our auras intersect and she obviously needed some lift." She paused briefly and then added, "I'm very sorry about your husband."

In the days and months to come Ismail Kanasani would recall that brief exchange as the oddest moment he had experienced during the most bizarre yet enthralling day of his career. Everyone in the antechamber became suddenly aware that their own lives continuously intersected with the lives of other human beings whether they recognized that reality or not. At that moment Kanasani also prayed to Allah that it be his will that all of those standing in the antechamber be spared.

Priscilla Stengel also listened to the words of Julianne Carson and momentarily stopped taking photographs with her iPhone. She wondered if this story that was unfolding would ever end. Inversely she also wondered if there was such a thing as a never-ending story.

Almost as quickly as it had reclaimed the attention of the group of seekers at the Munson farm, Hurricane Jesus passed through the vicinity of northern Mobile and continued on in a northwesterly direction. The water stopped rising in the antechamber. At the first prolonged sign of a lightening sky and an ebbing wind, the group that were hunched together in the antechamber resurfaced and began to assess the wreckage.

Meanwhile seated in the Range Rover, even before the others had resurfaced, Carol Mays turned toward Tim Hanlon and said, "Let's get out of here. I don't want to answer questions right now. All I want to do is see Russell. You said he was in Birmingham. Let's go."

"Do you want to see if we can get you some dry clothes first?"

"No. Let's just go."

It took almost ten minutes to fully navigate the Range Rover back across the soaked surface of the farm. They finally passed the leveled Munson farmhouse and made it out onto the state highway. It was approximately 6:25 PM and the late afternoon sun had appeared as Tim Hanlon started back on the roadway that he had travelled just hours earlier, in the opposite direction. Hanlon couldn't help but think that his life was running in circles.

〜✺〜

Melech:	5:47 PM Thinking about u & worried.☺ M.
Melech:	6:01 PM Tried calling yr phone. No answer. Call when u can. M.
Melech:	6:11 PM Newscasts r showing devastation in Mobile. Very worried. ☺
Melech:	6:51 PM News reports r saying: Rev Will Brand has died. No details r u there?
Melech:	7:01 PM Still can't get through 2 u. Weather = fine here ☺
Melech:	7:01 PM Sorry about that. Still very worried. ☹ M.
Melech:	7:57 PM News says HJ death toll in Mobile is 17+. R U OK? Plez ☽.
Melech:	8:33 PM Realize that ☎ lines r down up there. Plez ☽ when u can
Melech:	9:07 PM News says that Carol Mays has been found alive!!!! What's going on?
Melech:	9:09 PM Reports now say PD, Fire Dept, FBI etc swarming over Munson farm.
Melech:	9:09 PM What's up? ☽☽☽ !!! Please!!!!!!!! ☽☽☽

Melech Katz had grown increasingly concerned as he saw news reports of all kinds of different things going on in Mobile Alabama. The various news agencies were operating satellite news feeds from the area and were able to put out the story but apparently communication for the local folks had been either knocked out completely or overwhelmed by sheer volume. Finally a little more than a half hour after his most recent text he got several gruesome pictures sent to him that he had not seen on any media outlet. The pictures came from Priscilla and they were followed by her text.

Priscilla:	9:51 PM Tried 2 cll 4 many hours. Still no ☽ voice line.
Priscilla:	9:51 PM Just got yr txt's. Sent #'s of pix.
Melech:	9:51 PM Jst got them.
Melech:	9:51 PM Unbelievable. Especially Munson making like Jesus on the cross.
Priscilla:	9:52 PM ???

Melech: 9:52 PM Munson: Loin cloth? Feet nailed? Arms spread? Making like ✟ Right?

Priscilla: 9:52 PM ???

Melech: 9:53 PM Come on. I'm a Jew & even I can c it.

Priscilla: 9:55 PM Took another look. Certainly makes u think.

Melech: 9:55 PM Can you call yet? Keep trying.

Priscilla: 9:56 PM I will. So far, no luck.

Melech: 9:56 PM Is the world coming to an end in Mobile or what????

Priscilla: 9:56PM No!!! Storm has passed through. Me and Mobile r still here. ☺ Melech: 9:56 PM Thank God 4 that.☺

Priscilla: 9:57 PM U can say that again.

Melech: 9:57 PM Can u tell me what's going on?

Priscilla: 9:57 PM Not in a txt. Way too much too tell.

Melech: 9:57 PM Well u said u wanted 2 write a book. I've saved the pix here 4 u.

Priscilla: 9:58 PM The book has already begun writing itself.

X

Bramaylon House

"**Y**ou are watching *The Brady Focus* and I'm Kenneth Brady. Good evening. Tonight on the one year anniversary of Hurricane Jesus we are happy to have best-selling author Priscilla Stengel as a guest on our show to discuss the astounding confluence of events that connected last July's Terrifying Thursday with the awe-inspiring arrival last August of Hurricane Jesus.

"So then, Priscilla, tell our viewers, how does it feel to be at the top of The New York Times bestsellers list with your book, <u>The Downpour & The Deluge</u>: *Death & Deliverance*?"

"It's awesome, Kenneth, absolutely awesome. I can't believe that so many people have such a strong interest in my story. Frankly it's quite flattering. I only wish that my father was still alive to share the limelight with me. He was a strong supporter and always encouraged me to follow my dreams."

"I can relate to that. I lost my own father a few years before I started *The Brady Focus*. I know he would've been proud. But you know what they say, 'Life is for the Living.' "

"Are you bating me with that remark, Kenneth? Do you want me to respond as though I don't realize that is the name of one of the chapters in my book?" They both laughed easily.

"No I wasn't bating you, he said with a smile. It's just that I'm fascinated by how you cope with all of issues of life and death that you captured in your book, and you do speak briefly about your father in the chapter I just mentioned."

"Let's just say thanks to both of our parents then for giving us guidance and helping to make us the people that we are, and then we can move on from there."

Brady thought about this for a second and didn't respond. It was true that his own father would've been proud of him had he lived to see his success, but Brady wasn't overly close to his father when he was living. Rather than getting into all of that he simply chose to go another way with his questioning.

"Now I have read your book completely two different times … which by the way I normally never do … and I have to admit that I'm still not sure what it is about. Don't get me wrong … it is a riveting and fascinating book … but I don't think of it as a real life crime story. On the surface you appear to be chronicling several loosely related contemporary crimes … but it's much more than that isn't it?"

"Well I certainly hope so. And the feedback that I have been getting from my readers also indicates that they have enjoyed my writing on a number of different levels."

"You know, on *The Brady Focus,* we often do extended interviews with bestselling authors. Sometimes we talk about the books and sometimes we talk about the authors themselves. In your case let's start with the book … better yet let's start near the end of your story. That seems fitting as we're now recognizing the one year anniversary of Hurricane Jesus. Take us back to the scene on the farm when you're all out at underground bomb shelter where Carol Mays was being held captive. From what I've read in your book, that's a strange amalgam of characters. I understand how the two detectives got there and how and why you travelled up to Mobile with them. And I also understand how and why Father Hanlon and Mrs. Munson were there. And you covered the rationale for Reverend Brand's comings and goings, but I don't quite understand how this woman, Julianne Carson got involved."

This was a touchy topic for Priscilla right at the top of the interview. After meeting at the Munson farm Priscilla and Julianne had formed a spontaneous friendship. Priscilla was fascinated by the personal journey that Julianne had undertaken. She got to know Julianne well. Priscilla learned that Julianne truly devalued material possessions and Priscilla admired the authentic largesse that Julianne exhibited with regard to the many charitable organizations she supported. Priscilla also genuinely respected Julianne's quest for spiritual fulfillment. Finally Priscilla was enthralled with Julianne's comfortable acceptance of her own sexuality. But that also became the larger issue that had temporarily derailed their friendship. Still Priscilla wanted to be honest and straightforward when answering Brady's question.

"Julianne would describe herself as a seeker and some people have described her as a spiritual savant. She has told me and others that she had some sort of precognition about the whereabouts of Carol Mays. The police investigation corroborates her assertion that she told several people, including Hawk Richter's chauffeur, Paul, that she was going to Mobile to help find Carol Mays."

"You mention this in your book. You also tell us that Ms. Carson was coincidentally in Mobile accompanying the deceased physicist, Hawk Richter and that Richter had scheduled a meeting with the Reverend Billy Brand that unfortunately never took place."

"Yes that's right. And you also know from reading my book that I find it fascinatingly coincidental that God took the lives of three men in Mobile that day, whose lives were interwoven through a complex tapestry of people, places and events."

"Yes, but you also point out that there were a total of thirty-six deaths in Mobile that day including twenty-nine that were classified as being caused by Hurricane Jesus. But let's get back to the specifics surrounding Julianne Carson. They seem to suggest that she is an unusual woman to say the least. According to some of the details that you provide, she had been more or less co-habitating with Hawk Richter for about a month or so before they travelled to Alabama together with two separate objectives in mind. Then the hurricane hits; they have sexual relations in their hotel room, and the 39 year old scientist has a heart attack and dies while his girlfriend is out chasing down some theory about the whereabouts of a woman she has never met. Don't you think that these facts are almost too bizarre to be true?"

"When you couple it all together in a statement like that, yes it sounds bizarre. But it is what it is. Things happen for a reason."

"It's nice to throw clichés around. But even after reading your book, I find it difficult to understand exactly how this woman came to believe that she could find Carol Mays and then actually did find her. It's fascinating. I should also tell you that when our production staff tracked down Ms. Carson and asked her to come on our show, she declined our invitation."

Priscilla began to wonder how much Brady knew. Did he know that Julianne refused to go on *The Brady Focus* because of Brady's less than charitable treatment of Melech Katz in the past? And did he know that Melech Katz and Julianne Carson had recently been sharing more than a simple distrust for the controversial commentator?

"I've had extensive discussions with Julianne over the past twelve months and she has taught me a lot, or maybe I should say that she has caused me to think quite differently about a number of things. Julianne would tell you that she tries her best to be living in the moment. So while we are here talking about my book and the events of last summer, Julianne is out there somewhere just being Julianne"

"Another person that you have written about quite extensively in your story is Carol Mays. And on that I want to congratulate you for your fine work as a reporter, because Ms. Mays has not been available to most members of the media since she was found and set free. By now, of course, everyone in America and many people around the world are aware of the harrowing experiences that she endured at the hands of the Mobile Monster, Cabbage Patch Munson. But your book paints a somewhat more sympathetic view of Mr. Munson than the way others have portrayed him. Does Carol Mays share your views of this man who chained and tortured her for several weeks?"

"The perspective I use to portray Patch Munson *is* Carol's perspective. I don't have a perspective of my own because I never met the man. As you know from my story, our paths crossed literally, one time on Terrifying Thursday, and then the next time I saw him he was dead. I never spoke to the man. I never knew him. But Carol has characterized him as a "misunderstood soul." And I should tell you that Carol read every word of my manuscript before it was published and has been quite supportive of my characterization of Munson. Carol also rejects the notion that the so-called "Stockholm Syndrome" has played any part in her assessment of Munson."

"Stockholm Syndrome is the phenomenon that causes victims to somehow support the people who have abducted them. They start to view them as heroic and such garbage. Is that it?"

"Well, that may well be an oversimplification of Nils Bejerot's theory, but yes that's the general idea behind Stockholm Syndrome. The Patty Hearst kidnapping case back in the 1970's is probably the best known example. But Carol Mays says that her situation was much different. She never, at any time, believed that Munson was virtuous in any way with respect to the things that he did, from killing Aaron Fein to her own kidnapping. She was however grateful to Munson for stopping Bubba Looney's attack on her. And as you know she has said that Looney's shooting was accidental."

"Yes, and I think that certainly adds to the overall credibility of Mays' account of her captivity. When the authorities recovered all of the bullets and bodies, the forensic evidence certainly supports her explanation also. But there's something else that has certainly captured the prurient interest of many folks. Carol Mays gave birth to her second son this past April 17th. Maggie Munson gave birth to her first son on April 30th. Can you confirm for our viewers that these two children are not half-brothers?"

"The only thing that I can tell you for sure is that Carol Mays son, James Lawson Hanlon, is a full blooded brother of her first son, Russell Hanlon. As for Mrs. Munson … well I was not able to interview her in the course of writing my story, and I believe that she has said she might want to write her own story about her husband. But as you know, when her 10 pound baby boy was born he was proudly given the name Harry Munson IV, although I believe she has apparently nicknamed him PJ which evidently stands for Patch Junior. Go figure."

"Your testimony in <u>The Downpour & The Deluge</u>: <u>*Death &*</u> <u>*Deliverance*</u> tells us that Ms. Mays was pregnant the whole time that she was in captivity, but that she didn't recognize this reality until several weeks after she escaped. This had to frighten her. Was she at all concerned about the health of her unborn child?"

"Obviously when they learned about James, both Carol Mays and Tim Hanlon were quite concerned for the health of their child. I don't know all of the details but I can tell you that Carol and Tim could have obtained the finest medical help in the world. There was no shortage of financial resources to make certain of that."

"How sadly ironic it might have been if Mays' child had not been healthy because of all that she had been through and that she then ended up terminating her pregnancy. After all wasn't the abortion debate the impetus behind all of the bedlam that you describe in your book?"

"That's a crude assessment on your part Mr. Brady. I don't know why you would try to sensationalize the events of last August any more than they have already been dramatized. Nowhere in anything I have written nor that I have heard in my discussions with Carol Mays indicated that abortion was ever considered by Carol and Tim. As you know they are both devout Catholics and steadfast advocates of the Right-to-Life."

Brady had gotten the agitated reaction that he was looking for. He believed that there might still be a news story yet to be uncovered with respect to Hanlon and Mays. And if that were at all possible Brady wanted to lay the groundwork for claiming that he had been the one to uncover the story. He knew that he would cause his viewers to think. This also opened up the opportunity for him to grill Priscilla Stengel more directly because she was not only the author of the best-selling book but she was also an integral part of the news story.

"Well I'm not so sure about that Ms. Stengel." The audience was now well aware that they had dropped the familial first name basis for their discussion and were now engaged in a formal debate of some sort. Brady tugged at his tie in a nervous tic manner and then continued. "This story was and still is very much about the abortion debate in this country. You opened up this can of worms in your book by telling your readers that you, yourself, had an abortion at the Fein Center for …"

"And I also called in the biggest tragedy of my life." Priscilla interrupted the news commentator before he could finish his statement.

"Yes you did say…"

"And I also acknowledged my role in fanning the flames over the debate with the article that I wrote for my paper just prior to Terrifying Thursday. But what appalls me even more is your suggestion that good people like Tim and Carol would ever even consider an abortion because their child might have been developmentally compromised by the trauma of her captivity. As you know I have a son who is considered handicapped by those people and institutions who choose to label certain conditions of life in particular ways. But let me tell you this, God certainly forgave me for my past transgressions because my son Michael makes me happier than you could possibly ever believe. He is the best gift God could ever have given me."

Priscilla was aware that many of the questions that she would be asked by Kenneth Brady might be painful to answer. However she wanted to appear on *The Brady Focus* for the simple reason that the news show had a large viewing audience and she had an appeal to that audience that she wanted to make. Meanwhile she tried not to be too off-putting to Brady. She was simply glad that Brady himself had no children. She remembered her father's contention that God had fully intended for some folks to have children and that there were others, like Brady, who neither wanted nor deserved the blessing of parenthood.

"Well that's all well and good Ms. Stengel and I'm happy that you're making full disclosure about many of these things because your readers probably deserve to know all of the facts behind your story so that they can read your account of the events of Terrifying Thursday and Hurricane Jesus while understanding the viewpoint that you bring to the story. With that in perspective, would you mind telling our viewers why Tim Hanlon also paid you $100,000.00?"

"That was the reward money that Tim had offered to pay for information leading to the safe release of Carol Mays. Indirectly the information that I provided about seeing Munson in Tampa, then led to a search for Fein's killer in Tampa which in turn led to finding Carol out on the Munson farm. And even though Carol had technically already escaped by the time we arrived on the scene, Tim Hanlon graciously paid me the reward without a moment's hesitation."

"And speaking of Tim Hanlon and Carol Mays and their two sons, what are we to assume has happened to them as a family? Is there any truth to the rumor that they are no longer together and that Hanlon has returned to the priesthood?"

"I'm not in a position where I feel comfortable commenting on that."

"But you have been in regular contact with the Hanlons and can confirm that they were indeed married?"

"Yes, That's accurate."

"Can you confirm that they are still together?"

"I can confirm that when I last spoke to them eleven days ago they were together but they have also been very good to me ... sharing elements of their story. In deference to their privacy on certain matters, that's all I want to say about Carol and Tim and their children."

"Alright then, there is still one matter I'd like to ask you about. Your book is openly critical of the police in Southern Alabama. In addition you paint a picture of racism, and anti-Semitism as well as anti-Catholicism and other latent prejudices as well. Do you feel that your portrayal is fair and balanced?"

"Regardless of the progress that has taken place, I think that there is ample evidence that there are pockets of racism in the South. To deny it would be less than truthful. But eventually the water will wear away the rock. People like Reverend Billy Brand and Reverend Lawson Mays are making a huge difference. I only wish that Reverend Tim Hanlon was still working as a Catholic cleric in his parish in Mobile."

"Okay Ms Stengel, we're just about out of time for this segment but I promised you an opportunity to talk to our viewers directly about the proceeds from your book. Go ahead."

"Thank you Kenneth. As you mentioned many of the events in my book are rooted in the debate over the dignity of life, and so in one small way, I will be trying to give back to others for the help that they have given me. So I would just like to announce that the profits from my book between now and the end of the year will be going to help the work of the Bramaylon House in placing orphaned children in Ethiopia with loving families here in the United States."

Neither Kenneth Brady nor his producers had bothered to investigate who was behind the Bramaylon House. They were not providing any funding themselves so they just assumed that Bramaylon House was another of the many worthwhile charities that solicited funding through some of the guests who appeared on their show.

Julianne Carson walked slowly along the beach and brushed her long auburn hair away from her face. It was a beautiful morning on the island of Taha'a in the Pacific Ocean's French Polynesian Islands. The sun was already baking down on the island before many of the natives and visitors were ready to start their day. Julianne was getting ready to start her trip back to California later in the day and wanted one last contemplative stroll along the beach before going back to her room to pack for her trip home. She would be returning after a two week spa retreat that she had spent mostly by herself, not counting the two amorous nights she had spent enjoying the romantic company of Ka'eo, a local vanilla merchant.

As she walked along the white sand of the beach she looked out across the ocean to the horizon and saw the spot where the eternal dark blue ocean met the endless light blue sky. She saw no ships sailing at this particular moment and no planes flying in the sky. The only non-blue colors in her immediate visage were the white sand beneath her feet and the black bikini bottom that covered her butt. However her mind was a sea of gray. For the first time in many years, she was worried about her self-image as a seeker. It had been a year since her short relationship with Hawk Richter had come to screeching halt. She never felt any profound sadness or sense of loss at the time. She liked Richter a lot. However she knew that mourning his death and posturing like she would eventually meet him again as they wandered together in The Elysian Fields would merely be making a mockery of his belief system and his thirty-nine years on earth. She was simply content to accept his atheistic position, at least as it pertained to Richter himself. There was one thing that surprised her however about Richter's death. His autopsy revealed significantly elevated levels of anti-depression drugs and that he was combating the dysfunctional sexual side effects of these drugs by also using heavy doses of Viagra. Richter had never mentioned any of this to Julianne but she theorized that the combination of prescription drugs had allowed him to delay his own sexual response while still possessing the wherewithal to be a bodacious lover. Unfortunately this quest probably contributed to his premature death. She resolved that the things that she would remember most about Richter would be the passionate physicality and the fact that the blind man regarded her as beautiful.

She strolled a little further down the beach and her thoughts went to her equally brief relationship with Melech Katz. He was different from Richter. She knew that she had lusted for him from her first brief meeting with him in the bar in Ybor City with Richter. She knew that she would eventually experience his virility and she had done so. She had made the mistake of not recognizing the impact that her decision to "live in the moment," would have on her fledgling friendship with Priscilla Stengel. She had misunderstood the relationship between Stengel and Katz to have been a professional one. Katz had helped Stengel with drafts of her book while he was getting her a part time teaching gig at BITSY. Both Katz and Stengel had stated in so many words or less that their friendship was platonic. It seems that only Katz really believed that. Julianne hadn't tried to hide the relationship from Stengel. She didn't think it was necessary. But it turned out to be messy and confrontational, not at all what Julianne had wanted or expected. She now knew that had been quite naïve on her part, but what was done was done.

The sun was gradually rising higher into the northeastern sky. Even though she was walking alone, Julianne managed to feel sexy and attractive. She sucked in her miniscule stomach and stuck out her high-riding breasts. She put her hands around her waist, one on either side of her 24 inch midsection. She was self satisfied, but no one other than Julianne noticed. She smiled anyway. She had always worked at keeping her figure attractive. She just wasn't always sure who she was trying to attract. She waded into the clear surf up to her ankle tops, then up to her knees and then to her narrow waist. Finally she dived straight out into the surf and took several strong strokes through the incoming tide. She felt physically vigorous but drained emotionally. She thought again about her relationship with Priscilla. They had spent much time together during the last year and had learned from one another. Priscilla had gone to yoga classes with her and had made some significant changes in her diet. Julianne felt that she had helped her friend to learn more about her body and as a result Priscilla had shaped up a bit. Priscilla wasn't a physically attractive woman but Julianne had helped her make major strides with her physicality.

Julianne took several more strong strokes out toward the horizon. She was still thinking about Priscilla. Priscilla had helped Julianne also. Stengel had helped Julianne understand her seeking in a much more human way.

In the past a good deal of Julianne's search had been an intensely personal quest. Others had helped her with technique and format, but her meditation and her ultimate quest were deliberately devoid of dependence on others. Yes she had learned to live in the moment. And yes she had been able to achieve fleeting moments of ecstasy, but these had too often proved to be isolated and ephermal moments of rapture. Their duration was indefinite but rarely prolonged.

During her most recent meditation sessions Julianne began to think more about Priscilla's postulate that true happiness was found through other humans. Priscilla had also said that it was more important to trust God than it was to find God or prove God's existence. It was just these thoughts that were going through her mind when she turned her head to see how far she had swam. It was a significant distance. She could just barely see the shoreline. She felt some fatigue and then some cramping high up in her right thigh. At first she felt some pangs of fear and started taking strokes toward the shore, but these movements aggravated the cramping. She thought again about Priscilla's statement about the importance of trusting God. She relaxed her stroke and elevated her feet to the surface of the heavy salt water. She floated on her back as the succession of swells of the incoming tide took her gradually toward the shore.

The billboard outside the Christian Ascendancy Community Church indicated that Billy Brand's Sunday's sermon would be about "Love." It was a theme that Billy had not addressed passionately until this past year. His growing congregation had occasioned the addition of a new wing on the church and several new affiliates on the CACC network, worldwide. When Billy Brand stepped to the pulpit he knew that it was only days since the first anniversary of his father's passing. On a much more positive note it was also the day that his son and his daughter, Dawit and Jalene, became three years old. He wished his parents had lived long enough to see the next generation of the Brand family come to America, even if they didn't have Brand blood. He knew that the twins were going to be very special people. He took a deep and thoughtful breath and then began his sermon.

"A *li'l* more than a year ago, God called *mah Daddeh*, Reverend Will Brand, home. It was *signif'cant* that He chose the same day to call home two of his *otheh* children as well: Bertrand Richter and Patch Munson.

"We all *remembeh* the pain *an' sufferin'* from last *summeh* when the rain never seemed *t' stop fallin' an' Ah'm* sure that *maneh o* us are *wonderin'* where that rain is this *summeh* as we *suffeh* through this three month long drought. Lord knows that it's been *draher* than *Happeh* Hour at the *Betteh* Ford Clinic. But we must know that the Lord has his reasons for all of these *thaangs. An' maybeh* it's *jes'* his way *o teachin'* us the *thaangs* we need *t'* know. *Yew* see, even in hardship, God teaches us love. So last *summeh whahle Ah* was *preachin' t' y'all 'bout* the evil deeds of men *lahke* Hawk Richter, *Ah* was *shamefulleh* not *listenin'* to the word of the Lord who tells us *'bout* love. L-O-V-E, love."

"In Matthew 5:43 *an'* 5:44 we are told *'bout* love." Even though he knew the verses by heart Brand flipped through the pages of the bible in front of him on the pulpit to fortify the fact that these words were truly inscribed in the good book. "*An' Ah* quote:

> *Yew have heard that it was said, 'Yew shall love*
> *yer neighbor an' hate yer enemy.' But Ah say t'*
> *yew, love your enemies and pray for those who*
> *persecute yew.*

"So *Ah* confess that *Ah* may well have been guilty of *chastahsing* the man rather than *chastahsing* his deeds. And if *Ah* had followed the gospel and loved *mah enemeh, Ah wuddah* seen the good in a man such as Bertrand Richter, because the Lord uses His love to save us one *an'* all.

"Now *sem* of *y'all* may know that when Bertrand Richter *dahd*, he was on his way *t'* see *meh 'bout sem o mah preachin' 'cause Ah* hadn't always said the *kahndest thaangs 'bout* his views on *A-bortion an'* the existence of God. What *yew* may not know is that it was *mah Daddeh* who encouraged *meh t'* receive Mr. Richter in *mah* home *an'* talk *t'* him *'bout* our *diff'ences. Mah Daddeh* was *trahin' t'* teach *meh* how *t'* love those *wit'* whom *Ah* had *diff'ences. Ah* guess *yew* could say that *Ah* still had *sem learnin' t'* do.

"*Ani'weh*, what *y'all* also *mahght* not know is that the day after Hurricane Jesus had left a mark on our *lahves, Ah* found an email that Mr. Richter had sent *t' meh jes' b'faw* he left *Tamper t'* travel up *t'* see *meh*. Let *meh* read that *t' y'all*." Billy read the scientist's email with his own southern accent.

> *"Reverend Brand, Thank yew fer agreein' t' see*
> *meh 'bout our diff'ences. As yew are aware Ah*
> *am a scientist who does not share yer beliefs in*
> *God, spiritualiteh, an afterlahfe an' the lahke.*
> *Ah hope yew will agree that our diff'ences o*
> *opinion should not be the impetus behahnd*
> *vah'lence o aneh kahnd. Ah have had a friend*

tell meh that science is mah God. An' whahle Ah believe this to be a dramatic ovehstatement, or at least semantic silliness o sem kahnd, Ah will tell yew, however, that recentleh Ah have begun t'reevaluate mah position on A-bortion, not fur aneh religious reasons but because o simple scahentific reasons. There is vereh lit'le doubt that sentient lahfe begins in the womb. Therefore Ah will vereh lahkeleh elect t'liquidate mah fahnancial position in the Fahn Cenneh, in the neah future. Ah look forward t' our discussion on this matteh an'otheh iss'yews o mutual interest, even those where mutual agreement is hahghly unlahkely. Ah'm sendin' this email t'yew now in the hope that our discussion this evenin' cain move faster in the dahrection of mutual respect an'understandin'.

Sincerely,
Hawk Richter.

"So now, even though *Ah* have not changed *mah o-pinion* one iota on the *A-bortion iss'yew*, *Ah cain* now understand that it *sem tahmes* takes the Lord a *whahle t'git* His message through *t'ever'un. An' Ah onleh* wish that God had left Mr. Richter on the earth a *lit'il longeh, b'cause Ah* know that we *mahght* have been able *t'*bring *'im 'round t' acceptin'* the Lord as well."

Brand was much less volatile in his sermon pattern than he had been in the past. For the last eleven months or so, he was preaching less about hell fire and eternal damnation. He didn't use the term murderer (although he still referred to abortion as murder.) He was preaching about healing. He was preaching about forgiveness. He was preaching about discipleship. And he was preaching about love. He paused for a full five seconds before continuing on in his Sunday remarks.

"Now *Ah* mentioned that there were three of God's *chil'ren* who *dahed* during the visit from Hurricane Jesus, that *Ah* wanted *t'*talk *t'* *y'all 'bout. B'sahdes, mah Daddeh an'* Professor Richter, there was another man who *dahed* that day who was a *membeh o* our congregation. *An'* it *sem 'tahmes* troubles *meh* that *jes' lahke Ah cudden git t' mah Daddeh* in *tahme an' Ah didden git t'* Richter in *tahme,* Ah also *didden git t'* Patch Munson in *tahme eitheh.* Please God *furgive 'em;* bless *'em; an'* keep *'em* all. Now *havin'* said that much, *Ah'll* tell *y'all* that *Ah* seemed to be in the wrong place at the wrong *tahme.* Now *Ah* have thought *'bout* that a bit *an' Ah* have looked *t'* the scriptures *fur sem* explanation. In Ecclesiastes 2:22 *Ah* found *sem* wisdom.

> *"There is a tahme fur ever 'thaan' an' a season*
> *fur evereh activiteh undeh heaven: a tahme t'*
> *be born an' a tahme t' dahe, a tahme t' plant an'*
> *a tahme t' uproot, a tahme t' kill an' a tahme t'*
> *heal, a tahme t' tear down an' a tahme t' build,*
> *a tahme t' weep an' a tahme t' laugh, a tahme*
> *t' mourn an' a tahme t' dance, a tahme t' scat-*
> *ter stones an' a tahme t' gather them, a tahme*
> *t' embrace an' a tahme t' refrain, a tahme t'*
> *search an' a tahme t' give up, a tahme t' keep*
> *an' a tahme t' throw away, a tahme t' tear an' a*
> *tahme t' mend, a tahme t' be silent an' a tahme*
> *t' speak, a tahme t' love an' a tahme t' hate, a*
> *tahme fur war an' a tahme fur peace.*

"*Howeveh* the *onleh* problem *wit'* Ecclesiastes is he *dudden'* tell us which *tahme* is which. We are told that there is a *tahme fur* all *o* these *activitehs,* but we are left *wit'* our own free will *t'* tell what *tahme* will be when. Therefore *Ah'm sayin'* that we have *alreadeh* had our *tahme t'* kill; our *tahme t' dahe;* our *tahme t'* give up; *our tahme fur* war; *an' our tahme t'* hate. Now is our *tahme t'* be born; our *tahme t'* embrace; our *tahme t'* mend; our *tahme fur* peace; *an'* most *importantleh* our *tahme t'* L-O-V-E, love."

Billy Brand was ready to finish up and he chose the most basic tenet of love that his faith could offer. He slowly looked around the entire church with a sweeping yet penetrating glance and then thundered the final words of his sermon,

"*An'* so as we all *endeaveh t'* make this the season *o* L-O-V-E, love, *Ah'll* finish *wit'* a verse we all know *onleh* too well, from John 3:16.

> "*Fur God so loved the world, that He gave His onleh begotten Son, that whoever believes in Him shall not perish, but have eternal lahfe.*"

The Bramaylon House orphanage in Ethiopia had been a wonderful place for Father Tim Hanlon and his wife Carol Mays Hanlon to work through the many unusual twists their lives had taken in the last year. Their second son, James Lawson Hanlon was born in the East African country far from the hospitals and clinics in the United States that might have provided a more secure medical environment for Carol to give birth. However after all that she had been through in Southern Alabama there was no way that she would ever doubt the grace or the providence that God had in mind for her and her family. At the moment she was more concerned about the impact of the drought in the East African country than she was about her healthy three month old son.

Mays began to compose the weekly letter to the two southern preachers who had made such a big difference in their lives. Billy Brand and her father Lawson Mays together with her husband had each contributed three letters from their names and thousands of dollars from their wallets to create Bramaylon House. The orphanage was one of the last few projects that had been envisioned by Reverend Will Brand, before his dementia interrupted his dream, and his death delayed its deployment for a couple of months.

Tim Hanlon walked behind his wife and rubbed her shoulders.

"Do you mind if I read over your back?" These weekly letters were a joint composition that they utilized to keep Reverend Lawson

Mays and Reverend Billy Brand updated on the many events that continued to shape all of their lives.

Carol Hanlon looked up at her husband and smiled. She scrolled up on her computer to the top of the page and let him lean in to read what she had written so far in their letter.

Dear Dad and Reverend Brand,

The last few weeks have been difficult for a lot of us here at the orphanage. We now have fifty-one children here. The youngest child is eight days old and, at nine years old, Dula is the oldest. Dula and Russell have become very close friends as they are only seven days apart in age. Our biggest concern continues to be the water supply which we have had to ration carefully. We are working with the local leaders as well as with the Ethiopian government to get the water and supplies that we need but you know how these things go. We are also processing the paper work to get Dula to the United States to join his brother and sister. But once again you know how these things go.

Hanlon looked up for a second recognizing that the phrase, "you know how these things go," was simply a code that they had worked out that meant that they needed to provide more funds to the corrupt locals to ensure that the health and welfare needs of the residents of their orphanage were met.

We know that Dawit and Jalene miss their brother as much as Dula misses them, but we hope that their reunion will occur within a month. We received your correspondence indicating that the adoption paperwork had been completed on your end, and that Dula will

*soon be Dula Brand. We also intend to be fly-
ing back to the United States at that time, to
begin our fund raising tour. I have been in con-
fidential contact with Jude Royale in New York
to help us with the fundraising in the fashion
and financial industries in the Big Apple, but he
is being hampered a bit by the fact that I have
asked him to keep our names out of the media
for at least another month. He may be calling
you to discuss some of the details that he has
planned. He is a wonderful man. Please continue to accept him as our friend and confidant.*

*On another note, Tim has had some ongoing
dialogue with the Catholic Church, in Alabama,
with the Papal Nuncio in Washington DC and
with members of The Church in Rome. As you
know, Tim is no longer considered a Catholic
cleric, but the Catholic Church will always consider him to be a Catholic Priest. In a very fortu-
nate turn of events, that we consider a blessing,
Father Goethe, the pastor of Tim's former parish
in Mobile, The Most Holy Tabernacle Catholic
Church, has been acting as a liaison for us with
The Church's hierarchy. These deliberations
have been intriguing, and almost frustratingly
slow. The Catholic Church does not recognize
our marriage that was performed in your Baptist
Church, Dad, as a Catholic marriage, so they
don't consider Tim to be married. In the past
this may have served to be just the convenience
they needed to allow Tim to return to his clerical
duties, simply by confessing his "sinful" ways.
However the enormous media interest in our
lives has apparently caused a lot of discussion
about the right way to handle the disposition of*

Tim's request to continue the clerical duties of his vocation as a Catholic Priest. We have no reason to expect an answer anytime soon, although we do believe that God will answer our prayers in due course and on His time schedule. Meanwhile Tim continues to baptize new Christians here at the orphanage every day. And we are happy to report that it is not only the orphans who are seeking baptism.

Love, Carol and Tim

Carol looked back over her shoulder and up at her husband and said, "Does it sound okay to you?"

"It sounds wonderful," he answered. "But we've got much of God's work yet to do, and we're only human."

"Yeah, I know what you mean. Let's not screw it up."

When she was no more than 50 yards from the spot where the ocean waves broke upon the beach of the island of Taha'a, Julianne had made up her mind. She would seek out her friend, Priscilla, and ask her to forgive her for her insensitivity with respect to her feelings for Melech Katz. She would also look to explore more closely the possibility that her seeking could be more interpersonal in its approach and still serve the purpose of self fulfillment.

She drifted in a little closer and although she still felt a tight cramping in her upper thigh, she was now able to stand in the shallow water. As she walked gingerly out of the blue surf and onto the white sand, she saw another person in the distance walking toward her. He was bare-chested and wearing a mid-calf length multi-colored bathing suit. Within moments they drew closer together and she noticed that it was the muscular young bronze-skinned vanilla merchant, Ka'eo. He flashed his warm gap-toothed smile and held out his hand, to help her as soon as he noticed her limping slightly.

"Will you be staying a few more days?" Ka'eo's question was sincere and his magical invitation was obvious, but Julianne's mystical calling was coming from somewhere else. She once again experienced a spiritual connection that was undeniable.

"No I don't think so," she said. "There are others who need my help and it's time for me to move on."

THE END

Acknowledgements

Family is the most important facet of this writer's life. And I am blessed. My family has been tremendously supportive of my desire to write meaningful fiction. My wife Debbie, my son Andrew and my daughter, Kieran were early reader/editors, whose careful perusal of some of the content led me to look at certain events from different vantage points and helped me bring the final copy to life. In a similar manner I would particularly like to thank my brother, Mike and his wife, Gloria, for their insightful suggestions after reading one of the earlier drafts of the manuscript.

I also want to thank the online reviewers of my previous novels for their encouragement to keep writing about the events and characters that often kept me awake at night.

I have often been asked about my own spirituality, and I will meekly acknowledge that at any given moment I could describe myself as a seeker, a sinner or a simpleton. I do have trust in the existence of a Supreme Being. However, I can offer no new evidentiary information to substantiate this belief. I have often felt that the delta between what I can prove … and what I believe … is *Faith*. Therefore I should state that I was raised in the Roman Catholic faith, and I have passed this religious affiliation along to my own children and grandchildren. Consequently I would also like to acknowledge and thank the many men and women of the Catholic clergy who helped me formulate my own belief system over the past sixty years. One of those strong beliefs is that human life has dignity that should be recognized from the moment of conception until the moment God calls his sons and daughters to an afterlife.

Finally if I have inadvertently been offensive to any spiritual group or religious congregation, I apologize profusely. That certainly was not my intent.

Other Novels by Jim Lynch

The Rhapsody Players: *The Sensuous Pursuit of Health Happiness and Longevity*

Amazon 5 Star Review - *Jim Lynch's first novel blends the reality of an emerging corporation with deeply painted fictional characters acting out a plausible conclusion to real events just now beginning to unfold. The strength and drive of the female characters is an interesting twist in that these characters succeed in a male dominated business world without sacrificing their femininity and family values. Mr. Lynch's story includes intrigue, murder, sex, business, hope and despair in a novel that attempts to capture and define the direction humanity is heading as we move forward in the 21st Century.* – By Dr "CEP" (Upton, NY)

The 2020 Players: *A Futuristic Account of the 2020 Presidential Election Years*

Amazon 5 Star Review - *Lynch develops his characters well and I became involved in all of their stories, rooting for several of them at the same time.* – PT Cruiser | 5 other reviewers made a similar statement

Amazon 5 Star Review - *The story moves so fast you really can't put the book down or you'll lose the feeling of being right there with everyone.* – Lisa Lisa | 3 other reviewers made a similar statement

Amazon 5 Star Review - *I thought the book was very engaging and well-written, and seemed very realistic.* – Lyda Alexander | 2 other reviewers made a similar statement

Amazon 5 Star Review - *It is a brave new world, indeed, in author Jim Lynch's spellbinding, compelling and thought-provoking, futuristic novel, "The 2020 Players." To call this a political novel would not do it proper justice (although politics play a serious role). Because this thrilling and imaginative look at America in ten years covers so much territory, including espionage, the media, worldwide terrorism, the agents of change and so much more. In short, it is a vision of America and the world as it might exist in 2020 and it is a thrilling and adventurous roller-coaster of a ride into the deepest heart and soul of this country – past, present and future.*

-John J Kelly